CITY WOMAN

Patricia Scanlan

BANTAM BOOKS

LONDON · NEW YORK · TORONTO · SYDNEY · AUCKLAND

CITY WOMAN
A BANTAM BOOK : 0 553 409468

Originally published by Poolbeg Press Ltd, Dublin, Ireland

PRINTING HISTORY
Poolbeg edition published 1993
Bantam edition published 1999

Set in 11½/12½pt Garamond 3 by
Kestrel Data, Exeter, Devon.

Bantam Books are published by Transworld Publishers Ltd,
61–63 Uxbridge Road, London W5 5SA,
in Australia by Transworld Publishers,
c/o Random House Australia (Pty) Ltd,
20 Alfred Street, Milsons Point, NSW 2061,
in New Zealand by Transworld Publishers,
c/o Random House New Zealand,
18 Poland Road, Glenfield, Auckland,
in South Africa by Transworld Publishers,
c/o Random House (Pty) Ltd,
Endulini, 5a Jubilee Road, Parktown 2193.

Reproduced, printed and bound in Great Britain by
Cox & Wyman Ltd, Reading, Berks.

There is a destiny that makes us brothers,
None goes his way alone,
All that we put into the lives of others
Comes back into our own.

Acknowledgements

Thank you, God above, for getting me through number four.

To Michael, who listened to seven months of moans and still wants to teach me how to use my new computer!

To Margaret and Chris, only a phone call away.

To Jo, for the last four years.

To Deirdre, who knows *exactly* what it is like.

To Jean Kelly and Carol in the NI Tourist Board, Nassau Street, Dublin.

To all my friends who are still putting up with me.

And especially to my wonderful family who give me so much love and support.

Contents

Prologue

'Well, girls, we had a ball. It's back to the grindstone now,' said Devlin, smiling as the trio climbed out of Caroline's car, which she had just driven into the private car-park of the City Girl health and leisure club. It was a lovely sunny Monday morning and they had just returned from their first weekend together in years. No husbands, lovers or boyfriends; no children – just the three of them. And they had thoroughly enjoyed it. 'I can't believe it went so quickly; it seems like only hours ago that we were setting off.'

Caroline locked the car and gave it a little pat. 'My first long journey. I wasn't bad for a beginner, was I?'

'Caro, I can see a future for you in Grand Prix racing,' Maggie teased. 'When we overtook that tractor, you were going all of forty-five miles an hour. Girl! I was nearly on the Valium.'

'Come on. Let's go and have a cup of coffee,' suggested Devlin, not wanting to face into work immediately.

'We'd be better off doing an aerobics class after the way we've eaten this weekend,' Maggie retorted, feeling the tightness of her waistband.

'Ah don't be a spoilsport: come on, let's be really bad and have a cream slice,' Devlin snorted.

'You're on,' declared Caroline, leading the way to the Coffee Dock on the first floor.

At reception, women variously dressed in business suits, sports gear, expensive leotards and other kinds of leisurewear, were making appointments for the enormous variety of services offered by the City Girl complex. Movers and shakers, career women, wealthy wives – all came in their droves to enjoy the pampering provided by the handpicked staff. Business was booming; it had taken off and was successful beyond Devlin's wildest dreams, but it wasn't enough for her. She had plans, great plans, for the future, and with a characteristic singlemindedness she was going to make those plans succeed. She had been telling the girls about them during the weekend and they had been very impressed. Sipping their coffee in a secluded corner of the Coffee Dock they made arrangements to meet the following Friday for their weekly early-morning workout. Then they went their separate ways.

Devlin

Devlin strode along the grey-carpeted corridor to her office. Now that she was back, her mind was buzzing with ideas. She greeted Liz, her PA, took the list of messages awaiting her into her office, left instructions that she was not to be disturbed for the next half-hour and closed the door firmly behind her.

Devlin had learned from experience that if she

wanted to get her priority work done it was imperative that she be not disturbed. Otherwise she had an open-door policy that was much appreciated by her employees. She flicked through her messages quickly and read one in particular with considerable satisfaction. Good, she thought: that was exactly the response she had hoped for. She must phone Luke; he wasn't too happy about what she was planning next. Luke Reilly, her partner, was a very good businessman, and over the years he had learned to be cautious. Devlin, in business only a short time, was still finding her feet and inclined to rush into things. But this idea she'd had was a good one. She knew it was a good one – one of her best – and she knew it was going to work. Tanned fingers dialled the digits on the phone, as Devlin sat on the edge of her desk, her long legs swinging.

As she waited for a response, she observed the rush and bustle of St Stephen's Green below her. Down the square she could see a sleek black limousine pulling up outside the Shelbourne Hotel. Liz had told her that a well-known pop-star was arriving in the city that day and had booked a private workout and aromatherapy session for later on. It often happened that visiting celebs did that and it gave Devlin a great sense of satisfaction that City Girl had become 'the' place. God knows she'd worked really hard to get it going. If it hadn't been for City Girl and Luke and the girls she would have gone crazy. Sadness welled in her and tears smarted her eyes.

It had been hard at the graveside when the three of them went to pray on the Saturday. It didn't really get any easier. She had to push the pain away almost

15

physically. 'Oh, my baby. My darling child. I love you. Why did it happen?' Don't think about it! Stop. Stop. Stop, she silently screamed. She heard Luke's voice on the line. He had answered himself because she had dialled his private number. 'Hi! It's me.' Devlin strove to keep her voice cheerful. Luke was so kind to her and if he knew she was feeling sad, his sympathy would have made her bawl. She was having none of that. Grit your teeth and get on with it was Devlin's motto.

'Hi, you!' Devlin could sense that Luke was smiling at the other end of the phone. 'Did you have a good weekend with that other pair of nutters?'

'Oh it was great. Listen, Luke: I got word from Arthur Kelly and he's very interested. I think we should go ahead.' Devlin wasted no time in getting down to business. There was a silence at the other end of the phone.

'Is that so?' said Luke, an edge to his deep voice. 'I'll be in Dublin on Wednesday. I'll get my PA to talk to yours to arrange a meeting. I'll see you then, Devlin, and we'll talk . . . business.' There was a click at the other end of the line and the phone went dead.

Devlin stared at the silent phone in her hand. What the hell was wrong with him now? And why had he made the word business sound like such a dirty word? Men! She'd never understand them. Well, he could just go and get lost; she had work to do. She wasn't going to waste all day worrying about why Luke Reilly had got into a huff just because she had mentioned Arthur Kelly. All the same, it wasn't like him.

'Oh drat!' she muttered, pressing her intercom

button. 'Liz, would you come in and collect these letters I've just signed. I want to go through my diary for the week.'

'Sure, Devlin, I'm just arranging a meeting for you with Mr Reilly. I'll be in in a second,' Liz responded. Devlin sat glumly behind her desk. At that moment she wished Mr Bloody Reilly would go to hell.

Luke

Luke Reilly sat behind his desk, his face dark with anger. There were times when he felt like strangling Devlin Delaney. At this very moment he wished he had never laid eyes on her or got himself involved in her business venture. Not that City Girl wasn't doing well. It had exceeded all their expectations and that was part of the problem. Devlin was consumed by the business . . . and he was consumed by her. In his entire adult life, he had never been so . . . so rattled by a woman and it was infuriating at times, to say the least. Here he was trying to establish a romantic relationship with the woman and just when he thought he was having some success, off she goes again.

This blowing hot and cold was getting to him. That was it! From now on it was going to be business only with Ms Delaney. She couldn't even be bothered to tell him how she'd got on on her weekend away with Maggie and Caroline. Straightaway into business and what Arthur Kelly was interested in. Who cared about Arthur Kelly? What about Luke Reilly and what he was interested in? Didn't Devlin care enough even to ask him how he'd got on on his trip to Holland? He'd been dying to tell her that the firm had secured the contract. Was she interested? Obviously not! All she saw him as was her business partner in City Girl. Nothing else. And it hurt.

Luke couldn't believe how hurt he had felt by her phone call. Was he getting sensitive in his old age or something? 'No, you're just in love, you fool!' he muttered, scrunching up a page he'd been doodling on and aiming it at the waste-paper basket. It missed. Even his aim was gone to pot, he thought, feeling very sorry for himself. 'Well, just snap out of it, mister,' he ordered himself sternly, picking up another page and taking aim.

'Sorry, did you say something?' Dianne, his highly efficient PA, remarked as she walked in.

'Just talking to myself, Dianne,' Luke said grumpily. Dianne's eyebrows rose imperceptibly. In her book, MDs of highly successful companies did not go around talking to themselves. She knew Devlin Delaney had been on the phone. She had been in the office when the call came through and had exited discreetly although she'd been dying to earwig. Why Luke Reilly was wasting his time with DD, as she called her, was beyond Dianne. She had seen her once, looking like a schoolgirl with no make-up on and wearing just a pair of jeans and a T-shirt. A far cry from the glamorous image she portrayed on the glossy brochure of City Girl. Luke needed somebody sophisticated and sexy. Someone just like herself.

Dianne had fallen for Luke the moment she had

met him at her job interview and she was damned if she was going to let the blonde bombshell from Dublin swipe him from under her nose. 'I've arranged for you to meet Miss Delaney at 9.30 a.m. Wednesday at the Forte Crest Hotel in Dublin Airport.'

Luke looked at his PA in surprise. 'Why didn't you arrange the meeting for her office?'

'I thought it would be less time-consuming for you to meet directly off your flight,' Dianne informed her boss calmly. 'Miss Delaney has a very busy schedule, it seems. Her PA agreed it would be best to meet you there. Anyway, Miss Delaney is travelling to Drogheda to a business lunch following her meeting with you.'

'Is she indeed?' Luke said coldly, his eyes like flints. So he could be fitted in only to a meeting at the airport. He was sorely tempted to get Dianne to call and say the venue did not suit him. But that would be the height of childishness. Look what she had reduced him too. It was pathetic. Cop on to yourself, Reilly, he urged.

Dianne noted the expression on her employer's face, glad that his ire was not directed at her. It was obvious Luke was miffed about something DD had said or done. This did not please Dianne. His anger was too strong, too powerful. It meant that there was serious emotional involvement here.

'Thank you, Dianne. That's all for the moment,' Luke said politely, his thoughts obviously miles away. That's what you think, you gorgeous hunk, Dianne thought longingly to herself, as she left the office as unobtrusively as she had entered it, leaving Luke staring out over London's skyline, his mouth still a

19

hard line of anger, his fingers drumming impatiently on his desk.

Caroline

Caroline couldn't quite decide what to do with the rest of her day off. She didn't particularly want to go home to the penthouse in Clontarf. She had phoned Richard at his office to tell him she was home safe and having coffee in City Girl but he hadn't been there. He wasn't in court either. His PA said he had just told her he was taking the rest of the day off. That was most unusual behaviour for Richard. Caroline couldn't remember her husband ever taking a day off from his thriving legal practice for no reason at all. She felt a vague sense of unease. Well, he's not seeing another woman, that's for sure, she thought, a wry smile playing around the corners of her lips. It was strange how she had accepted his homosexuality almost with relief. After the years of tormenting herself, of wondering what she was doing wrong, of knowing that no matter what she did her husband had no interest in her sexually, realizing that she was not to blame had been a turning point in her life. She had stopped drinking, stopped taking Valium and started living again.

There were days that she felt quite shaky, times when she longed for a drink or a Valium to calm the fluttery feelings of fear, but on the whole she was managing well. And her relationship with Richard was now so different. True, she had hated him when she found him in a loving embrace with his lover Charles Stokes – not because he was homosexual but because he had betrayed her, made her live a lie and brought her to the edge of despair. That night had been the worst night of her life: she had told her husband she never wanted to lay eyes on him again and she had tried to commit suicide.

But she had lived. She had been given time to think and eventually she had been able to forgive Richard. Now her husband and she had a much better relationship than they'd ever had before: no more beatings, no more rows, he living his life, which included Charles, she living hers, which included no-one at the moment. Some day, Caroline promised herself, she was going to fall in love like any normal person and have the children she had always wanted. It was her dream and she held on to it tightly. Of course she'd have to get a divorce and annulment first. It would have to be one of those foreign divorces since you couldn't get divorced in Ireland. But not right now. Things could go on as they were with she and Richard keeping up the pretence of marriage. It was much easier to drift for the time being. 'Typical,' she told herself as she strolled down Grafton Street and had a look in Acquiesce to see what was new.

Caroline was notorious for putting things off. It was one of her worst faults. Devlin was always on at her about it. Devlin wouldn't consider hanging around letting life pass her by. Just looking at her in City Girl, observing the way she behaved as owner/manager of the club, really impressed Caroline. Devlin, who had once been so spoilt and pampered, had grown up and made something of herself. She was a real career woman now with aims and ambitions. It would do Caroline good to emulate her friend. And what about Maggie getting her first novel published! What an achievement that was! Maggie, too, was getting up off her butt and doing something.

Well, Caroline would just have to haul herself out of her little rut and do something about her own situation. The trip to Rosslare Harbour with the girls had been such a treat. Just being with her two best friends, confiding and talking things through, had been a tonic. They had been so shocked when she had told them about Richard. Well, she'd had to tell someone. And Devlin and Maggie were like sisters to her. She wouldn't tell anyone else. No-one else needed to know. It was hers and Richard's business but she had never kept anything from the girls, nor they from her. Their friendship was a great bond that had seen them all through many trials and troubles. She thought of poor Devlin, standing at her baby daughter's grave. Caroline knew she wasn't yet over the shock of Lynn's death. Devlin was suppressing her grief, throwing herself into her business, not allowing Luke to get close to her. But that was Devlin, too self-sufficient.

That's a problem you'll never suffer from, my girl, Caroline thought crossly. The trouble with her was that she couldn't stand on her own two feet. Tomorrow she'd look at the jobs section in the paper, she decided. She wanted to work full-time again. That would be one small step forward. Deciding that there was nothing that she particularly fancied in the boutique, Caroline headed back to the car-park. On her way, she stopped at a phone and rang Richard's office again. 'I think he's gone for the day, Mrs Yates,' his PA said politely. There was something up. Caroline just knew it. The best thing to do was to go home, she supposed. She wished Devlin and Maggie were in the car with her: they always gave her a sense of reassurance, especially in the city traffic. Hands gripping the steering wheel of her brand-new Fiesta, Caroline edged her way timidly out of the car-park and into the fast flow of traffic around the Green.

Richard

Richard was glad the weekend was over. He had missed Caroline and the apartment seemed very empty and unwelcoming. It had been a lonely few days. Charles had gone to London the previous Thursday and wasn't due back until later that morning, so he hadn't even been able to spend time with him.

All he'd done was take his mother shopping and listen to her moans. In the end, he was sorry he had ever mentioned the fact that Caroline had gone away with the girls for a few days. Sarah had seized on the snippet of information and like a dog with a bone she had gone back to it over and over, stating her opinion that it was not proper for a wife to go away without her husband in the company of female friends. It was just 'not done', and Caroline was behaving in a most selfish and unwifely manner, according to her mother-in-law.

If Caroline was unwifely, she'd been driven to it, Richard admitted ruefully as he put some Alpen in a bowl, poured milk on it, and sat down to eat his breakfast. His mother didn't know the half of it. No doubt if she did, she'd still find some way of blaming Caroline for everything. Sarah would have apoplexy if she ever found out about him and Charles.

Richard sighed. It was all such a mess – himself, Charles and Caroline – but after all the trauma of the past, at least the three of them were friends. He wished Charles was home; he'd missed him these past few days. Something was not right with Charles. These past few weeks he had not been his usual cheerful self. And he was holding back from telling Richard something, whatever it was. Well, he'd call him in an hour or so – he should be home from the airport by then – and arrange to meet him. Richard was determined to find out once and for all what was the matter with his friend. Maybe later Caroline could meet them for lunch, if she was home from her trip to Rosslare.

Maggie

Maggie couldn't resist slipping into Hughes & Hughes bookshop on her way to Dunnes foodhall where she wanted to buy a few groceries before going home. No doubt Terry wouldn't have remembered to get nappies and the like, and although she had done a big shop before she went away for the weekend there were some items you never had enough of. She loved this cheerful bookshop with its elegant green fixtures and fittings. Since her novel had been accepted for publication, she couldn't resist bookshops. Just think, in a few months her own novel would be sitting on the bookshelves, looking as bright and glossy as any of those currently on display.

She studied the covers and titles of the newest bestsellers, approving this one, disliking that. Soon she'd be having discussions with her publishers about her own cover. A little frisson ran through her veins. This was the most exciting thing that had ever happened to her. Her own achievement, something that she had succeeded in, not as a wife, mother or daughter, but as a person in her own right. Maggie Ryan. Author. And today had been the icing on the cake. This very morning, in the company of the greatest pals a woman could have, her novel had finally acquired a title. From now on she would no longer call it the *novel*. From now on it would be called *City Woman*, the name Devlin had suggested.

Maggie felt like dancing a little jig in the book-shop, but managed to restrain herself. No doubt her husband, Terry, would have something sarcastic to say when he found out about her good news, but that was his problem. In fact she was seriously considering not telling him for the time being. How she wished Adam was home so she could tell him. He would be so delighted and, after all, it was thanks to Adam Dunne, in a way, that she had got this far. His guidance and encouragement had been just what she needed at that time when she had been at one of the lowest points in her life. Smiling at the thought of his reaction, Maggie strode briskly out of Hughes & Hughes and on to Dunnes.

As she pushed the trolley between the shelves she thought of the nice fat cheque that she had deposited into her newly opened personal account. It was lovely to have money of her own again. Not that Terry was mean. But to have money and know she had earned it herself was very satisfying. And she had great plans for it too. She popped a bottle of red Piat d'Or into her trolley. Terry liked it so she'd cook him a nice dinner tonight and make a bit of a fuss of him for letting her have the weekend with Devlin and Caroline. Mind, knowing Terry, she'd be repaying the favour for weeks to come.

The thought came unbidden to her mind and the old familiar anger flamed as she thought of how he had betrayed her with Ria Kirby when she was pregnant with their youngest child. Yes, minding the children for a weekend was the very least he could do after carrying on an affair for God knows how long. Oh, how she hated that woman's guts! That two-faced, conniving little bitch. Maggie had never known she had it in her to feel such hatred, such anger. It frightened her. But for her children, she would have left him and never gone back. But she couldn't break up the home and take her twins away from their father. Whatever else he might be, Terry was a good father and provider. Mind, if her writing career took off she might very well end up being able to provide for them all herself. Anyway, that was all water under the bridge now, she chided herself. Maggie thought of Adam. Could she do to Terry what he had done to her? As she paid for her

26

shopping, Maggie knew she was going to have to decide, and sooner rather than later.

Terry

Terry Ryan was working himself into a slow rage. It had been bad enough having to look after three kids for the weekend without this happening. Maggie was really something else, swanning off with that other pair down to Wexford and leaving him with the lads. It was all right for Devlin and Caroline. Devlin was a free agent and Caroline had no children to look after but Maggie had responsibilities and it was about time that she started taking them seriously. If it wasn't gadding off with her friends, it was having her nose stuck in a typewriter writing her great novel while the house turned into a shambles. Novel indeed, Terry snorted as he paced up and down. Let her write her novels when she had reared her children. Hadn't his own mother, and hers, had to rear their kids without any of this crap about having time for themselves and fulfilling their own needs. God knows, he slaved day and night to give them a good standard of living.

OK, he might not be earning as much as Richard Yates and no doubt Devlin would be a millionairess by the time she was thirty, the way she was going on. But Maggie wasn't doing too badly. They had a four-bedroom detached house in Castleknock. And in the posh part of Castleknock too! She had her own car, plenty of money for food and clothes, the fees for that blasted gym club of Devlin's. What more could she want? Wasn't she ever satisfied? She was getting her own back, of course. Ever since she'd found out about that fling with Ria, Maggie had slowly been turning the screw. First of all it was employing Josie, the child-minder, on Fridays so she could have 'time for herself'. Then she'd started attending some writers' group or other one night a week. Was the woman ever home? She'd probably spent a fortune on the weekend, too. It was just a bit much. If she wasn't careful he'd go off and start seeing Ria again. He'd heard she was back in town. Not that he was vain or anything, but he knew he was still a pretty good-looking guy.

Now, Ria was a woman who understood a man's needs. She knew how to pamper a man after his hard day's work. Nice soothing massages, long lazy baths together. Good lusty sex. No excuses about getting pregnant and moans about having some time to herself. Ria had always made a fuss of him, always appreciated the flowers and champagne and little bits of jewellery he'd bought for her. It had been worth every penny he'd spent.

Well, whenever Maggie got home – *if* she ever got home – he was going to lay down the law. Because she hadn't been there this morning when she was needed, he had to take the morning off. Possibly the afternoon too if she didn't get a move on. How was a man expected to run his accountancy business with this kind of carry-on? Well, he'd had it! She could forget this writing crack and taking off for trips with the other two.

He marched out to the door to see if there was any

sign of her. It was just after eleven. Surely she must be home by now and have got his note. Well, by God, he'd have something to say to her when she got here . . . *if* she ever got here. Terry Ryan resumed his pacing.

PART ONE

Devlin's Story – I

One

Devlin sat in the Arrivals Hall of Dublin Airport, visibly impatient. She had left home extra early so that she could greet Luke off the plane instead of waiting for him in the foyer of the Airport Hotel — and now the damned plane was delayed.

Once more she checked the monitors and saw that Luke's flight would not be in for another twenty minutes. It would be at least a half an hour before he cleared customs. She might as well go and have a coffee. She could take another look at the figures for her meeting with Arthur Kelly, the Belfast business-man whom she was seeing later in the day. As she took the escalator up to Departures, she remembered that *Woman's Way* magazine had an article about City Girl that she hadn't yet seen. She'd buy a couple of copies and give them to Arthur, to keep for when they were arranging publicity.

In Hughes & Hughes, Devlin hastily thumbed through the magazine. Her eyes widened with pleasure as she saw the pictures the photographer had taken of the complex. He'd done a great job and the place looked a million dollars. The accompanying interview was very nicely done and Devlin was more than pleased. She took five copies of the magazine and paid for them at the cash desk. Five minutes later, she sat drinking a cup of coffee in the lounge bar overlooking the apron and runways. Dublin was a lovely airport to land at, she thought proudly, as she gazed out at the tapestry of green and gold fields and the purple-blue haze of the Dublin mountains in the distance. Devlin liked airports. She loved the air of hustle and bustle, the buzz of arrivals and departures and the roar of the jets. Her impatience dissipated as she sat watching planes taking off and landing. She saw a Ryanair jet land and guessed it was Luke's. In spite of his coolness on the phone the other day she was looking forward to seeing him. She just couldn't wait to talk to him about her great new idea. Surely he'd be enthusiastic once he'd seen the projections!

Finishing her coffee, she took the escalators back down to Arrivals and sat in a front-row seat waiting for Luke to emerge from customs. She saw him before he saw her and smiled to herself as she saw him stride through the doors. He frowned as he glanced at his watch and saw how late he was. He looked good — very good, she thought — in his casual grey trousers and soft grey leather jacket. Luke had a permanent tan, not the lounge-lizard look of the sunbed user but the rugged, weather-beaten look of a man who was used to being outdoors in all kinds of weather. Luke, who had once been a seaman, loved water and he had a sailing boat on the Thames, where he spent his precious and rare free time.

'Hi, Luke!' Devlin stood up and called his name. He did a double-take at the sight of her and then his frown was replaced by a broad grin as he dropped his briefcase and overnight bag and held out his arms to give her a hug.

'I certainly wasn't expecting to see you here. I thought you'd be dancing a jig of impatience over at the hotel. I was preparing myself to do battle,' he teased, enveloping her in a hug. 'Sorry I was cranky on the phone.'

'It's all right.' Devlin hugged him back. She had meant to be ever so cool, but in spite of herself she was really glad to see him. His gaze caught hers and then, taking her by surprise, he lowered his head and kissed her, a long lingering kiss that made her heartbeat quicken as to her own surprise she found herself kissing him back.

'Luke, stop,' she said, half-laughing, half-dismayed.

'I don't want to stop,' he said with a grin. 'Look, let's do a bunk. You cancel your meeting and I'll cancel mine and we'll spend the day together and forget all about business and just concentrate on us.'

Devlin, for reasons she could not explain, always felt panicky when Luke started talking about 'us'. She knew he wanted much more than she was prepared to give. Ever since the disaster of her relationship with Colin Cantrell-King, the suave gynaecologist who had fathered her baby and wanted her to have it aborted, Devlin did not want to get involved again with a man. And yet she trusted Luke implicitly. He had treated her with such kindness after the death of her baby. He had been so good to her when she was starting up City Girl. He was a terrific business partner and if ever she needed anything, he was always reliable. It wasn't that she wasn't attracted to him, either. Just kissing him now had brought back long-suppressed memories of desire. Since Colin's time, Devlin rarely thought about sex. Her experience with him had been disastrous and she had felt utterly used. She had gone right off men and indeed felt a deep distrust of them. Although she wouldn't admit it, Devlin was scared: scared of being hurt, scared of losing control, and very scared of getting into a relationship with Luke Reilly because she knew if she did, she would end up falling in love with him and falling in love was the last thing she wanted.

Devlin was quite happy with her life as it was. She had her independence and was in no danger of being hurt by anyone. Her present detachment suited her just fine.

'Come on,' he urged, his heavy-lidded brown eyes smiling down at her with an expression that made her breath catch in her throat.

'Luke, you know we can't do that,' Devlin said, as lightly as she could.

'I can, and you could too if you really wanted to,' Luke argued. 'We never have time to ourselves: it's always business, business, business. And I'm getting damn well fed up with it, if you want to know.' There was more than a trace of anger in his voice and her heart sank.

'Luke, don't be like that,' Devlin pleaded.

'Don't you think we should talk about us? You know I want us to . . .'

'Luke,' Devlin said firmly, 'we're very late; here isn't the time or the place . . .'

'It's as good a place as any, Devlin. I'm sick of this carry-on!'

'Luke, please . . .' Devlin said agitatedly, 'I've only got an hour. I must be on that road to Drogheda. I thought we were going to talk about the Belfast proposal.'

'I couldn't give two hoots about the Belfast proposal,' Luke retorted angrily.

'Luke!'

'Well, right this minute I couldn't care less if you wanted to take City Girl to the moon. I want to know where I stand with you. I deserve that much at least.' Luke's eyes were flashing and the thin line of his mouth left her in no doubt of his annoyance.

'Luke, you're not being fair,' she snapped, beginning to feel angry and trapped.

'No, Devlin. *You're* not being fair. And you're not being honest with me or with yourself. Stop running away and face up to things. You could be as attracted to me as I am to you if you'd let yourself. Why are you holding back?'

'For God's sake, Luke! People are looking.' A blush rose to her cheeks as she saw people giving them curious stares.

'Let them!' Luke was not concerned, but he drew her aside to a more private place so that the stream of people coming out of the customs couldn't see or hear them.

'Look, can't we talk about this later tonight when I get home from Drogheda?' Devlin said wearily. Why did he have to keep pushing her! Why couldn't he just be happy with the way things were!

'Is that a promise?' said Luke, his face stern and unsmiling.

'If that's what you want . . .' Devlin said, thoroughly exasperated.

'Don't sound too enthusiastic, for Christ's sake.'

'Ah, don't annoy me, Luke! Just knock it off. I've enough hassle without this. I don't know what's wrong with you lately. You're always in such an argumentative mood; you never want to discuss business. I was dying to tell you all about Belfast and now you've ruined it.'

Luke stared at her in silence and then he said coldly, 'Maybe we *should* discuss business – as to whether we should continue as business partners. Maybe this whole thing was a mistake. Not from a financial point of view but personally. I don't know if I want to get involved in any new ventures. Maybe you're right: it *is* too much hassle.'

Devlin couldn't believe her ears. Of all people, she never imagined that Luke would resort to emotional blackmail; she had always thought of him as one of the straightest men she had ever known.

Disgust tinged her voice and disdain flared in her eyes. 'Don't try emotional blackmail with me, Luke; it's beneath contempt. I thought you were more of a man than that.' If she had slapped him in the face, Luke could not have been more shocked. She saw it in his eyes and then anger replaced the shock, an anger so fierce that she quailed beneath his gaze.

'Is that what you think?' he said through gritted teeth, taking her by the shoulders, his thumbs digging into her flesh.

'Luke, you're hurting me,' she said heatedly. He dropped his hands immediately and drew several deep breaths as if to try and calm himself.

40

Picking up his bag and briefcase, he said in the coldest tone she had ever heard him use, 'Let's end this now. My solicitors will be on to yours about dissolving the partnership. City Girl is yours. I want nothing to do with it or you. I'm sure that will make you very happy.'

She saw red. 'It will. Believe me, that suits me just fine, mister,' she retorted.

'I'll get working on it immediately.'

'Do that!'

Turning, he strode over to the exit and disappeared through the Arrivals doors. Devlin was left angry and deeply shaken.

Two

'To hell with you, Luke Reilly!' fumed Devlin as she revved her engine and roared out of the multi-storey car-park. How dare he talk to her like that! How *dare* he! 'Bastard,' she swore as she drew up to the car-park exit and slid her ticket into the barrier control. As she drove out of the airport and on to the Belfast road she was fuelled by self-righteous anger. Luke Reilly wasn't the only businessman in the world; there were plenty of others who'd like to be associated with a success like City Girl. Look at Arthur Kelly: he was more than ready to get involved with her proposed Northern venture. If Reilly thought for one second that she was going to go crawling to him to beg him to reconsider, he could just think again.

She got stuck behind a tractor towing a trailer of hay, and cursed long and loudly using every expletive she could think of. She knew it was childish but she didn't care; it helped to vent the frustration that enveloped her after her fraught encounter with Luke.

What was wrong with that man? He had been so angry when she had accused him of emotional blackmail. It gave her the shivers to think of how enraged he had been: his eyes icy flints, his hands like two vice-grips. She had really hit a nerve to make him respond like that because normally he was very calm. He hadn't been all that calm when he had kissed her, she thought ruefully as she shot past the Donabate turn-off. A driver in the opposite lane of the dual carriageway flashed his lights at her. In an automatic reflex action she took her foot off the accelerator and hit the brakes lightly before gearing down. When she passed the speed trap Devlin was doing a respectable sixty miles an hour.

She'd been so looking forward to this trip. She just knew that the Belfast idea was a winner and smiled at how casually it had come about. She had been having a Turkish bath one evening after work and found herself sitting beside a petite blonde woman who confided that coming for a swim, sauna and aromatherapy session in City Girl was the thing she most looked forward to on her trips to Dublin. Her lovely soft lilting accent told Devlin she was from the North. She introduced herself as Lynda Jayne and explained that she presented a morning radio programme for Downtown Radio. When Devlin introduced herself, Lynda's eyes widened and she exclaimed, 'You're the brains behind all this! But you're so young. I didn't recognize you.'

'That's hardly surprising,' laughed Devlin, whose face was half-hidden behind a mist of steam. Her appearance was a far cry from the glamorous photo on the City Girl brochure.

'I'd love to do an interview with you,' said the woman enthusiastically. 'I take my hat off to women who make a go of things and prove that it can be done. I know my listeners would love to hear your story; I'd love to hear it myself.'

Devlin realized that her interest was genuine. 'If you like we can have coffee after your aromatherapy and we can chat about it then,' she suggested. One half of her wanted to talk to Lynda Jayne woman-to-woman; the other half was thinking that if Lynda broadcast the interview in Belfast, City Girl might gain a few more Northern customers. There were special membership facilities which enabled women from all over the country to avail themselves of its services when they visited Dublin.

The cup of coffee had turned into a meal and then Lynda and she had gone over to the Horseshoe Bar in the Shelbourne to have a drink and enjoy some people-watching. 'I love looking at the glam and the glitz; I love reading about the Ladies Who Lunch and all that kind of thing,' laughed Lynda as she sipped a Black Velvet. 'There's a whole scene down here that we just don't have in the North. Dublin always seems such an exciting city.'

'But I always think Belfast is exciting,' Devlin remarked. 'Look at all the shoppers who used to go up in their busloads. It was a chance to shop in Boots, BHS, Marks & Spencers. The other man's grass is always greener!'

'Hmmm,' agreed Lynda. 'We still don't have anything like this, though.' She waved a hand at the gossipy gathering that was crammed up against the bar waiting to be served. 'And as for City Girl . . . well, we could sure do with one of them. I'd nearly move down here to be able to visit once a week. It must be great for you to have all those facilities at your fingertips. I think I'd have aromatherapy or a facial massage every day.'

'Believe me, Lynda: running City Girl leaves precious little time for anything else,' Devlin said dryly. 'But I'll admit I make the most of it when I can.'

They had a most enjoyable evening, Lynda being the kind of woman one could listen to for hours. Devlin agreed, with no worries at all, to be interviewed. Lynda's researcher, Florence, arranged a link-up between an RTE studio and Downtown Radio. Sitting alone in the studio with a microphone in front of her, Devlin couldn't help feeling a little nervous. She had done many TV and radio interviews since opening City Girl but no matter how many she did, she felt butterflies in her stomach every time. People assured her that it was good to be a bit nervous; it was time to start worrying, they said, when you got blasé about it. Florence's calm tones as she arranged the sound-check helped a little. Lynda's voice came down the line asking if she were OK and then they were on the air. Lynda was so skilful that Devlin felt as though she were sitting beside her in the Coffee Dock having a chat.

As a result of the interview there had been many calls to City Girl from women wishing to avail of the special offer Devlin had organized for members from the North. Whenever Lynda came down south to visit, Devlin had coffee with her and enjoyed meeting the vivacious woman.

Several weeks after the broadcast, she had been having lunch with her father, as was their weekly custom. They had gone to the Coffee Dock in Jurys as Gerry was meeting some business men at the hotel, later in the afternoon. They were having coffee and

Devlin was teasing her father about how bank-managerish he looked when a male voice with a strong Northern accent hailed them. It was Arthur Kelly, a long-time friend and customer of her father.

'Sit and have coffee with us,' her father invited the jovial Derryman, shaking hands with him. Arthur grinned at Devlin as he leaned down and gave her a kiss on the cheek.

'Great interview with Lynda Jayne, kiddo! I nearly crashed the car when I heard your voice coming across loud and clear. Ach, I couldn't believe it was my wee girl.'

In the course of the conversation that followed, Devlin mentioned the interest in City Girl that the interview had created up North and in an almost off-hand remark had mused, 'I wonder how a place like City Girl would do in Belfast?'

Arthur sat up straight. 'Now there's an idea, lassie!'

Devlin's eyes widened. 'Arthur, do you think . . . ? Are you saying . . . ?'

'By golly I am.' Arthur's eyes were flashing with excitement, his ruddy face aglow.

'You pair!' laughed Gerry. 'Calm down now.'

'But Dad, this could work! I bet there's a market there ripe for exploitation.' Devlin was bubbling with excitement. This was just what she needed. Luke and she had discussed expanding and a feasibility study they had commissioned in Galway had been very encouraging. They were in the process of finding suitable premises. Having a City Girl in Belfast would be the icing on the cake.

Gerry left them to it and Devlin and Arthur sat for another hour discussing all aspects of the scheme.

They agreed the preliminary steps. Devlin's first priority was to have a chat with her accountant. She wanted to have all her facts and figures when she presented the idea to Luke.

Devlin sighed deeply as she arrived at the outskirts of Balbriggan. He would have been as excited as she was if he'd seen the file in her briefcase. She was sure of it. Now, because of their row, he hadn't seen one comma of the business plan and she was going to have to tell Arthur that she hadn't had a chance to get Luke's opinion. She was sure Luke hadn't meant it when he talked about pulling out of City Girl. That had been said in the heat of the moment. He was as committed as she was. When he cooled down she'd get him to go over the plan and meet Arthur.

If only they hadn't had that stupid argument. She supposed it wasn't all Luke's fault. He had a point about knowing where he stood. And she hadn't helped things by kissing him back. It had been a wonderful kiss, too. Devlin had been taken aback by the desire that had rippled through her. It had been a long long time since she'd felt anything like that. After being made pregnant by Colin and having her baby it was as if her sexuality and sensuality had shut down. After the accident she had become withdrawn. Even now when men – and there were many who wanted to get to know her – asked her out, she always refused.

But Luke was different. It was Luke who was responsible for her forthcoming lunch with her mother. He had persuaded her to try for a reconciliation with Lydia and she had been dying to tell him that she had taken the first step in that direction. She

47

knew that Luke would never hurt her like Colin did but she was as scared as hell of getting involved. If she could explain her fears to him maybe he would understand. When she got home tonight she would phone him and try to make him see. The thought cheered her up, because having rows with Luke made her miserable. She wondered if he would kiss her again. Part of her hoped he would, and she chided herself for her inconsistency.

The meeting with Arthur went better than she could have hoped. He had just come from a meeting in Dundalk with a colleague who had a site on the outskirts of Belfast that Arthur felt might suit their plans.

'I'm also looking at a premises near Donegall Square, which is the one I'd really like. It's central but I know an insurance company is after it as well as ourselves. If we can get it though, girlie, we'll have hit the jackpot. The market research report I commissioned showed a very positive response and the competition is nothing to be feared. Not for an up-market project like City Girl! Och aye! there's plenty of aerobics classes and gyms and the like but nothing that comes close to what we have in mind.'

'My accountant didn't turn the idea down out of hand as I thought he might. In fact, I've figures here that he's come up with. We could apply for grants under various business expansion schemes.' Devlin passed the figures over to Arthur.

'He's very thorough, this accountant of yours,' Arthur said approvingly as he read the figures. 'He's got it all covered. I see he's been in touch with CTT as well.'

'Kieran leaves no stone unturned, and if he didn't think there was something in this, I wouldn't be sitting here with these figures,' grinned Devlin. She was very fond of her parsimonious accountant, who kept her feet firmly on the ground and often poured cold water on her wilder flights of fancy. With the guidance of Kieran and Luke she had avoided quite a few pitfalls in the past, so she always listened carefully to what they had to say.

Full of enthusiasm, she and Arthur agreed to carry on costing and planning. They decided that Devlin should visit Belfast as soon as Arthur had firm information on the location of premises. Driving home late that afternoon, Devlin felt quite lighthearted. She wouldn't bother going in to the office, she decided: she'd go home, shower and change and phone Luke at his hotel.

As she stood under the shower soaping herself she actually felt a bit nervous. It was a bit like arranging a first date, she thought in wry amusement. She hoped he had cooled down. She would apologize for accusing him of using emotional blackmail. No wonder he'd been so insulted. That wasn't Luke's style at all. Wrapping herself in a soft towelling robe, Devlin walked into the bedroom and dialled the number of Luke's hotel.

'I'm sorry,' she heard the receptionist say. 'Mr Reilly cancelled his reservation; he said he was flying back to London this evening rather than tomorrow.'

'Thank you,' Devlin murmured, hanging up. She shivered a little, despite the warmth of the evening sun shining through her French doors. He must still be mad, she thought glumly, and a heaviness descended on her spirits. She felt terribly lonely all of a sudden. Impulsively she dialled his home number; he might be there already. She wanted to hear his voice; she wanted to say sorry; she wanted so much to tell him all her news about the meeting with Arthur and the phone call to her mother. There was no reply, only the recording on the answering machine. Uncharacteristically she was stuck for words as she heard his deep voice at the other end of the line inviting her to leave her name and number. She hated answering machines. She hung up and her finger hovered over the digits as she tried to make up her mind whether or not to call his office. Taking a deep breath, she dialled his private number. The line was engaged.

So he was there. It was hardly his highly efficient PA still working at this hour. A glance at her alarm clock told her that it was six-forty. She'd try again in ten minutes, she decided, as she switched on her hairdryer and began to blow-dry her blonde bob.

Five minutes later the phone rang and she nearly jumped out of her skin. 'Hello,' she said dry-mouthed, half-expecting it to be Luke. It was Maggie and she didn't know whether to be glad or sorry.

When she called his number again twenty minutes later the phone just kept on ringing.

'Oh Luke, why couldn't you be there?' she muttered unhappily.

She tried his home again around nine and got the machine again.

Thoroughly fed up she sat listening to her Mary Black discs.

She called again at eleven and he still wasn't home. Maybe he was seeing someone. Maybe he was out with a woman. The thought left her feeling miserable. She got into bed and lay tossing and turning until sleep finally came.

Luke stretched and yawned, rubbing his bleary eyes as he sat up and tried to work out where he was. 'God Save the Queen' was being played on the television and he leaned over and switched it off. He must have fallen asleep. He hadn't meant to spend the night on the boat but it was so late now he decided he might as well. He didn't particularly relish the thought of going back home anyway.

The waters of the Thames lapped soothingly against the sides of the boat and through the portholes he could see the lights of London twinkling like Christmas tree decorations. In all his life he had never felt so alone, so confused and so utterly browned-off. He buried his head in his hands, trying to erase the image of her face, that face that haunted him. When he saw her waiting at the airport so unexpectedly, Luke had felt ridiculously happy. When she had put her arms around him as if she were really glad to see him and kissed him back he had really thought he was getting somewhere at last.

'Oh Devlin, Devlin, what are you doing to me?' he muttered. When she accused him of emotional blackmail, he had felt such anger! He had actually wanted to shake her. Now, all he felt was a weary resignation that he was never going to have the relationship he longed for with Devlin.

He knew that she had been terribly damaged emotionally by all she had gone through. He had tried to be patient and restrained but after all these months it was obvious that he was making no headway with her. Luke was nothing if not a realist. You could bang your head against a stone wall for only so long. The time had come to call a halt. Now that City Girl was well established and Devlin had proved herself so capable, she no longer needed his assistance. It would be no trouble for her to find another business partner; her father would be able to help out there.

Anyway he had more than enough to keep him occupied on this side of the Irish Sea. With the downturn in property values, his company had been buying, refurbishing, letting, and eventually when the recession ended they'd sell and make a handsome profit.

No, he'd meant it when he told Devlin City Girl was hers. He'd had enough. He'd told Dianne to arrange a meeting with his solicitors first thing in the morning. He'd instruct them to start proceedings to dissolve the partnership.

With a heart heavier than the anchor of his boat, Luke switched off the lights of the saloon and went into his cabin. He undressed in the dark and got into bed. He wondered how Devlin was feeling. Had she even given him a thought? Knowing her, he guessed that she was up to her eyes in projections and costings and design layouts after her meeting with that Northern businessman. Imagine wanting to open a City Girl in Belfast! The woman was mad. He folded his arms under his head and lay back, listening to the creaking of the boat. Maybe she wasn't, though, he mused. There were great incentives for setting up a business in the North and maybe a City Girl there would take off as dramatically as it had in Dublin.

'It's nothing to do with you, so forget it,' he growled. 'And from now on, you're having nothing to do with her.' He turned over on his front and buried his head under the pillows but it was a long time before he slept.

'You're the one that I want . . . oh oh oooh, honey, oh yes, indeed . . .' sang Dianne Westwood as she smoothed pear and pawpaw moisturizer into her creamy skin. She was giving herself the works. Cleansing, toning, moisturizing. Plucking eyebrows, manicuring nails. She was in great form.

Luke had arrived back at the office totally unexpectedly and in a foul humour. He wasn't due back until the following day. She herself had made the flight and hotel reservations, and yet there he was as large as life striding through the office at five-fifteen, telling her to arrange a meeting with his solicitor first thing in the morning.

'Will tomorrow afternoon do?' she asked him calmly, after hearing Andrew Hunter's PA say that a morning meeting was totally out of the question.

'No it will not do!' Luke snapped. 'Tell Hunter's PA to arrange a breakfast meeting.' The meeting had finally been arranged although the woman at the other end of the line had been a bit miffed. But she knew it was more than her job was worth to discommode Luke Reilly, who was one of the office's biggest clients.

'How did the meeting with Miss Delaney go?' Dianne asked airily, thrilled that Luke had found her up to her eyes in work, despite the fact that the rest of the staff had left at five.

'It didn't go,' Luke gritted. 'Get me the City Girl file please, Dianne – contracts, everything.'

'Certainly,' she said, the very picture of calm efficiency. Privately she was agog. What was going on here? All was certainly not well with DD.

She got him the files he required and closed the door quietly behind her. Three-quarters of an hour later she had phoned the nearby deli and ordered thick-cut beef on rye, his favourite sandwich, and some salads and coleslaw. Setting a tray with a crisp linen tray-cloth and gleaming silver, she had made a pot of coffee and carried the meal in to her boss.

He lifted his head from his work and smiled at her, that gorgeous sexy smile that made his brown eyes crinkle up. She immediately wanted to plant a hot passionate kiss on that so sensual mouth. She wanted to tell him to forget Devlin Delaney, that she was here to fulfil his every need. But all she said was: 'I thought you might be hungry; you look as if you need some sustenance.'

'I'd be lost without you, Dianne,' he replied and she felt a surge of triumph. Had he ever said that to the blonde bombshell? She was sure he hadn't.

Beaming at the memory of the compliment, Dianne slid between her satin sheets and switched out the light. She could conjure up his image much more easily in darkness. Which fantasy would she have tonight? The wedding one, where she glided down the aisle in a fairytale dress far superior to anything worn by a royal bride, to be greeted by Luke, her husband-to-be, at the altar, and then to imagine him placing the gold wedding band on her finger, his eyes caressing her warmly? No. Tonight she wanted passion. She remembered the smile on his mouth and in his eyes. Tonight she wanted the seduction scene where his eyes smouldered into hers and he muttered thickly as he tore the silk camisole from her body, 'I want you, Dianne! God, how I want you!'

'Oh yes . . . yes, Luke . . . yesss . . .' Dianne breathed quickly in the dark. This was her favourite fantasy of all.

Three

'Oh shut up!' Devlin thumped the insistently chirping alarm clock that was guaranteed to set teeth on edge, and buried her head under the pillows. This was most unDevlin-like behaviour but she had not slept well and she knew she had a gruelling day ahead of her. She had three meetings to attend, two with personnel managers of firms that were negotiating membership terms for their employees and one with a PR firm that was anxious to persuade her to endorse a client's product. She was guest of honour at a chamber-of-commerce luncheon and she dreaded making a speech. Then she had to go out to RTE to record an interview for a current affairs and business programme.

For one moment she was sorely tempted to call her secretary, pretend she was stricken with flu and get her to cancel all her engagements. A day in bed with no-one to harass her seemed like such a good idea. Today she didn't feel like being Devlin Delaney, successful and ambitious businesswoman. She felt like keeping her head firmly under the pillow. It was just as she used to feel when she woke up on Monday mornings knowing she had a full week of school ahead of her.

People often said to her: 'It must be great being your own boss.' Well, that was the greatest misconception possible. She might be the boss, but she still had commitments that she couldn't ignore. It was easier by far for one of her employees at City Girl to duck out for the day than it was for her, she thought grumpily, as she slid unenthusiastically out of bed. Bleary-eyed, she caught sight of herself in the mirror, and thought – if only they could see me now. So much for the get-ahead businesswoman. It was tough going sometimes to live up to the image that the media had created for her. A shower and coffee refreshed her somewhat and as she placed the text of her speech in her briefcase, she was already mentally gearing up for her first meeting.

City Girl, even at eight-fifteen a.m., was a hive of activity. Lots of women came for early-morning workout sessions or swimming, before going in to work. Informal business meetings were often held over breakfast and as Devlin traversed the Coffee Dock to order some breakfast to be sent up to her office, she noted the presence of a prominent female politician, a high-profile business-woman and a board member of a government-sponsored agency, deep in conversation over coffee and croissants. A lot of networking went on at City Girl, especially over breakfast, and this pleased her enormously.

As she sat by her window overlooking St Stephen's Green, eating yoghurt and honey, Devlin toyed with the idea of phoning Luke. The longer the interval, the more her courage failed. She had never seen him so angry in all the time they had worked together. The least he could have done was to phone her and apologize for walking away at the airport. That had been the height of rudeness, she argued silently with herself. After all, they had had a meeting scheduled. It wasn't very professional of him, she decided, to let his personal feelings interfere with their business relationship.

Yes, but maybe you were sending out conflicting signals she chided herself, kissing him back that way. 'Oh this is ridiculous!' she muttered, as she rose and marched over to her desk. She dialled Luke's private number. They were adults after all; the sooner they cleared up this misunderstanding the better.

The PA answered. This did not surprise Devlin: she had met Dianne once and knew that this efficient young woman was not one to let the grass grow under her feet. 'Is Luke there, please?' she asked pleasantly.

'I'm afraid not,' came the crisp Sloaney voice. Dianne wasn't giving away any information.

'Well, this is Devlin Delaney. Could you tell him I called and ask him to call me back. I'll be in the office until noon; otherwise he'll get me at home tonight.'

'I'm not expecting him back at the office until this afternoon. He has a business meeting with his solicitors this morning and he'll be on site until lunchtime, but I'll certainly give him your message.'

'Thank you,' said Devlin, hanging up.

Dianne's news had disturbed her more than she cared to admit. Surely Luke wasn't meeting his solicitors about City Girl! He couldn't have been serious yesterday. Or could he? Suddenly, Devlin wasn't too sure.

*   *   *

'Any calls I should know about?' Luke appeared at her door, and Dianne devoured the sight of him in his jeans and T-shirt. He always wore jeans and a T-shirt when he was going on site and she loved the way the white material clung to his hard muscular body. She loved the way the dark hair curled at his throat and the idea of being held in his tanned muscled arms was her greatest dream.

'No calls,' she lied to her boss. She wasn't going to tell him Devlin rang. Something was going on between those two: they'd had a row of some sort or other. What other reason could Luke have for haring back to London when he was supposed to be staying over in Dublin. And wanting to meet his solicitors too.

No she wasn't going to tell him Ms Devlin Delaney called. If it ever came to light she could always say she forgot. Because she was so efficient as a rule, she was sure Luke would overlook it this once.

'I've prepared that report on the Shepherd's Bush project and it's being typed up. I have your itinerary for your trip to Holland. Your flight leaves from Heathrow at eight tomorrow morning. Would you like me to drive you to the airport?' Dianne asked, hoping against hope that he'd say yes.

'The Shepherd's Bush project already? That's good work, Dianne. Thank you. I appreciate the late hours you've worked on it.' Luke smiled and Dianne glowed. 'I'll get a taxi to the airport and save you the trek out; but thanks for the offer. Just hold the fort here for me until I get back.'

It's no trouble, she was tempted to say, but that would not be the way of a sophisticate and Dianne was nothing if not sophisticated. Let him take a taxi to the airport, but she'd be waiting for him when he got back. She was going to make herself indispensable to Luke Reilly, and DD was going to fade into insignificance – that's if *she* had anything to do with it.

'I'll organize some coffee for you, Luke – oh, and I got Sally to collect your suits from the cleaners. They're hanging up in your office.'

'Dianne, you're a brick,' Luke declared.

I know, she smiled to herself as she went to get the coffee.

Luke flicked casually through the itinerary Dianne had organized for his Dutch trip. Usually once he knew his itinerary, the adrenalin would start to flow for the business ahead. Right this minute the thought of going to Holland on a business trip was an irritation.

He had really hoped that Devlin would ring. Even as he sat listening to his solicitor tell him what dissolving their partnership entailed, he decided that if she phoned he would ask her if she wanted to discuss things. Obviously she didn't.

Flicking through his Rolodex, Luke found the number of his solicitor's office and picked up his phone to call him.

'When will he be back?' Devlin tried to keep her tone steady.

'I'm picking him up late on Friday night,' Dianne said crisply.

'Thank you,' Devlin replied.

'You're welcome, Miss Delaney.'

Was she imagining it, Devlin wondered as she hung up, or did Dianne sound almost insolent? She couldn't believe that Luke had gone to Holland without returning her call. He must really have meant it when he'd said he'd had enough. The thought left her feeling faintly sick.

Her secretary popped her head through the door. 'Are you ready to start interviewing? The first candidate has arrived.'

Devlin took a deep breath and nodded. 'Sure; ask Aoibhinn to come down, will you?' Aoibhinn was City Girl's chief beautician and the interviews were to fill two positions in the beauty salon.

The rest of the day passed at its usual hectic pace, and the following day, sick of the place, Devlin called on Maggie, who had her own problems just then. Seeing how preoccupied she was, Devlin kept her woes about Luke to herself.

She was going through the report Arthur had prepared for her the following morning when her secretary buzzed her to tell her that her solicitor was on the line. As if in a dream she heard Monica Finlay say that a letter from Luke's solicitors had arrived on her desk advising her that they had begun proceedings to dissolve their partnership.

Four

'We are making our final approach to London Heathrow. Please fasten your seat belts for landing and put your seats in an upright position.' At the stewardess's announcement Devlin felt knots of apprehension grip her stomach. It had been a real spur-of-the-moment decision to fly to London and, now that she was here, she wondered if she had made a big mistake. Maybe Luke would just tell her to get lost. He hadn't bothered to return her calls and their respective solicitors were currently working on the dissolution of their partnership.

She couldn't let it end like this. Not in bitterness and anger. Luke meant too much to her for that. But what would she do if he refused to see her? He had become so much a part of her life: always there, as a sounding board and supporter. She couldn't envisage running City Girl Ltd without him. She had taken him for granted for so long that it was something of a shock to realize just how much she depended on him. She had been so busy she had never really given too much thought to their relationship. But one thing she knew very well — she did not want to lose Luke's friendship.

She phoned his apartment immediately after

disembarking but there was no answer. She glanced at her watch and calculated that he was probably on his way to the office. It was just gone eight-thirty.

After she had cleared customs, she took a taxi and gave the address of Luke's office. It felt strange to be sitting in one of the big black London cabs again. Not that she'd been able to travel around in them that much when she'd lived in London. Money had been very tight: it had been the bus and tube for her then. To think that she had worked here, lived here and given birth to Lynn here. It all seemed so long ago. She had taken her baby home to Dublin to give her a better life. Perhaps if she had stayed in London, her daughter would still be alive. Tears smarted at the back of her eyes and her heart ached with an unbearable longing. Whoever said time healed was a liar. Subdued and getting more tense by the minute, Devlin was sorely tempted to tell the taxi-driver to turn around and bring her back to Heathrow.

By the time she got to the impressive block that housed Luke's offices she was feeling really nervous. A quick glance in her mirror told her that outwardly she looked fine and showed no hint of the turmoil that churned her up inside. She retouched her lipstick, paid the taxi-driver, took a deep breath and walked up the marble steps of the building. Now that *she* was here, she wondered where Luke was. He could be at a meeting or on site. But surely if he'd been away on a business trip until Friday night he would stop by the office first thing on a Monday morning. Well, she'd find out in just a few moments, she thought wryly as the lift rose silently to the top floor where Luke's offices were.

'Can I help you?' a pleasant young receptionist asked her.

'Sally, could you type this up immediately; Mr Reilly needs it.' A tall thin model-like blonde had come out from an inner office. Devlin recognized Luke's PA, Dianne.

The blonde woman's thinly plucked eyebrows arched questioningly. And then she too recognized Devlin.

'Oh Miss Delaney,' she said coolly. 'Can I help you?'

'I'd like to see Luke for a few minutes if you could tell him I'm here,' Devlin said, marvelling at how normal her voice sounded.

'He has meetings scheduled for the whole morning. I could try and fit you in later in the week – perhaps Wednesday?' Dianne said crisply.

'If you would kindly tell him I'm here, I'd be much obliged,' Devlin said firmly, holding the other woman's stare. She was damned if she was going to be intimidated by this creature.

'Dianne, I need Van der Voek's – Devlin! What are you doing here?' Luke was standing at the door staring at her.

Devlin's heart skipped a beat. 'I just need to see you for a few minutes – if you could fit me in.' Her eyes met his.

'Certainly. Come on in.' Luke held the door open for her.

'What about your nine-thirty appointment?' Dianne interjected coldly.

'Tell him I've been slightly delayed. Offer him coffee. Do what you usually do when this happens.'

He led the way towards his office and closed the door firmly behind himself and Devlin.

Just what the hell was *she* doing here, Dianne wondered furiously, as she sat at her computer and clattered the keys with much more force than was necessary. God, she'd nearly died when she had walked out to reception and seen the blonde bombshell in all her glory. And she had been looking glorious too, blast her, in her exquisitely tailored taupe suit and whiter than white camisole that showed off her tan. And the hair. The bob really suited her: it made her look sophisticated and vulnerable at the same time, if that were possible.

'Oh shit!' A thought struck her. Devlin would no doubt mention that she had called and left a message. Now she'd really be up the creek. Luke would be raging. Just when she thought she was getting somewhere with him, too. He had been really pleased that she had collected him at the airport. He had taken her for a meal at Scott's in Mayfair and the lobster bisque had been superb. She had asked him all about his trip and shown great enthusiasm when he'd told her all about the deal he'd made. He'd even bought her a present, a beautiful, carved jewellery box, and told her he really appreciated how hard she worked for him. Dianne had gone to bed that night on such a high. Even her discovery on coming into work that morning that he had also brought Sally back a present hadn't affected her great good humour. Everything had been going swimmingly until that Devlin had appeared, batting her big blue-green eyes and making Dianne look a fool.

What was going on in that office? She would give anything to know.

'Thank you for seeing me,' Devlin said, feeling more than a little awkward.

'Don't be daft, Devlin. Of course I'd always see you!' Luke expostulated.

'Well, I wasn't too sure,' Devlin retorted, 'especially when you didn't return my calls.'

'What calls? I didn't know you'd called.' Luke's brows drew down in a frown.

'Well I did; and I called you at home too. When I didn't hear from you and then when my solicitor told me about the letter from your solicitors, I figured that was the end of us . . .' Her voice trailed off.

'If I remember correctly, that didn't seem to worry you too much the last time we met,' he said dryly.

'Ah, Luke, don't be a pig! You told me you never wanted to see me again. Remember? Maybe you really meant it.' She turned to walk away, but Luke caught her by the arm and turned her back to face him.

'I didn't mean it. I'm sorry. You're right: I *am* being a pig. And I'm sorry about the other day at the airport. I don't want to be the one to end our partnership.' His amber eyes stared down into hers.

'I don't either,' she whispered. 'I need you as my friend.'

'Ah, Devlin, I'll always be your friend,' Luke sighed, putting his arms around her. It was as if a huge burden had evaporated and she rested her head on his shoulder, hugging him back tightly.

'I'd better call the solicitors and tell them we've changed our minds,' he said ruefully. 'We're like two

66

kids. You'd better tell me all about this Belfast deal we're getting into.'

'Luke, you'll love it.' Devlin's eyes sparkled with enthusiasm. 'I think we could be on to a winner.' A buzz on the intercom interrupted them. It was Dianne.

'Kenneth Major is on the line for you.'

'Tell him I'll call him back — and hold all my calls please,' Luke said briskly.

'Certainly,' came the frosty response.

Devlin smiled ruefully. 'We're upsetting your PA's carefully planned schedule. I know Liz, my secretary, goes mad when I upset her plans.'

'If I'd known you were coming I'd have rescheduled today's meetings,' Luke said regretfully. 'What time's your flight home?'

'I haven't booked one. I wasn't sure what time I'd get to see you; so I was just going to go back to the airport and hang around for a stand-by.'

'Look, why don't I try and get as much done here as I can? You take the keys of the apartment and go and freshen up. Or go shopping or whatever . . . and we'll go out to dinner. I'll get Dianne to book you a flight for tomorrow.'

'Liz will go spare,' Devlin laughed. But the idea was very appealing.

'Be a devil! I'll risk Dianne's wrath if you risk Liz's.'

'You're on,' Devlin said, smiling at him.

'I'm really glad you came, Devlin.' Luke's eyes were warm.

'So am I.'

Luke bent his head and kissed her very lightly on

67

the lips. It was like the fleeting touch of butterfly's wings.

'Go and have a lovely day to yourself and I'll try and get home by four.' He took a bunch of keys out of his pocket and slipped one off the ring.

'The key to the castle. I'll ring Raji the doorman and tell him to expect you. OK?'

'OK,' Devlin agreed.

He walked out to the reception area with his arm around her shoulder, quite unaware that Dianne was glowering at them both.

'See you later.' He pressed the lift button. The last thing she saw was his face smiling in at her, and then she was on her way down to the ground floor, her heart as light as a feather.

A huge fork of lightning streaked across the London sky and the heavens opened. By the time she had crossed from one side of Knightsbridge to the other Devlin was drenched. Laden down with parcels, she hailed a taxi, gave Luke's address and sank gratefully into the back seat. It had turned out a horrible day, muggy and thundery. Maybe after the storm the air would freshen up a bit.

She'd had a wonderful few hours browsing and shopping. There was nothing like a bit of a spree for lifting the spirits, she reckoned, especially since she hadn't been on one for ages. She had bought herself a gorgeous kimono. It was black with splashes of pale pink and turquoise, and the sleeves and neck were edged in pink. She'd also got the pale pink nightdress that went with it. She'd need it for tonight, she assured herself, as she hadn't come prepared to stay over. She'd treated herself to some silk and lace underwear while she was there. But the silk dressing-gown was exquisite, so feminine. It had just caught her eyes in the lingerie department of Harrods. Well, a girl was entitled to treat herself now and again, and it was certainly different from the terry-towelling robes she normally wore.

While she was in Harrods, after she'd had coffee and florentines, she'd gone to the opulent foodhall and bought some provisions. She planned to cook dinner for them tonight. It was cosier than going out. She knew Luke loved home-cooking. Like her, he had to eat out so often that it was no longer a treat. Whenever she cooked a meal for him at home, he relished it. She'd cook him a steak-and-kidney pie. His favourite.

She glanced at her watch. Two-thirty. Luke would be home soon. She was dying to hear what he thought of the Belfast project. She was so glad their tiff was over. It had made her downright miserable.

'You got wet already, Madam.' Raji, the doorman, held an umbrella for her as she alighted from the taxi.

'I sure did, Raji. That was some downpour.' Devlin's clothes clung damply to her and she was looking forward so much to getting out of them and having a shower.

'Mr Reilly left a message to say he'll be later than he thought; he sends his apologies.'

'No problem, Raji,' Devlin said cheerfully. It would give her a chance to get organized.

An hour later she was a different woman. Dressed in a borrowed shirt of Luke's, she padded barefoot around his kitchen, making preparations for the meal she was going to cook. She cut the steak in cubes, sliced the kidneys and chopped an onion and parsley finely, adding a few mushrooms because Luke liked the flavour, and whistling all the while. She had cheated and bought ready-made pastry because pastry-making was not her forte. But the ready-to-roll stuff was just as tasty. She had parboiled the potatoes to make another favourite of his, roasties.

In the distance, over towards Westminster, she could still hear the low rumble of thunder. It had stopped raining but it was still very overcast. Stepping out on to the balcony she inhaled the moist oppressive air. It really had turned into a horrible day and she was glad she wasn't still traipsing around the shops. Still, she could not help admiring the panoramic view of London and the Thames that Luke's huge balcony afforded. His penthouse was very expensive but he had worked very hard for everything he had and in her opinion he deserved the luxury.

She hoped he wouldn't mind that she had changed their arrangements about eating out. Anyway she had nothing to wear now: Raji had sent her clothes to the dry cleaners. The phone rang and she hurried back inside to answer it. It was Dianne.

'Mr Reilly asked me to phone: he's tied up at a meeting and it will probably be after five before he gets away.'

'Tell him not to worry, Dianne,' Devlin said cheerfully. 'I'm in no hurry now that I'm staying over. Did you organize a flight for me for tomorrow?'

'Mr Reilly has all the details,' Dianne said in her snooty accent.

'Great. Thanks. Cheerio.' Devlin hung up and

thought how lucky she was that as well as being efficient, Liz, her secretary, was very pleasant, and had a terrific phone manner.

She decided she would set the pine table in the kitchen rather than having the whole works in the dining-room. Anyway, she wasn't exactly dressed for a formal dinner! She grinned to herself at the thought. Luke's shirt was enormous on her and the shoulders came down nearly to her elbows. She had tied one of his ties around her waist to keep the shirt ends from flapping when she was cooking. A more glamorous specimen it would be hard to find! But she didn't mind with Luke. With him she could always be herself. He had seen her at her worst, when she had been so low that she wondered if life was worth living. It had been Luke who had got her going again and he was the one person in the world that she never felt she had to impress. He accepted her for who and what she was. Warts and all.

After she had set the table, she braised the steak and kidney and left it simmering slowly, made herself a cup of coffee and went into the lounge. Flicking through Luke's compact disc collection, she chose a Grieg compilation and sat back to let the evocative notes wash over her. She suddenly felt weary. She had been up at the crack of dawn to get to the airport and besides she hadn't been sleeping very well over the previous few days through worry about the situation with Luke. It was bliss just to sit relaxed, listening to the beautiful music.

That was how Luke found her, curled up in a corner of the sofa in his shirt and tie, fast asleep. He eyed her with some amusement and then followed his nose into the kitchen, inhaling the delicious aroma of the simmering steak and kidney.

'Hmmmm!' Luke's eyes brightened. Trust Devlin: this was a much better idea than going out to dinner. To tell the truth he was feeling pretty bushed himself. That trip to Holland had been a killer and he'd found himself tossing and turning a lot at night ever since his row with Devlin. Well, at least that was over, he thought with satisfaction, as he turned off the heat under the pan.

Twenty minutes later, he'd showered and shaved and changed out of his suit into a pair of jeans and a T-shirt. He had just made fresh coffee, when Devlin walked into the kitchen rubbing her eyes.

'Hi,' she said, giving him an affectionate hug. 'I meant to have your dinner on the table. I just fell asleep. Sorry about that.' She yawned.

'Only that it's steak-and-kidney pie you'd be sacked,' said Luke with a broad grin. 'Do you want me to do anything to help?'

'Yes: butter the brown bread for the smoked salmon. I'll just pop the pie into the oven. It won't take the pastry long to cook.' She busied herself with the pastry she'd already rolled out. She glazed the top with egg yolk, moved the roast potatoes, which were crisping nicely, down to the lower shelf and placed the pie dish on the top shelf of the oven. 'Are you sure you don't mind not going out? I thought this would be more homely and besides, I've loads to tell you.' Devlin sat up at the breakfast counter beside him and took a cup of coffee. 'Luke, I phoned my mother and invited her to lunch.'

'Devlin, that's great news. You won't regret it, believe me.' Luke gave her a comforting hug.

'I hope not,' Devlin sighed. 'I hope we'll be able to talk and that things won't be too awkward.'

'I'd say your dad's pleased.'

'Yes, he's really chuffed about it.'

'Don't worry; everything will be fine,' Luke assured her.

'Do you want to hear about Belfast?'

'Well, I can see you're bursting to tell me. Just don't get too excited. Don't you think we should wait until Galway's up and running first?'

'Oh, but Luke, wait until you meet Arthur. He's great! He's done a thorough business plan, including one of the best strategic marketing plans I've seen,' she declared. 'He's commissioned a survey in the catchment area to check our target market and find out about the disposable income of females in the twenty to mid-forty range . . .'

'What about cash flow? Have you sourced the finances that will be required? What about the fitting-out costs? Are you considering buying or renting? What about the financial institutions? Will the banks want personal guarantees? Are the interest rates going to be fixed or variable?' Luke, she could see, was enjoying himself. 'Have you considered insurance cover? What would our break-even point be?' Luke shot the questions at her like bullets from a machine-gun.

'Of course I've considered all the factors – you're not dealing with an amateur here,' Devlin replied calmly. She grinned at him. 'I was taught by the best. So you just sit there and I'll get the figures that

Kieran prepared for me; you'll soon see whether Belfast is a good idea or not. Don't forget,' she added, as she slipped off the stool to get her briefcase, 'the complex will be grant-aided as well.' Stick that in your pipe and smoke it, mister, she thought smugly, as she fetched the papers. The business plan was A1 – she knew it. Devlin had learned a lot when City Girl was being planned, especially from Luke and her father. She had expansion in mind, and Belfast was her target.

Dinner was a great success and, after reading her figures, Luke gave a cautious go-ahead to further work on the Belfast plan. Devlin was pleased; she knew Luke wasn't doing it to humour her. He was a hard-headed businessman and recognized a good opportunity when he saw one.

Nevertheless, she lay wide-eyed, unable to sleep. The nap earlier on had been a mistake, she conceded, but there was more to it than that. When she decided to fly over to London, she had wanted to safeguard their friendship. But more than that, much more, their row had focused her thoughts on what she wanted and needed from Luke and what he wanted and needed from her. For the first time they both wanted the same thing. And for the first time since her encounter with Colin, she finally felt she wanted to commit herself to a full and loving relationship. The only thing was: she was so nervous about it all. Beneath the veneer of sophistication she was very inexperienced. She had lost her virginity to Colin in a quick, furtive and painful encounter that had resulted in pregnancy. She had never had sex with a man since and she was a bit scared; scared that she wouldn't be any good at it, scared that it would be like the first time, painful and terribly disappointing, and not at all like the wonderful thing it was supposed to be. The only man she trusted enough and wanted enough to try again with was Luke.

She slid out of bed, slipped into the bathroom and washed her teeth. She caught sight of herself in the mirror, eyes as big as saucers, and smiled. God, people at home wouldn't believe it if they could see the self-confident sophisticate now.

She walked down the hall to Luke's room, padded over to the bed and slid in under the sheets beside him.

As he stirred and turned she whispered hastily, 'It's OK, Luke; it's only me.'

'Devlin!' He shot up in the bed and switched on the light. 'What's wrong?' He squinted in the glare. 'Are you afraid of the thunder?'

Devlin laughed. 'No, I'm not afraid of the thunder.' She met his puzzled gaze and said hesitantly, 'I . . . I . . . um . . . well actually, Luke, I came to seduce you. But I'm not very good at this kind of thing, and now I feel a bit daft.'

Luke lay back against the pillows and stared at her. 'You are daft, as daft as a brush, and that's why I love you, you mad nutter.'

'That's not very romantic — calling me a mad nutter.' She grinned back. 'Do you really love me?'

'What would you think?' He leaned up on one elbow and smiled down at her.

Devlin shook her head. 'Well, I guess if you've put

up with me this far, you've got to feel something for me,' she teased, feeling suddenly very happy.

Luke leaned over and kissed her on the lips. 'I don't want you to do anything you don't want to. I don't want to make you feel . . .' He hesitated and his gaze softened. 'I don't want you to feel emotionally blackmailed. I won't pull out of our partnership now or ever, no matter what.'

She silenced him with a kiss, a fierce passionate kiss that surprised him. 'I didn't mean it when I said that. I've regretted it ever since. I love you too, Luke,' she whispered. 'I want us to make love. And you don't have to worry about Aids or anything. I've only ever had sex with Colin and I had a test and I was fine,' she assured him a little breathlessly.

'And you don't have to worry about me. I've been tested too and I'm fine. I'm not promiscuous, Devlin,' Luke said gently. 'I'll wear a condom, of course.'

Devlin reached up and caressed the long lean line of his jaw. 'You don't have to: I've been on the pill for years because of my periods.'

'Don't talk to me about periods: mine are so irregular,' he said in an accent that was suspiciously like Dianne's. Devlin giggled.

'When did you find out you loved me?' Luke wrapped his arms about her and the heat from his naked body came through the thin silk of her night-dress.

'I suppose I've loved you for ages and didn't realize it. But when I thought everything was finished between us, I was scared of losing you and that's when I really knew. It's a bit of a shock!' She buried her face

76

against his chest, loving the feel of his rough black hair against her cheek and lips.

'I'd better resuscitate you then,' he murmured, raising her face and bending his mouth to hers. He kissed her slowly, exploring the velvet softness of her mouth, his tongue caressing hers so erotically that she felt a flood of desire, the like of which she had not experienced for years. His kiss deepened, became more passionate and her body responded instinctively, arching against him, feeling his need for her. Her fingers caressed him, touching tentatively at first and then more confidently as his breathing quickened and she could see how much she was arousing him. Gently he lowered his head and brushed away the wispy straps of her nightdress as his mouth sought the hard pink tips of her nipples.

'Oh Luke, this is lovely,' she breathed, her hands holding his head tight against her as he teased and touched and caressed her breasts. For a long long time he kissed and explored every inch of her, gaining her trust, exciting her body until she was calling his name out in pleasure. He was so gentle when he entered her that for a brief moment it was the most exquisite sensation she had ever experienced. Then all of a sudden she froze.

'Luke, Luke, stop!' she cried out in panic, her hands pushing him away as she struggled to sit up.

'God! What! What is it?' Luke exclaimed in alarm, his voice harsh with passion as he drew away from her.

'Oh Luke!' Devlin covered her face with her hands and burst into tears. 'I'm sorry . . . I'm sorry,' she sobbed.

'It's all right. It's all right. Tell me what's wrong.

Did I hurt you?' Luke didn't know what was going on, but he reached out and drew her close and stared down at her bent head in confusion as a flood of tears bathed his chest.

'No, you didn't hurt me. It's not you: it's me! It's me!' she wept, feeling ashamed of herself for being such a failure.

'Tell me about it,' he said gently.

'Oh, I feel so mortified behaving like this at my age,' Devlin muttered in embarrassment. 'You must think I'm terribly gauche.'

'I don't think anything of the sort.' Luke kissed the top of her head and his arms tightened around her. 'All I want is to make you happy and if you don't feel you're ready for a physical relationship yet, that's no big deal, Devlin.' He cupped her face in his hands and made her look at him. 'Sex is just one part of a relationship; it's not the be-all and end-all. It's not for the sex that I wanted us to become involved. The love and the friendship are just as important.'

'But aren't you frustrated?' Devlin asked, pink-cheeked. All she knew of men's sexuality was what she had read in romantic novels. She knew even less about her own.

'Oh Devlin!' Luke chuckled. 'Sure that's easily fixed. You wouldn't want to let any feminists hear you asking questions like that. They might picket City Girl.'

'Oh, you mean I should be concerned about my own satisfaction,' Devlin said glumly. 'I think I'm a bit of a disaster in that area.'

'Well, we were doing pretty well for a while,' Luke smiled at her. 'What happened?'

She bit her lip.

Seeing her discomfiture Luke said firmly, 'Look, we can talk about this another time – Devlin, please don't get into a tizzy – and don't get things out of proportion.'

'Luke . . . I lost my virginity to Colin Cantrell-King and that was the first and only time I had sex . . . I've never been with anyone since. When we were making love . . .' She sighed deeply. 'I know it's irrational but all of a sudden I just felt this awful fear that I would get pregnant . . . I can't really explain it.'

Luke lay back against the pillows and pulled her down beside him. 'I feel very sorry for women: they really get the rough end of the stick. I wouldn't presume even to try and imagine what you went through, or to try and imagine what it's like to wait and find out if you're pregnant after sex. And it's something women have to face all the time. Devlin, I know this sounds selfish but I'm so glad I'm a man. I'm not going to have you under this pressure. Let's forget about sex for a while. If you want to go for counselling or anything, I'll be more than willing to go with you. I just want you to be happy.'

'I love you, Luke,' Devlin whispered.

'I love you too. We'll work this out, don't worry,' he assured her, switching out the light and putting his arms around her.

She lay, listening to the steady sound of his heart-beat while her eyes grew heavy. Her last conscious thought was that Luke Reilly was the best thing that had ever happened in her life. She knew he was right when he said they would work it out. She wanted to work it out. She wanted to experience the pleasure she had felt with Luke until she had panicked. She had suppressed her own sensuality for so long, probably as a form of self-protection. Well, she trusted Luke implicitly. And because she loved him she wanted to give him great pleasure too: the next time would be different, she promised herself as she fell asleep.

Devlin slept really well that night. She had been pretty shattered, what with being up at the crack of dawn to get her flight, and then the shopping expedition, not to mention the emotional upheaval of last night. It was the first night she'd slept properly since her row with Luke at Dublin Airport and when she woke she felt totally relaxed, wondering sheepishly how she had got herself into such a state the night before.

Luke was still asleep, and she leaned on her elbow and studied him as he lay there beside her, limbs sprawled all over the bed. His crisp, dark hair, tousled in sleep, gave him a faintly boyish air that made her smile. She gazed at the long sweep of his lashes and his straight well-shaped nose, down to his mouth, usually firm, now relaxed in sleep. He had a nice mouth, she thought, remembering his kisses of the night before. He had a nice body, too, she thought with a tingle of pleasure, looking at the broad expanse of his chest with its tangle of dark curly hair that narrowed to a thin line over his lean stomach and disappeared under the sheet that covered them. The pressure of his thigh against her own was intimate, and Devlin decided that it was lovely to share his bed.

Luke's eyes flicked open and Devlin smiled down at him. 'Good morning, lazybones.' She bent her head and kissed him. 'I'm feeling terribly frustrated,' she

80

murmured against his lips, as her hand ran down the thin dark line of hair, past his waist and under the bedclothes. 'What are you going to do about it?'

Luke's hands slid down to her waist and then to the curve of her hips, as he moulded his body against hers.

'What would you like me to do?' he asked huskily, his eyes warm as he stared up at her.

'You're the expert. I'm just learning. Remember?' Devlin teased, as she kissed him again, a long, slow, satisfying kiss, that left him in no doubt as to what she wanted him to do.

'Are you sure?' Luke was still a little concerned. 'Don't feel you have to force yourself to do it again so soon, Devlin.'

'Do I look as if I'm forcing myself?' Devlin rubbed the tip of her nose against his. 'Luke, I really want to try again. I've missed out on so much; I've a lot of catching up to do. So stop playing hard to get . . .'

This time, because she was relaxed and knew that Luke was aware of her hang-ups, it seemed the most natural thing in the world to welcome him into her body. She gloried in every precious moment of it. Afterwards, they lay smiling at each other until Luke glanced at the digital clock on his bedside table and said, 'Well, Mata Hari, just as we were taking off, so was your flight from Heathrow.'

'Oh dear,' said Devlin happily. 'I'm starving. What's for breakfast?'

Five

For about the tenth time, Devlin rearranged the centrepiece of freesias on the table she had set for the lunch with her mother. She stood back and surveyed the effect. It did look nice, she had to admit, with its crisp fine linen tablecloth and starched napkins, and the silver and crystal sparkling in the mid-morning sun. It was such a beautiful day she had decided to have lunch outside on the big wide balcony that surrounded her penthouse on three sides, giving her a spectacular view of Dublin Bay and Howth. Big terracotta pots that matched the glazed Italian tiles were filled with a luscious variety of flowering shrubs, bedding plants and trailing ivies. Devlin loved her balcony: she always found it very therapeutic to slip into a tracksuit after a hard day at work and go out with her trowel. She would plant and feed and mulch and weed her pots, hanging baskets and window-boxes.

This was her little haven, her refuge from City Girl and from the fairly hectic social life that she was leading as a result of all the invitations that arrived on her desk, now that she was a celebrity of sorts. More than anything, Devlin had come to enjoy Sundays. No matter what the weather, whether wild and stormy in the winter or warm and balmy as it was now, she went for brisk walks along the length of the Bull Island or by the Bull Wall, enjoying the tangy sea breeze. Devlin had grown to love living in Clontarf. She had all the enjoyment of living on the seafront close to Howth and Malahide, the loveliest parts of the north County Dublin coastline, and yet she was only ten minutes away from the city and work. Back from her walk, she always bought the Sunday papers and after a long lazy brunch would settle down to read them. In winter, she would curl up on the sofa in front of the fire and listen to the rain beating against the big ceiling-to-floor patio doors but in summer, she loved to lie on her lounger, feeling the heat of the sun. It was bliss to have those few precious hours to herself after the frenetic pace of her life during the week.

It was Luke who had warned her that she was heading for a bad case of burn-out if she didn't take more care of herself. He had watched her work non-stop seven days a week, morning, noon and night, before, during and after the opening of City Girl. The excitement of it had kept her going for the first few months and then she found it had become very difficult to relax. She had become thoroughly immersed in the business.

One Sunday evening, Luke had called at the penthouse before flying back to London, to find her surrounded by papers as she worked on costings for shops in the mall.

'Devlin, I've been in business for a lot longer than you, and one thing I learned was that only fools give everything they've got to a business seven days a week. I did it myself for too long, Devlin. Don't make the same mistake. You need to unwind and relax and have time for yourself. You need to be able to set one day aside each week and say, "this is for me . . . and—" ' he paused, eyes twinkling, ' "—me." '

Devlin had ignored his advice until during the winter she had come down with a terrible dose of flu. She had had to spend three days in bed and for the rest of a week she was fit only for pottering around, flopping in front of the TV and catching up on the books, magazines and newspapers that had accumulated in an untidy pile in her bedroom. It was the longest period she had ever spent continuously in the penthouse and that week it was no longer a place where she slept and had the occasional meal: for the first time since she had bought it, the penthouse became home. She was quite enjoying doing nothing, she confessed to Maggie, who had called to visit, laden down with soups and casseroles and scones for the invalid.

'You shouldn't have had to wait until you were sick, you prat!' Maggie retorted. 'Try relaxing at weekends like us ordinary mortals.'

From then on Devlin had made a conscious decision to put City Girl out of her mind on Sundays and relax totally. It had taken a bit of time and a lot of effort of will but now she was an expert. If everything went all right today maybe she'd be able to have her parents over occasionally for a meal on Sundays. She considered the possibilities as she strode into the kitchen to put the finishing touches to the crème brûlée. It was ridiculous, she thought, as she crushed the caramel and arranged it decoratively around the rest of the dessert, to have butterflies in her stomach because her own mother was coming to visit.

She sighed, absentmindedly popping a piece of the caramel into her mouth. Despite the fact that Lydia Delaney had told her that she was an adopted child and that her real mother was Lydia's dead sister, Devlin would always think of Lydia as her mother. Not a great mother perhaps: a mother who had wanted nothing to do with her when she had found that Devlin was pregnant, a mother who had made the lives of her husband and daughter a misery with her binge-drinking. It was something that only the two of them knew about as Lydia wouldn't dream of getting drunk in front of her society friends. Lydia had her faults all right; nevertheless as far as Devlin was concerned Lydia was the only mother she had ever known and after all this time, she hoped fervently that things could improve between them.

Devlin slid the completed brûlée into the fridge and walked over to the cooker where her homemade tomato and tarragon soup was wafting out an enticing aroma. Blanched orange strips and freshly chopped tarragon were ready as garnish for the soup. In ten minutes she'd boil the water to steam the new potatoes and broccoli and diced carrots. The meal was under control: that at least was something. Deftly, she sliced the brown bread. Superquinn brown bread was one of her greatest weaknesses and she would normally have buttered herself a slice and eaten it as she cooked lunch. But today she couldn't face it. In spite of her best intentions, her stomach was tied up in knots. It was so long since she had seen Lydia, well over a year, and their last meeting had been one of bitterness: Devlin had lain injured and devastated in a hospital bed, recovering from the accident that had killed her daughter and aunt. She had told her mother she didn't want to see her again.

For so long, Devlin had carried the bitterness inside, despite the best efforts of her father, Gerry, to reconcile her with her mother. It was only in the last few months that her anger and bitterness had dissipated somewhat. Luke, who had been so close to his own father before he died, had tried to make her see that in her own way Lydia had suffered as much as Devlin. She had mulled over his words and at her weekly lunches with her father had gradually started asking after Lydia. Gerry had told her that after the accident she had gone in to St Gabriel's in Cabinteely for a couple of weeks of psychiatric care. She wouldn't admit that she was an alcoholic but at least she had stopped drinking and hadn't been on a binge in months. The estrangement with Devlin was causing her great anguish, Gerry had told his daughter, and Lydia blamed herself totally.

Coming to the decision to phone her mother and arrange to meet her had not been easy, but after she had taken the step, Devlin had felt a keen sense of relief. Lydia had been uncharacteristically nervous on the phone, something that surprised Devlin. There had been a stunned silence when Devlin had said, 'Hello, Mum,' and when she had suggested they meet for lunch, Devlin realized that Lydia was crying. This had shocked her. Her mother was not a person who showed her emotions easily, let alone cried. At first, Devlin had planned to meet in a restaurant, but then impulsively she had suggested that Lydia come to lunch in the penthouse. Thinking about it afterwards, Devlin decided it had been the right thing to do: it was much more personal than meeting in a restaurant.

She walked from her grey-and-green kitchen into the lounge and tried to view it as Lydia would, seeing it for the first time. Her mother had superb taste and the family home in Foxrock was a model. She hadn't done too badly herself, Devlin decided, as she viewed her large bright lounge with its French doors framed by gold brocade curtains that made the room cosy in winter. The gold of the curtains was picked up in the cream and gold of the carpet. Two sofas in cream chintz with hints of peach were placed in an L-shape by the fire and in front of them she had a lovely square glass-topped coffee table on which, that day, reposed another vase of freesias. The alcoves on each side of the chimney breast contained fitted cream bookshelves on one side and a television and video unit and stereo deck in the other. Slim peach candlesticks and wide pleated peach lampshades stood in the corners of the room and at night their glow gave an atmosphere of comforting warmth. It was a feminine room, light and airy in summer, warm and cosy in winter.

The dining-room was decorated in pink and grey with elegant black ash furniture. Devlin used it only on the rare occasions she had a formal dinner. When Maggie and Caroline visited, they always ate in the kitchen unless they were guests at one of Devlin's dinner parties.

She slipped into the bedroom and cast her eye around. The restful green-and-white room with its matching en suite bathroom was looking far tidier than normal. No longer did sheets of figures and files from the office clutter up the top of the fitted drawers that edged two walls. The panelled doors of her Sliderobes had been dusted and polished and the mirror panels gleamed and sparkled after a good application of Windolene. Devlin had been shocked at the dust that had come off the screen of the portable television set which sat on top of the long bank of drawers and, shamed, she had promised herself that she was going to polish and dust at least once a week.

The second bedroom, decorated in cream and yellow, had got the same treatment and at least, thought Devlin in satisfaction, her spring cleaning, though a tad late, had been completed. Devlin straightened the bedspread that matched the curtains and lampshades and, spotting some dust on the top of the headboard, she picked a cream tissue out of the box on the bedside locker and flicked it off.

She caught sight of herself in the mirrored wardrobe. Was she too casually dressed, she wondered, eyeing her white cotton trousers and cerise shirt dubiously. Her sleek blonde bob would come as a surprise to her mother, she thought with some amusement. Anxious not to be seen as a bimbo Devlin had taken stock of her public image. The reappraisal had been occasioned by the gossip columnist of the *Sunday Echo*, who had written a piece headed, '*Blonde! Beautiful! But has she the Brains to keep it going?*' that had enraged her. Gone was the flowing blonde mane, gone were the two-tight and too-short skirts. Now she wore well-tailored suits and skirts that ended barely above the knee for business meetings or interviews. She had to admit ruefully that the image she presented was of someone older and more sophisticated than her mid-twenties. But then that was the business. At home, she much preferred casual clothes and used very little make-up.

Maybe she should put on a bit of lipstick and mascara. Lydia, who was always perfectly groomed, might think she did not consider her mother worth the bother if she used no make-up at all. A lightly tanned face with troubled aquamarine eyes, a full determined mouth and good bone structure stared back at her from the mirror. She could see a line at each side of her mouth that hadn't been there this time last year, and when she smiled she noticed faint creases around her eyes. It didn't bother her: she had earned them; she had gone from being a spoilt, immature, selfish young girl to a thoughtful and very independent woman.

Having a baby and losing her had had the most profound effect on Devlin. She knew she would never ever get over Lynn's death. A wave of despair swept through her even at the thought of it. Her heartache had a physicality about it that only someone who had experienced it could understand. There were times when the desire to hold a toddler in her arms was overpowering. Playing with Mimi and Shona, Maggie's two little girls, was such a bittersweet experience. There wasn't much difference between Lynn's and Mimi's age – just a few months. They could have been pals and grown up to enjoy a great sustaining friendship like their mothers had. When she saw Mimi and heard her chatting away nineteen to the dozen and saw the personality she was developing, she couldn't help wondering what Lynn would have been like at that stage.

It was so painful that Devlin rarely allowed herself to think of her daughter. She buried the grief deep inside, keeping herself totally occupied with City Girl. She had kept a few of Lynn's clothes, including the dress she was wearing the day of the accident. She had never washed it. Sometimes when the ache was too much to bear and wouldn't be denied, she would take it out and bury her face in it, smelling the sweet talcy scent of her daughter. 'Oh God, why did you do this to me? After all I went through to have her? I could have aborted her and I didn't. Why did you take her away from me?' It was an anguished howl that came from her lips and she sank to her knees and bowed her head and wept. Why did this have to happen today, just when she needed to be in control! Devlin took several deep shuddering breaths. Her mother would be here any minute. What would she think if she saw her like this?

She went into the bathroom and splashed cold water on her face and red-rimmed eyes. She sat on the edge of the bath, holding a damp cloth to her face, and when she took it away it was covered in lipstick and mascara. She redid her make-up and brushed her hair and soon she looked all right again. Devlin tidied up the bathroom and went back to the kitchen to boil the water for the potatoes. What was she going to talk to her mother about? There was such a chasm between them.

Well, at least the view and the gardens that surrounded the apartment complex would be a talking point. Lydia had a great interest in gardening: her own looked good enough to feature in a glossy magazine. They could talk about Gerry, too, about City

Girl, maybe. Lydia had never been to the complex. Devlin would like to offer her membership. Many of her mother's friends had joined and they were always asking when Lydia was going to take the plunge. There were loads of things they could discuss, Devlin reassured herself as she buttered the brown bread. Honestly, it was pathetic having to think of things to talk to her mother about. How she envied Maggie her relationship with Nelsie. Nelsie might moan a bit and take advantage now and then but at heart they had a truly close relationship, and whenever Devlin had been in their company she had enjoyed listening to them natter. She and Lydia had never had that kind of a relationship, even when things were all right between them. Now they had no relationship to speak of. Would today help? It was hard to know.

Glancing at the clock on the wall she saw that it was almost twelve forty-five. Lydia should be here any time now. They had agreed that she would arrive between twelve-thirty and one. Well, at least everything was organized. The soup was simmering, the bread buttered, the potatoes and vegetables ready for steaming and the salmon steaks for popping in the pan. The dessert was in the fridge and the wine was chilling nicely. Just as well she had come home at eleven, though; having time to spare was much better than rushing around like a lunatic.

A troubling thought struck her as she opened the fridge to get the cream for the soup and saw the bottle of wine. Should she offer Lydia some? Gerry had said she wasn't drinking now. Would a glass of wine set her off? Would it be too obvious if she didn't offer her a drink? Maybe she should ring her father at work and ask him. The chiming of the intercom sent her heart lurching up to her throat and down again. Devlin's palms actually felt sweaty as she walked over to the intercom and saw the screen image of her mother standing waiting to be let in.

Her hand was shaking as she rang Devlin's doorbell. She had stood for several minutes trying to gather the courage to press the button. Lydia Delaney couldn't help the apprehension she felt. When she woke up that morning and thought of the ordeal ahead of her she was half-tempted to ring Devlin and plead a migraine. How was she going to face her daughter? After letting her down all along the line and failing dismally as a mother?

When Devlin's baby and her own sister Kate had been killed in that horrific accident in Wexford, Lydia had really gone to pieces. Devastating guilt, grief, and the knowledge that she would now never see the grandchild that she had refused to acknowledge had brought her to the brink of a breakdown. When Devlin had told her from her hospital bed that she never wanted to see her again she had gone on the worst bender of her life and to this day could not remember those three days. Gerry, unable to cope any longer, had told her that if she didn't do something about her drinking and get some treatment he was going to leave her. That had shocked her so much she had sought psychiatric help and gone into St Gabriel's.

After a dark time of near-despair she had come to realize that she had been a most selfish wife, unworthy of Gerry's years of patient loving kindness, and a disaster of a mother to Devlin. She had vowed to herself that she would make it up to her husband but remembrance of the bitterness and anger of Devlin's words had prevented her from contacting her daughter. It wasn't that she didn't want to. More than anything, Lydia had longed for Devlin's forgiveness. She had believed that Devlin had spoken the truth when she said she wanted nothing more to do with her and then, when Devlin had been so spectacularly successful with City Girl, she had been afraid to call her and congratulate her in case Devlin would think she was making up to her now only because she was successful and famous.

When she had picked up the phone and heard Devlin's voice at the other end inviting her to lunch, it was as if a huge burden had been lifted from her shoulders. Gerry had been so pleased when she had told him and did his best to calm her fears that she wouldn't say the right thing to her daughter and that the whole thing could end up in disaster.

She had nearly lost her nerve that morning; only the knowledge that she would never have such a precious opportunity again had kept her going. Three times she had changed her outfit, not wanting to look either overdressed or underdressed. She had dithered about whether to bring champagne or even wine, not wanting Devlin to think that she was still a drinker. In the end she had bought a bouquet of roses and some handmade chocolates.

Driving across the East Link bridge she had got increasingly nervous and as she turned right on to the Alfie Byrne Road, she longed to pull in and have a cigarette to gather her scattered wits. The tide was in, boats bobbed up and down and windsurfers scooted along the waves. Clontarf, nestling among verdant trees, looked very pretty. She pressed on. Devlin had said any time between half-past twelve and one. It was twelve-forty.

'Jesus help me!' Lydia prayed from the heart as she stopped at the traffic lights before turning on to the Clontarf Road. 'Put the right words in my mouth; let me show my child that I love her and that I'm sorry. Let me try and make up to her for what I've done. O Sacred Heart of Jesus, I place all my trust in Thee!' It was strange how for years she had gone to Mass every Sunday, helped church charities, done good works, was highly thought of in the community; and yet when the test came and Devlin had told her she was pregnant, she had almost pushed her on to the plane to London for an abortion.

That betrayal of her daughter, herself and her religion should have distanced her from God, and yet, when she had been in that nursing home in dark despair, she had felt closer to Him than ever before. Nowadays when she heard of girls and women having abortions, she did not judge them as once she would have. She knew through personal experience why some women were driven to do this fateful thing. But, despite the awareness of the circumstances and the understandable desire of women to have the right to choose, Lydia had decided that if ever she could persuade a girl or woman not to have an abortion, she would.

She had done a course in counselling and now twice a week she talked to women who had to make that decision. She always started off by telling them of her own experience: how she had insisted that her unmarried daughter go for an abortion. 'It was the biggest mistake of my life. My brave daughter left that clinic and had her baby and I was not there to support her. But I am here to support you in any way I can,' she would assure the upset woman. And support them she did, whatever their decision. It helped her more than it helped them, Lydia often believed, but it could not assuage the aching sense of loss and guilt she felt over Devlin.

Following the directions Devlin had given her over the phone, she drove along the seafront until she came to the address. As she drove up the tree-lined drive Lydia was impressed. This was a very elegant complex indeed, she thought, as she viewed the flowering shrubs, the beds of heathers and the ornamental central pool with its arrangement of waterlilies and reeds. Several of the tenants sat reading or sunning themselves on garden seats, and in the distance she could see some tennis-courts and hear the rhythmic whack of ball and racket as a foursome played an enthusiastic game. It was as nice as any complex one would find on the southside, Lydia thought approvingly, and then shook her head at her silly snobbery.

She parked the car and, taking a deep breath, walked up the steps to the entrance. Locating Devlin's bell, she paused with her finger on the button and then let her hand fall to her side. She could see her reflection in the glass panels of the doors. Nervously she patted her hair with her free hand and clutched the flowers tighter to her with the other. What if everything didn't go well? She had to do this right: it was her only chance to make it up to Devlin. 'God give me courage,' she said under her breath, pressing her finger against the bell.

For what seemed like an eternity there was silence and then Devlin's voice seemed to float down over the intercom. 'Hello, Mum. I'll send the lift down to you. It's the first one on the right.' Then the door swung open and Lydia, following Devlin's directions, found herself in a lift, which glided swiftly up to the penthouse where her daughter lived. As it came to a halt, she swallowed hard. When the door opened and she saw Devlin standing in front of her, she tried to smile.

Six

'Hello, Mum.' Devlin tried to keep her voice normal.

'Devlin . . . dear.' Lydia attempted a smile as she proffered the roses and the chocolates but to her horror her lip started to tremble and tears spurted from her eyes.

'Oh Mum, Mum. It's all right. Don't cry! Don't cry, Mum, there's no need!' Devlin flung her arms around Lydia and held her tightly.

'Devlin, I'm sorry, I'm so sorry. I can never forgive myself for what I did.'

She suddenly felt very sorry for Lydia. It wasn't that she was a saint full of turning the other cheek and dispensing forgiveness or anything like it! But she had never been one to harbour a grudge and it was clear that while Devlin had been going through hell, Lydia had had her own trauma. As far as Devlin was concerned, the past was the past; nothing would change it, but she and her mother could now pick up the pieces and go forward to a new and more en-riching relationship.

'I didn't know how I was going to face you.' Lydia took an immaculate linen-and-lace handkerchief out of her bag and dabbed at her eyes. 'I didn't mean to end up like a weeping willow.' She gave a sheepish smile.

'I was a bit nervous myself, Mum,' confessed Devlin, 'but we've done it now and that's the worst part over. And I'm sorry for the things I said to you in the hospital that time. I . . . I was in bits.'

'I know you were.' Lydia squeezed her daughter's hand. 'And I was no help to you when you needed me most. I've thought about it every day and cursed myself. Maybe if I'd acted differently your baby would still be alive.'

'Oh, Mum.' Devlin started to cry. She couldn't help it. 'Mum, she was beautiful. She had the most gorgeous golden hair and the biggest blue eyes and the heartiest chuckle. She was such a little dote. I miss her so much.' Devlin sobbed her heart out as the pent-up grief of many months was released like a tidal wave. Lydia cried with her and held her close in a way she would never have been able to do in the old days.

'Have a good cry, my love. It's always good to cry. And then tell me all about my grandchild,' she murmured.

'I'm sorry,' Devlin apologized a little while later when she had cried herself dry.

'Don't be, darling,' Lydia soothed. 'It's only natural for you to cry. I've learned a lot since the old days. If you bottle grief up you only make yourself ill. Some day it will all come at you. So grieve as long as you must and don't keep it all inside. Look at the way I kept things inside. I was so unhappy myself; I made your father dreadfully unhappy — and look what I did to you. I turned to drink to blot it out. It didn't: it only made things worse. I keep away from it now, Devlin, and your father and I are much closer. I want to try and make up to him for the dreadful life I've given him and if you will let me, I'll try and be as good a mother as I can to you.' Lydia's tone was pleading as she stared into her daughter's pain-filled eyes.

'I'd like that very much, Mum. I've never really talked to anyone about Lynn since the accident, I just couldn't: it was too painful. I'd like to talk to you about her and show you her photographs.'

'Thank you, darling, for wanting to share your memories with me.' Lydia stroked her daughter's cheek tenderly and Devlin marvelled at how changed her mother was.

The lunch lasted for hours. 'I didn't realize you were such a good cook,' Lydia declared as she ate the last spoonful of the brûlée with relish.

'When I went to London I couldn't cook an egg,' Devlin laughed. 'I used to live out of the frozen food compartments when I was in a flat here. But I just couldn't afford that over there. It was a case of having to learn or starve.' Lydia looked stricken and Devlin could have kicked herself. 'I'm exaggerating, Mum,' she said gently. 'I'm glad I learned how to cook. I learned a lot of things, I learned how to stand on my own two feet and that's the best lesson a girl can have. Mum, some of the things that have happened to me were for the best. I was a spoilt brat when I lived at home. All I had to worry about was where to spend my allowance and to decide whether to go to Leggs or the Pink Elephant on Friday and Saturday nights. I was very shallow and totally immersed in my own

99

petty little problems. I really wasn't a very nice person.'

'Don't be so hard on yourself, dear,' Lydia responded, taking a cigarette out of her bag and lighting up. 'You were a good daughter to both of us. And though I've no right to say so, I'm so proud of you. You know I envy your generation so much. All mine aspired to was getting married and having a nice home and a successful husband, if we were lucky. Our status was tied to our man's. If he did well, we didn't have to worry about not being well provided for. If he didn't, we suffered hardship with him. But your generation—' Lydia exhaled a long thin stream of smoke '—you just get out there and take control of your own lives and finances. I think it's wonderful. I wish I were a young woman again.'

'You don't have to be a young woman to take control of your own life,' Devlin pointed out gently. 'Look how you've stopped drinking. Look at the way you've done your counselling course; and there's the voluntary work you do.'

'I know that,' Lydia sighed. 'And I feel a lot better. But . . .' Lydia turned her fine eyes to her daughter. 'I feel I've really achieved nothing significant with my life. Looking at you makes me ashamed. You've done so much in such a short space of time.'

'Yes, but at what cost?' Devlin said sadly. 'I'd give up all this tomorrow to have Lynn and Kate alive.'

'I know you would, dear,' Lydia murmured. 'I'm sorry: that was thoughtless of me.'

'Have you never thought of setting up a little business? You'd be great at interior design. Or even opening a boutique? You've got such taste, Mum.'

100

'I don't think I'd have the nerve, Devlin,' Lydia laughed. 'Anyway what would I know about setting up a business? I'm a bit long in the tooth now, don't you think?'

'What did *I* know about it?' Devlin declared. 'And you're never too old. It's not as if you're Methuselah!' A thought struck her. 'You know one of the shops in the mall in City Girl is closing down because the woman who opened it just couldn't be bothered to put the time in. She's far more interested in swanning around the Coffee Dock in her designer gear. You know Vivienne Kearney? It's her place. She decided she was going to open this exclusive boutique. All she wanted to do was take off to Paris and Milan to stock it. She was very enthusiastic at the beginning but it's such a hard slog; the glamour of it has worn off.' Devlin's eyes sparkled. 'I was in London with Luke recently and I got the most beautiful lingerie in Harrods. I think something like that would go down very well in the mall.' Devlin sat up straight. 'Mum, why don't you take it over? We haven't let it yet. Lease it and do what you want with it.'

'Devlin, I couldn't,' Lydia demurred.

'Of course you could,' Devlin said excitedly. 'You could stock lingerie and soft toys and knick-knacks like that. Little treats.'

'Maybe pot-pourri and stationery and chocolates – gifts . . .' Lydia, infected by Devlin's bubbly enthusiasm, started getting excited herself.

'Oh Mum, go home and talk to Dad about it. It's so handy having a bank manager in the family.'

'Will I?' Lydia's eyes were wide with excitement.

'Yes. Do. Tonight!' Devlin urged.

'Oh all right,' Lydia chuckled. 'I'd better get going soon anyway. Gerry will wonder where I am.'

'I've something for you before you go,' Devlin said shyly. She went into her bedroom and took a framed photograph out of a drawer. It was a photo of Lynn that she had kept on the chance of such an occasion.

'Oh, Devlin! Oh, my dear, she's beautiful.' Lydia took the photograph and gazed at her grandchild. Tears coursed down her cheeks. Devlin too started to cry and the two of them stood hugging each other tightly.

'I wish you had known her, Mum, but you don't know how happy it makes me to be able to give you this.' Devlin brushed the tears from her cheeks and tried to smile.

'She's so fair, isn't she? I thought she'd be much darker,' Lydia reflected, tracing a finger gently over the photo. Devlin was puzzled by the comment then suddenly remembered that Lydia had always believed that Devlin had become pregnant by a Portuguese during a holiday fling.

'Mum, I didn't get pregnant on holidays that time,' Devlin said quietly. 'It wasn't a foreigner. It was Colin.'

'Colin Cantrell-King! Oh my God!' Lydia exclaimed, utterly shocked. 'Oh, the bastard!'

'Forget it, Mum. I just thought you should know.'

'Oh Devlin, to think that every time he sees me he asks after you and he's so sweet and charming. I could kill him,' Lydia said fiercely.

'It wasn't all his fault,' Devlin sighed. 'I was flattered by his interest and very smitten. I was a silly young girl playing with fire and I got badly burnt.

He's a bastard but he's the loser. At least I can look myself in the eye.'

'That's very true, dear,' Lydia agreed. 'And you're right to put the past behind you.' She put the photograph in her bag and held out her arms to her daughter. 'Thank you, Devlin, for today, for lunch, for talking to me and for putting our past behind us. It means more to me than you'll ever know.'

'You're welcome, Mum. It means a lot to me too.' Devlin kissed her mother's cheek. She went down in the lift with her and walked her to her car.

'This is a beautiful complex, darling, and I'm mad about your penthouse. You've decorated it beautifully, and those views . . . Aren't they magnificent?'

'I like it here very much,' Devlin smiled, holding the car door open for her mother. 'Tell Dad I send my love. We'll get together soon about the shop?'

'Of course, dear . . . ' Lydia hesitated. 'I was wondering if you'd like to have lunch with us on Sunday?'

'I'd love to,' Devlin said and was rewarded by a smile of pure happiness on her mother's face.

'Lovely; we'll look forward to that, so.' Lydia was clearly delighted and as she watched the car going down the drive, Devlin was heartily glad that everything had gone so well. It was incredible how changed her mother was. Even in her readiness to cry and the warmth of her affection, she was so unlike the brittle, tense woman she had been. Seeing her as she was now had banished any lingering resentment that Devlin had felt. She had been able to talk to Lydia in a way never possible before and reflected that it was probably because for the first time Lydia had treated her as an adult. They had met as equals. She'd be able to tell Luke that it hadn't been an ordeal at all. The worrisome lunch had been a real success, Devlin decided with immense satisfaction, as the lift travelled swiftly upwards to the penthouse. It was as if a great weight had been lifted from her shoulders and she was sure the same was true of her mother.

She tidied up and went outside. In the block to her left, she could see Caroline on her balcony.

'Come on over,' she called. 'Mum's been; I've loads to tell you.' Caroline waved in acknowledgement, and ten minutes later the pair of them were sitting having coffee as Devlin confided in her friend the details of the long-awaited reunion.

'I can't believe it went so well, Luke.' Devlin lay back on her lounger and watched the evening sun slant slowly over the Wicklow hills turning the waters of the bay to gold. She had called Luke to tell him all about the meeting with Lydia.

'That's great news. I'm delighted for you, Devlin.' She knew he was smiling at the other end of the phone.

'She's so changed, you know, it's hard to believe. She's so much more—' Devlin searched for an appropriate word, '—much more human. I was able to talk to her about Lynn and you know I never talk about my baby.' Despite herself a tear rolled down her cheek.

'That's very good, Devlin,' Luke said gently. 'That will surely help a lot.'

'It just hurts.' Devlin's voice wobbled. 'But Mum said I should talk about Lynn much more. She's done counselling and she says it's very bad to keep things all bottled up inside.'

'I've been telling you that for ages and Maggie and Caroline have been telling you too. You should listen!' Luke urged.

'Luke, will the pain ever go away?' Devlin started crying, great big sobs that shook her body.

'No, my darling, it won't, but it will get easier. I promise you. Now that you're facing it and acknowledging your loss you're going to cope much better.' Luke's reassuring tones made her wish so much that he was there to hug and comfort her as only he could.

'Are you all right, Devlin?' she heard him ask in concern. She took a deep breath and sat up straight.

'I'm OK. I guess it's just talking about it that sets me off. That's why I never talked about it before.'

'You just keep talking as long as you need,' Luke said. 'I'll always be here to listen.'

'I know you will,' Devlin said, comforted. 'I love you, Luke.'

'I love you, too,' he echoed down the line.

Later that evening, when her doorbell rang, Devlin was working on a speech that she had been invited to give to a women's political association group. She glanced at the clock on the kitchen wall in surprise. It was nearly eleven o'clock. She wasn't expecting anybody at this late hour. And she certainly wasn't dressed to receive guests. She'd had a shower and got into her nightdress and dressing-gown about half an hour previously. Maybe it was Caroline wanting to stay the night. She often stayed when she was feeling a bit down.

She went over to her intercom and pressed the button. It was a great invention, she reflected, as the screen focused on the entrance area. It gave great security too. You could see who was there and any caller didn't have the same advantage.

'Yes?' Devlin ran her fingers through her hair and tied her robe around her.

'Hello,' said a familiar and much-loved voice.

'Luke!' Devlin exclaimed in pleasure as she saw him standing smiling into the camera. She pressed the buzzer and went out into the hall and sent the lift down to him. Two minutes later she was in his arms.

'I just wanted to be with you. I hated your being upset, so I took a standby seat and here I am.' He smiled down at her.

Devlin was overwhelmed by joy at being loved so much. She hugged Luke tightly. All these years she had been searching for she knew not what. Now at this very moment, Devlin knew her search was over. She had found this faceless, nameless thing that had eluded her for so long. It was like coming home after a long, long voyage. A great peace enveloped her.

'Come in, Luke. Come in,' she cried, happier than she had ever been in her life.

Seven

'Well? What do you think?' asked Arthur, beaming.

'Looks good,' assented Luke.

'Good! I think it's fantastic. You've got so much done since I was here last,' Devlin declared, her eyes dancing with pleasure as she walked around the foyer of the Belfast City Girl. 'And that was only two weeks ago! Arthur, you're a genius.' She turned to Luke. 'Come on, you have to admit it: this man is a miracle-worker. You haven't seen the place since the summer and look at it now. We'll be opening soon.' She rubbed her hands with glee.

'We hope,' Arthur said cautiously. 'We've still got a problem with the swimming-pool filter and the damn suppliers of the gym equipment went bust, taking our deposit with them. But I've organized a new supplier, so we should be taking delivery of the gear next week.'

'Do you think we'll get our deposit back?' Luke asked as he ran his hand along the grain of the shiny reception desk.

'Ach, we haven't a snowball's chance in hell,' Arthur grimaced. 'They've left creditors from here to Donegal.'

'You win some; you lose some,' Devlin said,

determinedly cheerful. True, there had been a few setbacks since they decided to go ahead with the project but opening up a new business was never all plain sailing.

Luke winked at Arthur and grinned at Devlin. 'Tell you what. You can pay Arthur and me back the deposit out of *your* share of the profits, seeing as you're so unmoved by the loss of it.'

'Ha, ha,' Devlin retorted. 'Come on. I want to see the beauty salon and the library.' She led them up the green-and-grey-fern-patterned carpet to the first floor. The small library was an oasis of peace and quiet with plush sofas and easy-chairs arranged around an inviting fireplace. Lamps and vases spread around gave the room a domestic air and Devlin felt that the young Belfast interior designer she had commissioned to decorate City Girl had done a very impressive job. The whole tone of the building was one of discreet opulence.

The beauty salon, which Aoibhinn had organized, looked superb. While it wasn't as big as the Dublin City Girl salon, it was very well laid out, and the pretty pink-and-green curtains that fronted the individual cubicles and hung on the floor-to-ceiling windows gave the room a sunny atmosphere. Across the square, Devlin could see the Portland stone City Hall, its imposing Classical Renaissance copper dome the most familiar landmark in the city. The superbly laid-out gardens were ablaze with late autumn colours and Devlin thought they would be a lovely sight for clients as they were pampered by the beauticians and hairdressers.

They had paid a lot of money for the building that

now housed the Health and Leisure Centre but the three partners agreed that it was worth it. It was situated in the city centre, close to the new bus station, the exquisitely restored Opera House and the Europa Hotel. Northern Ireland Rail's Central Station was less than a mile away. The trio agreed that the money had been well spent if only because of the building's accessibility.

After they looked around, chatted to the workmen, and saw what progress had been made, Arthur took them for coffee in the famous Crown Liquor Saloon, the Victorian pub that was in the care of the National Trust. Located at the start of what was known as 'the Golden Mile' of restaurants, bars and entertainment centres that led on to the elegant areas around Queen's University and the Botanic Gardens, the Crown was full of atmosphere and charm.

'Isn't Belfast a very classy city?' Devlin observed, as she gazed admiringly at the Opera House through the window.

'The people of Belfast are very conscious of their heritage,' said Arthur, as he paid the waiter who had arrived with their coffee. 'You won't catch them hauling down historic buildings the way they do willy-nilly in Dublin. I mean, how your Corporation got away with erecting those monstrosities they call the Civic Offices, after all the controversy about Christchurch and the sites surrounding it, is beyond me!'

'That was outrageous,' Devlin agreed, sipping her coffee. 'The wishes of the people were ignored completely.'

'Well, they wouldn't have got away with it here.

We wouldn't have been allowed to change one square foot of the façade of City Girl, even if we had wanted to,' Arthur said.

'It's a very elegant building anyway,' Luke reflected. 'It suits the ambience of City Girl very well. It's not brash and brassy as a modern building might be. It's very soothing, even reassuring, if you know what I mean. The Stephen's Green building is in the same style. It would be interesting to see how a high-tech, California-style City Girl would do.' He looked at Devlin questioningly.

She wrinkled her nose. 'It might suit the young types. But we have a very broad membership and I think our clients value the sense of leaving their cares behind and being petted and pampered in luxurious surroundings. I've seen some high-tech leisure centres. They're not that relaxing, and I think relaxation is one of our main selling points.'

'I think so, too. I've been getting very positive feedback about what we're doing,' Arthur said enthusiastically, 'and the great thing is that I'm having no problem at all promoting it. Everybody's very eager to get on the bandwagon because it's new and different, and people think it's going to work. I've three companies prepared to do an advertising promotion with display bins, posters, flyers and so on, and they'll be stocked in the major multiples like Dunnes, Stewarts and Wellworths as well as the CTNs . . .'

'The whats?' Devlin had heard the term before but just couldn't remember what it meant.

'Sorry, lassie, I get carried away,' Arthur chuckled. 'The confectioners, tobacconists and newsagents.'

'Oh, right,' Devlin nodded.

110

Arthur continued in his exuberant way: 'The promotion will be the same in all three cases: there'll be a competition with a main prize of a day in City Girl sampling all the services. It's a great way of advertising and getting into people's consciousness. And I've lined up Lynda Jayne to perform the opening and of course she'll be doing an interview with you on Downtown. I've a publicist organizing the rest of the media interviews. We'll be doing either *Anderson on the Box* or *Kelly* as well, and Sean Rafferty's radio programme. So, lassie, you're going to be up to your eyes. As we're going to be opening before Christmas, I'm going to take up your suggestion of gift vouchers too.'

'Maybe you should have special offers for the first month of operation,' Luke suggested. 'After all, the idea is to get customers in and talking about the place. We did that with the Dublin City Girl and it worked very well.'

'Definitely,' Devlin agreed. 'And I want to get working on the corporate business; it's really booming.'

'Folks, we can't fail,' Arthur said, beaming. He was such an optimist, and Devlin was fond of him. 'I'll see you tonight for dinner, then.' He stood up and held out his hand to Devlin and Luke. 'Enjoy your lunch with Lynda and Florence. Tell them I'd have loved to come, but some of us have to work.'

Back in their bedroom in the Europa Hotel, Devlin put her arms around Luke. 'Well, what do you really think?'

'What do I really think? Hmmm.' He pretended to ponder. He smiled down at her. 'Devlin, from the minute I heard you had targeted Belfast, I felt so sorry for the poor citizens . . . they're not going to know what's hit them and that's the truth.'

'Do you think it's going to work?' She thumped his chest.

'Well, if it doesn't it won't be yours or Arthur's fault: you've done a great job. Listening to Arthur, I can't see how it can go wrong. But don't forget, we *are* in the middle of a bloody awful recession.'

'Yeah, but it hasn't affected membership of City Girl: there are still people on the waiting list, and Belfast in parts is a very affluent city. Did you see those houses on the Malone Road? Mansions! I believe it's called "Millionaires Row". There's money here, Luke, as there is in every city. I think we'll have no problem attracting customers.'

'Well, the market research has certainly been pretty positive,' Luke agreed. 'We'll know soon enough.'

'It's exciting though, isn't it?' Devlin's eyes sparkled. She loved this kind of buzz: she was in her element plotting and planning and getting things moving.

'*You're* exciting,' Luke said wickedly, tightening his arms around her.

'We'll be late for lunch,' Devlin demurred.

'We've lashings of time,' Luke murmured, bending his head to kiss her.

'My God! I'll never get through all that,' Florence exclaimed wide-eyed as a portion of lasagne that would have fed the four of them was placed in front of her.

'I'm starving,' Devlin declared, as she prepared to tuck into a mountain of scampi. Luke caught her eye knowingly and Devlin blushed. Fortunately Lynda Jayne who was sitting opposite her, at Luke's side, was smiling at the waitress as she placed a steaming plate of ravioli in front of her. 'I told you the food here was great,' she laughed.

They were having lunch in the Cultra Inn, which was set in the grounds of the magnificent Culloden Hotel, a classic nineteenth-century Scottish baronial palace. It was a beautiful place, recommended heartily by Arthur. Set in the wooded slopes of the Holywood hills, it had stunning views of Belfast Lough and the Antrim coastline. The inn itself was separate from the main hotel and it had a charming rustic atmosphere, emphasized by the black wooden beams and the small lanterns hanging from them. The atmosphere was very convivial and relaxed and Devlin sat back and prepared to enjoy herself. It was Luke's first time to meet Lynda and Florence and they were all getting on like a house on fire.

'Did you know that the hotel was once the official palace of the bishops of Down?' Lynda said, as she attacked her ravioli with gusto.

'Wow! Lucky old bishops!' Devlin exclaimed enviously. 'How come they always end up with a palace? Our fella in Dublin has one in Drumcondra.'

'The Church must have been loaded,' Luke remarked, 'to have been able to afford a pile like this.'

'You should see the beautiful antiques and paintings,' Florence remarked, 'and, Devlin, the Louis XV candeliers are out of this world. You and Luke should take a walk in the grounds after lunch and then have a drink in the Gothic Bar . . .'

'. . . and you should take Luke home past Stormont,' Lynda interjected. 'At this time of the year it is something to behold. The trees have all turned and the colours are amazing.'

Lynda and Florence declared that they were dying for the opening of the Belfast City Girl. Devlin knew that in Lynda's capable hands the opening ceremony would be a great success. After they had gone, Devlin and Luke took their advice and strolled arm in arm through the picturesque grounds of the hotel and then down a quiet country lane that brought them right on to the shores of Belfast Lough.

'Isn't it beautiful here?' Devlin gazed at the peaceful panorama. 'You never see this side of the North. It's always the horror of the Troubles.'

'It's hard to reconcile this with the sight of the soldiers and the armoured cars. I wonder how people ever get used to them?' Luke mused. He found it hard to adjust to the military presence on the streets. Devlin, who had been a regular visitor to Belfast, had come to accept it.

'I suppose you get used to anything,' Devlin murmured. 'I suppose it's a case of having to. But it's such a shame. The people are so friendly and helpful. One man said to me he's lived here all his life and he's never even been caught up in a bomb scare. But if it's not bad news it will never get on TV.'

'Well, that goes for most of the media worldwide. It's in the nature of the beast, isn't it?' Luke expertly skimmed a flat stone across the waves. 'I wonder would a newspaper that reported only good news sell at all?'

'It could be our next venture,' teased Devlin as she tried to copy him. But to her dismay her stone sank beneath the water without so much as one hop.

'Let the expert show you how it's done,' Luke said smugly repeating his previous success.

'Show-off!' retorted Devlin, as she tried again and had the satisfaction of two hops before her stone sank. Half an hour later she had mastered the skill, though only after much laughter and teasing.

'I'm really enjoying myself,' she said, smiling, as they walked back to the car.

'Me too! We'll have to go away somewhere for a few days that isn't business.'

'Definitely!' Devlin agreed. 'As soon as Belfast is up and running.'

'I meant for Christmas,' Luke said firmly.

'OK,' Devlin agreed, leaving her companion speechless.

'Without even an argument?' he murmured, hiding his amazement.

'I'm a changed person, don't forget!' Devlin said with a grin. 'I think I'd like to go to Bali.'

'I was thinking in terms of somewhere a bit nearer, darling. Paris maybe. But if it's Bali you want, then Bali you'll have.'

'I'll get the brochures,' Devlin laughed. She wasn't serious, but it gave her a warm glow to know that if she really wanted to go to Bali, Luke would take her there. He really did spoil her.

They drove back to Belfast via Stormont as Lynda had suggested and sat for a while admiring the stupendous view of Parliament House that both of them had seen so many times on television. The rolling lawns sweeping up to the bank of steps fronting the elegant white colonnaded building looked like something out of a picture postcard. The trees, green, gold and russet in their autumn glory, were breathtaking, and the sun, sinking in a red-gold orb behind the hills, turned the sky to crimson.

'It's very very impressive in real life, isn't it?' Luke murmured.

'Mmm,' Devlin agreed. 'I'll look at it with new eyes when I see it on the news now and say to myself, "I've been there." I'm really glad you came to spend the few days in Belfast.' Devlin leaned over and planted a big kiss on Luke's cheek.

'I wouldn't have missed it for the world,' he assured her.

It had been a bit like a honeymoon, Devlin told the delighted Caroline and Maggie. They were having breakfast in their usual spot after a very strenuous workout. 'I've put on loads of weight,' Devlin moaned. 'I never stopped eating when I was up there.' She was eating a prune and making a face at the same time.

'Sure, you'd have got rid of that in bed,' Caroline murmured as she tucked into cinnamon toast. 'They say love-making is a great way to get rid of calories.'

'Oh yes!' Devlin brightened. 'I never thought of that. Here, give me a slice; it looks gorgeous.' As she spoke she pushed the offending prunes away.

Maggie laughed. 'Devlin Delaney, you are something else.'

'Oh stop being a goody-goody with your grapefruit

and yoghurt. Have a slice of this. It's yummy. Then go and ring Adam and you'll be fine: you won't gain an ounce.'

'I will in my hat!' laughed Maggie, 'I haven't a bit of Christmas shopping done and I swear to God I'm going into town today on a blitz and that's the end of it. And if Mimi changes her mind as she's done forty times this last week about what she's getting from Santa, I'll swing for her.'

'Ah, Maggie,' remonstrated Devlin, 'that's half the fun.'

'Oh funny, ha ha. It's hilarious. I've already re-turned a Polly Pocket dressing-table set that cost a fortune and bought the last My Little Pony Wedding Set in the shop. And my editor in her innocence thinks I'm madly writing.'

'All will be well,' soothed Devlin. 'What are you doing, Caroline?'

'I'll go home to Dad and the boys.'

'Well, you'll be coming over to me after Christmas, won't you?' Maggie urged. 'And you too, Devlin?'

'Wouldn't miss it!' Devlin exclaimed.

'Sure thing,' agreed Caroline with pleasure.

'And when I come back from Paris, Caro, you're going to stay with me for a few days, aren't you?' Devlin cocked an eyebrow.

'Yep,' Caroline said cheerfully eating another slice of toast.

'Have you no shame?' Maggie enquired.

'Nope.'

'Ah, to hell with it, Devlin! Order another plate of that toast. I'll need it to keep my strength up in town.' Devlin needed no second urging.

It's going to be the best Christmas ever, she promised herself, as she took the elevator downstairs to where her mother's shop, Special Occasions, had opened in the mall. Devlin was delighted that Lydia had taken her up on her suggestion. Leasing the unit and starting up the gift shop had done wonders for Lydia, whose business flair had come as a very pleasant surprise both to Devlin and to her father. Special Occasions was trading very well and now in the lead-up to Christmas, business was booming. Devlin intended to do most of her Christmas shopping there and had earmarked some exquisite lingerie for the girls and for Liz, her secretary. Lynda and Florence were getting some of the very pretty scented stationery that Lydia stocked and the staff of City Girl were each getting a large box of scrumptious handmade chocolates. So Devlin was very happy in the knowledge that several hundred pounds' worth of business would be going her mother's way and at the same time people would be getting lovely gifts.

'Hi, Mum.' She bounded in and gave Lydia a kiss. 'Here's my shopping list. I'm giving it to you well in advance so you'll have plenty of time. Can I have them gift-wrapped as well?'

'Good Lord,' exclaimed Lydia as she scanned the typed pages. 'You'll be bankrupt and I'll be in profit. Oh excuse me, dear, I've a customer,' she said, all businesslike as she went to the till. Her assistant didn't come in until eleven.

'Come up and have your lunch with me in the Coffee Dock,' Devlin suggested. 'We'll have a natter. I want to hear what you think of my idea for Dad's Christmas present.'

'Right, I'll do that,' Lydia promised as her customer took out her credit card and began to point to a variety of items she required. Obviously someone else doing her Christmas shopping, Devlin thought approvingly.

There was a spring in her step as she ran up the stairs to her office. In two weeks' time, all going to schedule, Belfast City Girl would be opening in a blaze of publicity. Then it was off to Paris on Christmas Eve with Luke. She could hardly wait! Then she'd have Caroline to stay and there would be dinner parties and the crack would be mighty. She was definitely going to make sure it was a good Christmas this year. She had earned it, she told herself, as she walked into her office humming.

Liz turned a worried face in her direction. 'Devlin, there's a bit of bad news, I'm afraid. Arthur Kelly's had a heart attack. He's in intensive care in the Royal Victoria. It's not looking too good.'

Eight

It was a warm July morning seven months later. They were waiting patiently at the entrance to Johnson's Mobile Caravan and Camping Park. When they saw her there were screeches of excitement and they danced up and down waving at her. Devlin rolled to a halt and felt a balm envelop her. This was just what she needed. And it was such a beautiful place: the hills of Wicklow all around and in this natural little hollow a haven for the weary soul.

'Hiya, Auntie Devlin!' said Michael with a beaming face. 'Follow us and we'll show you where our mobile is.'

'You have to go slow: there's ramps,' Mimi said importantly as she stuck her head in through the car window and kissed her 'aunt' enthusiastically.

'Right, I'll follow you,' said Devlin, starting the engine again. Like two outriders Mimi and Michael swept ahead on their scooters, their little brown legs in rhythm and Devlin, feeling as important as if she were President Robinson, followed behind them. To her right she could see a children's play area with swings, roundabouts, see-saws and a swimming pool that sparkled blue and silver in the early-morning sun. To her left were the reception area and shop, and then, as she drove down into the hollow, she could see the mobile homes in their own neatly tended, spacious plots.

Her outriders hung a left and she passed the showers and washrooms and then climbed a little hill. Then again another turn – a sharp right this time – into another field. Devlin followed them down to the end of it, past a tennis-court. She smiled as she saw Maggie hanging out clothes on a small line while Shona handed her the pegs.

'Oh God, I need this.' Devlin climbed out of the car and flung her arms around Maggie.

'Are you staying on your holidays, Manty Devlin?' Shona tugged at Devlin's skirt and held out her plump little arms to be lifted.

'Yes, darling. Yes, I am! Isn't it great!'

'Look at mine own bed.' The toddler eagerly dragged her up the steps of the veranda.

'And mine too!' Mimi was hotfoot behind them, scooter flung on the grass.

'Are you sure this is what you need? You won't get much of a rest here.'

'Maggie, I've been so looking forward to this,' Devlin said fervently. 'Oh it's lovely!' she exclaimed as she stepped inside the mobile. 'Maggie, it's fabulous. I've never been in a mobile home before.' She stood gazing around at the compact lounge with its comfortable sofas, built-in units and neat fireplace. Further down was the kitchenette and dining area and at the very end she could see through the open doors bedrooms and a shower and toilet.

'Congratulations, Maggie, you really deserve this! God knows you worked for it.'

'You can say that again,' her friend said dryly. 'You'd better let them show you around. I'll put the kettle on.' The next ten minutes were spent ooohing and aahing at the children's lovely cheerful little bedrooms with built-in units and matching curtains and duvet covers.

'OK, that's it!' Maggie cried as she carried in the tea and produced homemade brown bread and cheese and biscuits. 'The sun is shining, and you know the rule: out to play when the sun is shining.'

' "The sun has got his hat on; hip, hip, hip hooray," ' trilled Mimi as she waved at her aunt. 'See you later, alligator.' Devlin burst out laughing.

'In a while, crocodile,' she responded, as the three of them tumbled out the door and went off to play.

'That one is a hoot,' Devlin chuckled.

'Tell me about it!' laughed Maggie. 'Yesterday she informed me that she wanted to be a nopra singer and could she please have singing lessons. You'll hear her warbling away. I'm telling you, Maria Callas would have had nothing on her.'

'How's your own career?'

'I'm just going to concentrate on my writing and win as much independence as I can. That's one of the reasons I bought this mobile with my last advance. This is mine; it's my bolthole. Nobody can annoy me here. And the only people I have here are the people I love dearly.' She reached across the table and squeezed Devlin's hand. 'Actually, since I've bought this place I've perked up an awful lot. At the moment I'm quite happy. But what about you? Tell us all the news.'

'News! Huh! I'd need a whole hour on Sky News to tell you all that's going on,' Devlin groaned. She sipped her tea and took a satisfying bite of fresh brown bread, topped with rich yellow cheddar cheese. 'All I can say is: Maggie, I'm totally exhausted. As you know, I haven't had a minute to myself since before last Christmas, what with Arthur having his heart attack, and Luke and I having to cancel our trip to Paris.'

'That was unfortunate all right,' Maggie sympathized.

'Well, it just meant that we had to postpone the launch of the Belfast City Girl for a week. I had to spend a lot of time there, coordinating everything and getting all the publicity done – and dealing with all the things Arthur would have been handling.'

'So, is everything all right with Belfast now?' Maggie asked.

'It's going great guns now; doing really well, thank God,' Devlin exclaimed. 'But I just don't want ever to go through something like that again. The pressure was incredible and I felt responsible because I'd sort of railroaded Luke into it.'

'Don't be daft,' grinned Maggie. 'No-one could railroad Luke Reilly.'

'But you know what I mean,' argued Devlin. 'I was gung-ho to get Belfast going but really it was Arthur who was the driving force behind it all. He had all the contacts and he had made all the publicity arrangements. When he had his heart attack I really felt totally lost, as you can understand. It was scary, I can tell you, trying to carry on where he left off.'

'But Arthur's OK now, isn't he?' Maggie queried.

'He's fine, as good as new. You should see him. He's a reformed character. Doesn't drink, doesn't smoke, walks six miles a day, has dropped three stone. He's sickening, so bloody smug. You know how I love chocolate. Well, I daren't touch the stuff when he's around or I get a lecture on my cholesterol levels.'

'I had quite a few patients who had heart attacks who really changed their bad habits and developed a healthy lifestyle,' Maggie reflected. 'And they've never looked back. The quality of their lives improved tremendously.' Her preaching was spoiled by her spooning more sugar into her second cup of tea and devouring a Club Milk with indecent haste.

'I see it hasn't rubbed off on you,' Devlin teased.

'Give over!' grinned her friend, passing the packet to her.

'Arthur's incredible, though,' Devlin remarked, as she bit into the chocolate snack. 'He had loads of energy before his attack, but you should see him now. I just can't keep up with him. He was very seriously ill for the first couple of days but he pulled out of it and fought his way back to health. He did everything he was told by his doctors and dieticians and I raise my hat to him. Do you know what he thinks we should do next?'

'What?'

'Mr Arthur Kelly thinks we should open a . . . wait for it . . .' said Devlin with a smile, '. . . a City *Man*.'

'Good thinking,' approved Maggie. 'What do you think?'

'Oh, I think it's a great idea,' laughed Devlin. 'At least we'll be able to refute the accusation that we're sexist. But right now I'm up to my eyes getting Galway organized, so it will have to wait. He's going to look into financing and the like up in Belfast. But

I just can't get involved yet: we're going too fast and I'm barely able to keep up.'

'You should be careful,' Maggie warned. 'You could get burnt out very easily.'

'I know; I feel a bit whacked,' Devlin sighed. 'The last six months have been hectic.' She quickly brightened. 'And that's why I came down here. And thanks for asking Luke at the weekend, you're a real pal, Mags.'

'You mightn't be saying that by the end of the week,' Maggie laughed, as Shona raced through the door and launched herself at Devlin.

'Manty Devlin, Manty Devlin, will you bwing me for a swing by mine own self?'

'Everything is mine own self these days, as in "I can do it mine own self," ' Maggie explained.

'Come on, then.' Devlin lifted the toddler in her arms and held her close. Shona snuggled in tight and patted her on the shoulder.

'I lub you, Manty Devlin.'

'I love you, too.' Devlin kissed the fine gold curls under her chin. 'I'm off to the swings,' she said to Maggie. 'Expect me when you see me.'

'This is the life, gang.' Devlin stretched golden limbs out along her lounger and revelled in the heat of the sun.

'It's a bit like old times,' Caroline remarked, as she lifted her head out of Deirdre Purcell's blockbuster.

'Old times!' guffawed Maggie, as a gang of children danced and shrieked behind them in the great rolling dunes of Brittas Bay.

'Ah, you know what I mean,' said Caroline, who

125

had arrived down from Dublin that morning and had lost no time in joining the relaxed holiday atmosphere that Maggie and Devlin had already eagerly embraced.

'It's a long time, all the same,' said Devlin reflectively, 'since the three of us were away together. The weekend in Rosslare a year ago was our last little holiday.'

'It's been some year — and there's been some changes,' Maggie said ruefully and rather ungrammatically for a writer.

'Imagine,' said Caroline, 'the step I'll be taking in less than four months. I wonder am I mad to have agreed to go?'

'You're *not* mad: it's a fantastic opportunity and just what you need,' Devlin retorted, gently flicking at a bee that was hovering over her left breast.

'I'm really sorry I'll miss your launch, though, Maggie,' said Caroline regretfully.

'Can't be helped. You just go. Mind it won't be the same not having the third musketeer there. If things had gone to plan, it might have been *my* novel you were reading on the beach today.'

'Your day will come,' Devlin said comfortingly. 'Lying on a beach, being warmed by the sun, and listening to the sea just has to be the most therapeutic thing in the world. I feel so totally relaxed it's incredible. It took me about two hours to wind down. I thought it would take me two days.'

'It's such a simple pleasure and simple pleasures are always the best,' agreed Caroline, lashing on Nivea suntan milk.

'Mammy, will you tell Shona to stop throwing

sand: it's getting in my eyes and it's not fair.' Mimi had galloped up, scattering sand all over them.

'For God's sake, Mimi!' Maggie exclaimed in exasperation. 'I've told you to be careful. Look at Auntie Caroline: she's covered in sand.'

'Sorry, Auntie Caroline.' Mimi looked crestfallen.

'Not to worry,' Caroline said, dusting herself off. 'It was an accident,' she added kindly, giving the little girl a hug.

'It was an accident!' Mimi shot a triumphant look at her mother.

'Tell Shona to come up here; and if there's any more rows we're all going home and we're not having our picnic. OK?'

'OK.' Mimi threw her eyes up to heaven and went slithering back down the dune to get her sister.

'Mammy wants you 'mediately, Shona, you're in *big* trouble,' they heard her tell her younger sister.

Shona came panting up to them, her little legs sinking into the fine sand. She was pouting. ' 'S not sair, Mammy, 's not sair,' she complained. Devlin and Caroline hid their smiles behind their hands.

'Were you throwing sand?' Maggie asked sternly. Shona hung her head and stubbornly refused to answer. 'If I catch anyone throwing sand I'll get the wooden spoon! Do you hear me, Shona?'

The toddler nodded.

'Am going to play with Piona an Triona by mine own self, so I nam,' she said defiantly as she trotted off down the hill in a huff.

'Don't throw sand,' Maggie called after her.

She smiled at the amused Caroline. 'You were saying something about simple pleasures . . .'

'What the hell is wrong with your man there?' Devlin sat up and glared at a clean-cut young man in his twenties who was peering in over the top of the windbreak.

'You'd want to mind those nipples don't get frost-bite,' he said hastily and took to his heels.

Devlin sat with her mouth open, not sure if she had heard right.

The three of them stood up and stared after the man as he darted through the dunes.

'Pervert!' shrieked Maggie. 'God, wouldn't they just sicken you! Isn't that pathetic! What a way to get your kicks. You should see them on Sundays, out with their binoculars pretending to be bird-watching. It's disgusting. That kind of thing really bugs me: it's so offensive to women and there's nothing we can do about it.'

'We could have chased him and kicked him in the goolies,' Devlin hissed.

'He probably hasn't *got* any goolies,' Caroline snorted. 'That's why he's sneaking up on women hoping for a free look. He's probably a eunuch.'

'Well, if he comes back here, he's in trouble,' Maggie vowed. 'When we were kids we used to cycle here by ourselves and my parents felt we were perfectly safe. I wouldn't let my kids out of my sight for a minute – here or anywhere else. Isn't that an awful reflection on the society we're living in,' she added gloomily.

'Oh come on, don't let him spoil our day. What time is our picnic at? I'm starving!' Devlin grinned.

'You've only had your breakfast!' Maggie exclaimed indignantly.

'I know. It's the fresh air,' Devlin said unrepentantly.

'You can have a bag of crisps.'

'And a Club Milk?' Devlin pleaded.

'Don't push your luck. Come on, let's bring the lads for a swim,' Maggie suggested.

There was great excitement when the children heard about this. As well as Maggie's trio, they brought five pals from neighbouring mobiles. Michael and John, his new buddy, were studying a crab shell intently. 'Mind them claws,' Michael warned, much to Devlin's amusement. She overheard Fiona confiding in Mimi as they splashed around in the water, 'This is the best day of my life.'

'Me too,' agreed Mimi.

Shona was squealing with delight as Devlin dunked her in the waves. Devlin found herself thinking that, although she didn't have Lynn, she was blessed with the love and affection lavished on her by Maggie's children. Caroline was right: the simple pleasures were best. Luke would be here at the weekend to share them, she thought happily, as Shona urged with delight: 'Do it aden! Do it aden!'

The picnic was a riot. It was all new to Devlin: she had never been on a picnic as a child. The beach had not been Lydia's scene.

'What is it about banana sandwiches and orange juice?' said Maggie, grinning as she demolished a sandwich in two bites.

'Oh no! I love the egg-and-onion ones.' Caroline leaned across and helped herself to two more.

Devlin was engrossed in making the tea from the

129

water she had boiled on the little kerosene stove, ably assisted by Michael and John. It tasted divine.

It was a weary but happy gang that trudged through the dunes towards the car-park quite a few hours later. They had had their picnic and then gone picking shells on the beach. Then they had had another dip before playing a great game of rounders. At that, the three adults had said *enough* and returned to their loungers to recuperate.

'Isn't it great that they have picnic tables and everything here?' Caroline remarked carrying Shona on one arm and a lounger on the other.

'Oh, they do beautiful burgers and chips here,' Maggie announced, towing a plastic canoe weighed down with beach-balls, swimming rings and wet towels and togs.

'Burgers and chips?' Devlin said. 'Mmmm!'

'Devlin, you're incorrigible.' Maggie couldn't help but laugh.

'We wouldn't have to cook dinner then,' Devlin retorted.

'Who wants burger and chips?' Maggie eyed the eight eager children.

'Me!'

'Me!'

'Deadly!'

'Yippee!'

'Goody!'

'Yes, please!'

'Can I have sausages?'

'Can I have some chips mine own self?'

Devlin guffawed. 'I think the ayes have it.'

It was a very happy crew that tucked into burgers,

sausages, onion-rings and deep-fried mushrooms. Devlin brewed up again and there was lots of licking of fingers and sippings of teas and murmurs of great appreciation. The banquet was rounded off with a '99' cone for everybody. No meal in a five-star restaurant could have tasted so good.

This is the perfect end to a perfect day, Devlin thought, as she sipped her Bacardi and Coke and, leaning back in her chair, smiled at her friends. They were sitting on Maggie's veranda, gazing at the panorama of countryside. All that could be heard in the deepening dusk was the sound of birdsong and the soft lowing of the cows in the adjacent fields. There wasn't a child to be seen. Maggie's three were fast asleep in their beds, showered, ruddy-cheeked and exhausted after their day in the fresh air. 'I never want to go back to Dublin.'

'Me neither,' agreed Caroline. 'Maggie, this is paradise.'

'As near to as you'll get,' Maggie said, smiling. 'I love the peace here. Digby and Marjorie really run this place well. I stayed in a park once where the kids used to be out around shouting, screaming and kicking ball until all hours. That's not allowed here. You never see a child out after eleven.'

'I don't think our gang would be able to stay up and play even if they wanted to,' said Devlin. 'Did you see them? They were asleep nearly as soon as they hit the pillows? Shona fell asleep in the car coming home.'

'It's a great place for children,' Caroline reflected. 'They can play out in the open and you know they're safe from traffic and strangers. I wouldn't mind having a place here myself if I am ever lucky enough to marry again and have children.'

'There's a waiting list,' Maggie warned. 'Marjorie and Digby are very particular about whom they allow to park a mobile here. I don't think a pair of riff-raff like you would be suitable at all.'

'The cheek of you!' laughed Devlin.

'You've really taken to it, haven't you?' Maggie eyed them in amusement. 'I wasn't sure if you two high-fliers would take to the laid-back lifestyle. You didn't even bring your mobile phone, Devlin! You haven't phoned the office once. I thought you'd have terrible withdrawal symptoms, you the well-known workaholic!'

'I know. I'm chuffed with myself,' Devlin said proudly. 'I'm telling you, after two hours of being here I couldn't have cared less. This is just what I needed, and I'm going to come down again, if you'll let me.'

'You can stay for the summer if you want, the pair of you,' Maggie laughed.

'Wouldn't that be bliss!' Devlin sighed. She was so relaxed she couldn't keep her eyes open. 'Girls, I'm awfully sorry but I'm going to bed. It's this sea air: it knocks me out.' She yawned mightily. 'See you in the morning.'

'Night, Dev,' said the other pair, laughing in unison.

Ten minutes later, snuggled down in her sleeping bag on one of the soft sofas, Devlin was snoring gently.

*   *   *

'The few days in Wicklow did you the world of good,' said Luke as they drove back to Dublin the following Sunday evening.

'God, Luke, I feel like a new woman!' Devlin said happily. 'It was perfect. We had a great weekend, didn't we?' she smiled at him.

'I enjoyed myself immensely. Those kids are great. And that barbecue was super. Caroline really enjoyed it too.'

'I'm glad she's staying a few days longer with Maggie; it's tough for her at the moment with this business of Richard and Charles,' Devlin observed. 'But she's so much more her own woman now than she was when I first met her. Caroline will be fine.'

'I'm glad you like my friends, Luke. It was very important to me that you should,' Devlin said seriously. 'We're as close as sisters, you know.'

'I know that,' laughed Luke. 'Offend one and you offend them all.'

'Yeah, but wouldn't it be awful if you didn't get on with them. I don't know what I'd do: it would be an awful dilemma.'

'Well, that's one dilemma you don't have to contend with.'

'You made a great hit with Mimi, I've never seen you with children before. You've a great way with them.'

'I like children, I love their honesty. Whatever's in their mind they say it straight. Mimi's as straight as you'll get. Did you hear her telling that obnoxious kid on the beach who made Shona cry that he had no manners? That was before she pulled his hair. I felt like standing up and cheering.' Luke smiled at the memory. 'Let's take them to Funderland this Christmas,' he suggested as they turned left at Rathnew.

'Oh yes! that would be great fun!'

'That's a terrific place Maggie's got there.' He cast a glance at her. 'We must ask her to see if we could go on the waiting list. Wouldn't it be nice to have a place beside her for when we have a gang of our own?'

'Luke Reilly!' exclaimed Devlin, not sure if he was joking or not. But the more she thought about it, the nicer the idea seemed.

Nine

Devlin was talking to Antoinette Phillips, the organizer of the charity fashion show to which she had been invited, when they were interrupted by a scruffy young man with shifty eyes and a pimply chin.

'Excuse me, ladies,' he said cockily. 'I need to speak to Ms Delaney.'

Antoinette threw him a scornful look. 'It's important,' he declared, unimpressed by this subtle intimidation.

'We'll talk when you've finished with this . . . person,' Antoinette said haughtily. She did not like being interrupted when she was in full flow. And she did not like her VIPs being shanghaied by scruffy little chappies.

'Certainly,' Devlin said politely. In fact she was bored and dead beat. The day had been hectic and all she wanted to do was go home to her bed. She certainly didn't want to stand here yapping to this unknown personage who had something important to discuss with her, nor did she want to spend the rest of the night listening to Antoinette rabbiting on.

'How can I help you?' she asked with superficial politeness.

The young man shuffled uneasily and held out a

hand. 'I'm Larry Dempsey,' he said chummily, in a tone which suggested to Devlin that it was a name she should know and, what was more, that she should be honoured that he was speaking to her. It *was* a vaguely familiar name but she was too tired to try and remember where she had heard it before. He had a limp handshake, too. Devlin hated people with limp handshakes.

She stared blankly at him.

'Larry Dempsey, columnist with the *Sunday Echo*.'

'Nice to meet you,' Devlin murmured, wishing he would shove off.

'Well, the thing is, I'm doing a series coming up to Christmas called "A Drink with Larry",' he simpered, 'and basically like, I invite well-known celebrities of the female sex to come and have a drink with me and like, see how we get on, kind of thing. I've been considering you as one of my like, guests.' He chuckled inanely.

Oh shit! thought Devlin in dismay, suddenly identifying the nuisance she was talking to. Not even if City Girl were to go under in the morning because of lack of publicity would she do an interview with Larry Dempsey!

'No, thank you,' she said. She was sorely tempted to say: 'It's like, not my scene,' but she restrained herself.

'Aw come on! Be a sport.' Larry was leering now. 'You successful women always play hard to get.'

'No,' Devlin said firmly. 'Excuse me.' She turned on her heel and walked away. Sexist pretentious little git, she thought. She wasn't going to have herself humiliated in his sleazy column, thank you very much!

'Stuck-up bitch,' Larry muttered, blushing to the roots of his lanky blond locks.

Devlin stayed for another half-hour before making her excuses and escaping to her bed.

Larry Dempsey was not used to being turned down. Most women he approached, after the initial playing hard to get and coy refusal, were perfectly happy to have him treat them to a night on the town. The details then appeared several Sundays later in his widely read and even more widely admired column.

Larry was a name to be reckoned with in journalism – at least in his own mind. He just couldn't figure this Delaney woman out. The way she had looked at him as if he had crawled out of a piece of cheese! Who did she think she was? And what was he going to tell his editor? He had been very keen for Larry to get an interview with Devlin Delaney. Larry rather suspected that Mick Coyle had a fancy for the leggy blonde. The dirty old lecher. Well, he might not be too impressed when Larry told him of her rudeness. Devlin Delaney was a stuck-up snob who thought she was too good for Larry Dempsey. Well, he'd just see about that, Larry decided. Nobody made him feel like a worm and got away with it. He'd heard talk about Ms Delaney around town. And he was just the lad to get to the bottom of a rumour. The pen was mightier than the sword. A little bit of malice here, a soupçon there – just enough to make mischief. Especially for one as delectable as Madame Delaney. He had been looking forward to having his photo taken with her. Especially as he always made a point of having very close contact with his guest when it was photo time.

Everybody thought he had women falling all over him. If the truth were known the nearest he ever came to close contact with a woman was at those damned photo sessions. No matter how hard he tried, he just couldn't score with a broad. It was infuriating, decided Larry, drowning his inadequacies with another free drink.

'Devlin, there's a Kevin Shannon on the line. He wants to do an interview with you. He's from the business page of the *Sunday Echo*.' Devlin came to with a start to hear Liz speaking to her. She had been daydreaming, remembering the precious week she had spent in Paris with Luke at Christmas. It had been a wonderful holiday, a year late maybe, but that had made it all the more special, and ever since she had come back she had found it hard to settle down.

'Well! What shall I say?' Liz asked patiently.

'Sorry, I was in Paris,' said Devlin. 'The *Sunday Echo*? That's an awful rag, isn't it?' she grimaced.

'I know,' soothed Liz, 'but it is the business page. They can't do much harm on that and it's not good to say no to a business interview. You never know when you might need publicity, especially now that Galway will be opening.'

'Why are you always right?' Devlin said in mock-irritation.

'That's the reason you hired me, boss,' Liz saluted. 'I'll tell him sometime next week?'

'As long as it's not that sleaze-bag Dempsey who accosted me at Antoinette Phillips's charity thing before Christmas,' Devlin sighed. 'If you really feel it's a must, then go ahead.'

'I do,' Liz said firmly and closed the door behind her.

'Bully,' Devlin called after her, as she lifted the phone to call Luke. She just wanted to tell him that she missed him and was thinking of him.

Dianne answered his phone, much to Devlin's disgust. She had wanted to hear his voice; she had wanted to tell him that she loved him and missed him.

'He's on site. Any message?' Dianne asked snootily.

Yes, tell him I love him! Devlin was tempted to say. She knew Dianne didn't like her and had a sneaking suspicion that Luke's PA had a crush on him.

'Just tell him I called,' Devlin answered.

'Certainly,' came the frosty response.

'Happy New Year, Dianne,' Devlin said wickedly. There was a long pause.

'The same to you, Miss Delaney,' came the cool tones.

'Thanks. Bye.' Devlin hung up, smiling.

How dare that dame wish her Happy New Year as if they were bosom buddies or something, Dianne thought furiously. It really was galling to have to speak to that woman on the phone. To think that she and Luke had been canoodling in Paris for a week. It was pretty clear that Luke and Devlin had become very close companions. Luke had come back from Paris looking totally relaxed and happy. It had sent Dianne into the pits of a depression.

Suffering from unrequited love must be the most

painful thing in the world. It was even hard to keep her fantasies going. Last night she had been watching a cowboy film starring William Holden. He had been a captain in the US cavalry and he had looked magnificent in his uniform. She had spent a good part of the night imagining Luke as a cavalry officer in the blue uniform and lovely high dusty leather boots, making passionate love to her under the stars in the desert, but it had been hard to concentrate. She kept imagining him and Devlin together in a four-poster bed in Paris.

Dianne considered whether she should let Luke know something of what she was feeling. She sat at her desk, chin propped on her hands, and pondered the problem. Then she sat up straight. She'd tell him, that's what she'd do. She'd tell him right to his face that she loved him. And then see how soon he'd forget Ms Devlin Delaney. Luke was just passing time with the blonde bombshell. Dianne was sure of it. No, once Dianne had declared her love for him he'd have eyes for no-one else.

What would she wear when she told him? Something that was easily removed. Just in case Luke decided to make love to her there and then. She'd leave work early today, plead a headache – that would make him concerned. And on the way home she'd treat herself to some really sexy underwear. Black stockings and suspenders. Dianne was sure Luke was a black stockings and suspenders type. She was getting randy just thinking about it. She wasn't going to wait a minute longer: she was going out right now to buy her treats.

'I'm going home: I feel dreadful,' Dianne told

her astonished secretary. 'I don't know if I'll be in tomorrow; it depends on how I feel.'

That should give Luke something to think about. In the three years she had been working for him, she had never once missed a day.

Feeling strangely exhilarated, Dianne left the office and began her quest for black suspenders and fine silk stockings.

The *Sunday Echo* had become a sleazy sensationalist rag that could compete with any tabloid of the gutter press. Of that there was no doubt. Though masquerading as a quality paper, its ethics were non-existent, its news reporting pathetic, and its dirt-dishing far steamier than that of any other paper in the country.

That was why it sold so well! Peddling the details of people's private lives was its stock-in-trade and nobody peddled so well or so thoroughly as did the hacks (who called themselves journalists) of the *Sunday Echo*. Certainly, there were good articles by well-thought-of contributors, but in the main it had gone from a good newspaper to a rancid tabloid in disguise.

The *Sunday Echo* now had a brand-new sacrificial victim to help them on their way – Devlin. It had been decided at the last editorial meeting of the features department that Devlin Delaney, who had kicked the gossip columnist of all gossip columnists, the *Sunday Echo*'s very own Lucinda Marshall, out of the exclusive City Girl Health and Leisure Club and who had refused point-blank, and with even a hint of distaste, to go out on a date with Man About Town

Larry Dempsey for his Christmas column, was to be the next victim of a hatchet job.

There were rumours circulating the hot spots about Ms Delaney, businesswoman and media celebrity, that were too juicy to be ignored. And one thing the *Sunday Echo* never did was to ignore juicy rumours. Hell, when they had no juicy rumours, they just made some up themselves! But *these* rumours were really hot. She was supposed to have had a baby! Supposed to have lived in Ballymun. Then there was supposed to have been a terrible accident. There were rumours that it hadn't been an accident at all and that Devlin had got a massive insurance pay-out with which she had opened City Girl. Rumours that no self-respecting hack could ignore.

Larry and Lucinda were dispatched with instructions to leave no stone unturned, no gutter unexplored, in the quest for the goods on Ms Delaney. Kevin Shannon of the business section was going to be told to do a business interview which would give the article an air of respectability and around which they would slip in their juicy titbits. With all the resources of their horrible little trade, Larry and Lucinda set off on the trail of the 'to-lie-for' scoop.

Caroline's Story – I

Ten

Her idea had been to go home and lie out in the sun for the rest of the day, to top up the tan that she had got in Rosslare Harbour. But as Caroline drove along past Connolly Station, out towards Fairview and Clontarf, she decided that she didn't want to go home just yet.

She didn't know where Richard was. Presumably he would be home for dinner; he hadn't said otherwise. Maybe she'd pop in and see her dad in Marino, and she could get some steak from the local butchers and do Richard steak and onions for his dinner. Now that she had a plan in mind, she didn't feel so low.

When she got to her father's house, she decided against driving in the gate. Caroline didn't feel quite proficient enough to turn in between what she considered excessively narrow gate-posts. Her father was working out in the back garden. Tony Stacey was a keen gardener; his little plot had helped to occupy his mind when his wife died suddenly and left him with the task of rearing three teenagers alone.

Caroline watched him stooping to dig out a particularly stubborn weed from between his cabbages. He was still a sprightly man at sixty-four. It was hard

145

to believe that he'd be retiring the following year from his job as a maths teacher. 'Hi, Dad.' She walked down the path and smiled at her father.

'Ah, Caroline, I wasn't expecting to see you.' Tony wiped his hands on his gardening trousers and greeted his daughter with a smile. 'You look well. Did you have a nice time in Wexford?'

'I had a great time, Dad.'

'Well, you got a good tan, anyway,' her father observed. 'Have you time for a cup of coffee?'

'I'll make it,' Caroline offered. 'Have you had your lunch?'

'Well, now that you come to mention it, I *am* a bit peckish,' Tony admitted, glancing at his watch. 'I didn't realize it was so late.'

'You carry on there; I'll rustle you up something,' Caroline said, glad of something to do. She picked a pod off a stalk, squeezed it open and ate the sweet-tasting peas. 'These are nice. You've a good crop. And the broad beans look very healthy,' she remarked. Her father's garden was a credit to him. He grew all his own vegetables and when she lived at home she had always enjoyed going out to pick fresh cabbage or parsley or lettuce or other vegetables in season.

She went into the kitchen and opened the fridge door. An unpleasant smell assaulted her nostrils and she raised her eyes to heaven. Her father and two brothers lived in the house, and while they kept it clean and fairly tidy, any time she went to the fridge she would find something that was going off, or past its sell-by date. She started on the top shelf. Two yoghurts, a week out of date; they went into the bin. Next shelf: a lump of cheese that was rock-hard. Out.

Two sausages in their plastic packaging didn't smell great; she got rid of them. The rashers were fine.

The next shelf had a carcass of a chicken and a leg and a wing, obviously the remains of Sunday's meal. Caroline took that out. She would give it to her father for his lunch. She opened the salad drawer and found the source of the pong, a green pepper that was beginning to grow a fluffy white coating on the inside. The tomatoes and cucumber were all right. Caroline took them out to accompany the chicken, filled the sink with hot water and washed out the salad drawer. Just as well she dropped in once a week or those men would poison themselves, she thought in amusement.

Her father popped his head around the back door. 'How would you fancy a few nice potatoes and some scallions and lettuce and a few peas and beans?'

'Oh, Dad, I'd love them! Thanks,' she exclaimed.

'I'll just go and dig the spuds for you, so,' he said cheerily.

Twenty minutes later Caroline called him in for his lunch. She had put a wash in the machine and had run the hoover over the sitting-room and hall.

'Aren't you having anything?' he asked, sitting down to his chicken salad.

'I ate earlier at City Girl. I'm not hungry so I'll just have the coffee.'

'How's the mad Devlin one?' Tony grinned. He had a soft spot for his daughter's friend and was very appreciative of how both Maggie and Devlin had been such a help to Caroline when it came to her drinking problem.

'The mad Devlin one is fine and full of ideas for

expanding City Girl. Although,' Caroline admitted, 'it was a bit harrowing when we went to visit her baby's grave.'

'That was very tough on her. Be extra kind to Devlin, Caroline – it will take her a long long time to come to terms with that tragedy,' her father said sadly, remembering how he had felt in the years after his wife's death.

'I will, Dad, don't worry,' Caroline promised. She brightened. 'And guess what? Maggie's having a novel published. Isn't that a great achievement?'

Tony was delighted with the news. 'Well, good for Maggie. She's a gas woman. I'd say she'd have an interesting story to tell.'

'Well, she's being published; Devlin's succeeding beyond her wildest dreams. I'll have to pull up my socks to keep in the same league as them,' Caroline said with a wry smile.

'You have your own talents,' her father said kindly.

Yes, I was a great drunk, Caroline thought glumly, but she said nothing, just poured her father another cup of coffee.

'Hello! Hello!' Sarah Yates barked imperiously down the phone. All she got was Richard's voice on the answering machine telling her to leave her message after the bleep.

'Bah!' she expostulated. She had no time for these new-fangled machines. Where on earth was Richard? Five times she had called his office. *Five times!* And left a message that he was to call her urgently. 'Have you given him the message? It is extremely important. I'm his mother, you know,' she had informed the girl at the other end of the phone.

'Yes, Mrs Yates, but I'm afraid I don't know where he is. If he rings in, I'll certainly give him your message.'

'Tsk, you're not much of a receptionist if you don't know where your boss is,' Sarah had retorted after the last phone call.

It wouldn't have happened in his father's day. Reginald Yates was a complete professional, as Sarah was constantly reminding her son. The very time she needed Richard, he wasn't there. Those dreadful new people who had moved in next door, with their barking dog and brazen children, were causing her sleepless nights. The children were deliberately trespassing into her gardens, back and front, to get the balls they were always throwing in. What the neighbourhood was coming to was nobody's business.

She had never allowed Richard to play on the street, no matter how much he pleaded. That was 'common' behaviour as far as Sarah was concerned. And the Yateses were not of common stock. That was more than she could say for her son's in-laws, she thought grumpily, as she straightened up the antimacassars on the sofa and chairs in the parlour. Why Richard had wanted to get married to Caroline, she could not imagine. And look at the way she had ended up. In a drying-out clinic. The shame of it! Richard hadn't meant to say anything, but he'd let it slip one night he'd been taking her shopping. She'd known her daughter-in-law was in a private hospital for 'tests' and she asked Richard how Caroline was.

'Suffering badly from withdrawal symptoms,' he'd

149

said tiredly, and of course she kept at him until she found out what the addiction was.

She wasn't the slightest bit surprised to hear that Caroline had a drink problem. It probably ran in the family. Hadn't her uncle been tipsy at the wedding, that awful wedding that was too dreadful to think about. Caroline's father had looked ridiculous in his top-hat and tails. Just like a dumpy little penguin. Now Reginald had always looked superb in tails. He could carry them. He had class, not like the Stacey family. That aunt of Caroline's who gave herself such airs, Sarah had seen her on the day of the wedding eating her melon-and-kiwi starter with her soup-spoon. And as for that silly little cousin of Caroline's who had simpered at Richard and said she'd love to meet some of his friends if they were as good-looking as he was! A social climber without a doubt, Sarah sniffed, as she removed some dead leaves from her geranium plants.

Richard should have taken her advice and stayed single. The two of them had been perfectly happy when he lived at home and she took care of him. He'd never had to worry about coming home and not finding his dinner on the table. Imagine a wife going away with her friends for a weekend and leaving her husband to fend for himself. It was outrageous. Some wife, Caroline's mother-in-law thought in disgust, as she picked up the phone to call her son's penthouse once more.

This time she left a message on the despised machine. 'Ring your mother immediately, Richard. It's of the greatest urgency.'

That should get a response, she thought grimly, as

she sat down in a red-velvet-covered armchair and prepared for the afternoon watch. If that ball came into her front garden *once* this afternoon she was going to confiscate it and by jingo she'd see her neighbours in court.

'Can I have two T-bone steaks, please, Robert,' Caroline asked the young butcher as he diligently wiped down the weighing scales.

'Ah it's yourself, the lady of leisure,' Robert grinned. Caroline grinned back. She always enjoyed the slagging she got from Robert and David, the two butchers who now worked in the shop where she'd always bought meat when she'd been cooking for the family.

'Don't mind his cheek,' David advised. David was in charge of the shop, which was always kept immaculate.

'What happened to your wrist?' Caroline asked Robert, noticing that it was bandaged.

'He was on the beer again,' David said with a grin.

'Don't mind him!' Robert exclaimed indignantly. 'I was not.'

'How did you do it? Fighting off the women, was it?' Caroline teased.

'I fell over the hoover,' Robert informed her, 'and me ma was more worried about the blooming hoover than she was about me. She comes rushing out and roars, "Is the hoover all right? I hope it's not broken." And my lying in a heap. I ask ya!'

Caroline and David guffawed.

Robert took the tenner she handed him. 'Here's your steaks and don't cremate them.'

She left the shop smiling. Most customers did. The two lads were always ready for a bit of a laugh. Now she was *not* going to get down in the dumps, she told herself, as she drove towards Clontarf. She had spent a lovely weekend with the girls. She had passed a nice couple of hours chatting to her father, which was something they had never done before she'd ended up in hospital with her alcoholism. Their relationship was much stronger than it had ever been. The same was true of her brothers, Declan and Damien. They'd got *such* a shock when they'd heard she was an alcoholic. They had always taken her for granted when she'd been at home taking care of them. She'd been someone who'd cooked their dinner, washed their clothes and kept the house clean. It had given them a bit of a land when she left home and they had to start doing it themselves. Not that she left them completely in the lurch. Once a week, come rain or shine, she'd come home and do the housework for them. And still they took her for granted. It was only after they'd seen her shaking and ill and suffering the most awful withdrawals from drink and Valium, that her brothers came to realize that behind their drudge of a sister was a very fragile, vulnerable person. Now they were much more supportive of her, and she was enjoying their new relationship.

It was just, she thought with a sigh, as she drove along the seafront, glancing at the palm trees waving in the breeze — it was just that she was feeling a bit restless. Listening to Devlin and Maggie making their plans had made her realize that her own future was a void.

She would have to make up her mind whether she

wanted to continue living with Richard or finally admit to the world that their marriage was over. Richard didn't want her to leave; it suited him to be 'married' to her. Just imagine the shock waves that would crash around the law library if its denizens knew that Richard, high-profile married solicitor Yates, and Charles, eminently respectable barrister Stokes, were lovers.

Would she have the nerve to live on her own and stand on her own two feet? This was the question that Caroline frequently asked herself. So far the answer was no, but looking at her friends and seeing the success they were making of their lives despite having their share of troubles had made her think. Maybe she'd talk to Richard about it after dinner tonight. Yes, that would be a start, she decided, as she drove into the apartment complex. Devlin's penthouse was in the block opposite theirs, but no doubt her friend was still in the office making plans and decisions in her usual businesslike manner. Well, Caroline was going to start making a few decisions about her own life soon, she promised herself, parking her car and taking her bag of fresh vegetables from the boot, as well as her weekend luggage. Her father must have thought she would be cooking for an army, she grinned, weighed down by the bulging bag. She'd cook Richard some of the new floury potatoes, she decided.

After she had unpacked the groceries and the vegetables and dumped her weekend case in the bed-room, Caroline switched on the answering machine. She'd noticed the light flashing and thought that maybe Richard had left a message for her. Her heart sank when she heard the imperious tones of her mother-in-law. Now, what on earth was wrong with her that was such a matter of great urgency? That woman was the greatest notice-box going. And utterly selfish. Caroline detested her. No matter how much Richard and she did for her, it would never be enough. Of course, Sarah Yates had never forgiven Caroline for marrying her precious son. No woman in the country was good enough for her Richard.

Caroline had realized this very early on in her marriage and had tried to accept it. It was under-standable to a degree. After all, Richard was Sarah's only child, and after his father had died she had come to depend on him utterly. That was fair enough. Caroline could cope with that and also with the fact that Sarah clearly had no time for her daughter-in-law. But what really annoyed her was the way Sarah treated Richard. She had never accepted the fact that her son was a grown man and even though he was in his mid-thirties she continued to treat him as though he were a ten-year-old. And worse again, Richard allowed her to get away with it.

'Don't argue with me, Richard; I'm your mother,' was a frequent saying of the mega-martyr Sarah. 'If only your father were still alive *he'd* look after me.' This infuriated Caroline because, whatever his faults, her husband was an exemplary son and always had been.

He looked after Sarah's financial and legal affairs; he listened to her complaints about her daily and her gardener and often had to soothe their ruffled feelings when they threatened to give notice. He took her to the doctor whenever she needed to go, although she was as healthy as an ox. He phoned her twice a day and visited several times a week. But was her mother-in-law in the slightest bit appreciative of what was done for her? She was not! She accepted it all as her due and was constantly looking for more.

Once a week Richard and Caroline used to take Mrs Yates shopping to Superquinn in Sutton. This was not a simple matter. Mrs Yates was a pernickety shopper, picking items up, putting them down. Up and down the aisles they went, waiting patiently while she made her selection, Caroline pushing her trolley, Richard pushing his mother's. Anything Caroline put into her own trolley was commented upon.

Richard had a weakness for Superquinn pizza, accompanied by tuna salad from the supermarket's salad bar. Invariably, Sarah would comment that her son would be a whole lot better if he ate 'proper' food instead of that kind of modern stuff.

'Of course, I always cooked the best of food for him when he lived at home. Wives these days aren't very good in the kitchen,' she sniffed one evening after Caroline had bought chicken Kiev, another favourite of Richard's. Caroline was furious. She had been cooking meals since the start of her teens and had never poisoned any of her family. Nevertheless, she had swallowed her annoyance in her usual timid fashion, not anxious to have a confrontation with the formidable woman. After she had been hospitalized for alcoholism and Richard had admitted his homo-sexuality, she had simply stopped going late-night shopping with him and his mother. It was the one stand she made, and her husband didn't press her. Caroline did her own household shopping by herself, and thoroughly enjoyed meandering up and down the aisles putting whatever she liked into her trolley without fear of disparaging comment. She didn't go to Superquinn in Sutton, although it was a lovely shop, because Sarah had ruined it for her. She went to Finglas instead and made it hers.

When they'd got married first, Richard used to moan about Caroline going home once a week to clean the house for her father, until she pointed out to him that, just as he had a mother who depended on him, she had a father who valued what she did. And, while she didn't mind going shopping with her mother-in-law, or visiting her, or having Sunday lunch with her every so often, the least she could do was visit her father once a week. He couldn't argue with that.

Now, Caroline wondered what matter of great urgency Sarah was referring to in her message. She wondered if there was anything seriously wrong? Had she fallen, maybe, or cut herself? If she cut herself it wasn't blood that would flow – it would be something more like Tabasco! But Caroline thought she'd better phone the old bat just to make sure everything was OK.

'Yes? Hello?'

Caroline winced at the bellow that came down the phone. Mrs Yates was a bit deaf and inclined to shout. 'Hello, it's Caroline. I got your message on the machine. Is anything wrong?'

'Of course something's wrong. I wouldn't have said so if it wasn't,' Sarah snapped.

'Can I do something for you?' Caroline asked politely, holding the phone slightly away from her ear.

'Where's Richard?'

'I'm afraid I don't know, I haven't been able to get in touch with him today.'

Mrs Yates gave a snort of derision. '*That's* not surprising, since you were off carousing with your friends for the weekend. In my day, wives didn't go off without their husbands. No wonder the world is in the state it is. When Richard comes in, oblige me by asking him to telephone me immediately.' There was a peremptory click at the other end of the phone as her mother-in-law hung up, leaving Caroline half-amused and half-furious.

'Old crab,' she muttered, heading out to the kitchen to prepare the dinner.

But where *was* Richard? It was most unlike him to take off without leaving a message or telling his secretary where he could be contacted. She toyed with the idea of ringing Charles. He might have some idea what was going on. But she decided against it. It might look as if she was checking up on Richard. Once she had got used to the idea that they were committed long-time partners, it no longer bothered her. In fact it was a huge relief to realize that it was not her, or what she considered her lack of sex-appeal, that had made Richard so loth to share her bed. She was as feminine and sexy as any other woman, although she had spent the years of her marriage doubting her appeal. Once she knew the truth behind her husband's behaviour, it made a lot of things clear to her. No, she wouldn't phone Charles, she decided, as she chopped the onions, trying to keep her mouth open so she wouldn't cry. She'd let Richard tell her in his own good time where he'd been.

About an hour later, she heard his key in the door. That was really good timing, she thought with satisfaction, lifting a big floury potato out of the pot.

'Hi, Richard,' she called out cheerfully. 'I'm just dishing up.' Her husband appeared at the kitchen door and she was shocked when she saw his ashen face.

'God, Richard! What's wrong?' she exclaimed as the vague sense of unease at his uncharacteristic behaviour that had been with her since she came home, suddenly coalesced into a leaden knot of apprehension.

Eleven

'What's wrong, Richard?' Caroline repeated the question, her voice rising in concern.

Richard's eyes flooded with tears. 'Charles has got cancer of the spleen. It's terminal.'

'Oh, Richard!' Caroline rushed across the kitchen and put her arms around her husband. 'How long does he have?'

'They say a year at the most. I can't believe it,' he wept. 'How will I manage without Charles?' He drew away from her and rubbed his eyes like a child. 'Did you hear what I said? There I go, thinking of myself again. How is *he* going to manage? How do you cope when you're told you've less than a year to live? I'd crack up! Imagine counting the days on a calendar?'

'That's awful,' Caroline murmured, her heart like lead. It was so hard to believe that the seemingly healthy man that she knew and cared for was being eaten alive by that most hideous of diseases. She had to fight to stop herself breaking down. Charles would be a great loss to her also. By right she should hate her husband's lover, but she knew that Charles understood her and Richard better than they understood themselves. He could see why they were drawn to each other and, knowing that it would end in grief, he had tried hard to prevent Richard from marrying her. Charles had the most empathy of any man she knew, and he had been genuinely kind to her, in his avuncular way, ever since the dreadful night she had tried to commit suicide. He knew how fragile she still felt. He could understand her fluttery feelings of panic when she didn't think she'd make it on her own without a drink or a Valium.

If Charles would be such a great loss to her, Caroline just couldn't imagine her husband's feelings. He loved Charles with a great and abiding love. They had been together for most of Richard's adult life. To him, Charles was a father figure, confidant and adviser, as well as being his lover. How would her husband face the world without his love and support?

'What's Charles going to do?' Caroline asked gently.

Richard sighed and sat down at the kitchen table. 'I don't know. I'm not sure if he knows himself yet. He's reviewing his options, although, God knows, there aren't many,' he added bitterly. 'Oh Caroline, what will I do? I want to die myself.'

'Well, that's *not* an option,' Caroline said firmly. 'You'll do what we all have to do. You'll pick up the pieces, dust yourself off and get on with it – and be very thankful for the privilege of having had someone like Charles in your life for as long as you did.'

Richard hadn't expected this from his wife.

'I mean it, Richard,' Caroline declared. 'If you're going to give in to yourself and be melodramatic, you'll be no help to Charles when he needs you most. Just think how remorseful you'll be about your selfish behaviour when he's gone, and that will keep you on the straight and narrow.' She sat at the table opposite him. In the old days she would never have addressed her husband in such a fashion. She had held him in far too much awe. But these were not the old days; now they were equals and she felt no such constraints.

'Look, Richard,' Caroline said calmly. 'The trouble with you is that ever since you were a child, you've been spoilt in the worst possible way by your mother. You were the focus of her existence and she raised you to think that the world revolved around you. Well, it doesn't. It isn't your fault that that's the way you were brought up, but you've got to realize that right now it's not *your* feelings that are important. You've got to put yourself in Charles's shoes. You've got to be there as long as he needs you, and that's going to be tough. And if you think for one minute that I'm going to let you give in to self-pity while he needs you, or even when it's all over, then you can think again.'

Richard's face flushed, and for one frightening moment Caroline felt the old fear rise up, as during the time he used to beat her. In the old days, he would not have tolerated such straight talking. Maybe she had gone too far. Caroline stared at her husband as his hands clenched on the table in front of her and then, to her surprise and relief, he leaned across and took one of her hands in his.

'Thanks, Caroline, I needed that kick in the arse. This time, I can't think about myself; I've got to think of him. Please help me, Caroline. I don't think I'm strong enough to get through this by myself. Promise you'll help me,' he said urgently.

'I will, Richard, I will. I promise.' Caroline hoped that she, too, wouldn't go to pieces herself before the

161

ordeal was over. She, who had never coped with any trauma in her life without resorting to some sort of crutch, was promising her husband that she would help him in his hour of greatest need. Charles had always assured her that if she dug deep enough she would find all the resources she'd ever need within herself. Well, maybe he was right. Maybe this time, drink- and drug-free, she would cope with a crisis all by herself for once in her life. She had lectured Richard about his self-pity; well, it was time she grew up as well and started taking responsibility for herself. Just like Devlin and just like Maggie. She would make herself ignore those fluttery feelings of panic that enveloped her. It was only self-indulgence giving in to them, lying there listening to her heart pound more and more loudly. The next time it happened, she was going to say, 'I don't have time for this,' and make herself do something to forget about it, no matter what time of the day or night it was. She was going to control the panic, rather than allowing it to control her.

'We'll get by, Richard.' She squeezed his hand. 'Charles would be terribly disappointed if we didn't.'

'You're right,' her husband said stoutly, taking strength from her support.

'Why don't you have some dinner and go back over to him? Stay the night if you want; maybe he could do with the company.'

'Don't you mind being here on your own?' Richard asked in amazement.

Caroline gave a wry smile. 'I think, Richard, it's about time I started trying it out. I'm a big girl now. Besides, when Charles gets really ill, he'll probably need you there, so I might as well start practising now.'

'Well, if you're sure,' he said hesitantly.

'I am. Now eat your dinner and off with you.'

'I'm not really hungry.'

She put the plate in front of him. 'Well, just try a bit. I cooked steak and there are some lovely peas and broad beans and potatoes out of Dad's garden.'

'I had it all planned that some day you would find a nice straight man who could give you everything I couldn't and I would go and live with Charles and we'd all be happy for the rest of our lives. Things don't work to plan, do they?'

'No, Richard, they don't,' Caroline sighed. To tell the truth she wasn't feeling that hungry herself now after hearing his news. Richard toyed with his meal just to please her, but eventually he pushed away the barely touched food. They were having coffee when the phone rang.

Caroline's hand flew to her mouth. 'Oh heavens above, Richard, I forgot to tell you. Your mother left a message that she wanted you to phone her urgently. I rang her to see if anything was wrong, but she just wanted to speak to you.'

Her husband raised his eyes to heaven and went to answer the phone. After a minute or so, Caroline heard him say brusquely, 'Mother, I haven't time for a lecture. I have to go out now, so tell me what's the problem.' There was a long pause and then she heard him say in exasperation, 'Mother, I suggest you try and get on with your neighbours rather than start a whole sorry saga by bringing them to court. You never know, you might need them some time.' From fifteen paces, Caroline could hear the shriek of outrage that followed this pronouncement, and she turned away to hide her amusement.

'For God's sake, Mother,' Richard interrupted angrily, 'I don't have time for this kind of crap!' Caroline's eyes widened. Imagine Sarah at the other end of the phone, listening to her precious son using vulgar language and brushing aside her matter of great urgency. It's about time for the worm to turn, Caroline thought with satisfaction. Good on you, Richard, she mentally applauded.

'Look, Mother, if you want to bring them to court, do so. But I'm not getting involved, so go see another solicitor. Now, I'm going. I'm going to spend some time with Charles, who has just been told that he has less than a year to live. When you hear something like that, it puts petty little arguments with the neighbours into perspective, doesn't it, now? I'll call you tomorrow if I get time.' Richard hung the phone up very decisively.

'She probably won't talk to me for months,' he said ruefully. 'She wants to start proceedings for trespass and nuisance against her new neighbours. They're nice people, Caroline. I met them,' he said in irritation. 'The children are only toddlers.'

'Why don't you get her to put up a fence?'

'That's a good idea,' he reflected. 'I know her garden is precious to her and the next time I see those people I'll ask them to try and get the kids not to kick the ball in because it upsets her. But to start going on about going to court at this stage . . .'

'Well, at least it wasn't a medical emergency,' Caroline said diplomatically.

164

'Huh,' snorted Richard. 'My mother has the constitution of a horse, but I'll tell you one thing – I pity any doctor who has to look after her.' A note of self-doubt crept into his voice. 'I suppose I should ring her back. Maybe I was a bit harsh with her.'

'Why don't you leave it until she's cooled down a bit,' Caroline advised. 'Give her a call first thing in the morning.'

'Maybe you're right,' he said, giving her a kiss on the cheek. 'Are you sure you'll be OK?'

'I'll be fine,' she assured him.

When he had gone, she cleared off the table, scraping the remains of their meal into the bin. What a waste of a lovely meal. Richard was right: things never did go to plan. Here she was, alone in the penthouse. Well, she'd better get used to it, because she couldn't hang on to her husband's apron strings for ever. Or he to hers. They were going to have to decide about their future.

She got an attack of the collywobbles and her heart started to palpitate. Caroline swallowed hard. Right now the last thing she needed was a panic attack. There weren't even any Valium in the house now. Why did it happen? Every time she thought about her future and being independent, this awful fluttering started inside, making her palms go sweaty and her head turn dizzy. Dr Cole, her GP, had explained it to her and she knew that she must keep her breathing calm and even. No-one had ever died of a panic attack, he had told her reassuringly.

What use were all her fine words now? What was all that about taking control? What a spoofer you are, she thought unhappily, as she stood gripping the sink.

A more positive thought pushed its way through: *this is your big chance; try it*. Breathe evenly the way you were taught. In, out, in, out. Keep it up. Slowly, her heartbeat settled down. Gradually the intensity of the panic diminished and eventually it ebbed away. It was still there, but it wasn't in control. 'I did it, I did it!' she congratulated herself aloud. 'Now I'm going to clean up the kitchen, and then I'm going to unpack my bags and do some washing. I'm going down to the pool for a swim and then I'm going to come back and have a bath and some hot chocolate and I'm going to read my *Hello!* in bed.' She instructed herself in loud, firm tones, the sound of her voice oddly reassuring. 'I just don't have time for a panic attack.'

Nothing answered her back. The panic attack had no voice to argue with her. 'Just go away,' she said, emboldened. She gave a shaky grin. 'You're a nutcase, Caroline Yates. Talking to yourself in the kitchen!' But it had worked.

Wasn't that better than a drink or a Valium, she thought with relief as she put the dishes into the dishwasher and wiped down the counter tops. For the first time ever she had stood up to a panic attack. She had taken control. It was a great feeling that she had taken the first big step in her new life with courage. And that was the way it would be from now on. Her new life started from now.

Twelve

'Couldn't you get a second opinion?' Richard suggested, as he made coffee for Charles and himself that evening.

'This *is* a second opinion, Richard. That's why I went to London for the weekend,' Charles said gently. 'And I must accept it and deal with it, just as you'll have to.'

'Why didn't you tell me before now? Why did you keep it to yourself? How long have you kept this from me?' Richard was nearly in tears as he ran his fingers through his well-cut tawny hair.

'I've told you, Richard, I didn't want to burden you,' the older man said wearily. 'With Caroline trying to commit suicide and then drying out and the way you and she were for a while, I thought you had enough on your hands. I didn't want you to go to pieces. Caroline needed you.'

'You needed me too, and as usual I wasn't there for you. I've ruined Caroline's life. I've been ashamed of us, terrified of any whiff of scandal. I'm pathetic. I don't know how you put up with me.'

'Oh, it's a bit of a trial, I admit, particularly when you're being theatrical like this. But I cope,' Charles retorted.

Richard caught his eye and laughed in spite of himself. 'God, I'm sorry, Chas. Here I am being sorry for myself as usual – and you must be feeling like death.' The colour drained from his face and he shook his head. 'Oh Christ, what an insensitive remark. I'm sorry . . . I don't know what to say.'

Lighting up his pipe, Charles said, 'It's something we've all got to face. Some of us sooner rather than later. I don't want you to start considering every word before you speak, for fear of saying something inappropriate. I'd hate that, Richard. Please promise me that we will continue to talk as freely as we've always done about what is in our minds and hearts. Our honesty has been one of the most enriching things in our relationship for me.'

Richard came over to the sofa and put his arms around the other man. 'I promise, Charles. It's as important to me as it is to you. But I . . . I just don't know how to handle the new situation.'

'Neither do I, Richard. We'll just have to learn as we go along. Don't worry; we'll muddle through. We have until now, haven't we?'

'Well, don't go putting on a cheerful face just for me. Promise me that if you're scared or in the dumps or in pain you'll tell me,' Richard requested earnestly.

'I will.'

Richard took a deep breath. 'Could they be wrong about the time-span?' he asked hesitantly.

'Who knows,' Charles said gruffly. 'All I want is time to put my affairs in order.'

'What are you going to do? Do you mean you're thinking of finishing up work?'

'I think I will, Richard. I had the idea of going over

to Boston; my brother's an oncologist there. Even though I love the law and I've worked hard at it, I feel I've given enough of my life to it now. I've made a hell of a lot of money in the past few years — would you mind if I left a whack of it to charity?'

'Charles, please, just leave your money to whoever or whatever you like. Whatever makes you happy.'

'*You* make me happy,' the older man smiled, and Richard hung his head. He had been *so* selfish about their relationship, particularly when he insisted on marrying Caroline against Charles's advice. But then, Charles had always been able to accept without any shame that he was homosexual. Unlike Richard, who did not have the courage to face the truth.

Well, Charles had six months to a year to live, and Richard was going to make sure that it was the best possible time for him. He hoped that Caroline would understand the reasons for the decision he was about to take. Right now, Charles needed him and he was determined to be by his side. If his wife didn't accept that, it would be hard, but he had to make a commitment for once in his life.

Caroline sat up in bed and glanced at her alarm clock. Seven-thirty. Well, she'd survived the night. Not too bad for a woman on her own, who was subject to panic attacks. It had been a good move to go for a swim; she had swum twenty lengths and really worn herself out before going to bed. True, it had taken her a while to get to sleep, as the events of the day weaved in and out of her mind. It was hard to accept the news about Charles.

Richard had phoned about eleven to see if she was

all right and then he had passed the phone to Charles, who had thanked her for sending Richard to spend the night with him. She had choked up completely at the sound of his deep voice, and could only say brokenly, 'I'm so sorry, Charles, I'm so sorry.'

Charles offered her words of comfort. 'I've had a good life and a lot of love. I'm a contented man, so please don't take it so hard, my dear Caroline.'

She had pulled herself together for his sake but when he hung up she cried. She felt better for it, the lump in her throat dissolving with her tears. Having a cry was good for you, a therapist in the clinic had once told her, and ever since she had taken her advice. Instead of suppressing feelings of anger and grief, she was learning to express them, and it was helping. When she recalled how she had spoken to Richard at dinner that evening, she knew she was much more assertive, in fact a completely different woman from what she had been even six months earlier.

Yawning, she thought how funny it was that the noises that she had grown used to over the years seemed different when she was in the apartment on her own. But it had been a long day, what with the drive back from Rosslare Harbour, the news of Charles and then her marathon swim, and eventually she had drifted into sleep.

She was sitting down to breakfast when the phone rang. 'Put me on to Richard,' Sarah Yates ordered.

'I'm afraid he's not here, Mrs Yates.'

'Not there! Where is he at this hour of the morning?'

'He had to leave early,' Caroline replied. 'You

170

even bothered to clean the bathroom! She noted in disgust the dribble of toothpaste down the side of the avocado wash-basin. Did the vendors not stop to consider that a favourable first impression was of the utmost importance? She had seen people put completely off houses by dirt and untidiness. In one house that she had sold recently, the owners, who had already vacated the premises, had left a bin in the kitchen overflowing with refuse and soiled nappies. Well, it wasn't up to her to go tidying up, so she went back downstairs to the lounge to await the first viewers.

They arrived about ten minutes later, a young couple with a child in a push-chair. Caroline showed them around, then brought them out the back to view the garden. By then, two further sets of viewers were on the doorstep: a middle-aged couple and a woman in her thirties who worked in the airport and was a first-time buyer. The middle-aged couple were very pleasant, and Caroline honestly didn't think the house would suit them at all. She said, as diplomatically as possible, 'This is a fairly new estate and in another couple of years you're going to have lots of children and teenagers kicking ball and playing on the streets and greens. Do you not think you might be better off going for a more mature area?'

'There, Joan, didn't I tell you that?' the husband said triumphantly.

'I don't want to move too far from Jill and the children,' the woman explained. Caroline nodded sympathetically when she heard that Jill was their daughter and lived in Santry. 'My son's a pilot and he lives off Griffith Avenue, so I want to be near them both. Our own house has dry-rot, and we thought we'd move rather than go through all the hassle of getting a job done on it. Besides,' she confided in Caroline, 'we've dreadful new neighbours for the past year or so. They've made our lives a misery and we just want to get out.'

'We happen to have three properties for sale in a mature estate in the Ballygall area,' Caroline suggested. 'That's between Glasnevin and Wadelai. I think somewhere like that would suit you much better and it would be no distance from Santry or Griffith Avenue. Why don't I arrange a viewing for you?'

The husband looked hopefully at his wife. 'That sounds just the ticket.'

'That's very kind of you, dear,' the woman beamed. Caroline took their phone number and promised to get back to them with the arrangements. She waved them off happily, very pleased with herself. One thing she had never done in her career as an estate agent was to sell a property that she knew did not really meet a client's needs. It just wasn't her style. If she lost a commission because of it, so be it. It would have bothered her far more if she'd been tossing and turning at night feeling guilty – which she certainly would have been had she sold that couple a house more suitable for a young family than for a pair nearing retirement.

The Aer Lingus woman was quite interested, and told Caroline she would get back to her as she had several other houses to view. The young couple weren't too happy with the location of schools and although there were several large shopping centres

174

nearby, the wife didn't like the idea of the nearest local shop being twenty minutes' walk away.

After all the viewers had left, Caroline had a good half-hour to spare before her next appointment. As she drove along the Ballymun dual carriageway, she thought she might as well pop into a shop and get something for her lunch. She turned left into Pappin's Road and parked outside Network News. She could buy a few goodies for Maggie's two elder children as she was going to be babysitting them later on. She spent ten minutes selecting comics and colouring books, before buying a salad roll and yoghurt for herself in the supermarket, then another ten minutes in Chambers, looking at make-up, for which she had a great weakness. She emerged with a new eyeshadow, lipstick and a matching nail-varnish, feeling a little buzz from her spree.

The apartment in Glasnevin overlooked the Botanic Gardens and was in immaculate condition. Standing on the balcony overlooking the Tolka River and the Rose Garden, she knew she'd have no problems selling the property. Indeed, of the eight parties who came to view it, two, a young woman banker and a retired detective, informed her that they were willing to pay the asking price. She told them that it would go to tender and invited them to submit their highest offer to her at the office in a sealed envelope.

Caroline was about to leave the apartment when her mobile phone rang. It was Richard to say that he was taking the rest of the day off work to spend it with Charles, who was anxious to start putting his affairs in order.

'I'll be babysitting in Maggie's until around nine. Will you be home tonight?' Caroline asked.

'I will,' her husband said and then, 'Caroline, I need to talk to you about something. Can we discuss it when you get home?'

She was puzzled at the urgency of his tone. 'Of course, Richard.'

'Look, I have to go, Caroline. Charles wants to make a will. Because he's leaving me a bequest I can't act for him so we're going over to Shaun O'Rourke's. I'll see you later and we'll have a talk.'

'OK,' she said hastily. 'By the way, your mother phoned this morning.'

'I know. I got a lecture for using vulgar language.' Caroline could sense that Richard was smiling as he hung up.

She wondered what he wanted to talk to her about. Well, she'd find out this evening. The rest of the day passed in a flurry of activity. She went back to the office, had her lunch, completed her paperwork, made appointments for the following day's viewings, and arranged for her middle-aged couple to see the three houses she had told them about. Then she drove home, had a shower and changed into jeans and a T-shirt before setting off for Maggie's.

The children were delighted to see her and pounced on their goodies with squeals of excitement. By the time she'd fed them, played with them, and finally got them to bed, she was whacked, and she didn't delay when Terry arrived home. She was relieved to put the key into her own front door, all ready to relax in front of the TV with a cup of coffee.

Richard was already at home. He looked tired.

'How's it going?' Caroline hugged him. In the old days he would have rebuffed her expression of affection, fearing that she wanted an intimacy that he wasn't capable of sharing with her, but now he accepted her hug gratefully and hugged her back.

'Would you like a cup of coffee?' he asked.

'I'd love one,' she smiled, kicking off her shoes and flopping into an armchair. Five minutes later he handed her a mug of coffee and a Club Milk. 'Thanks,' she said appreciatively, taking a sip and unwrapping the snack.

'Caroline.' Richard started pacing the room. 'The thing is . . . I hope you don't think I'm an awful bastard . . .' He stopped short, then blurted, 'Charles wants to go and live in Boston. He has a property there and his brother is an oncologist in a hospital nearby, so he would be well taken care of . . .' Richard paused again, as if unsure how to continue.

'That sounds like a good idea,' Caroline remarked, wondering why Richard should imagine that she would think he was an awful bastard.

'Yes it is, but the thing is, I'd like to go and stay with him for as long as he needs me.' Her husband turned and met her shocked gaze. 'And that means leaving you on your own.'

Thirteen

'You want to go to Boston with Charles?' Caroline repeated, stunned.

'Yes, Caroline . . . I do,' her husband said quietly.

'When?'

'Whenever he wants to go.'

'I don't know what to say.' Caroline was completely taken aback by Richard's bombshell.

'Look, I know you probably think I've an awful cheek after all I've put you through to turn around suddenly and say that I want to go to Boston with Charles. But Caroline, it's the only chance I've got to make up to him for my selfishness in the past. Don't you see that?' he pleaded.

What about me? she wanted to shout.

Something of her feelings must have shown in her face because he said unhappily, 'I'm sorry, Caroline. I know I've no right to expect you to see it from my side. I've treated you every bit as badly as I've treated him. Why should I expect you to give me your blessing?'

'What does Charles think about it?' Caroline asked dully. Despite the fact that they hadn't much of a marriage, she couldn't but feel that her husband had betrayed her once again.

'He doesn't know I'm even *thinking* of doing such a thing. Charles would have a fit if he thought I was walking out on you for him.' He grimaced. 'I was kind of hoping that by saying you wouldn't mind, you might persuade him to agree.'

'What would you do about the practice?' Caroline was amazed that her husband would consider leaving his thriving legal practice.

'Well, I have Baldwin and Kenny there, and I'd let them get on with it. I would just wind down my own cases and not take on any more. Two solicitors in a practice is more than enough to keep it going,' Richard said eagerly, a glimmer of hope lightening his eyes. 'You'd get paid every week of course. I'd arrange all that,' he assured her.

Caroline said nothing. She couldn't think straight. Richard was proposing leaving the practice in the hands of the two solicitors he employed and going off to Boston for God knows how long so that he could be with Charles during his last illness!

She could understand his reasons and sympathize with them and indeed, if she had not been involved, she would have been full of admiration for this selfless gesture. But she *was* involved, very much involved, and it hurt her to think that Richard was so insensitive to her fragile emotional state that he did not realize the terrible effect the prospect of being left alone would have on her.

Oh, yes, all along she had been saying that she would get her annulment and a foreign divorce and start afresh, but she had always thought that Richard would still be there in the background – not thousands of miles away across the Atlantic. Making

179

plans had been all very well, but she hadn't thought that the moment of truth would come so soon. Now that the time seemed to have come for them to split up for real, it was a very daunting prospect.

'I know I've a bit of a cheek,' he said miserably.

'A *bit* of a cheek!' she burst out resentfully. 'I think you've a bloody big cheek. But what's new? Don't worry about good old Caroline; she won't mind; she's been a mouse for so long that she won't know the difference. Well, I *do* mind. I mind very much. I'm still your wife. If you take off for a year, apart from leaving me on my own, who's going to end up taking all the flak about our separation? Who's going to have to answer all the questions about where you are? Muggins here.' Caroline glared at her husband. A thought struck her. 'And what are you going to do about your mother?'

'Well, the firm will handle her affairs as usual. I was going to pay her daily to do her shopping if she wants it . . . and I was hoping you'd keep an eye on her,' Richard muttered.

Caroline's eyes widened at this, the greatest in-dignity so far. 'You were, were you? What a nerve! Richard, you just go and fuck off for yourself.' She got to her feet, picked up her bag and slammed the sitting-room door behind her.

She was *so* angry, so absolutely door-slamming, cup-throwing, chair-kicking *angry*. She marched down the hall to her bedroom, slammed that door, flung her bag across the room and threw herself on the bed.

What was it about her that no-one ever gave a shit about her feelings? How could Richard think that he

180

could even *propose* such an idea? Not when she was still getting over the shock of his homosexuality and recovering from her breakdown? It just wasn't fair!

Oh, don't be so childish, she turned on herself. It wasn't fair! Grow up. Nothing is fair. Look at Charles. What was the good of keeping Richard in Dublin, by clinging on to the pathetic idea that he was her husband. He wasn't her husband; he never had been. And if she truly was serious about making a new life for herself, it would have to be on her own.

'But I'm not ready for it, I'm not ready,' she muttered into her pillow, as fear, rage and resentment took hold of her and bitter tears spilled down her cheeks.

What would he do if he couldn't go to Boston to be with Charles? Richard paced up and down the sitting-room floor, frantically trying to find a solution. Maybe Caroline could come with them? If he had asked her to come, she might not have been so hostile to the idea.

'It wouldn't work,' he told himself glumly. What a *ménage à trois* that would be. He, his wife and his lover. No, it would be too awkward. It wouldn't be fair on his wife and it wouldn't be fair on Charles. Scrap that brainwave. He had made a right mess of things and now he'd alienated Caroline. In his haste to make his big sacrifice for Charles he hadn't stopped to consider his wife's feelings at all, assuming that Caroline would meekly accept his decision as usual and perhaps even admire him for it. His plan had greatly backfired. Caroline had been really angry — and let him see it, too. It was rare for her to raise her voice to him. Well, he couldn't blame her. Richard sighed. If he lived to be a hundred, he could never make up to Caroline for the grief he had caused her and the mess he had made of her life. Caroline had said that his mother had spoilt him. Maybe she was right, but now, when he *was* trying to make amends to Charles, it looked as if his great plan would come to naught. Charles would never agree to his accompanying him to Boston if he thought for an instant that Caroline was unhappy with the idea. And to say that she was unhappy was the understatement of the century.

Richard went out to make himself another cup of coffee. At times like this he could understand why people turned to drink. He wouldn't mind getting pissed out of his skull, now, and forgetting all the problems that were besetting him. Caroline had brought up the subject of his mother. How would *she* react to the news that he was going to Boston to be with Charles? Richard sipped his coffee and admitted to himself that his idea was a bit naïve. Sarah would definitely have something to say about him leaving what had been her husband's practice in the hands of junior solicitors. She would freak. No question. He had been fooling himself to think that he could just up and off and that people would back him up. Was he really planning to do this to make up to Charles for the cowardly way he had abused their relationship and to show how much he loved him? Or was it to salve his own conscience? If he were to be totally honest, he would have to admit it was a bit of both. Well, the way things were going, it looked as if he was going to get the chance to do neither.

*   *   *

'Here.' Caroline handed her husband a white form, an enclosure from one of the letters in the post that morning. It was three weeks since their acrimonious discussion, and tension still simmered between them. Richard had not brought up again the subject of his departure for Boston but it was something that had occupied Caroline's mind morning, noon and night.

At first she had been adamantly opposed to the idea, but hours of tossing and turning and, in the end, being very severe on herself, had made her rethink her attitudes.

She had had dreadful panic attacks, some of the worst she had ever experienced, and it was these that made up her mind for her. The longer she existed in a state of limbo and indecision the worse they were going to get. So, on one of her mornings off, she took her courage in her hands and followed a certain course of action. The white form that her husband was looking at in amazement was a direct result of that decision.

'Do you know what this is?' He stared at her with a shocked expression.

'Yes, Richard, I do,' Caroline said quietly. 'I do indeed.'

Fourteen

'This is a form from the Marriage Tribunal. This is an application for an annulment?' Richard was flabbergasted.

'Yes, I know, I applied for it,' Caroline said sadly. 'I figured, if you want to go to Boston with Charles, we should make a start at dissolving our marriage. You can start taking care of the divorce end of things.'

'But Caroline, why? I thought you didn't want me to go to Boston. Why take such an . . . an irrevocable step?'

Caroline sat down at the breakfast table opposite her husband. 'Because the longer we leave it, the harder it's going to get. If you're going to be gone, I'll have to get used to being on my own and so we might as well set things in motion. The annulment is going to take at least five years. You should know that; haven't you ever had a client who's applied for one?'

'Actually, I haven't,' he murmured. 'I know very little about them.'

'Well, the priest I went to see explained to me that after we send in the form, there will be an initial interview. As the petitioner I will be interviewed first and then you as respondent will do an interview exactly the same as I've done. Then we'll both undergo psychological assessment and they'll have to decide if we have a case before letting us on to the next stage.' Caroline could hardly believe that she was sitting here, calmly discussing the ending of her marriage. It was as if she was talking about someone else, a very weird feeling.

Richard interrupted her train of thought. 'Yes, but if I go to Boston, I don't know how long I'll be there.'

'I know, and I told that to the priest, but at least if we have the first interview over us it will be a start, and I won't feel as if I'm in a limbo.' Caroline's tone was curt. She was still feeling hurt about the way things had gone although she was trying to act as positively as she could.

'Look, you don't have to go through with this,' Richard said gruffly. 'I haven't mentioned anything to Charles about going with him to Boston.'

Caroline shook her head. 'I have to do it. If I don't, I'll never create a life or an identity for myself. I dread it but I've got to do it. And besides,' she grimaced, 'I don't want you resenting me for the rest of your life because I stopped you from being with Charles.'

'But you'll *feel* resentful; you do already,' Richard pointed out.

'Do you blame me, Richard?' Caroline said heavily, as she got up and walked out of the kitchen. 'I've an early appointment. I'll see you later.' She left her husband looking miserable, as once more he read through the form that might well lead to the dissolution of their marriage in the eyes of the Catholic Church.

Driving in to the office, Caroline felt like crying. 'Oh, for God's sake, stop being such a bloody wimp,' she muttered, as she turned on to the Malahide Road. She was wallowing in self-pity and it was getting her nowhere. Hers wasn't the only marriage that had ever broken up. If she hadn't been so petrified of ending up on the shelf she might never have married Richard. It was obvious from the very beginning that their relationship was in trouble, but she had deluded herself for years, so she was as much to blame as her husband was. She could go on feeling sorry for herself and carrying an extremely large chip on her shoulder, or she could start making the best of things; it was entirely up to her. Pulling into the parking area in front of Corpus Christi Church on Griffith Avenue, she dialled her home on the mobile phone. When Richard answered, she said quietly, 'Hi, it's me.'

'Yes, Caroline,' her husband answered.

'Look, I'm sorry I've been such a bad-tempered bitch the last few weeks. I know this mess isn't all your fault. Let's go for a long walk on Bull Island this evening, talk things over and see what we come up with.'

There was silence for a moment or two and then Richard said with a catch in his voice, 'Whatever happens, Caroline, in my own way I'll always love you.'

'I love you too, Richard. I'll see you tonight.' There were tears in Caroline's eyes as she clicked off but she felt much happier as she carried on into work. There was no point in letting anger and resentment drive them apart at this stage. They were both in this mess together and her husband was facing a very traumatic time. Staying friends was the best way to heal the scars and put an end to the bitterness.

*   *   *

'I won't allow it, Richard. You can't just drop everything to come to Boston with me — and by heavens you can't leave Caroline on her own,' Charles insisted.

'Of course he can leave me on my own. I don't need a nanny, Charles,' Caroline said lightly.

'Caroline, I'm not going to be the cause of any more trouble between you. It's unthinkable. I just won't have it.'

Caroline got up from her armchair and went over to sit beside him on the sofa. Putting her arms around him she said very gently, 'Charles, my dear, dear friend. You've never caused trouble in my marriage. The troubles were there from the very beginning and were as much of my making as they were Richard's.' She smiled at her husband, who was sitting across the room from them. 'Please let Richard go with you. I know it's what he wants to do more than anything. I want to tell you something and I don't want you to feel one bit bad about it, because for me it's a very positive step.' Caroline took a deep breath and held Charles's hand. 'I've petitioned for an annulment. I want to start afresh and have a life of my own. Whether Richard goes with you or not, we are separating. We'll always be friends but we can't stay married; we're living a lie and it's not doing either of us any good. I want Richard to go with you, I want you both to have as much happiness as you can, and I want to move on with my own life. And if you take him off my hands, I'll be eternally grateful.' Caroline smiled at her horrified friend.

Tears glistened in Charles's eyes. 'This is incredible. I . . . I don't know what to say!' Caroline hugged him tightly, feeling great affection for this kind man, on whose shoulder she had cried many times.

'All you have to say is that you'll let Richard go with you. It would mean so much to both of us. I wouldn't have to be worrying about you being alone so far away. I'd know that Richard would be there taking care of you – and he's not a bad old stick.'

'I'm overwhelmed,' Charles murmured.

'And I'm parched for a cup of tea, so I'm going to make a pot while you two start making plans,' Caroline announced, giving Charles another hug and a kiss and feeling certain that she had made the right move for all of them.

'I'll never be able to thank you enough for that, Caroline. You were wonderful!' Richard said earnestly as they drove home that night. 'Did you see the expression on Charles's face? He was so moved.'

Caroline nodded. 'I know he was. And I'm glad it's worked out like this. Charles is one of the best, kindest, most Christian men on this earth. He deserves every bit of happiness he'll have, and I'll always be glad we did this for him,' Caroline said softly.

'It's funny the way life works out,' Richard reflected, as they drove across the East Link in the deepening dusk. The setting sun touched the turbulent grey-blue waters of the Liffey with orange-gold. Autumn had come early and the trees in Fairview Park were already turning.

'You should try and visit New England before the autumn ends. I've heard it's very beautiful,' Caroline observed, as they drove along Alfie Byrne Road, admiring the beauty that was practically on their doorstep. Each of them was thinking that this was probably the last time they would make this journey together for God knows how long. Richard had made all the arrangements for his practice and already acquired his visitor's visa for the States. He and Charles had decided to go to America in mid-October. For Caroline and Richard, the first interviews with the Marriage Tribunal were in a fortnight's time. After that, all that remained was to inform Sarah Yates of their separation.

They had decided to say that Richard was taking an extended leave of absence to go to America with a view to opening a practice there to service the huge Irish community. There was no point in telling Sarah that her son was making the journey in order to be with Charles for his final days. She would not understand, never dreaming that Richard was homosexual.

Telling Sarah was a task they both dreaded, and although Caroline could have let Richard deal with his mother alone, her intense loyalty to him made her want to face the ordeal with him. Caroline was determined that this time Richard would be firm in his resolve and carry out his plan, whatever the views of Sarah Yates.

'What was it like?' Richard was waiting for Caroline after her first interview with the Marriage Tribunal. He had taken the afternoon off to drive her to the interview and she was glad she hadn't had to face the dreaded event alone. He held the car door open, noting the pallor of her face and the tiredness of her eyes.

Caroline gave a great sigh of relief that this first trial was over. 'There was just one priest and he was very nice and compassionate. But I've an awful longing for a drink, Richard,' she confessed. 'I think I'd better go to an AA meeting tonight.'

'I'll go with you,' he offered immediately, as he started the engine and drove towards Drumcondra. 'Was it awful?' he asked sympathetically. Caroline rooted in her bag and pulled out a packet of Polo Mints. For some reason they were a help when she craved a drink.

'It wasn't as bad as I expected,' she said. 'As I said, there was just the one priest and he was extremely nice. We went through the form, you know, name, address, where we grew up, details of studies. He asked about our courtship and engagement and about the pre-marriage course.' She sighed, and in spite of herself, her voice shook and a tear slid down her cheek. She swallowed hard and continued. 'Then he asked when things started to go wrong and if we'd sought help, and about the divorce proceedings – and that was it really. I got a bit upset and he was very kind to me and told me to take my time and go at my own pace. But I'll tell you, I'm glad it's over. It was hard going back over the bad times but I tried to be as honest as I could.' She broke down and Richard turned left up Millmount Avenue and parked in a quiet spot just below the library. Taking Caroline in his arms, he held her until her sobbing had stopped, knowing that he was going to face the same inquisition in a few days' time.

His heart ached for his wife. Not only was she undergoing the trauma of speaking to a complete stranger about the most private, most horrible moments of their marriage; she was also trying to fight her alcoholism, which was obviously much more of a problem at such a stressful time. One thing he was sure of: Caroline had more courage than he would ever have.

She raised her tear-stained face to his. 'If Maggie wrote our story she'd have a bestseller for sure,' she said shakily.

Richard smiled down at her. 'Yes, and with Mother thrown in, she'd win the Booker Prize. I don't know which I dread more, the interview at the tribunal or telling her about going to America.'

Caroline gave him a sympathetic hug. 'I had only one ordeal to go through. Don't worry, Richard. I won't desert you in your hour of need. We'll face your mother together and if we get through that alive, we'll get through anything!'

Fifteen

'You're *what*?' Sarah Yates snapped. 'Don't be ridiculous, Richard! You're doing no such thing, I'm not allowing you to leave your father's practice in the hands of two whippersnappers.' The indomitable elderly woman sat in her hard chair, her back as stiff as a ramrod, her grey eyes flinty with anger.

'Mother, John Baldwin and Martin Kenny are two qualified solicitors in whom I have the utmost faith,' her son explained patiently. 'Since I took them on, business has almost doubled. I'll be keeping in close touch with them by fax and phone.'

'I'm not interested in hearing that kind of nonsense.' Sarah waved a dismissive hand. 'You're not going and that's that. I absolutely forbid it.' She glared at Caroline, who stared back at her in disgust. One thing was sure, Caroline thought – she was going to have as little as possible to do with that woman in the future. Caroline concluded that her mother-in-law was the worst kind of bully. In her mid-seventies, she looked a decade younger. Tall, like her son, spare and angular, her fine grey hair drawn back in a bun at the nape of her neck, Sarah Yates would have made a good reverend mother. She had that austere air about her. In all the years Caroline had known her, she had never once seen her laugh heartily or give even a hint that she enjoyed life. To Sarah, life was a battle to be won, and lightness of heart and gaiety and fun did not count. In a way, Caroline pitied her mother-in-law. How awful it must be to have such a dour outlook on life, viewing everyone with suspicion and convinced that no-one else was ever right but yourself. Even the way she dressed signalled her killjoy nature. Brown twinsets and tweeds were her usual outfits, with nothing but pearl earrings and a single strand of pearls to soften the effect.

In the beginning, Caroline had bought Sarah lovely jumpers and scarves for birthdays and Christmas, but she had never once worn any of them, so Caroline had stopped buying them. She had stopped buying her chocolates as well, after her mother-in-law told her bluntly that they were a waste of good money. Sarah always ate frugally, never indulging in dessert. Her only concession was a slice of Oxford Lunch. No wonder Richard was emotionally damaged, after being reared by such a joyless soul.

She came out of her reverie to hear her mother-in-law snap at her. She was now directing her haughty patrician stare at Caroline. 'I suppose you thought a junket to America would be a great idea. Wouldn't it just suit you to be off spending his hard-earned money there? Well, you can forget it, my girl, if it was you who put such a daft idea in my son's head. The pair of you can stay put.'

'I'm not going with Richard, Mrs Yates.' Caroline had to control a powerful urge to tell her imperious mother-in-law to get lost and mind her own business.

'You're not *going*? What kind of a carry-on is that?

He's *going* and you're *staying*? Have the two of you lost the run of yourselves? It would behove you better to start a family, one of the reasons you were supposed to have entered the holy state of matrimony.'

Richard shot up out of his chair. 'That's enough.'

'Don't talk to me like that. I'm your mother.' Sarah pointed a long bony forefinger at her son. 'I just don't know what's got into you. Before you got married, you were always courteous. Now, it grieves me to say, you behave like a corner-boy at times,' she rebuked him.

'Don't be ridiculous, Mother. I'm not a child. I'm a grown man and I've made up my mind. I'm going to America on business whether you like it or not. There's one other thing Caroline and I have to tell you and kindly remember that it's our business, whatever you think of it,' Richard said sternly, his face flushed. He would rather face down a dozen judges than his mother, but she had to be told.

'Caroline and I are separating. For reasons that will remain known to us alone, our marriage is over. We have started annulment proceedings and will be getting a divorce.'

Sarah went white with shock. She opened her mouth to say something and closed it again.

'I know it's a shock, Mother, but it's the best thing for us,' Richard said. Sarah gasped as if she'd been struck. Then she stood up and, advancing on Caroline, her grey eyes slits of venom, she said in a voice that shook with fury, 'It's all your fault! I never wanted you to marry my son. I knew you weren't good enough for him, you and that . . . that dreadful family of yours.'

194

'Be quiet, Mother. I won't let you talk to Caroline like that,' Richard cried.

'Don't you tell me to be quiet in my own house.' Sarah was livid, two bright spots of red mottling her cheeks. 'I warned you. I warned you but would you listen to me? I knew it,' she ranted. 'I knew it would end in tears. All she's done is bring disgrace to the family name by her drinking. She's a slut, do you hear me, a drunken slut who doesn't know how to behave.'

In two steps Richard was across the room, and Caroline saw him raise his arms as if to shake Sarah. 'Richard!' she grabbed his arm. 'Don't touch your mother!'

'I'll kill her!' He was white with temper as Caroline came between them.

'Stop it! Stop it!' she shouted, sick with fright.

'I hate her.' Richard started to cry. 'She's made my life a misery. She never let me have any friends. She always claimed that she was above everyone else and so was I. It's all her fucking fault. She interfered in everything. I wanted to be a botanist but she wouldn't hear of it; it wasn't good enough for her precious son. I had to be a solicitor like Father. Didn't I?' he roared at his horrified mother. 'Don't you dare blame Caroline. Blame yourself, Mother, for all this mess, because you're right – I should never have married her. And I'll tell you why, you mean-minded, selfish, horrible woman—' He was almost incoherent with anger. '—I should never have married my wife because I'm a homosexual, Mother. Do you know what that means? I love men, not women. I love Charles and I'm going to America to be with him because he's dying. If I never see you again, I'll be happy.' He pulled his arm from Caroline's grasp and rushed from the room and out of the front door, slamming it behind him.

'Oh,' Sarah moaned, her hand clutching her throat. 'Oh, Richard, what has she done to you?' She sank to her knees and Caroline caught her as she fainted.

She thought she was going to faint herself. Dry-mouthed, trembling, she tried to haul her mother-in-law on to the sofa but she was too heavy. Leaving her stretched on the floor, she ran out after Richard, who was sitting in the car staring into space.

'You've got to come back in,' Caroline pleaded. 'She's fainted. We can't leave her like this, Richard.'

He was beside himself. 'I hope she fucking dies.'

'Richard!' Caroline yelled at him. 'Stop it. Come into the house with me now and help me lift your mother on to the sofa.' Biting his lip and wiping the tears from his face, he followed her back, and between them they managed to lift his mother. 'Put some cushions under her feet,' Caroline ordered, 'and get me a glass of water.' Sarah was moaning on the sofa as she started to come round, and when Richard returned from the kitchen with the water, Caroline held the glass to her mother-in-law's lips and raised her head so that she could drink.

The elderly woman sipped the water, then lay back and closed her eyes. 'Get me the priest,' she moaned. 'Get me the doctor. I'm dying.'

'You're not dying; you just fainted,' Caroline said brusquely. 'Lie back and relax, you'll be all right in a minute.'

Sarah opened her eyes and glared at her. 'And I

don't want any help from you,' she hissed, and Caroline felt quite relieved that her mother-in-law was returning to her usual form and obviously in no danger.

'Leave me.' She waved a limp hand. 'I want nothing to do with either of you.' Caroline cast a glance at her husband. He shrugged his shoulders. He was a great help, she thought in irritation.

'We'll just stay for another while to make sure you're all right,' Caroline said steadily.

'I want to go to my room,' Sarah said stiffly, and in spite of herself, Caroline felt sorry for her. This visit must be like a nightmare for her. First to be told of their separation, then to have Richard raise his hand to her and finally to have him declare his homosexuality.

'Would you like me to come up with you?' she asked.

'No, thank you,' Sarah said curtly and, drawing herself erect, walked out of the room with immense dignity.

Caroline turned on her husband. 'You know, you'd want to go and see a therapist about that temper of yours. How could you even think of raising your hand to your mother? You should be ashamed of yourself. That's not normal behaviour, Richard.'

'Well, when she called you a slut, I just saw red,' he muttered.

'Nothing justifies violence to a woman. Your own *mother*, for God's sake!' Caroline said, utterly disgusted.

'But you don't know how she makes me feel,' he burst out. 'Like a two-year-old, powerless, frustrated.

She's always done this, as long as I can remember. It's not right, it's not fair.'

Caroline sighed and shook her head. She was suddenly very tired of it all. Richard's fraught relationship with his mother had caused him serious psychological damage, and unless he sought professional help he would never learn how to deal with it.

'Richard, for your own sake please see someone who can help you to work through all this anger. You'll never be happy otherwise.'

'All right, Caroline, I will. When I'm in America I'll do something about it,' her husband promised. 'Come on; let's go home.'

From an upstairs window, Sarah Yates watched them go. She felt terribly shaky after that dreadfully angry scene. She had never seen her son so much out of control and it had frightened her. If Caroline had not intervened, he would have shaken her. Her own son would have laid hands on her. It was unbelievable. And the language he had used. And the names he had called her. He wasn't himself. She must have driven him to it, that no-good wife of his. God knows what kind of pressure he was under because of her drink problem. No wonder the poor boy thought he was . . . she shied away from that horrible word he had used to describe himself. He had been pushed to the limit, obviously. If he'd met the proper girl none of this would have happened. Maybe this annulment and divorce were blessings in disguise. When he was finished with that woman he'd go back to his old self, the loving, kind, obliging son he had always been. Let him go to America with Charles Stokes. Charles had been like a father to Richard; no wonder he was upset that the poor man was dying. He was so unhappy and confused he didn't know what he was saying.

How could he say he hated her, his own mother? Had she not made him her life's work, caring for him, trying to guide and encourage him to be as good a man as his father was. Everything she did had been done for him. Why was he so angry now? Sarah sat on the edge of the bed, twisting her hands together. Showing emotion was anathema to her, and a lot of emotion had been shown that afternoon. It was at times like this that people took a medicinal brandy, but she had no alcohol in the house. She didn't drink and she never offered it to others either. She felt the need for something – but what? Her gaze alighted on the bottle of Lourdes water by her bedside. Her daily had brought it home to her after her last visit to the shrine. With trembling fingers, Sarah twisted off the blue-crown and took a few little sips of the miracle water.

'Help me carry this cross,' she prayed. 'Thy will, not mine, be done.' Two tears plopped down on to her hands followed by two more, as Sarah bowed her head and wept.

'Did you phone her?' Caroline asked her husband the following day.

'Yes, I did.'

'And?' Caroline said in exasperation.

'She told me to go and see a doctor about the stress I was under and said that maybe a trip to America would be a good idea after all.'

Caroline's eyes widened as she digested this piece of information. 'Well, that's good news.'

'Hmm,' Richard said non-committally, unable to recount to Caroline that his mother had also said that the Lord above would fully understand his reasons for seeking an annulment from his totally unsuitable and unwifely wife. Caroline was the cause of all his problems, according to his mother, and once she was out of the way everything would be back to normal. Richard just hadn't bothered to argue; he hadn't the heart. If his mother chose to deny what he was, and blame Caroline for everything, nothing that he was going to say would change her mind one iota. Sarah Yates was an expert at denial — he had learned that skill from her.

'Is Charles all organized?' Caroline raised her eyes from the shirt she was ironing and glanced at her husband.

'He's closing the sale of his house today. That will be a sad moment for him. He loved that old house.'

'I wish he'd come and stay with us for the couple of weeks before you go,' Caroline said. 'I feel awful thinking of him going to a hotel. It's so impersonal.'

'I know,' her husband agreed as he stapled several typewritten pages together. 'The O'Gradys asked him to stay with them too, but you know Charles, he can't bear to think he's putting anyone out.' He stuck the papers on the cork notice-board beside the phone. 'These are our telephone numbers in the States, and there's our address and also the bank manager's number and the number of Martin Kenny's mobile phone in case you need to get in touch with him. I've instructed Martin to lodge a cheque into your account

200

every month, and I've left John Baldwin instructions for taking care of Mother's affairs. I don't foresee any problems but if there are, call me immediately and I'll sort things out.'

'I'll be fine, Richard. I wish you'd stop fussing. I'm not a ten-year-old,' Caroline said irritably. Now that the time of their departure was approaching, she wished it would hurry up and come so that she could be finally done with it. It was unsettling the way things were.

'I'm only trying to help,' Richard said.

'Sorry, I know you are. I just feel a bit on edge, and no wonder, after yesterday.'

'Well, Mother's fine, believe me,' he reassured her. 'And I *will* go for some sort of therapy. I know my behaviour isn't exactly adult and rational. No doubt whoever I go to will unearth plenty of repressed fears and emotions; that's their game, isn't it?' he smiled ruefully.

Caroline put down her iron, went over to her husband and gave him a hug. 'But if it helps, it will be worth it, won't it?' she said comfortingly. 'And it might help you to be more comfortable about your sexuality,' she added.

Richard sighed. 'I don't think so. I bitterly resent being homosexual. Nobody could convince me they want to be like this. All it causes is misery.'

'Charles has always been at ease with it,' Caroline said gently.

Richard smiled. 'Charles is an exceptional man.'

'Yes,' his wife agreed, 'he is.'

*   *   *

'I want you to have this and when you have the collywobbles I pray that it will help you as it helps me.' Charles pressed a little leather folder into Caroline's hand. 'My mother gave it to me and I would like to give it to you.'

'What is it?' she asked, intrigued. They were standing waiting for Richard near the escalators in Departures.

Charles kissed her cheek. 'It's something that has been very special to me and there is no-one I would rather have it than you. You are very precious to me, Caroline, and your generosity knows no bounds.'

She opened the little leather wallet and saw a page of vellum with the finest, most beautiful script she had ever seen. As she read, tears welled in her eyes. It was a prayer, a beautiful prayer:

> *Count your blessings*
> *instead of your crosses:*
> *Count your gains*
> *instead of your losses:*
> *Count your joys*
> *instead of your woes:*
> *Count your friends*
> *instead of your foes:*
> *Count your courage*
> *instead of your fears:*
> *Count your health*
> *instead of your wealth:*
> *And count on God*
> *instead of yourself.*

'Oh, Charles, I'll always treasure it. It's beautiful. Thank you,' Caroline flung her arms around him and hugged him tightly.

'It got me through many a tight spot and it will do the same for you. God be with you always, Caroline.'

'And with you, my dear, dear friend,' she echoed warmly.

Richard, who had been buying some dollars, joined them. 'I think we should go to our departure gate.'

'I don't think I'll go with you,' Caroline murmured. 'It's best if I stay here.' As it was, she was having a hard enough time trying to maintain her composure. She didn't want to make a complete show of herself at the boarding gate.

'That's very wise, my dear.' Charles smiled at her. 'We'll phone as soon as we arrive.' Very quickly he kissed her once more and turned away. 'I'll go on and let you and Richard say your farewells,' he said briskly. 'Take care, Caroline.'

'And you too.' Caroline met his steady gaze and then he was walking away from them and she turned her head to hide her tears. 'Hurry after him, Richard. Don't let him go through on his own,' she urged, hating to see the lonely figure disappearing across the concourse.

Richard hugged her fiercely. 'I'll miss you, Caroline. Thanks for everything.'

'Look after yourself, Richard. Phone often.'

'I will,' he promised.

'Go on.' She gave him a little shove. 'Go and take care of Charles. Don't let him go to America on his own,' she smiled.

Only when she saw him hurrying away after

Charles did her composure break and when he turned to wave, she started to cry. She waved back and watched him disappear and was turning in the direction of the exit when she heard a familiar voice say kindly, 'It looks as though you need a shoulder to cry on. Here's four; take your pick.'

Through eyes blurred with tears, Caroline saw Devlin and Maggie standing in front of her. She didn't know whether to laugh or cry. 'Oh, girls, if ever I needed you both, I need you now.'

'You've got us,' Maggie assured her. 'Come on, let's have a coffee.'

'We thought you could do with some moral support,' Devlin explained, as they sat at a round table up in the lounge overlooking the apron. Just to the left of them, the huge green-and-white Boeing 747 with the distinctive shamrock on the tail was fuelling up for its long transatlantic journey.

'I'd be lost without you,' Caroline admitted, feeling much less alone.

'We know,' Devlin said smugly, then grinned at her friend.

'Ma Yates didn't come,' Maggie observed tartly. Caroline had told her friends about the events at her mother-in-law's house a few weeks previously.

Caroline shook her head. 'Richard went to see her this morning to say goodbye. She preferred not to come. I can't say I'm sorry.'

'And has she said anything more to Richard about his being gay?' Devlin enquired.

'She's pretending he never said it, that the whole episode never happened. She's blaming his

204

outburst on me and the stress I've caused him by my drinking.'

'The old bitch,' Devlin said with a scowl.

Caroline shrugged. 'I don't care, really. In a way I feel sorry for her. She's lost the one person she's devoted her whole life to, and if blaming me makes it any easier for her, let her. I won't need to have much to do with her from now on. I'm not going to let it bother me.'

'And you're right,' Maggie declared. 'From now on, you're going to put yourself first and you're going to start living your own life.'

'Yes, ma'am,' Caroline saluted.

'I mean it, Caroline,' Maggie said firmly.

'Listen to wise old Mother Hen. She knows what she's on about,' Devlin drawled. 'She's always practising what she preaches.'

Maggie laughed. 'Well, you know what I mean.'

'Yes, I do, and you're right,' Caroline said. 'And the first thing I want to do is treat you both to lunch. Come on, let's go over to the hotel. We haven't had a good natter in ages.'

'You *will* stay the night with me – that goes without saying,' Devlin said, as she and Caroline left to go their separate ways. Maggie had already left, to attend a meeting with her editor.

'Thanks, Devlin,' Caroline smiled. 'I appreciate the offer but I think I should sleep at home tonight. You know, good psychology and all that.'

Devlin nodded in agreement. 'Good thinking, Caro. But don't forget – I'm in the next block if good psychology fails and you get lonely.'

'I won't.' Caroline gave her friend an affectionate hug and received one back in return. Driving back to the apartment, she remembered a line from the prayer Charles had given her.

Count your friends instead of your foes.

Well, she had the best of friends. That was obvious. With Devlin and Maggie on hand to give her moral support, she'd manage fine.

Sixteen

'How are things?' The transatlantic line was so clear that it was almost as if Richard were just down the road.

'Good,' Caroline said cheerfully. 'I've been busy at work this week. I sold two properties, which isn't bad because the property market is in the doldrums. They're going to let me go at the end of the month until around February when things pick up again.'

'What will you do with yourself?' Richard asked.

'I'll keep myself occupied. I'm taking classes in Ballymun Comprehensive. I've taken up painting and I'm doing computer studies. I'm enjoying it.'

'That's great,' he said enthusiastically. 'Keep at it.'

'How's Charles?' she asked.

'He's not too bad at all. He's taking things easy. We followed your advice and went to New England one weekend and it was beautiful. Caroline, I wish you'd been with us. We're going to fly down to New York and do a cultural weekend soon, we've decided. He's not in any pain at the moment so we want to make the most of the good days. His brother is giving him excellent care, so that's a great help.'

'That's good. At least you've got someone to share the worry and you know that he's in sound hands.'

'I'm glad I came with him, Caroline. Our time together is very precious and I'll always be able to look myself in the eye and think that I didn't let him down,' Richard said. 'As long as everything is OK with you, I don't mind.'

'I'm fine,' she assured him. 'Give my love to Charles. We'll talk again soon.'

'I will,' he promised, and Caroline smiled as she said goodbye.

She hadn't been telling any fibs when she said she was fine, Caroline reflected, as she pulled the curtains in the sitting-room. It was lashing rain outside, and the nights had drawn in as winter took hold. It was five weeks since Richard and Charles went to America. She hadn't fallen to pieces and she hadn't turned back to the bottle and actually she was quite proud of herself.

Charles had been right: dig deep and you find reserves within yourself. She had been determined not to give herself time to brood and get depressed so she had taken the bull by the horns and joined a beginners' art class, something she had always wanted to do. She was thoroughly enjoying it. Caroline had always loved art at school. She had a creative streak that had never been developed and she found that, just as in her schooldays, she could immerse herself in her painting for hours and not feel the time go by.

The computer studies were far more taxing, but also something she wanted to persevere with. Caroline knew that if she wanted to work full-time again, she might have to look elsewhere than Foynes and Kelly, Estate Agents and Auctioneers. As she had said to

Richard on the telephone, they were letting her go shortly, until the spring. This would not cause Caroline any financial hardship because of the cheque Richard had arranged to be lodged for her every month. But now that she had set in motion the dissolution of their marriage, she wanted to work full-time and make her own financial way in the world. She was still a young woman with a whole life ahead of her. She couldn't go on working part-time and attending painting classes for ever.

She decided that she would invite Maggie and Devlin to dinner the following Friday. Devlin was in great form these days. Her relationship with Luke was bringing her happiness and Caroline was so glad for her after all the trauma she had been through. She was really excited about the new Belfast City Girl and buzzing with ideas about the launch. It was great to see her friend in top gear again.

Poor Maggie was a bit browned off, trying to get her second novel written. Time out away from the children would do her the world of good and it would be nice for the three of them to have an evening together. The other two were so busy these days that there were times they didn't even make their Friday morning workout. A dinner for three would be perfect.

Caroline opened the oven door and an enticing aroma assailed her nostrils. 'Very nice,' she murmured happily. She was cooking crunchy stuffed pork and it smelled delicious, even if she said so herself. She was serving buttered carrots, sprouts, baked parsnips and roast and creamed potatoes to accompany her main course. There was prawn cocktail for starter and a Pavlova for dessert.

Caroline was really enjoying herself as she diced carrots and parsnips, peeled the potatoes she was going to cook, and washed the lettuce for the prawn cocktail. Cooking for one was a bit of a drag, so she was really pulling out all the stops now that she was having company. To tell the truth, she was starting to feel peckish herself.

The table was set, the wine was chilling, and everything was under control, so she went into the lounge and sat in front of the fire with a cup of coffee. It was great being able to invite the girls over for dinner. She'd never entertained them when she and Richard were together. He and Devlin had never got on and it would have been too awkward. There was a strange kind of freedom in being on your own, she mused, staring at the flames as they leapt up the chimney. It was not at all the disaster she had thought it was going to be. It was nice being able to do exactly what she pleased without having to consider someone else's feelings. Caroline loved classical music but, as Richard had never liked it, she had rarely played her collection. Now *Madame Butterfly* was playing softly in the background. Little things like that were helping her to find her feet again and she was facing life with courage and a positive attitude.

The doorbell rang, interrupting her reflections, and she jumped to her feet and lifted the intercom. Devlin's image appeared on the monitor.

'Hi, it's me. Is dinner nearly ready? I'm starving,' her friend declared, as she stood shivering in the biting wind outside.

'Come on up, you gannet,' laughed Caroline, pressing the buzzer.

Devlin arrived with a bouquet of flowers and a bottle of non-alcoholic wine.

'Mmmm,' she sniffed the air appreciatively. 'That smells gorgeous! What is it?'

'Crunchy stuffed pork,' Caroline informed her.

'My favourite, oh yum, yum, yum,' Devlin did a little twirl of delight. The dish had been a favourite since their flat-sharing days, and was one of Caroline's great specialities.

'Come out into the kitchen and have a drink. I want to put the parsnips in the oven.'

'Baked parsnips as well! Oh double yum yum to you,' Devlin giggled.

Caroline cocked a suspicious eye at her. 'Are you tipsy already?'

'No, I'm just really looking forward to our evening. It will be like old times in the flat,' Devlin said with a happy smile.

'Yes, we were happy then, weren't we?' Caroline handed Devlin a gin and tonic.

'And we're not doing too badly now, either.' Devlin held up her glass in a toast, and Caroline clinked her glass of mineral water with her.

Unthinkingly, they slipped into their routine of several years before, Caroline cooking and stirring, Devlin washing up as they went along, chatting in that easy way of old friends. Shortly afterwards, Maggie arrived with more flowers and some goodies – for the 'Sin Bag', she laughed. They sat around the fire enjoying their pre-dinner drinks. All Caroline had to do was to pop the carrots and sprouts into the microwave, and make the gravy.

'Come on out into the kitchen until I tell you about this ould fella who came to view an apartment I was selling yesterday. He told me he was a bachelor with plenty of money in the bank if I fancied making a go of it.' Caroline grinned.

The other pair shrieked with laughter as they followed Caroline into the high-tech kitchen that was so different from Devlin's homely one across the way. Maggie and Devlin had just seated themselves on the chrome-and-leather stools and Caroline was pouring some of the sizzling juices from the pork into a saucepan when the lights went out.

'Oh shit!' Caroline exclaimed. 'Is it a fuse, I wonder?'

'It's not a fuse. Everything's out in my block as well. I think we're having a power-cut.' Devlin edged her way to the window and peered out.

'Ah, shag it,' Maggie said. 'I was really looking forward to my dinner.'

'Have you any candles?'

'Hold on, I'll get them. Oops, sorry.'

'Where's my gin and tonic?'

'That's right,' Maggie said, grinning at Devlin in the dark. 'Get your priorities right. Don't lose your gin and tonic, for God's sake.'

'Oh, girls, this is a disaster.' A crestfallen Caroline lit some candles and stuck them around the kitchen. 'The meat needed another half an hour at least. You know pork. The vegetables aren't cooked, the gravy's not made and the potatoes are still hard.' She stabbed one of the potatoes venomously with a knife.

'I wonder how long it's going to last,' Maggie said in disgust.

'Knowing my luck – hours,' Caroline replied glumly.

An hour later, Devlin had had enough. 'I can't last another minute. I'm starving. Come on, Caroline, let's see what's in the fridge.'

'Well, we can have the prawn cocktail and some brown bread . . .'

'And there's cream cheese and pâté.' Devlin was peering into the fridge, holding a candle up high. 'Oh, and what's this?' She pointed to a plate covered with tinfoil.

'That's a chicken breast. And I've tomatoes and cucumber,' Caroline said forlornly.

Devlin jollied her along. 'There's loads here. Come on; we'll have a picnic in front of the fire. Sure it's a bit of a laugh.'

'And most importantly,' Maggie murmured, 'we have the Pavlova for sweet and . . . *the Sin Bag*!'

It turned into an evening of great fun and laughter as the trio ate their makeshift meal by candle-light, sitting in front of the fire. Just as the lights came on, Devlin was telling them all about her plans for Belfast, and as they carried the dishes out to the kitchen, Caroline remarked that it was years since she'd visited the Northern capital.

'Well, you'll be finishing up work soon. Why don't you come up with me one of these days?' Devlin suggested. 'I'd love you to see the new place and you could do a bit of shopping.'

'I'd like that, Devlin, I'd like that very much,' Caroline replied.

'Right, we'll make an arrangement when you're free,' Devlin said cheerfully.

It was the early hours of the morning before Maggie left, and Devlin announced that she was staying the night. She just couldn't face 'the trek across the lawn', as she called it.

Caroline was delighted. It was nice to have the company and that night she slept like a log, knowing that Devlin was in the other room.

She woke early and lay listening to the rain beating against the window, as the wind whistled and keened between the apartment blocks. She snuggled down into the warm hollow in the middle of the bed. It was bliss not to have to get up for work on a day like today. Devlin had assured her that she was in no hurry to get up either, so a lie-in was on the cards. Today that suited her just fine. Her eyes grew heavy. Last night had been great fun and there was no reason why she should not have more nights like it. And she was really looking forward to her trip to Belfast, she thought, as she sank into a delightful state of lethargy that lasted until she eventually fell asleep again.

Seventeen

Caroline gratefully submitted herself to the ministrations of one of the beauticians in City Girl. She was having a steam treatment as part of her facial after a workout with Devlin and Maggie, and it was really the most relaxing experience. Her mind wandered and the muted sounds of the salon faded into her subconscious. Her little pink-and-green cubicle with the steamer hissing softly was like another world.

It was a Friday morning early in December and she was planning to finish off her Christmas shopping. It was hard to believe that Christmas was almost upon them. She had been living on her own for nearly two months now and she felt quite stable. She was controlling her panic attacks and their intensity and frequency had diminished greatly. Caroline had read somewhere that by facing up to your fear, you conquer it. Well, maybe that was what she was doing, she thought with some satisfaction. Even the imminent arrival of Christmas was not causing her the angst she had been expecting. But then she had so many plans for Christmas this year that she wouldn't have time for angst.

She would go to her father and the boys for Christmas Eve, Christmas Day and St Stephen's Day, then home to the penthouse to spend a few days on her own, painting. Richard and Charles had sent her the most beautiful easel, a selection of canvases and an array of oils and water-colours that Michelangelo himself would have envied. Caroline hadn't touched them at all; she was saving that treat for Christmas.

Richard and Charles had invited her to Boston, and she had given a lot of thought to their invitation. She would have liked to visit the city and see where they were living, but she wondered whether staying with them wouldn't be a bit awkward – an awkwardness, she admitted to herself, that would be entirely of her own creation. Caroline had come to the conclusion that it was the very distance between her and Richard that was enabling her to get on with her new life. She feared that if she went to America, all the old inadequacies would come surging in upon her and she'd be back where she started. She fretted about it until Devlin said in exasperation, 'For God's sake, Caroline, stay or go. Make a decision; then you'll only have to worry about the decision you've made.'

Caroline had there and then decided not to go and, amazingly, once she had made her decision, she ceased to worry about it. It was something she was going to remember in the future. From now on, decide and act was going to be her new year's resolution.

Once she made up her mind, she found herself quite looking forward to Christmas. When Devlin returned from her trip to Paris with Luke, she was going to spend a few days with her and then she and Devlin were going to visit Maggie, so it would be a busy little season. And a happy one too, she promised

216

herself, as she inhaled the faint scent of aromatherapy oils that permeated the air of the salon.

She hadn't much Christmas shopping left to do, so she was in no great rush. She had done most of it on her trip to Belfast with Devlin and she had thoroughly enjoyed herself, apart from her natural feelings of apprehension when she saw the soldiers and armoured personnel-carriers on the streets. How people lived with the constant threat of violence, she could not imagine. Devlin, who had been up North on numerous occasions, and had never been involved in even the most minor incident, had assured her that she would get used to it very quickly. By the end of that long, busy day, Caroline noticed that her anxiety had dissipated and that she had adapted to the situation, although she still felt a sense of physical relief when she crossed the border on the way home. But, she told Devlin, as they drove towards Dublin, her trip to Belfast was an experience she wouldn't mind repeating some time.

'Great,' Devlin declared. 'You can come up and help out with the launch.'

Caroline smiled to herself. Devlin was so decisive that it was no wonder she was such a successful businesswoman. That Belfast launch was consuming all her energies at the moment and if the new City Girl didn't succeed, it wouldn't be Devlin Delaney's fault. Caroline was looking forward to the opening. She remembered well the excitement of the Dublin one. She had helped out at that, too, so she thought it would be nice to get involved with the Northern venture.

'Caroline?' she heard a voice calling.

'In here,' she called back. It was Devlin looking uncharacteristically harassed.

'Caroline, I can't go to the pictures with you tonight. I've got to go to Belfast. There's a bit of an emergency. Arthur's had a heart attack and it doesn't look too good. And City Girl is supposed to be opening in less than two weeks. I don't know whether I'm coming or going. It looks as if Paris is off as well,' she added forlornly.

Caroline sat up on the couch. 'Is there anything I can do? I'm finished working, I'm a free agent. I can type and make tea,' she offered. 'Do you want me to come up with you and give you a hand?'

Devlin's eyes widened. 'God, Caroline, would you? It would be brilliant just to have someone I could depend on. I'd pay you a salary, of course.'

'Oh, don't be daft, Devlin,' Caroline protested.

'Don't you be daft. By the time *I'm* finished with you you'll be demanding a salary. It's going to be hectic,' she warned. 'Are you sure you don't want to change your mind? I'll be staying up there for two weeks or more.'

'Fine,' Caroline replied with equanimity.

'I'd better get Liz to book us two rooms in the Europa, then. It's about the handiest to City Girl and it's very central. Are you *sure* you want to come?'

'For God's sake, would you stop blathering and get on with it,' Caroline said. 'And why do you want to book two rooms? Can't we share and save on the expense? We shared before – and if you start snoring, I'll buy some earplugs.'

'If you're coming to Belfast with me, you'll want a

bit of comfort. The budget will cope with it,' Devlin argued.

'It will be a bit of a laugh — like old times,' Caroline said, with a smile.

'Yes it will, won't it? Caroline, thanks. I really appreciate this. I was starting to panic for a minute there,' Devlin confessed.

'*You* panic . . . Impossible! Look, I'll just finish off here and go home and throw a few things in a case. You said we'll be there for two weeks?'

Devlin nodded. 'At least.'

'Right, I'll meet you at the apartments. Call me when you're ready to leave.'

'OK, but first things first. I'm going straight down to accounts to put you on the payroll. How does the title "Executive Assistant" grab you?'

'Wonderful. It'll look very impressive on my CV. Now, beat it and let me finish my facial.'

'Enjoy it,' Devlin warned. 'It's going to be the last bit of relaxation you'll have for the next fortnight.'

Her friend hadn't exaggerated, Caroline reflected, as she gazed at herself in the mirror in her bedroom in the Europa. The previous two and a half weeks had been among the most hectic, frenetic, exhilarating of her life. She and Devlin had started working the minute they had arrived in the city. Devlin had gone to visit Arthur in hospital, to reassure her partner that everything would be fine. She was relieved to find that his condition had stabilized and the critical twenty-four-hour period after the attack had passed with nothing untoward happening.

Caroline had gone straight to City Girl, introduced herself to the rest of the staff, found out what needed doing, and got to work.

She had taken over the administration, supervised workmen and organized deliveries of the remaining stock that was needed, leaving Devlin free to get on with the various promotions and marketing strategies that Arthur and his publicist had planned.

Caroline couldn't believe how much she was enjoying herself. She was too busy to be nervous or apprehensive or to dither over making up her mind. It was challenging and rewarding to be able to use her initiative to make decisions and follow through, knowing that Devlin was depending on her utterly because she was so busy with her side of things.

The staff that Devlin had employed were top-notch and, as the hectic days rushed forward to the planned opening day, they came together as a team and the atmosphere was tremendous, full of enthusiasm and goodwill. That was half the battle. Notwithstanding several minor hitches, like the wrong-coloured towels being delivered and one of the turbo sunbeds being faulty and a hiccup in the central heating system, by the evening of the big launch it was all systems go and, as Caroline eyed her glamorous reflection in the mirror, she was very satisfied.

She had mucked in and got on with it and been able to give Devlin all the support she needed to get the project up and running. She had learned that she could cope under stress and the whole experience had done wonders for her self-confidence. Even the fact that she'd had to stay a few nights on her own, while Devlin went back down to Dublin, had given her a great boost. She now knew without a doubt that she wanted to be back full-time in the workforce.

There was a knock on the door, and she opened it to find Luke smiling at her. He looked divine in his evening suit.

'Hi!' she greeted him. 'You look great.'

'You look pretty sensational yourself,' Luke said with a smile. 'That colour suits you. Are you ready?'

'I am,' Caroline replied.

She had chosen red, a glorious crimson sheath with black trim and a black silk bolero with matching crimson trim. It was very sophisticated. And with the professional make-up job that the beautician had given her and her hair newly cut and shining, she knew she looked her best.

Devlin emerged from her room, announcing, 'I'm ready,' and Caroline thought she looked stunning in an expensive and classy cerise cocktail dress that fitted her like a glove.

'I'll be the envy of Belfast with you two belles on my arm tonight,' Luke declared, as he led them down to the chauffeur-driven limousine. Tonight they were doing it in style.

It was a terrific party, and Caroline winked at Devlin as they noticed dozens of gorgeous ladies clamouring for the special opening offer at reception. The broadcaster, Lynda Jayne, had just made a very witty speech declaring City Girl open.

Arthur, who was out of hospital, had bullied his doctors to allow him to attend the launch for a couple of hours and although he was a bit pale and noticeably thinner, his bonhomie had diminished not one whit.

'Caroline, come here, I want you to meet someone. He's an old friend of mine and this is the kind of thing he'd normally run a mile from, but I wanted him to come and see what I'm up to now. Just to show off, like,' Arthur beamed.

'Caroline, this is Bill Mangan, at home on a few days' holiday from Abu Dhabi. Bill, this is Caroline Yates, who helped save our bacon here. She's done a terrific job helping to coordinate everything.'

'Hello.' She found herself shaking hands with a stocky, weatherbeaten man somewhere in his mid-fifties.

'How do you do?' he said, and looked alarmed as Arthur said ebulliently, 'Oh look, there's Jock Douglas and his wife. Excuse me for a minute. I must just have a few words with them.'

'Nice party,' Bill muttered, and Caroline felt sorry for him. It was obvious that this wasn't his scene at all.

'Can I get you a drink?' she offered. 'Come on over to the bar. I hate standing in the middle of a room,' she said lightly.

'Me too. I won't stay long. Arthur just wanted me to see the place. He's got a good business going here,' Bill remarked, as they edged their way through the throng.

'Well, we hope so.' Caroline caught the bar attendant's eye and asked Bill what he wanted.

'I'll have a pint of Guinness,' the older man said gratefully, smiling at Caroline.

Gradually, he relaxed in her company and she was so concerned with putting him at ease that she forgot to be shy herself. She found herself telling him about her broken marriage, although she didn't mention Richard's homosexuality, and remarked how she badly wanted to start working full-time again after her experience with City Girl. With her degree in languages she might look for something in that area, but she wasn't sure yet.

He told her about his building operations in the United Arab Emirates, and how his own marriage had broken up because he was always away from home, that his only daughter was married and living in Belfast and that he always came home to be with her at Christmas. He had given her a year's membership to City Girl as a Christmas present, and she was thrilled with herself. He pointed her out, a woman in her thirties who was chatting to one of the aromatherapists. Bill was on his third pint and telling her about the time he had been trapped in the desert in a sandstorm, when Arthur arrived over to them.

'The wife's insisting I go home,' he moaned, 'and I promised her I'd do as I was told. Will you come back for a bite of supper?' he asked Bill Mangan.

'I will surely,' the other man chuckled, 'just to see you doing as you're told.' He shook Caroline's hand. 'If you'll excuse me, I'd better let my daughter know I'm leaving with this old reprobate. It was a pleasure meeting you. I hope all goes well in the job search.'

'It was very nice to meet *you*,' she assured Bill with a smile, and then Arthur was kissing her and congratulating her again. As she watched them leave, she thought how interesting Bill had been about his life in Abu Dhabi. It sounded like a fascinating place.

She hadn't time to think any more about it, because it was time to pick some spot prizes. Devlin was insisting that she perform the selection, so, taking a deep breath, she walked to the top of the room and declared the winners, to great cheers from the gathering.

It was the early hours when she finally got to bed. The party had been really swinging and she had thoroughly enjoyed herself. Caroline fell fast asleep, chuffed that she had contributed so much to the whole venture.

Caroline was sitting on her balcony at the beginning of March, painting the view of Dublin Bay and the Wicklow hills. Spring had come. The early cherry-blossom was blooming and banks of daffodils waved resplendent beneath the trees and along the drive.

The glorious sight should have cheered her up — but it didn't. She was feeling a bit down in the dumps. After all the excitement and toing and froing of the Belfast City Girl opening, it was a bit of a shock to come back to earth again. She had stayed in Belfast for most of January and February to make sure that everything operated efficiently and to sort out the remarkably few teething troubles. But now she was back in Dublin doing her three days a week in Foynes and Kelly and she was feeling terribly restless. There must be more to life than this, she thought irritably, as she put a bit of yellow ochre on her palette.

Everything felt like such an anti-climax and she was back in her old familiar rut again. What had become of her great plans to get ahead? She had her name down in a dozen job centres, but so far, nothing. It was a real pain in the butt. She knew unemployment was a major problem but *surely* she should be able to get some sort of full-time job. She had a degree in languages; she had administrative experience. If she had more get-up-and-go, she'd land herself a job. She would just have to get out there and market herself, she told herself crossly.

The phone rang and, scowling, she got up and walked in to answer it. 'Hello. Is that Caroline Yates?' a man's voice asked, and she knew from the noise and echo on the line that it was a long-distance call. But it couldn't be Richard or Charles; she had spoken to them only an hour before.

'Hello, Caroline, it's Bill Mangan, Arthur's friend. I met you at the City Girl party. Arthur gave me your number. I hope you don't mind. But I have a proposition to put to you if you're interested.'

'Oh!' Caroline exclaimed. It was the man from Abu Dhabi. What on earth did he want with her?

'Hello. Are you there? Can you hear me?'

'I'm here, Bill, and I can hear you fine. What can I do for you?'

Oh my God, she thought to herself, her excitement laced with apprehension as she listened to his proposition.

'Well, what do you think?' he asked when he had finished.

Caroline took a deep breath. Without a second's hesitation, she said, 'Bill, that sounds like just what I need. I'd be delighted to accept your offer.'

'Great. I'll be home in two months and I'll get working on it then. Cheerio, Caroline.' Then he hung up.

'Oh my God,' she muttered, her eyes sparkling at her impetuosity. 'What have I let myself in for?'

Maggie's Story – I

Eighteen

The first thing she was going to do, Maggie decided, as she collected her car from the City Girl car-park and loaded her shopping, was to ring her newly acquired publishers. Her editor wanted to arrange their first editorial session and although she was excited about it, Maggie felt a little apprehensive. Marcy Elliot, the editorial director of Enterprise Publishers, had warned her newest budding author that there was a lot of work to be done on the manuscript.

The sales and marketing director, Sandra Nolan, wanted to arrange a meeting with Maggie and an artist about cover designs and she also wanted Maggie to meet Carol Lewis, the PR person who would be handling the publicity. It was all so new, so exciting. Never in her wildest dreams had Maggie thought her book would be published. If her husband hadn't had an affair with that slut Ria Kirby, Maggie would never have sat down and written a novel inspired by the diary she had kept in which she had recorded her pain and despair and anger. Terry had betrayed her but from that awful experience Maggie had emerged a much stronger woman. She had slowly started taking control of her life. And it was a good feeling. Next on her agenda was getting her tubes tied. Three children and two dreadful pregnancies were enough for any woman to go through, although she loved her twins and the toddler very much.

Terry certainly had no desire for any more children. Not that *he'd* take the responsibility and have a vasectomy. Her husband couldn't have looked more horrified when she had suggested it. 'Just say the kids and you were all killed in an accident and I wanted to get married again,' Terry blustered. 'Why can't you get that tube thing done?'

'Yeah, and what happens if I have a tubal ligation and something happens to you and the kids and *I* want to get married again?' she had countered.

'Well, go back on the pill then,' Terry retorted. He hated these discussions; he much preferred Maggie to take care of that business, although he wished she'd make up her mind and do something once and for all. He was fed up using condoms; he hated the bloody things.

Maggie knew she could argue until she was blue in the face and it would do no good. Terry would never agree to have a vasectomy. It seemed to be a threat to his manhood. If she didn't want to get pregnant *she* would have to do something about it. After all she was only in her mid-thirties, she had a decade of child-bearing years left and she didn't want to be worrying every time her period was late. Especially not now when such an exciting new prospect had opened up for her.

The way Enterprise were going on about her new book, she was going to be the next Barbara Taylor Bradford or Danielle Steele. Maggie grinned to herself as she drove past St Peter's Church in Phibsborough and headed out towards the Navan Road. She might as well dream here as in bed, she told herself wryly. Still, even to have got this far was an achievement and nothing and no-one was going to get in the way of her finally doing what she wanted. She had given of herself long enough. Maggie, the perfect wife, mother, daughter no longer existed. She was Maggie Ryan, writer. The next year at least was going to be devoted to her new career and having her tubes tied was the option that suited her the best. Her mother would be absolutely horrified. Flying in the face of God she would call it. Nelsie McNamara was of the generation that believed that sex was a duty of marriage and not a pleasure and that having children was part of that duty. And if God saw fit that a woman should have eight, nine or ten children or more, so be it.

Maggie sighed deeply as she turned left at the Halfway House and drove on to Castleknock. Surely God would be satisfied with the three children she had produced. She loved them passionately and was rearing them as best she could. Was it so selfish to want to devote a portion of her life to herself and her own needs? What was it about the female psyche that made guilt cling like a leech, no matter how liberated one pretended to be. Terry never agonized over anything. He didn't have to. She did it all for him. Well, enough was enough. From now on it was all systems go.

She was dying to phone Marcy and Sandra and ask them what they thought of the title *City Woman*. Maggie just loved it. It was so apt. Trust Devlin to come up with it. It was the hardest thing in the world to pick a title. Her editor and the sales and marketing director had made lists but none of the suggestions had seemed quite right. They had come up with *An Independent Woman* as a working title but Maggie hadn't felt comfortable with it. It was a bit long and too serious. Coming home this morning with her friends after their precious long-awaited weekend together, she had been chatting about this and that and Devlin had laughed and said she should call the book *Three Mad Women*. Then they had got serious and started tossing ideas around and Devlin had told them that she hadn't had a clue what to call her health and leisure club until she had heard Billy Joel singing 'Uptown Girl' and City Girl had just popped into her head and been perfect. 'It's a fabulous name,' Maggie remarked wistfully. 'Something like that would be perfect for my book.'

'Yes, but Nicola, your heroine, isn't really a girl after all; she is in her early thirties,' Caroline had interjected as she had driven on to the Newtown-mountkennedy bypass and increased her speed to all of 50 m.p.h. – daring driving for her on her second great journey in her new Fiesta.

'True, Caro, good thinking; it's got to be something with "woman" then,' Devlin had mused, a frown furrowing her brow.

'We've tried every permutation, believe me,' said Maggie. 'I think we're stuck with *An Independent Woman*.'

'Oh, Maggie, it's a bit . . . it's a bit contrived, if you don't mind my saying so,' Devlin retorted.

'Say what you like – that's what friends are for,'

Maggie had muttered glumly. Now Devlin had *really* succeeded in putting her off the working title.

'You need something that will grab your readers' attention, something sophisticated and savvy . . . something like . . . like . . . ' Devlin's eyes gleamed all of a sudden as she grinned at Maggie. 'Something like *City Woman*!'

'Wowie . . . I love it. Devlin, you genius!' Maggie yelled. It was perfect, perfect for her precious novel and its discovery at the end of their lovely weekend together had to be a good omen. She hoped Marcy and Sandra would go for it. Now they were two real City Women. Ambitious, intelligent, glamorous. Maggie was fascinated by them. Marcy, who had such original ideas and with a razor-sharp brain that could spot a mistake a mile off, and Sandra, who could sell sand to an Arab and who was so sophisticated that Maggie found her slightly intimidating. Just being in their company made Maggie feel exhilarated, their enthusiasm was so catching.

It was so interesting to see behind the scenes in publishing. She had never given the publishing business any thought before. She had just bought her books, read them and enjoyed or disliked them, and never considered the process behind it all – the hard slog that went into the creation of a book. From the idea in the writer's head to the bookshelves and into the reader's hands was quite a journey. Listening to her publishers discussing the text size, the cover design, the typography, the suggested price, the dumpbins and marketing strategies was an eye-opener for Maggie and she was eager to be involved and to learn all about it. After the last few years of staying at home with her children, she was ready for the mental stimulation. Writing the novel had been such a long, lonely experience. Only Adam had understood. Maggie's eyes lit up as she thought of Adam Dunne and how he had helped her change her life. Gorgeous, sexy Adam whom she had met while she was glancing at a book about novel-writing. Such an inauspicious beginning. Because of him she had joined a writers' group and now here she was about to be published, while the wild side of her, the side that buried guilts deep, was seriously considering an affair with him. Deep down she knew she probably wouldn't; she had invested a lot in her marriage with Terry. She had three children to consider but it was nice to have the fantasy. It kept her going, made her feel young and desirable, especially when he looked at her with that expression in his hazel eyes.

Adam understood her creative side because he knew what it was like. Terry had always dismissed her writing as 'scribbling' and it infuriated her. She was so sorely tempted not to tell her husband her news about being published until the night of her launch, just to see the expression on his face. Adam she couldn't wait to tell when he returned next week from the UK. She had really missed him for the time he had been away. Maggie had to admit her feelings for him were stronger than she had realized and it shocked her a little. She knew that if Terry had not had his affair she would never have encouraged this flirtation with Adam. Although on the surface she and Terry had put the past behind them and decided to make a go of the marriage, Maggie knew that she could never entirely forgive her husband. His betrayal of her had cut to the bone and only with Adam's arrival on the scene had her self-esteem begun to recover. Terry would never again have such a hold on her loyalty. He didn't know that though. He suspected nothing of her attraction to Adam. It was her secret and when the time came she would make her decision and her husband's feelings wouldn't enter into it at all.

Stopped at the traffic lights in the village, Maggie rolled down her window. It was a hot day all right. It had been a shame to leave Rosslare Harbour with the sun shining so brightly. Her tan had come up beautifully. Maybe she would sunbathe this afternoon while the kids played out the back. She was looking forward to seeing them. It had been lovely to have the few days to herself with no children to worry her, but she was looking forward to a few kisses and cuddles, especially from Shona, the baby. Not that she was a baby any more, really: she was walking now and had her head stuck into everything and as for the gobbledegook she uttered . . .

Of course having the twins for company was great stimulus for her. Everything they did, she had to do too. Her real name was Fiona, but Mimi her elder sister could not pronounce her 'f's and so it came out as Shona. It suited her so well that the name had stuck. Terry hadn't been too cheerful any time she had phoned home. He had found it hard to accept the idea of Maggie going away with the girls for a weekend. It just wasn't what wives did! But tough! Maggie had been looking forward to a break for a long time and she bloody well deserved it. Swinging into the drive, she noticed that the lawn needed a mow. Typical! If she didn't do it, it would never be done. It would never dawn on Terry to cut the grass.

She checked her watch. Almost midday. The twins were at summer school until twelve-thirty so she'd have Shona to herself for half an hour. She was dying to feel the little arms around her neck and to smell the lovely sweet baby scent of her and have her soft blonde curls tickling her cheeks. Maggie loved her youngest daughter's hair. It was like spun gold, so soft and fine. Devlin's baby had had hair like that, she remembered sadly. Poor Devlin, she had pitied her so much at Lynn's grave. Devlin would never get over her baby's death. No mother would. God grant that her three would live to grow up healthy and strong. Rooting in her bag for her keys, she remembered the chocolates she had bought for Josie, her baby-minder. Josie had been great about her long weekend. 'I'm home,' she announced cheerily, letting herself in. 'Josie, Shona, I'm home.'

The house seemed strangely quiet. 'Josie. Shona,' she called heading into the kitchen. They must be out the back, she decided, but a frisson of uneasiness disturbed her. She couldn't explain it but she just knew something was wrong. There was no-one out the back, just a line of clothes fluttering in the breeze. Maybe Josie had taken the baby for a walk or on a trip to the shops. Yet Maggie had told her child-minder she'd be home before noon to collect the twins from their summer school. Her eye caught the note on the kitchen table and she read it with dismay. 'Oh Christ Almighty!' she groaned. Why this weekend when she wasn't here? Of all weekends in the year for this to happen . . . God, she should have known she couldn't expect to go off with the girls and get away scot-free. Terry would really go on about it now. Maggie read the note again with a sinking heart. 'God, please don't let it be anything serious,' she murmured aloud as she headed back out to the car. Her heart was beating fast and her palms were sweaty as she got behind the wheel and scorched down the drive and back in the direction from which she had just come.

Nineteen

'Pneumonia!' Maggie was aghast.

'And tonsillitis,' Terry added grimly.

They were standing in the corridor outside the casualty ward in Temple Street Children's Hospital. Maggie shook her head in disbelief. Shona had had the sniffles on the Friday before Maggie left but she'd been playing happily. She'd certainly had no temperature. 'How did she get that?' She spoke to herself more than to Terry.

'Don't ask me. You're the nurse . . .' her husband retorted sarcastically.

'There's no need for that, Terry,' Maggie said sharply.

'Well, if you hadn't been gadding about down in Wexford, you might have been able to prevent it.' Terry glared at his wife. 'I don't know what to do with temperatures and coughs. You do. You weren't here and I was left on my own with them. And it's just not on, Maggie.' Her husband's voice rose and people looked curiously in their direction.

'Oh for God's sake, Terry, don't start here.' Maggie struggled to suppress the fury and resentment that surged through her. What was she? A one-parent family, for crying out loud! He was the father; that meant taking half the responsibility. But Terry never saw it like that. As long as he provided for them, that was his job done. Let Maggie look after everything else.

She felt like crying. All the euphoria of the morning evaporated and a weariness of spirit pervaded every inch of her. 'Where's Shona?' she asked dispiritedly. 'Tell me what happened.'

'I just came out to have a fag; she was seen by a doctor only twenty minutes ago. This place is packed. The nurses are sponging her down. They're waiting for a bed up in one of the wards. She was very hot and flushed and restless all night. I gave her Calpol but it didn't help. I phoned you early this morning but there was no answer; so I brought her here as soon as Josie arrived. I figured it was the best thing to do, rather than waiting for a doctor to come. I had to cancel an important meeting this morning because of it, too,' he added, accusingly. 'Where were you this morning anyway? I rang at eight-thirty. It couldn't have taken you all this time to get home, even with Caroline driving.'

'We went for a swim, Terry; that's where I was at half eight this morning,' Maggie faced her husband squarely. Damned if she was going to let him make her feel guilty. She moved down towards the ward and as she got there she could hear a pitiful little voice saying, 'I want my Mammy. Where's my Mammy?'

Burning daggers of guilt stabbed her heart. It was Shona.

'She's been calling for you all night and all morning.' Terry twisted the knife with pleasure, heaping the coals of guilt on her head. While she was swimming languidly in the clear warm waters off Devlin's private little beach, Shona had been burning up with a fever and calling for her.

She swallowed hard and went over to where Shona lay quietly with just a nappy on. Her blonde curls stuck damply to her head, her face was flushed, her eyes bright with fever. She lay submissive to the ministrations of the nurse who was sponging her down.

'Hello, baby, hello, my pet.' Maggie leaned over and kissed her daughter's forehead. It was burning to the touch. Shona reached out her arms to her and Maggie took her up and cuddled her and whispered endearments. The toddler laid her head limply on her mother's shoulder and Maggie could feel the heat from her body.

'How high is her temp?' she asked the young student nurse.

'Almost forty. We've given her a suppository to try and bring it down. She's had a chest X-ray, and she's for admission. She's a bit dehydrated so they'll be putting her on a saline drip as soon as we get a doctor available,' the nurse said. Maggie's heart sank at the thought of the drip. She couldn't bear the thought of the needle piercing her baby's vein. As a nurse, she had never been squeamish about giving needles to adults but children were another matter.

The twins had so far avoided hospital and apart from the odd temperature and cold had never been sick. Having her child in hospital was a new experience for Maggie, and none of her nursing experience was of any help to her. She couldn't think rationally. All she knew was that her child had pneumonia and a

240

temperature of forty, which, if they didn't get it down, could result in convulsions, and she felt very apprehensive and helpless. People often said to her, 'Ah sure, it's great you're a nurse; you know what to do.' And in any emergency she *would* know and deal with matters competently and professionally. But when it was your own child it was a different thing and all her competence and professionalism were in danger of deserting her completely at this very minute.

She drew a deep breath and laid Shona back on the bed. 'I'm a nurse myself. I'll take over the sponging if you like,' she told the younger woman.

'Oh fine. We're up to our eyes here so that will be great.' The nurse smiled as she handed Maggie the sponge. 'As soon as there's a bed free we'll let you know.' Maggie dipped the sponge into the tepid water and gently patted it over Shona's body, willing her temperature to come down.

'I might as well push off, now that you're here.' Terry had joined her. He didn't say 'at last' – he didn't have to. She knew what he meant. 'Is Josie going to look after the twins?'

Maggie didn't look at him. 'Yes,' she said shortly.

'Fine. See you. Ring me at the office if you have to. I'll call in on the way home.' Terry bent down and kissed Shona. She started to wail as he walked towards the door.

'Want Daddy, Mammy.'

'Daddy will be back soon. He has to go to work for a little while,' she soothed.

'No,' Shona said petulantly. 'Want my daddy.' She twisted away and kicked out at the sponge and started to cry again. A child in the bed next to her joined in and a little boy opposite who was getting his temperature taken anally was yelling blue murder.

A sister of the child, who was bored and fed up with the long wait in the stiflingly hot ward kept saying in a whiny voice that was setting Maggie's teeth on edge, 'I wanna go home, Ma. Ma, I wanna go home.' Another child was playing with a computer game and the tinny beeps out of it added yet another element to the cacophony. Maggie could feel the beginnings of a headache. She wouldn't have minded a cup of tea but she knew if she left Shona even for a minute there'd be ructions. Across the way, the little boy puked right over his whingeing sister and she started to yell. Casualty was always a nightmare. It would be much better when she went up to the ward, Maggie comforted herself.

It was late afternoon by the time a bed finally became available and as she carried her daughter up the interminable flights of stairs to St Camillus's ward, Maggie was fit for nothing. She was baked alive; her clothes stuck to her; rivulets of perspiration ran down between her breasts. She had forgotten just how warm hospitals were. And it was even worse in children's hospitals. She was starving, her head was pounding and she was wondering how she was going to organize herself for the rest of the week. Josie was not available for the next two afternoons. The mornings would be OK; Michael and Mimi would be at summer school until twelve-thirty. But after that she was stuck until Terry came home. She wanted to stay with Shona. The nurses had told Maggie that the toddler would be in hospital for at least four days and that there were facilities for parents to stay overnight if they wished. It was reassuring for the child and Maggie knew she'd only be worried sick if she was at home, knowing that Shona was ill and fretting for her.

But she had Michael and Mimi to think of as well. She didn't want them to feel excluded. Mimi had been a little bit put out by the arrival of Shona and always made sure that she got her fair share of attention. Michael, God bless him, was a placid child and she'd have no trouble with him. Maggie laid Shona into the cot as the nurse arranged the drip beside the bed. She had chickened out when they were inserting the drip. The nurse in the observation room had asked if she wanted to stay and hold Shona down but Maggie had said no. She had stepped outside as the doctor got to work and had to put her hand over her mouth to stop her lip quivering as she saw her daughter struggling and squirming against the nurse, her howls heart-rending.

Now when a nurse or doctor approached, Shona's lip started to tremble and she clung to Maggie. Consequently, Maggie was now even more reluctant to leave her. When Terry came in tonight, she'd go home and see what she could organize. Then she'd come back and stay the night. It was after six when Terry arrived, and Maggie was starving. 'What the hell is that? What's going on here? What's wrong with her?' Terry looked horrified as he pointed to the drip strapped on to Shona's hand.

'Calm down, it's a saline drip; they're giving her antibiotics through it as well. I'm going home to see the kids, have something to eat and shower, and I'll come back and stay. Will you get the kids off to summer school in the morning and I'll arrange for someone to pick them up tomorrow?'

'Don't be too long, will you, Maggie? I've a lot of work to do for tomorrow.' Terry was not in the best of humours.

'I'll be as long as it takes,' Maggie said evenly, taking her bag and edging her way out the door. She didn't want Shona to get upset about her leaving. As she ran down the stairs past Intensive Care, grateful that at least her child wasn't in there, Maggie fumed at Terry's attitude. He could be such a pig sometimes. You would think from the way he was going on that it was all her fault. Whether she was at home or not, Shona would still have contracted pneumonia. It was a virus. Outside, she paused for a second and drew some deep breaths. A slight breeze had blown up and after the airless heat of the ward it was such a relief. Across the street, a gang of teenagers sat smoking and listening to ghetto-blasters. Oh, to be them without a care in the world, Maggie thought as she walked along to where her car was parked.

Wearily she walked around to the driver's side and went to insert her key. A windscreen-wiper blade protruded from the lock and Maggie's jaw dropped as she looked in and saw that her car radio had been ripped out and there were wires dangling from the ignition. Across the street, someone laughed. She turned to see the gang watching her. Anger ripped through her. Fucking little bastards, she swore. As if people weren't miserable enough having a child in hospital. The last thing they needed to worry about was where to park their cars. She felt like going over and thumping the daylights out of them. She wanted to rake her nails down their jeering faces and pull chunks out of their hair and kick the fellows hard in the balls. All her anger and frustration at the whole sorry day coalesced into a vicious desire to inflict violence on these so-called victims of deprived backgrounds. It wasn't they who were victims but people like her who were at the mercy of every criminal Tom, Dick and Harry. It was she who was being deprived right now, deprived of the car she needed to get home to her children. By God, that lot would be deprived when she got her hands on them she thought, too furious to think straight and be intimidated by the gang of them.

She was just about to cross the street when a shabbily dressed old man stopped her. 'I wouldn't, ma'am, if I were you. They're a tough shower that lot — I know — I live around here and I've seen them in action. You'd only end up getting battered and mugged. The next time, park up the way as far as you can, although Eccles Street is getting as bad: three cars were done there on Sunday. What kind of rearing is on them at all? God be with the days when you could walk the streets in safety and, if you were in trouble, be sure of a helping hand. Good evenin' to you, ma'am.' He raised his hat at her and his kind old eyes smiled into hers before he shuffled off towards Hill Street.

His words and mannerly way diffused her anger a little and made her rational again. That old man was right; she wouldn't have a chance and if she did strike any of them, she'd probably end up in jail for assault. Those gurriers always knew their rights. A thought struck her. Where was Terry's car? The last thing she

245

needed was for *his* car to get robbed. She'd better go in and tell him to move it and give the AA a call. She'd have to phone Josie and tell her she'd be late. It was a totally harassed woman who finally got home that evening. Michael and Mimi, with that instinctive facility that children have for knowing that their parents are pushed beyond the limit, were playing up. 'Mammy, he called me a maggot. I'm not a maggot, aren't I not?' her daughter whined.

'Liar! Liar! knickers on fire,' Michael taunted.

Mimi's eyes grew round. 'Oh, Mammy, he said—' the voice was lowered dramatically, '—*knickers*,' she declared, horrified, ever the little lady.

'Stop fighting this minute,' Maggie warned.

'Where's our presents from your holiday?' Mimi changed the subject to one that interested her far more.

'That's lovely,' Maggie declared, as she smiled at Josie. 'No-one even gave me a kiss or a hug or a cuddle. Poor Mammy, no-one loves her any more!' Immediately she was enveloped in two pairs of arms as the twins scrambled on to her lap to give her the required kisses and cuddles.

'By the way,' said Josie, as she prepared to leave, 'a woman named Marcy Elliot called several times in the hopes of getting you. She wants you to phone her at the office tomorrow and she said you are to keep Wednesday afternoon free to meet her. I told her you had a child in hospital but she said if possible she'd like to meet you on Wednesday.'

'Oh Lord, I was supposed to give her a call today. It just went stright out of my head.' Maggie ran her fingers through her hair. 'Fine, Josie, thanks, I'll look after that and thanks for today. You're a brick.'

'You're welcome. There's a bit of shepherd's pie in the oven for you. See you tomorrow.' Josie waved at the children and let herself out.

'Mammy, can I have my hair in a tail-pony tomorrow?' Mimi enquired. 'My friend Joanna is having hers done in a tail-pony instead of plaits.'

''Course you can.' Maggie kissed her little daughter on the top of her head and smiled to herself. Mimi could be such a little madam. And the things she came out with! Only last week they had gone to Mass and a coffin was lying at the Altar of Repose and at the top of her voice, her three-year-old had enquired, wide-eyed: 'Mammy, why is there a treasure chest over there?' Maggie had been speechless. She cuddled her children close to her. They were so precious and at this age so adorable – when they weren't fighting. 'Come on, let's get you pair into your pyjamas and as soon as I've had my dinner we'll have a game of Matching Pairs.' Cheers of delight greeted this pronouncement as the pair scurried off to get undressed. Limp, Maggie sat flopped in the chair. Thanks to the brats who had broken into her car, she was going to have to wait for Terry to come home and then get a taxi into the hospital. Before she did anything else she decided she had better try and make some arrangements to have Mimi and Michael looked after the next day. Picking up the phone, she dialled Caroline's number.

'It's imperative that we meet very soon, Maggie.' Maggie stifled a yawn as she listened to her editor at the other end of the phone. She had been up since

247

six-forty-five, when the nurses had called her to say that Shona was awake and fretful. So far her temperature had not been brought under control and she was a very sick little girl. 'We're anxious to have you out in time for the Christmas market and that means a very short lead-in period,' Marcy continued. 'So we've got to get working on the rewrites. That's why I want to meet you tomorrow afternoon. I've kept it free so that I can start going through the manuscript with you. Isn't there someone else you can get to sit with your little girl for a few hours? It's not that I'm unsympathetic to your plight, Maggie, believe me. I know it's tough. But we have so little time, we've got to get working,' Marcy's crisp voice came down the line.

'I know, I know,' Maggie said hastily. 'It's just that I can't really leave here. She frets terribly and she's so sick.'

'Just for an hour, even,' Marcy urged. 'I could come and pick you up and we could pop down to the Gresham and then I could leave you back.'

'OK, OK,' Maggie agreed. 'I'll fix something up.'

'Great, Maggie, that's the spirit. I'll pick you up at three. I'm going to put you on hold; Sandra wants to talk to you,' Marcy said brisky.

'Tell her to hurry,' Maggie urged, 'I haven't any more change and I don't want to be cut off.' She saw the professor going up the stairs on his rounds and she wanted to be there when he got to Shona. Come on, Sandra, she thought impatiently.

'Hi, you poor thing.' Sandra came on the line. 'Look, I know you're up to ninety but I've got to set up a meeting with yourself, myself and Carol. We need an author biog from you and I want you to meet someone I think might suit us for the cover. That's very important, Maggie. We need a cover urgently so I can start selling in to the shops. When can we meet? This week, if possible. Normally we wouldn't publish a novel as quickly as this. But I think this is going to be big and I want to hit the Christmas market.' Sandra was as always very enthusiastic.

'Look, Sandra, could I get back to you?' Maggie was utterly harassed.

'Sure, sure, but soon, Maggie.'

Maggie was just about to hang up when she remembered. 'Wait, Sandra. I forgot to mention it to Marcy. I've a title that I prefer to *An Independent Woman*.'

'Hmmm?' Sandra was cautious.

'I'm going to call it *City Woman*,' Maggie said firmly. After all it was *her* novel. There was silence at the other end of the phone. Maggie waited anxiously.

'Hey . . . I like it. I like it,' said Sandra enthusiastically. 'Let me run it by the others. OK?'

'Right. See you, Sandra.' Maggie replaced the phone and raced up the stairs, anxious to get back to the ward in time to see the professor. Terry would never agree to taking a half-day, so there was no point in asking. Josie wasn't available to look after Mimi and Michael; Caroline had promised to do that for her. She'd have to leave Shona alone for an hour while she was with Marcy and that was that. Sandra would just have to wait until things had calmed down a bit before she could even think of meeting her. And as regards sitting down to rewrite, how the hell was she

249

going to do that? Maybe she should phone her mother and ask her to come up for a few days. But that would be more trouble than it was worth; it would end up with her looking after Nelsie as well as everyone else. Scrap that brainwave. She could hear Shona crying from the top of the stairs and with a heart as heavy as lead she went back into the ward to try and comfort her.

'Hello,' a familiar voice said in her ear several hours later, and Maggie turned to find Devlin smiling down at her. 'How is she?' Maggie looked down at her daughter, lying with her head against her shoulder, fast asleep. She looked worn out and still had a high temperature. As well as everything else she had developed blisters and mouth ulcers and she couldn't eat, and trying to get her to take her oral medicine was a nightmare. Every time she saw a nurse coming she buried her face into Maggie's neck, clinging tightly to her, and Maggie had had to hold her struggling in her arms as the nurse had forced a syringe into Shona's mouth. Most of the medicine landed on Maggie and the nurse as Shona spat it out and they'd had to repeat the exercise. Shona had fallen asleep, still sobbing, her eyes reproaching her mother for her act of betrayal.

'Not too good: they can't get her blasted temperature down. It's fluctuating between forty and thirty-eight,' Maggie sighed.

'What's that in the old system?' Devlin pulled up a chair beside Maggie and deposited a large fluffy koala bear on the bed.

'Thanks; you shouldn't have.' Maggie was touched.

'Forty is 104 Fahrenheit. That's the highest it's gone. It's 102 at the moment.'

'Jesus,' breathed Devlin. 'One hundred and four! That's high — but at least it's dropped two degrees. Can't they do anything?'

Tears stung Maggie's eyes. 'They're doing everything they can. They're very kind here. It's just so frustrating that the antibiotics aren't working yet. She's so sick, Dev; it's awful to see her like this. You know what a little live wire she is usually. I know they'll get it down eventually. I'm a nurse. I know these things, but I can't help worrying.'

'Of course you can't! You're her mother, for God's sake. I remember once, Lynn—' Devlin stopped short. 'Ah, nothing . . . don't worry, Maggie, you know kids: one minute they're as sick as a parrot, the next they're jumping around.'

'Yeah, I know. It's just that this pneumonia worries me.'

Devlin put an arm around her shoulder. 'She'll be fine, Maggie, believe me. Caroline phoned me last night after you were on so I called the hospital and they said I could come in any time after eleven. So I just popped up. It's handy being your own boss at times like this.'

'You don't know how lucky you are, Devlin. God, I'm running round in circles trying to sort things out. My editor wants to meet me tomorrow afternoon; my sales and marketing director wants a meeting; the car's in the garage. Terry won't take time off so I'm up the creek.' Maggie grimaced.

'Is Terry up to his eyes at work?' Devlin asked sympathetically.

'No more than usual,' snorted Maggie. 'Do you know something, Dev: he blames me for this. Because I went away for the weekend Shona got pneumonia. How's that for logic? He's been a real pig about it. If I tell him I need some time to go to a meeting at my publishers, he'll just tell me to get lost. Anyway I haven't told him yet I'm being published. The time just wasn't right and I don't think he'll be that impressed anyway.'

Devlin shook her head. 'That's not one bit fair. I'm surprised at Terry. Men! They're gas, aren't they? I phoned Luke yesterday and he went into a huff and hung up – why, I don't know. Wait until I see him tomorrow, I'll be just as cool.'

'Ah Devlin, you can't be cool to Luke; he's crazy about you,' Maggie remonstrated. 'He's a very nice man.' Maggie knew if it were Luke Reilly she was married to she would be getting a hell of a lot more support from him than she was getting from Terry.

'I know he is,' Devlin sighed. 'Listen, I'm just thinking here: what if you could reschedule your meeting with your editor for now? I could stay here for a couple of hours. You can take my car. It's open drive. Go and do your biz and back you come.'

Maggie smiled. 'Devlin to the rescue. You're a great old buddy.'

'Don't worry. I'll get my own back one of these days. Give me that child and go on and phone your editor.'

Maggie hesitated, for she knew Devlin was a very busy lady.

'Now!' ordered Devlin.

Twenty

Twenty-five minutes later Maggie was parking Devlin's Sierra in the forecourt of the complex just off the Santry bypass that housed her publishers' offices and warehouse. Marcy had rescheduled an editorial meeting so she could fit her in. Maggie couldn't help a little buzz of excitement as she parked the car. To be going to a meeting at her publishers! Thousands dreamed of getting this chance and *she* had succeeded. How many times had she passed this way and never really noticed the smart yellow-brick single-storey building, with its well-kept forecourt decorated with tubs of flowering shrubs. It was part of a small industrial estate that was well laid out and maintained. Enterprise Publishers were to the front of the complex. In fact to Maggie's biased eye, theirs was the nicest building in the estate. The enormous warehouse, a long low building, was behind the office building and on her first visit to Enterprise House, Jeremy Wilson, the managing director, had given her a guided tour and presented her with a selection of books from the shelves. By the end of the year, with any luck, copies of *City Woman* would be reposing on those shelves.

The first person Maggie saw when she entered the

plush foyer was Sandra Nolan and she groaned inwardly. Her cotton summer dress was creased and clung to her. She hadn't had time to wash her hair over the past few days, she had no make-up on apart from a touch of lipstick and she just felt she looked a sight. Sandra was perfectly groomed and looked every inch the young executive in her cream Betty Barclay suit. Her jet-black hair gleamed in a shining bob; her make-up was subtle but perfectly applied. She was one of these people who are naturally glamorous, and no matter what the circumstnces, are always perfectly groomed — the type of person you would love to hate but couldn't because she was so nice.

'Hi! how's the baby? You look a bit tired, Maggie. Can I get you some coffee?' Sandra said solicitously. 'Come on into my office and we can have a chat. Everybody here loves *City Woman*. I've some great ideas for the cover design. The feedback in the trade is good too. I think we're on to a winner here, Maggie!' Sandra's exuberance was infectious. Maggie found herself smiling, even though she had only been there for a minute or two; her adrenalin was starting to flow. Sandra always had that effect on her.

'Shona's not responding to the antibiotics. It's a matter of getting one that will control her infection. It will take a while. A friend is sitting in for me so I was able to come up. But I won't have coffee; Marcy's expecting me.'

At that moment Marcy came out of her office and saw her. 'Is Sandra trying to poach you? Typical!' she laughed. 'She's mine today, Sandra. Make your own arrangements and stop trying to steal a march on the editorial department,' she said with mock-severity to the sales and marketing director, as she ushered Maggie into her office. 'I'll organize coffee for us and we'll get down to work,' Marcy declared, as she pressed a button on her intercom and asked the receptionist to bring them in a pot of coffee. 'And hold all my calls for the next hour, please,' she instructed crisply. 'I prefer to work on a manuscript with an author away from the office if possible, because this place is a madhouse!' Marcy explained as she took Maggie's manuscript out of a file. 'I know the circumstances are exceptional but perhaps when your little girl is better we can arrange to meet where neither of us will be interrupted. You'll get much more work done, quality work.'

The editor sat behind her desk and pulled a chair up beside her. 'Sit down, Maggie, and take a deep breath,' she said, smiling. Marcy, like Sandra and Maggie, was in her mid-thirties. She was a brisk businesslike woman with a sharp brain that impressed Maggie. Tall and very thin, Marcy was superbly fit and her skin and hair glowed with good health. She never ate junk, didn't drink, didn't smoke, her only indulgence being coffee. She jogged daily with her partner, a vice-president of a meat exporting company, and was always in bed before midnight. It paid off, Maggie thought admiringly. Marcy Elliot had the energy of ten; her workload was enormous but it didn't faze her one bit. One of these days, *she* was going to get herself in hand, start eating properly and become more fit than she managed with her weekly workout and swim in City Girl. Definitely . . . one of these days . . .

'Now Maggie——' Her editor interrupted her

musings. '——here's a pad and paper. I know you haven't your copy of the manuscript, so we'll use mine and, by the way, I love the new title.' Marcy tapped a pen approvingly on the title page, and Maggie hid a smile. Her editor was so authoritative. Maggie knew full well that if she hadn't liked the new title she would have made her protests loud and clear. Because Maggie knew nothing about publishing she felt at a disadvantage sometimes in discussions with her publishers but she had decided if she felt really strongly about something she was going to stick to her guns. It was good that Marcy liked the title but even if she hadn't, Maggie wouldn't have changed it. 'I just want to make some general comments first and then get you organized for the rewriting.' Marcy sat back in her chair, her bright intelligent blue eyes staring at Maggie reflectively. 'Just as an aside, Maggie, I suggest, indeed I believe it vital that you get yourself a word processor. Apart from the fact that it's very expensive having work typed, it's much easier to edit on screen and we do all our work on disk now. The typewritten manuscript is obsolete in this tech-nological age, I'm afraid. So definitely for your next novel you should invest in a word processor.'

'I wouldn't have a clue how to use one,' Maggie said in dismay.

'Of course you would, you're an intelligent woman; there's nothing to it,' Marcy said bracingly and Maggie felt like a ten-year-old. 'Now at all times while we're editing, remember that I am on your side and my criticisms are for your own good and the good of your novel. I know first-time authors often find it difficult to listen to someone pointing out errors and flaws but if you keep a positive attitude you will learn a lot, Maggie, and life will be much simpler when you are writing your next novel.' Marcy was sweetly patient. As she gave her discovery a summary of the improvements necessary in her novel, Maggie tried not to cringe inwardly. Maybe she shouldn't have bothered submitting her novel for publication. Maybe it just wasn't up to scratch if all these adjustments had to be made.

'We need more verisimilitude,' Marcy was saying.

Holy Divinity, thought Maggie in dismay. What on earth was verisimilitude?

'More true to life,' Marcy explained, seeing her puzzlement.

Maggie nodded as she assimilated what she later realized was to be some of the best advice she would ever receive in her writing career. This woman, with her brisk businesslike way, was good at her job, Maggie had to admit. Everything she had said was absolutely spot on, even though it had been difficult to take it on the chin. 'Thanks, Marcy,' Maggie said calmly. 'That will give me a lot to chew on. It's very helpful stuff.' Now that she had got over the shock of having her flaws pointed out, she was beginning to be enthusiastic about things again.

'Well, I think you've enough to be going on with for now if you do the work I've marked up for next week. We'll carry on from there.'

'Sure, I'll be in touch.' Maggie gathered up her notes. It was like getting her homework marked, she thought in amusement.

'When we've gone through the script we'll have

lunch. I like to bring my authors to lunch every so often. It's nice to get to know the person behind the writer,' Marcy remarked as she stood up and straightened her skirt. 'Maggie, you must excuse me now. I've to attend an in-house meeting, but keep in touch if you've any difficulties. I'm always here.' She added gently, 'I hope Shona will be well soon.' With that, she was striding out the door, a file under her arm, and Maggie knew that she was instantly forgotten. Marcy's racing brain was already dealing with the next item on her agenda.

Driving back to Temple Street, Maggie didn't know whether to laugh or cry. How she was going to manage to sit down to rewrite with Shona still in hospital, and two other children at home – and a husband who was in a huff with her. Marcy, being childless, obviously had no conception of the difficulties Maggie was having to contend with.

For the first time Maggie realized that her writing was no longer a hobby. This was business. It was like having a job again. Now that she had signed a contract she was going to have to produce the goods and within the time required. She was a working mother now, although she had always thought that was a silly term since all mothers worked. She was just going to have to cope, like millions of other women who juggled motherhood and careers. At the moment it was a thought that gave rise to some apprehension. Writing was such a solitary occupation and how could she, the mother of three small children, ever hope to get the time she needed to write. But in spite of herself she felt exhilarated. I'll manage somehow, she assured herself. As she sat waiting for the red lights at

Whitehall Garda station to change, she was already planning the decor of the apartment of her heroine, as per Marcy's instructions.

'Please, God, let Shona be feeling better when I get back,' she beseeched the Almighty. But for Caroline stepping in to take care of Michael and Mimi, she would have been in a hell of a pickle, because her next-door neighbour who was good at helping out in a fix was in Corfu for a fortnight's holiday. Maggie parked the car in the car-park where Eccles Street College had once stood. She could still see the markings of basketball and tennis-courts where the schoolyard had been. It had started to drizzle and she had to sprint the rest of the way so she wouldn't get too wet.

She was puffed when she reached the hospital. No doubt it wouldn't have knocked a feather out of superfit Marcy. In the distance she could hear the rumble of thunder. It was so heavy and muggy, maybe a good thunderstorm would clear the air. Hot and thirsty, she walked down to the canteen and bought a can of Coke and a sandwich. She held the ice-cold can against the side of her neck as she walked up the several flights of stairs to the ward. It was refreshing. She'd love a swim right now, she thought longingly. Devlin was sponging Shona down when she went in. 'Her temperature's climbed back to 103, Maggie. I'm sorry,' her friend said ruefully.

'Shit!' cursed Maggie in frustration.

'Oh and ah . . . well, Terry called in. He was going to a meeting across town. He was wondering where you were. I didn't say anything about your meeting or anything. I just said I was giving you a break for an

259

hour. He'll be back at teatime,' Devlin murmured diplomatically.

'Thanks, Dev,' Maggie said heavily, as she took the sponge from her.

'Aren't you going to tell him about the book?'

'I don't know what to do, Dev. If I tell him I was at a meeting with an editor today, he'll freak and say I'm neglecting Shona. I can't keep it a secret much longer. I've a lot of rewriting to do in a very short space of time.' She grimaced. 'Ah to hell, I suppose I'll have to tell him one way or another. Tonight is as good a time as any.'

Twenty-One

'You're not serious!' Terry gazed at his wife as they sat in the dingy hospital canteen having a cup of coffee and a sandwich. Shona was asleep and they had slipped away for a little while before Maggie went home to shower and change her clothes and put the twins to bed.

'I am,' Maggie grinned, enjoying the look of stupefaction on her husband's face.

'You're having a book published? Well, fair dues to you, Maggie, and all the time I thought you were wasting your time sitting at that typewriter. What's it about?' Terry asked.

Pleasantly surprised at his attitude, Maggie was just about to bubble enthusiastically that it was about a woman whose husband has an affair while working in Saudi, when discretion stopped her tongue. No point in antagonizing her husband by reminding him about his past. He'd never read it anyway. Terry wouldn't read a book to save his life.

'Ah, it's just about three women,' she said off-handedly.

'When will the money start rolling in?'

Maggie laughed. 'It's started already. I got a

cheque for the first instalment of my advance last Friday before I went away.'

'For how much?' Terry was flabbergasted.

'Two thousand five hundred,' Maggie said airily.

'Good God, that would pay off the loan on your car.' Terry rubbed his hands as a broad grin creased his handsome face.

'Well yes, maybe I could pay fifteen hundred off it but I need to keep a bit. I have to do some rewriting and I was thinking that, when Shona gets out of hospital and the lads are finished summer school, I might rent out a mobile in Redcross for a month. It will be good for them and I can concentrate on my novel at night when they're in bed.'

'Why don't you stay at your Ma's and save yourself the expense of a mobile? They aren't cheap to rent at the height of the season. It seems like an awful waste of money to me, especially when your parents have the big farmhouse and loads of room,' Terry argued.

'No, Terry!' Maggie was adamant. 'I never have a bit of peace when I'm at home with the children. Ma gets into too much of a tizzy, and starts going on about the way she did things when we were small and I end up simmering with frustration and anger with a touch of inadequacy thrown in. I'm always afraid they'll break something and I spend my time telling them not to do this and to be careful of that. It's just not worth it. If I rent a mobile we'll be able to visit a couple of times and that will suit me fine.'

'OK, OK, keep your hair on,' Terry growled. 'How long more do you think Shona's going to be in here? Are they doing anything with her at all? I think I'll get on to them. There's no improvement.'

'They're doing their best, Terry. The professor told me if there's no improvement by tomorrow he's going to put her on Erythromycin. It's a superstrong antibiotic; the only thing about it is that it sometimes makes children sick.'

'That's not much use then, is it?'

'If it takes her temperature down and clears the chest infection it will be worth it.'

Maggie placed the dirty cups and plates on her tray and stood up. 'I'm off. I'll see you later. Caroline cooked a lasagne so you can bake a potato in the microwave and have that with it when you get home.'

'I suppose I'll have to fend for myself, when you're enjoying yourself on your month's holiday,' he moaned.

'I won't be on holidays, Terry,' Maggie retorted. 'I'll be working. I'll be looking after three children, cooking for them, washing their clothes, entertaining them. On top of that I'll be trying to concentrate on my rewrites. If you'd like to swop places with me and go down to the mobile for a month and let me stay at home in peace and quiet to get my work done, you're more than welcome.'

"Aw, come off it, Mags,' Terry scoffed. 'You're not going to stand there and tell me that sitting at a typewriter writing whatever comes into your head is hard work?'

It's as hard as sitting at a calculator working out a tax return, she thought, and was sorely tempted to tell him so, but she restrained herself. There was no point in getting upset by her husband's attitude. She remembered something she had heard at one of the sessions in the writers' group of which she was a member. A writer who had achieved great success had told them how annoyed he had been when one day after he had become a full-time writer, a close friend said, 'Tell me what's it like not to have to work any more?' The writer had been so angry he had snapped, 'What are you asking me for? I don't know. I work bloody hard.' Only a writer could understand how hard it is, he had told the class. 'So,' he said, 'don't let people's attitudes upset you. Just keep writing.'

In a million years Terry would never understand. Adam would, but not her husband. Nevertheless, even if he didn't understand, Terry should be much more supportive of her. It was this lack of support that riled Maggie so much. It didn't matter whether her interest was writing or painting, he should be behind her every step of the way — just as once she would have been his greatest champion. No matter how much she kidded herself, Maggie knew that ever since his affair with Ria Kirby their marriage was a continuing disappointment to her. She found herself constantly comparing their relationship with that of other couples, and it didn't compare well with a lot of them. Even Caroline and Richard were more content than she was.

'You're a gas woman, Maggie.' Her husband was smiling and Maggie realized sadly that Terry didn't even realize he had hurt her feelings.

She kept her tone light. 'I must be to have married you!'

'Oh, you didn't do badly for yourself,' Terry said, grinning. He leaned over and gave her a kiss and a pat on the behind. 'God, you've a great ass, Maggie. I wish this was all over. I'm as horny as hell and I miss you in bed at night.'

'Stop it, Terry! People are looking at us!' Maggie extricated herself from his embrace.

'Let 'em look! A man can kiss his wife, can't he, especially when she's as good-looking as you!' Terry was unabashed.

In spite of herself Maggie had to laugh. In mind and heart her husband was still sixteen years old.

'I'm going. I'll collect the car from the garage. Caroline said she'd wait until you got home, so I can come back sooner. Maybe we could nip off somewhere for a court and a bit of nookey,' Terry whispered hopefully. 'It's been ages, Maggie.'

'Give over,' she said indignantly. 'It was last Friday morning before I went away.'

'That's ages,' he exclaimed.

'Ever ready! That's you.' Maggie grabbed the tray and followed the notice that directed them to the kitchen where people were requested to help by leaving out their dirty crockery to be washed – the staff shortages were that bad.

'I'd want to be to make the most of the rare occasion when you're in the mood,' Terry muttered.

'That's not fair, Terry Ryan,' Maggie exploded. 'Christ Almighty, as if I haven't enough on my plate at the moment! You're totally fucking insensitive.'

'Sure, I'm as knackered as you are. I'm looking after the kids and getting them up and dressed in the morning, as well as doing my stint in here. Besides which I've got a day's work to do. It's no joy-ride for me either, Maggie.'

'I didn't say it was,' Maggie argued hotly.

'Well then, don't start acting the martyr,' Terry snarled. 'All I wanted was a bit of love-making and you carry on as if I'd asked you to do the pilgrimage at Lough Derg or something. Typical, making a big deal out of everything.'

'Listen, buster, one day I *will* make a big deal about something and then you'll know about it.' Maggie tramped up the stairs in fury and swept out the front door, leaving her spouse equally angry as he headed up to St Camillus. He was just in time for Shona to puke all over him as he lifted her in his arms to kiss her.

'Are you all right there now, Mr Ryan?' a young blonde nurse asked after she had helped him wipe off his trousers.

Terry smiled at her. She was a very pretty young girl and it was nice to have a woman smile at him after the way Maggie had jumped down his throat a while ago. 'Thank you, Nurse . . .' He peered at her badge. 'Thank you, Dolores, you're very kind.' He gave his most charming smile. He could see that she liked him. It made him feel good about himself. A man needed to feel good about himself and it certainly didn't help when his wife made it quite clear that making love to her husband was the last thing in the world she was interested in. He was thinking of her as much as himself. A nice kiss and a cuddle would have relaxed her and taken her mind off things. Didn't she appreciate all he was doing in the crisis? And the way she snapped his nose off when he suggested that writing wasn't work! She could argue until she was blue in the face; sitting at a typewriter making things up out of her head was a doddle compared to working out complicated figures and tax-relief scams. And now she was talking about going away for a month of leisure and leaving him to his own devices. Honest to God, talk about being neglected! Was it any wonder men had affairs? That nurse definitely fancied him. He knew by the way she was smiling in at him. Oh well, no harm in a little flirtation to keep his confidence up. If Maggie didn't want him, there were plenty of women who did.

'Maggie, you look wrecked! Go up and have a shower,' Caroline said solicitously, shooing her up the stairs. 'I'll have your dinner on the table in ten minutes. The twins are all ready for bed.'

Her kindness almost made Maggie cry. After her row with Terry she was fit for nothing. Why couldn't he see she was under pressure, she fumed, as she stood under the steaming jets of water, trying to erase the ache of tension that knotted her neck and shoulder muscles. They were always rowing lately and she admitted it was as much her fault as his. Was she being super-sensitive? Was she deliberately concentrating on his faults rather than his good qualities? And he *had* good qualities, she admitted to herself. He was a great father and thought the world of his kids. He wasn't mean with money. He would do anybody a good turn. He had always been very kind to Devlin and Caroline in their hours of need. He was good to his mother. He worked all the hours God gave him to make a success of his financial consultancy. Why couldn't he just give her the support she craved? 'Because he's a selfish insensitive shit,'

Maggie muttered, as she soaped herself all over, still fuming at his infuriating remarks.

'Dinner in five minutes,' Caroline called up the stairs.

'OK,' Maggie yelled. Caroline was such a pet and the kids loved her. When this was all over she was going to treat her friend to a really nice lunch in a good restaurant. She looked a bit tired and pale today. Richard had better be behaving himself, she thought grimly.

'You OK, Caroline? You look a bit off,' she enquired of the younger woman five minutes later as she sat in a robe of soft pink towelling, ready to eat the tasty lasagne and side salad Caroline had served up. 'The kids aren't playing up or anything?'

'No, no, they're great, Maggie. I'm fine,' Caroline assured her, pulling up a chair and pouring herself a cup of tea. 'How's Shona?'

Between mouthfuls of the creamy feast, Maggie told her friend the latest about her daughter. 'I wish the news was better,' she sighed. 'With luck the Erythromycin will work. It's heart-breaking looking at her. I know she's hungry; she was dying for the Petit Filou I got for her but after the first spoonful she started to cry. Her mouth is in bits with the blisters and she can't eat anything.' Suddenly, Maggie's throat constricted as she thought of her little daughter unable to eat even a yoghurt while she was stuffing herself with lasagne. She started to cry and great big tears plopped on to her dinner plate.

'Ah Maggie! Ah Maggie!' Caroline leaned over and put her arm around her.

'Oh Caroline, it's awful, it's awful, and when they

give her the oral medicine by syringe and I have to hold her down it breaks my heart. The poor little mite! I feel so useless; I feel I'm letting her down,' Maggie sobbed bitterly. 'And then Terry and I had a row, a terrible row. Caroline, I know this is an awful thing to say but I don't think I love him any more. Things haven't been good between us for ages. He thinks everything is OK after his affair but it's not. It's not OK for me, I've tried to put it behind me and I can't. I bet if Ria Kirby was writing a book he'd be kneeling holding her goddamned typewriter,' she wept bitterly.

'Maggie, Maggie, you're just overwrought,' broke in Caroline. 'You're tired and worried sick over Shona, and things seem to be much worse than they are. Honestly, when she's well again they will get into perspective. You're at a low ebb now and believe me, I know from experience that everything always looks much blacker when you're at rock bottom.' Caroline was glad she hadn't confided her own problems in Maggie, although she had been sorely tempted to.

'It's ironic, isn't it? I should be on cloud nine, getting my novel published and all, and I've never been so unhappy.' Maggie wiped her reddened eyes.

'It *will* be a happy time. I'm sure that super-antibiotic will fix Shona,' Caroline said kindly. 'You shouldn't take any notice of Terry. Men react differently to women when they're under stress. He didn't mean anything he said. I know he didn't, so don't take it to heart. Look, the twins are watching The Little Mermaid. Why don't you go in and sit with them for a while? I'll clear up here.'

'You're very good to me, Caroline.' Maggie hugged her friend.

'One good turn . . .' said Caroline, smiling.

Michael and Mimi were sitting round-eyed looking at Ursula the Sea Witch, mixing her magic potions as she huskily boomed, 'Poor unfortunate souls, in pain, in need.' I know the feeling, thought Maggie wryly as she plonked herself down on the sofa and allowed herself to be kissed and cuddled. 'This part's real exciting, Mammy; 'Itsom an' Bitsom are being very bold,' Michael said seriously.

Maggie hid a smile. 'You mean Flotsam and Jetsam, pet?'

'Yeah and they made the Little Mermaid follow him to Ursula's cave . . .'

'But Flounder an' Sebastian are tryin' to save her,' Mimi chimed in. 'Mammy, do you think I look a bit like the Likkle Mermaid?' her daughter enquired, flicking back her auburn hair and gazing at her amused mother with huge blue eyes.

'Oh, I think you're even more beautiful than the Little Mermaid.' Maggie hugged her and reflected ruefully that she had inherited some of her father's vanity. 'And you're even more handsome than the Prince.' She smiled down at her son, making sure not to leave him out.

'Mammy, are you staying at home tonight?' Michael asked seriously. 'I miss you.'

'Me too! I wish Shona was home.' Mimi snuggled in closer.

'She will be soon, but I have to stay with her when she's sick. Just as I'd stay with you if you were sick,' Maggie explained patiently.

270

'I do feel sick,' Mimi said sorrowfully, 'here in my tummy, so will you stay at home and mind me tonight?' Oh Lord, Maggie thought miserably, why are you doing this to me?

'How about if I stay until you are fast asleep?'

'That's not fair; you only care about Shona,' Mimi said petulantly, going into one of her dramatic huffs, her lower lip stuck out stubbornly. Maggie realized that it wouldn't surprise her one bit if Mimi ended up on the stage. Even at this age, she had a flair for dramatics.

'Don't be silly. You know I love you and Michael as much as I love Shona. Now let's watch *The Little Mermaid* and then I'll read you a story in bed,' Maggie said firmly.

'Will you read us the one about Higgledy Piggledy Hilda?' Mimi cast a sideways glance up at her mother. Maggie's heart sank. 'Higgledy Piggledy Hilda' was a very long story and normally Maggie did not read it at bed time, keeping it for a rainy Saturday afternoon, when all other forms of childish entertainment had been exhausted. Mimi was perfectly well aware of this, but little manipulator that she was, she knew she had played her trump card by her accusation of not caring. If Maggie refused to read 'Higgledy Piggledy Hilda' that would also constitute a not-caring offence and Mimi would go into a mega-huff. Mother nil, daughter one. Game, set and match to Mimi.

Maggie could not help but be amused at how her daughter had, as many times previously, completely outmanoeuvred her. Mimi was an extremely strong-willed little girl and Maggie knew that rearing her was not going to be an easy task. Her daughter had a mind of her own and was frequently openly defiant of her mother. Because she was the apple of her father's eye, most of the chastising was left to Maggie, which she felt was totally unfair, but she also knew that Mimi needed a firm hand if she wasn't to grow up into a wild undisciplined brat. She was the dominant twin, always ordering her brother around and making the decisions, and Michael, who was generally a placid, cheerful little boy, was perfectly happy to be bossed around by his sister. It was something Maggie kept a watchful eye on. She didn't want her son to become a submissive child and she was always trying to get him to be a little more assertive and a little less dependent on his twin. Rearing children was fraught with such difficulties, she thought. Maybe she was just a worrier but she wanted to raise her children to be well-rounded individuals with a sense of their own worth.

Perhaps if her mother and father hadn't made her feel she was inferior to her brothers, she might not now be in such difficulties in her relationship with her husband. If she had grown up to have more confidence in herself, to be more assertive, she wouldn't have these ridiculous feelings of guilt at taking a weekend break with her friends or about her writing career. Well, at least Mimi would never feel inferior to anyone; that was something. Maggie turned to her son. 'What would you like me to read, Michael? I think it's your turn to choose the story tonight,' she said, hoping that he might ask for his favourite, 'Ivor the Engine'.

'He'd like "Higgledy Piggledy Hilda" too, wouldn't you, Michael?' Mimi butted in.

'Now Mimi, let Michael make up his own mind,' Maggie instructed.

Michael shot his twin a look of triumph. 'I think I'd like . . . mmmm . . . maybe "Ivor the Engine" . . .' Maggie gave a smug smile. Thank you, my son, she thought fondly. 'Or maybe I'd like "Postman Pat".' He looked up at Maggie, his wide hazel eyes with their long sweep of black lashes gazing trustingly at her. 'Achurly, Mammy, I'd really like, really really, *really* like "Pinocchio" if you don't mind,' he added politely. Oh crikey! thought Maggie in dismay. 'Pinocchio' was even longer than 'Higgledy Piggledy Hilda'.

'Oh yes, "Pinocchio".' Mimi brightened up. 'Please, Mammy, please,' she wheedled.

'Come on, the pair of you then,' Maggie said, smiling. You just couldn't win.

By the time she had read them their story, given them their last drink of water, got herself dressed and dried her hair, it was almost eight-thirty. Terry would probably think she was delaying on purpose after their row but there was nothing she could do about it. With a heavy heart she bade goodbye to Caroline. She really was not looking forward to going into that hospital and spending another night there. She was certainly not looking forward to another hostile encounter with her husband. Was this how a marriage broke up? Did every couple go through stormy patches like these? Looking back she couldn't remember her parents ever arguing that much but they were different times. Her mother's expectations in no way compared with Maggie's. Nelsie had been quite prepared to rear her children and help her husband on

273

the farm. Having a career other than that of mother and wife was something that had never crossed her mother's mind. Or that of Terry's mother either.

But these were different times. Maggie was lucky that having a career was a choice rather than a necessity. She knew many friends and ex-colleagues who had to work outside the home to pay the bills, whether they liked it or not. Mind you, Terry hadn't turned up his nose at the prospect of a bit of extra cash. As long as her writing didn't put him out in any way, he didn't care, but if she started expecting him to take over household chores and look after the kids every so often, that was a different matter. It was the unfairness of his attitude that annoyed Maggie so much, but nothing would make him change his mind. She knew her husband of old and she wasn't sure if she was going to be able to spend the rest of her life living with his selfishness. The shrill tone of the phone brought her back to earth and she answered it, half-expecting it to be Terry. The voice that greeted her at the other end of the phone made Maggie's heart skip a beat and involuntarily her hands tightened on the receiver as upstairs she could hear Caroline trying to mediate in an argument about ownership of a colouring book.

Twenty-Two

'Can you talk?' Adam asked, and Maggie longed to be able to say yes, longed with all her heart to tell him about *City Woman*. But it was too awkward, what with the children misbehaving, Caroline upstairs and the realization that she was late for the hospital.

'Not really. When did you get home?' She tried to keep her voice steady.

'Ten minutes ago,' Adam laughed down the phone and her spirits rose effervescently. 'I missed you, Maggie,' he said softly.

'Me too.' She couldn't keep the smile off her face.

'When can I see you?' He sounded so eager that Maggie was touched.

'Can I call you? Is it still the same phone number?' She tried to keep her voice calm and even.

'Yes, Maggie, everything's the same,' Adam assured her, and she knew it wasn't just his phone number he was referring to. 'I'll be at home all day tomorrow. I've taken a few days' leave; maybe you could meet me in the afternoon or something.'

'I don't think so. My little girl is in hospital,' Maggie said regretfully. 'I'm just heading off there at the moment. I'll call you when I can.'

'I'm sorry to hear that, Maggie. I shouldn't have

phoned. I was just dying to hear your voice and hear how things were going. If you get a chance and you feel like it, get in touch.'

'Oh I will, I will!' Maggie assured him hastily. 'I've some news for you.'

'What kind of news? Are you getting a foreign divorce or something?' She could sense that he was smiling down the other end of the phone.

'I'll tell you when I see you. I'll be in touch. OK?'

'Soon?'

'Soon,' she promised. 'Bye and thanks for calling.'

Maggie hung up and took a deep breath. Her heart was racing and her palms were sweating and she couldn't think straight. 'See you, Caroline,' she called and raced out the front door. Terry would be going bananas. She was in such a tizzy she dropped her keys, and then, when she finally turned on the ignition, forgot that the car was still in gear. It jerked forward and cut out with a shudder. Take a grip on yourself, you daft woman, she admonished herself as she started up again. And she *was* being daft, wasn't she? Adam Dunne was a gorgeous, sensitive, good-humoured six-footer. Adam Dunne was also single, almost a decade younger than her, and what he saw in her she could not imagine. Maggie, you're a married woman with three children. You've got responsibilities and commitments and you're treading very dangerous waters, she argued with herself as she stopped at traffic lights in the village.

She saw a man in the car opposite her giving her a rather strange look. Well, *you'd* talk to yourself if you were considering having an affair with a man ten years younger than you, she thought, and was quite relieved when the lights turned green and she sped off. She knew her face was the colour of a tomato. Imagine! Ringing her only ten minutes after he got home. He must have been thinking of her all the time he was away. Wait until he heard about *City Woman*. He'd be delighted for her. She was dying to see him again, dying to see that lovely way his mouth curved into a smile and his hazel eyes crinkled up at the side. That time he had kissed her before he had gone over to England to work he had made her feel like a young girl again. He had been so gentle and loving and passionate. Just thinking about it made her feel sexy. What would it be like when she met him again? Would they stare into each other's eyes? Would he take her in his arms and kiss her passionately, hungrily — wanting her there and then? No, that would be more Terry's style. Adam would seduce her, kissing every inch of her, sliding her clothes off her eager body, kissing her with long slow hot kisses.

Her mouth parted, her eyes glazed and her hands tightened on the steering wheel. She would take his shirt off, running her fingers over every inch of his tanned muscled torso, and then she would follow the line of hair that snaked down from his chest to his navel. Slowly, teasingly she would unbuckle his belt and unzip his jeans and . . . The driver behind beeped impatiently and Maggie came to with a start to realize that the lane of traffic had moved on and she had not moved with it. He beeped again. 'Oh keep your hair on, buster,' she muttered, sorry to have been jerked out of her gorgeous fantasy. She'd better keep her mind on her driving or she might end up as a patient in hospital and not a visitor. It was amazing, though, she reflected, as she drove on towards Phibsborough, she hadn't felt like sex for ages. Even when she and Terry *had* made love, it had done nothing for her lately. But just knowing Adam was home, even listening to his voice made her feel as randy as hell. It was true: sex really was all in the head. Right now she was sorely tempted to turn left off the North Circular Road, and drive up to Adam's house in Drumcondra and . . . and jump on him.

'Oooh,' she groaned in frustration. She wouldn't say no even to Terry right at this minute. Regretfully she carried on straight through Phibsborough and turned right at Berkeley Road where she intended parking the car. She had a big lock and chain and hoped that would prevent any attempt to steal it. The walk down to Temple Street was never-ending in the deepening dusk and the clip-clopping of her heels seemed to say Adam, Adam, Adam, Adam! Stop it, right now! she ordered crossly. Grow up! You're not a teenager; you are a married woman. Married. Married. Married. You made vows. You can't break them just because your hormones are jumping around.

That's what Terry and Ria did, she reflected; you're not going to sink to their level. But I want to, she thought longingly. I don't care any more. Adam appreciates me: he understands what my writing means to me. He's tender, loving, sensitive and kind. So was Terry when you met him first, her conscience argued. Maybe if you were married to Adam you'd be going through exactly what you are going through with Terry. No you wouldn't be; I know you wouldn't be: Adam's totally different to Terry. He's not that different, the voice would not be silenced. He knows you're married and he's pursuing you. Where are his ethics? Men are all the same, you know, especially where sex is concerned. Oh shut up! She gave a mental growl, and a priest who was passing the Mater Private and about to salute her with a good evening, deemed it prudent to step smartly out of her way and keep his salutation to himself, when he saw the fierce expression on her face.

Her high had evaporated as she struggled with her over-active conscience. Why could she just not go off and have an affair and enjoy it without complicating things? Thousands of people, millions of people had affairs every minute of the day. Look at Ria Kirby: it hadn't cost her a thought to get involved with Terry, right under his wife's nose. Ria had flirted brazenly with Terry in front of her, when they had been living in Saudi. Look at Marcy Elliot. Sandra Nolan had more or less insinuated that Marcy and Jeremy were having a rip-roaring affair, despite the fact that Marcy was living with someone and Jeremy was married. Of course, Jeremy's wife, Claudette, was having a fling with Finian MacMahon, who was twenty years her junior and Sandra's PA to boot! Claudette, a tall, slim, ash-blonde sophisticate, was showing all the signs of satisfaction with the affair. It was definitely working for her, much to Sandra's chagrin. She didn't like the idea of her PA sleeping his way to the top and possibly into her job.

The internal intrigues and politics of Enterprise Publishing were enough to write a novel about, Maggie thought to herself as she ran grinning up the steps into Temple Street Hospital. But all these people were having affairs, doing themselves the world of good and obviously not suffering from any guilts or complexes about it. Couldn't she just do the same? Couldn't she just have a nice loving affair with Adam? And then they could go their separate ways and she could stay married to Terry and rear her children and write her novels.

Don't be such an idiot, she chided herself as she queued up to buy a can of Coke. What happens if you fall in love with Adam and he falls in love with you? How are you going to cope with that? What happens if Terry finds out? You know then he'll feel he'll have carte blanche to have an affair every time he fancies someone. What about the children? How would it affect them? Children sense things. It could undermine their security. What if anyone saw you with Adam? She sighed. What if? What if? Who? How? Why? Where? You can keep on like this until you're blue in the face!

Maggie handed the girl at the cash desk a fiver and took her change. She walked slowly up the first flight of stairs towards ICU, still in turmoil. She continued silently to harangue herself: the question is which will you regret more: having an affair and all it entails or not having one and regretting it for the rest of your life? Only *you* can make the choice; so make it one way or another.

Twenty-Three

Three weeks later, Maggie and her children were ensconced in a mobile home in Wicklow. The Erythromycin had proved almost miraculous and Shona was out of hospital within forty-eight hours of going on it. Maggie had not phoned Adam. She had lost her nerve. When she went into the ward that night, Terry had been waiting for her with a big bunch of flowers, a box of chocolates, a bottle of champagne, and a sheepish grin. 'Sorry, Mags! I didn't mean to upset you. Here.' He thrust the flowers and champagne at her. 'Congratulations on your book!' She felt such a heel and when he had put his arms around her and given her a hug she had hugged him back warmly. From that moment, she had tried to put Adam out of her head — as a matter of self-preservation. Any sneaky thought of him was swiftly banished because she could not allow herself to think about him or fantasize about him — that would be fatal. Nevertheless there were times her heart ached and she had to resist a powerful urge to phone him, if only to let him know about *City Woman*.

In any case, she had her hands full. As soon as Shona's temperature returned to normal the specialist had told Maggie to take her home. She had been a bit taken aback because the child was still very sick but the professor assured her she was much better off in her home and far less prone to infection than in the hothouse environment of the hospital. They'd had a few sleepless nights with her and it was a while before her wheeze lessened. A fortnight after her discharge, she had a check-up and X-ray and it was found that the pneumonia was gone. The doctor had given Maggie the all-clear to go off to Wicklow.

Maggie looked out the window of the mobile at her three offspring, all in shorts and T-shirts. She heard Shona chuckling at Michael doing handstands to entertain her and marvelled again at the resilience of children. Apart from a pallor that a few days in the sun and fresh air would clear, Shona was almost herself again, and for that Maggie was deeply grateful. This was their second day here and Maggie was not too enamoured of the site. She had wanted to rent a mobile in Digby Johnson's in Redcross, but he had no vacancies. She was not really surprised as it was a superb site, very clean and well kept. It even had a swimming pool.

Here the grounds weren't very well kept. The grass between many of the mobiles was uncut, the shower rooms and laundry were so dirty that Maggie decided to hand-wash her clothes in her own mobile. At least it had hot and cold running water and a shower. She lasted three days on the site. Barking dogs, noisy kids out until all hours at night and a gang in the mobile next to her who used to come in singing every night from the pub proved too much for her. In desperation, she drove around every other mobile-home site in the area. She tried Johnson's again and Digby promised that if he had a cancellation he would let her know. In the meantime she took a mobile in a site along the coast which would cost an arm and a leg but was worth it until she could go to the one in Redcross. At least when she was settled into the new luxury mobile she was able to sit down and start working on her novel.

Marcy had been quite displeased at their second meeting to discover that Maggie had got little or nothing done. However, they had finished editing the rest of the manuscript so now she was able to settle down to some serious work. It was such a beautiful day that she decided to bring her typewriter out on the veranda in front of the mobile. The children were playing happily with a few new friends so Maggie slipped into her bikini, got her notes and very soon was immersed in her characters.

She worked away happily until she came to the chapter introducing Ira Kingston, the bitch who stole her heroine's husband. Marcy had insisted that Maggie make her a more rounded figure. I can do that all right, Maggie had thought viciously, visualizing Ria Kirby, as she always did when she thought about the character. Ria was a fat tarty little slut, as was Ira. There'd be no problem rounding her off: just add another couple of inches to her waistline. 'She'd the look of one who'd seen too many ceilings,' Maggie typed; then reflected on it, and crossed it out. 'She had been an early bloomer but she was fading fast.' Maggie smiled to herself; that was much better.

She worked diligently, pausing only occasionally to look up and see if the children were all right or to feast her eyes on the sparkling blue sea that she could see just across the sand dunes. Later on she'd bring the children to the beach. They'd love that. She might even go for a swim herself. Tomorrow was Friday; she'd have to go shopping. Terry was coming down for the weekend so she might have more time to herself to get really going on the revisions. She wondered what Adam was doing. She cupped her chin in her hands and stared into space. She should have phoned him, she thought sadly. She knew he would be very hurt that she had not called him back. But it was a risk she dared not take. What was the point in getting involved with him if they weren't going to have an affair? Maggie was enough of a realist to know that they could never be just friends. The attraction was too strong between them. They would only end up putting themselves through torment and undoubtedly at some stage would end up in each other's arms, and that would be her undoing. Let sleeping dogs lie, she decided, with a vague ache somewhere under her ribcage. Bending her head to her work again, she carried on with her task of making Ira Kingston a more rounded character.

'Hey! It's a nice pad, isn't it?' Terry poked his head into the double bedroom which had built-in wardrobes, bedside lockers and wall lamps. 'Look at the kitchen. Fitted, all mod cons. I think we should sell up and buy one of these to live in. I could always commute.' He smiled at his wife as he enveloped her in a bear-hug. 'You look good, Mags. The tan's coming up a treat.'

'Daddy, Daddy, look look what I can do!' Michael

was dancing up and down on the lawn with excitement, thrilled that his daddy was here.

'I'm looking, I'm looking,' Terry assured his son as he scooped Shona up in one arm and Mimi up in the other and kissed them both. Michael did a handstand that he'd been practising for hours, in preparation for this moment. 'Brilliant! You're going to be an Olympic champion,' he promised his little boy, who was very chuffed. Maggie smiled. Whatever the ups and downs of their relationship, Terry really was good with the kids and they adored him.

'What's for dinner? I'm starving! The traffic down was brutal.'

'I did pork and pineapple with cashew nuts and I've a side salad.' Maggie sprinkled a few sesame seeds into the salad.

'Oh good. Let me at it.' Terry took off his jacket, loosened his tie and sat down at the table. 'I've a couple of bottles of wine in the car and goodies for the kids. Mimi, run out and get me a bottle of wine out of the box in the back – and bring in those pink Snacks.' Shona clambered up on his knee. 'And how are you, Miss Mathilda?'

'*Not* Tilda,' Shona said indignantly, sticking out her tongue as far as it would go.

'Oh, that's naughty. Nice little girls don't stick out their tongues; only bold bad girls.'

'Amn't,' said Shona, as she pinched her daddy's cheeks.

'This is the latest caper,' Maggie said to her husband as she served up dinner. 'Ask her how's her chest and see the carry-on.'

'How's your chest, Shona?'

The little girl panted and the faint wheeze that she still had became more pronounced.

'Could you be up to her, the little minx. She's as cute as bedamned: she arrived in the other day and asked me to do her physio,' Maggie said proudly, as she mashed up a dinner for her.

'She's her daddy's little girl,' said Terry, beaming as Maggie set his dinner before him and called the twins.

Afterwards, when the washing-up was done, and they'd had their coffee, Maggie suggested a walk on the beach. It was a lovely warm evening and Terry was more than agreeable. 'I missed you,' he said as they walked along the strand, with the children galloping ahead in front of them.

'Me too,' she murmured, almost automatically. Had she missed him, she asked herself. Not really! She had been quite happy being by herself with the children, doing as she pleased, eating as it suited her. It was nice having a whole double bed to herself. It was nice being able to sit down at night after the children were in bed and write away to her heart's content and not feel guilty about it. It was nice, then, just to sit and watch whatever she wanted on the TV without listening to moans and groans if an American soap or mini-series came on. It was *wonderful* not to have to listen to or watch sport.

If she was perfectly honest, Maggie hadn't missed her husband one whit. But now that he was here, she was glad to see him. He had enjoyed his dinner and been appreciative of the effort she'd made and that was something. He'd brought magazines and choco-lates for her; he'd even asked her how she was getting on with her writing and been quite interested in the process leading up to publication. He had also brought a message from Sandra Nolan asking her to phone her urgently. The sales and marketing director had given Terry her home number. He put his arm around her shoulder and she smiled at him. Yes, she was glad he was here for the weekend. It was good for the children and it was nice to have some adult companionship for a couple of days. But it was just as nice to know that he was going home on Monday morning and that she'd have a week to herself again.

'We're having a barbie. You'll come and join us, won't you?' It was Cathy Roche, from two mobiles up, who called as Maggie and Terry were strolling after their walk on the beach along the winding flower-tubbed path that led to their own place. Maggie's spirits lifted. She was feeling so much better and she liked Cathy and her children. A barbie was just the thing to finish off a perfect summer's day. 'What do you think, Terry? Are you on?'

'Great stuff,' said her husband, beaming. 'I'll nip into Wicklow and buy a few more bottles of wine and a couple of six-packs.'

'That would be lovely, Cathy. I'll just get the gang to bed,' said Maggie with a smile.

'Easier said than done,' groaned Cathy, who had three children just a little older than Maggie's trio, 'especially when they know there's a barbie in the offing, but I'm doing one for them tomorrow so you can tell your lot if they behave themselves tonight they can come.'

'Excellent psychology,' said Maggie.

'Oh, a bit of bribery works wonders. I learned that the hard way, believe me,' laughed the other woman.

'But I want to come too,' Mimi whinged. 'It's not fair! We never have any fun. You and Daddy have all the fun.' It was twenty minutes later and she was sharing a bath with her sister.

''S not sair, Mammy.' Shona's big eyes reproached her mother as she added her tuppenceworth in support of her sister.

'Ten o'clock is too late for you to be out and besides it's for adults only. Cathy is being very kind and doing a barbecue for you tomorrow so I don't want to hear another word,' Maggie said firmly as she washed the sand from between Shona's toes.

'Tomorrow's no good,' sulked Mimi, her bottom lip thrust out stubbornly. Maggie sighed. She knew the signs. Mimi was going to start her shenanigans and Shona, who idolized her older sister and imitated everything she did, wouldn't be slow to follow suit.

'Don't be silly now, Mimi. You had a lovely day: you played all day; I took you to the beach and we went swimming and you had an ice-cream for a treat and then we had fun with Daddy tonight, and tomorrow you're going to a barbecue with your new friends. Think of the poor little boys and girls who aren't as lucky as you are,' Maggie retorted and, with a little shock of dismay, realized that she sounded exactly like her mother. She had always sworn she would not make her kids feel guilty about what they had and here she was doing precisely that.

'Don't care about them. I want to go tonight. I don't want to go to bed.'

'Don't *want* to go to bed,' echoed Shona.

'You're going to bed and that's the end of it.' Maggie had had enough. She whipped her younger daughter out of the bath, wrapped her in a soft bath towel and began to dry her.

'Tickle my toes,' Shona commanded, and Maggie laughed as she hugged the wriggling little body tighter to her. It was so good to see her precious child herself again and when she tickled her daughter's tiny toes she relished her great chuckles of laugher.

As she powdered the baby's bottom and put on her nappy, Maggie cast a surreptitious eye at her elder daughter. Mimi was pouring water out of a bath bucket over her toes, with a surly expression. Being a twin wasn't that easy, Maggie mused, as she pulled on Shona's Little Mermaid pyjamas. Because there were two children, they both missed out on the individual attention that is traditionally lavished on the first-born. Then with Shona coming so soon after the birth of the twins, it was no wonder that her eldest daughter got a bit stroppy sometimes. Terry had taken Michael into Wicklow with him as a treat. Maybe she'd take Mimi into Arklow tomorrow morning and go to Lally Stafford's bookshop and buy her a book. Mimi loved books and Maggie could see that she was going to be a good reader when she was older. They'd have coffee as well, and that would make her daughter feel all grown-up.

'Go and tidy up your toys, Shona,' Maggie instructed her toddler as she prepared to dry Mimi. She didn't want Shona to hear of the proposed visit to Arklow. 'Time to get out, Mimi.'

'Don't want to,' sulked the little girl.

'Come on! I have a treat for you tomorrow, just for you and me,' Maggie said coaxingly as she lifted her out and wrapped her up in a fresh towel.

'Not for Michael and Shona?' Mimi brightened immediately at the idea of a treat for her alone.

'Just you and me,' Maggie assured her. 'We'll go in to Arklow and buy a book for you and go and have a cup of coffee. Won't that be nice?'

'Can I have a Slush Puppy as well?' Mimi pressed her advantage.

'Yes, if you're good.' Maggie despised herself for her craven submission to blackmail. Where were all her good intentions of being firm in the face of tantrums! She'd be spineless just for this weekend. From next Monday on she'd stand no more nonsense. She dried carefully under Mimi's arms and gave her a cuddle. She was looking forward to the barbecue. It was nice when something unexpected like this happened. Cathy had been friendly since Maggie had arrived on the site and the children got on well together. The fact that Cathy's mobile was only two down from her own meant that Maggie and Terry could check on the children every so often and that they wouldn't need a babysitter.

An hour and a half later she stood humming under the shower. She was really pleased with the way her tan was coming along. Of course she had got a good basis that weekend away with Devlin and Caroline and the few pounds she had lost when Shona was in hospital really made a difference. She must try and keep her weight down, she reflected, as she shampooed her hair. She felt she'd need to look her best when her novel was launched. If she could stay as she was now she'd be doing fine. She'd call Sandra from Árklow tomorrow and see what she wanted her for. Maggie was smiling as she stepped out of the shower and dried herself. It was great to be writing again and whereas when she had been at home and under pressure the revisions had seemed like a daunting task, down here in the fresh air where she was able to plan her days as she pleased they were much less onerous. The children were always within sight and she was actually enjoying the work. If she got through as much next week as she had this week, she'd have most of it done. She just hoped that Marcy would be pleased. The next afternoon, she was going to take herself and her typewriter off somewhere quiet and really get a few hours' uninterrupted work done.

'Hurry on, Mágs.' Terry looked round the door. 'Hmmm,' he murmured appreciatively as he saw her standing naked drying her hair. 'You know tans always turn me on.' He reached out and stroked a finger lightly between her breasts and down her navel to the silky gold pubic hair where droplets of water from her shower still glistened.

'I want to do a wee-wee, Mammy.' Mimi marched through the door and giggled, 'Oooh, Mammy's in her nudies.'

'You should be asleep, miss,' growled Terry. 'Michael and Shona are.'

'I'm drawing a very portant picture, Daddy, achurly,' Mimi informed her father with great dignity as she pulled down her pyjama bottoms and perched on the loo. Maggie hid a grin as she wrapped the towel around her and headed into the bedroom to get dressed. Children were the most effective

291

contraceptives and for reasons she did not care to examine too closely she was glad of her eldest daughter's interruption of the moment in the bathroom.

'Be good now and don't get out of bed. Daddy and I will be just across on Cathy's veranda so we'll be able to see through the window,' Maggie whispered to Mimi a short while later as she sat in her bed, colouring a picture neatly. In the bed across from her, Michael slept soundly, his brown cheek resting on one hand, the thumb of the other stuck securely in his mouth. Maggie's heart melted with love and she bent down and tenderly pulled his light summer quilt up around him before brushing her lips lightly against his downy cheek.

'You look beautiful, Mammy. Can I have some of your lipstick?' Mimi whispered back, puckering her lips. Maggie smiled down at her and pressed her pink-iced lips against her daughter's.

'There, you've got some now. Be a good girl, won't you?'

'I will, Mammy,' Mimi assured her solemnly as she bent her head industriously over her colouring book.

In the next room, Shona lay on her back with her head turned to one side, her little rosebud mouth curved in a smile. Maggie pulled her quilt up over her although she knew it was a futile exercise. In five minutes she would have kicked it off. Maggie longed to lean into the cot and kiss her baby daughter but she knew it was too risky. If Shona woke up now, she could forget her evening out. Regretfully she closed the bedroom door. Since the hospital episode, Maggie seemed to have a greater need to kiss and cuddle her infant. But that was only natural. What Devlin felt when she held her, Maggie couldn't begin to imagine. If any of her children had died as Devlin's baby had, Maggie knew she could never cope with it. Throwing herself into her business had been Devlin's way, but Maggie knew her friend well enough to be certain that Devlin really hadn't come to terms with Lynn's death. She hadn't given herself time to grieve and it was affecting her, especially in terms of her relationship with Luke. Maggie shook her head ruefully. Luke was nuts about Devlin but Devlin couldn't cope with it.

'Are you ready, Maggie?' Terry said from the kitchen where he was having a beer. 'I can smell the food from here.' Maggie came over and stood behind him and inhaled. The delicious scent of outdoor cooking wafted along on the balmy evening breeze and in spite of the fact that she had had her dinner only a few hours before, Maggie's mouth began to water.

It was a beautiful summer's evening: the sun, beginning to dip in the western sky, lightly tinged lacy wisps of cloud with pink and crimson softening the sharp outlines of the gently rolling Wicklow hills. The distant fields and forests coloured the countryside like a great patchwork quilt. The sea shimmered beneath the pink and crimson sky, the gentle shushing of the white-tipped waves making a soothing lullaby. Her home county was the most beautiful place on earth and Maggie felt a great sense of renewal as she stood looking at the beauty that surrounded her.

At the mobile opposite she could see a man taking

luggage out of the boot of a dark green Mercedes. 'Nice car. They must be coming on holidays. There's been nobody in that mobile since I've been here,' she murmured to Terry, who was viewing the proceedings with interest.

'One of these days that will be me, Mags.'

'I know it will,' she smiled.

'They must be loaded, whoever they are: that mobile is the biggest one on the site. There's twenty thousand quids' worth there or more. Imagine paying that for a mobile home!'

'Imagine the palace they must be living in, then,' laughed Maggie. 'Come on before the food's all gone.'

There were four other couples already on Cathy's veranda and introductions followed. Cathy's husband, Dan, was a jovial, gregarious man and Maggie and he hit it off immediately. Terry was soon deep in conversation with the glamorous raven-haired Sylvia, who was wearing psychedelic leggings and a body-suit that left nothing to the imagination.

'See the femme fatale is turning on the charm for Terry,' said Cathy with a grin as she turned the sizzling spare ribs and chicken pieces on the grill, 'but don't mind her; she's all talk and no action. She's harmless. Between herself now and Lady Muck you'd have two great characters for your books,' Cathy laughed. Maggie had told her about her forthcoming novel.

'Who's Lady Muck?' Maggie asked, intrigued, as she helped Dan to butter some rolls for the hot-dogs.

'She owns the mobile beside the one you're in. She must be coming down next week. I see hubby unpacking all the luggage.'

'Do you not like her?' Maggie asked curiously.

'Oh I can't stand her, with her airs and graces. She really thinks she's somebody. He's—' Cathy jerked a thumb in the direction of the grey-suited man '—a stockbroker and they're absolutely loaded. We're only in the penny-halfpenny place beside them and Dan's not doing badly.' She smiled affectionately at her husband. Dan was in computers.

'Well, at least you own your own mobile,' Maggie said cheerfully as she popped a black olive into her mouth. 'We're only renting ours.'

'Oh dear, Lady Muck won't bid you the time of day. "Renteds" are the lowest of the low in the hierarchy here,' giggled Cathy, who was getting slightly tipsy.

'There seems to be a bit of let's-outdo-the-Joneses here – or is it my imagination?' observed Maggie, who had passed a few pleasant hours people-watching during the previous week. In fact she had been thinking what a marvellous novel she could write about the various little rivalries that characterized mobile land. Who had the biggest veranda? Who had the most luxurious loungers? Who had satellite TV? Who drove the biggest car? It went on and on! Maggie had been vastly entertained.

Cathy deftly pronged the sausages and laid them on a plate. 'My dear,' she said drolly, 'one doesn't keep up with the Joneses here; one keeps up with the Montclares – your neighbours. Wait until you see herself and Sylvia outdoing each other in gear. They play tennis in their whites. Mind you, Sylvia is no Steffi Graf, poor thing. She's been lucky not to decapitate herself a few times.'

Maggie guffawed. She did enjoy Cathy's sense of

humour and it was going to be very interesting to observe the interplay between Sylvia and Mrs Montclare.

'Though,' added Cathy as she arranged the marinaded ribs artistically on a plate, 'they're really only blow-ins, you know, those Montclares. They arrived on site only last year but you'd think they owned the place. Alex, his lordship over there, spent a fortune in Arnotts on garden furniture for his new veranda as we were all informed one evening, and then . . .' She threw her eyes dramatically up to heaven. 'You'll never guess what they did?'

'What?' Maggie was still laughing.

'They got a landscape gardener to "do" the veranda. My dear, where you or I might stick a few night-scented stock and aubrietia in a flower pot, she had to have her huge terracotta pots planted with all kinds of exotica. I ask you! Poor Sylvia was only going bananas. It's a pity you aren't here for the summer; you'd get a bestseller out of it.'

'Yes, it is a pity, isn't it?' Maggie dipped a portion of chicken into the barbecue sauce and ate it with relish. 'I just couldn't afford it, to be honest. It's very pricey here but it's very well run.'

'Well, keep in touch anyway, won't you, when you go?' Cathy urged. 'I can keep you up to date on the goings-on here.'

''Course I will,' Maggie assured her as Dan called out for everybody to come and help themselves before Maggie had all the barbecue sauce eaten.

'Ah, Maggie, do I have to?' Terry moaned.

'Terry, I'm ovulating; condom or nothing! Sorry.'

'The sooner you have that tube thing done the better,' Terry grumbled, as he paused.

'Yes,' sighed Maggie as she tried hard to erase the fantasy of Adam Dunne making love to her, which was what it had taken to get any way aroused at all. Maybe if she had her tubes tied, it might be different with Terry. She wouldn't be on edge about getting pregnant again and she might recover her old zest for love-making with her husband. Lately it was becoming a real chore, much to her dismay. Maggie had always enjoyed sex until she had got pregnant. Once she no longer had to worry about contraception, she'd be fine.

Clinging on to that hope, she turned her attentions to her avid spouse, discreetly hiding a yawn against his shoulder. The barbecue had been great fun. She had drunk more wine than was good for her and all she really wanted to do was to turn over and fall fast asleep.

'Aw, Mags, this is great,' Terry murmured huskily against her ear. 'You're some woman! I'm going to make love to you all night. I missed you.'

Oh Lord! Maggie gave a deep sigh, which her husband mistook for a sign of passion. He congratulated himself on being an even better lover than he had given himself credit for.

Twenty-Four

'Well! What do you think?' With a flourish, Sandra Nolan handed Maggie the mock-up of her cover. It was the following Tuesday and Maggie was in Dublin for a meeting with her sales and marketing director. Her mother was taking care of the children for the day.

'You weren't around, Maggie; so Denis, the head of our art department, had to get going on it, and I needed something fast to get a package together to start selling in. Of course it's only a rough and if you have any ideas or suggestions we'll be perfectly happy to take them into consideration.'

Maggie gazed at the intended cover with awe. Denis had read some of the manuscript and she couldn't get over how he had put the perfect face on Nicola, her heroine. He had captured her vulnerability, her strength, her determination to be her own woman. Dressed in a smart tailored suit with a slim briefcase tucked under her arm, Nicola looked as if she was about to march off the cover. Emblazoned in big gold letters was the title, *City Woman*, and beneath it, her own name, Maggie Ryan, in royal blue.

It was indescribable the way she felt. As long as she

lived, Maggie knew she would never forget this moment. A fierce burst of pride surged through her. Her novel, hers alone, something she had achieved by herself through hard slogging and determination, that not Terry nor anyone else could take away from her.

'I take it you like it, then?' asked Sandra, beaming. That day she was looking extremely smart in a Michael Gall black-and-white check tailored suit. Maggie had come prepared, having learned from their last encounter. Knowing they were going to have lunch with Carol Lewis, the woman who would be handling her publicity, and who would, no doubt, be another glamour puss, Maggie had worn a simple but extremely elegant Jacques Vert pink-and-black dress that she had picked up in Stock Exchange, the smart swop shop in Baggot Street. It had cost her a fraction of the original price. With her make-up on and her smart new short hairstyle, Maggie knew without vanity that she was looking her very best.

'You're speechless — is it with pleasure or dismay?' Sandra queried a trifle anxiously.

'Oh, I think it's gorgeous! I love it. Just look at Nicola; he's pictured her perfectly. I can't believe that the face he has put on my character is just so right. Oh, Sandra, I'm so excited!' Maggie bubbled.

'I love it when an author sees her cover for the first time,' Sandra laughed, 'especially when the response is as enthusiastic as yours.' She glanced at her watch. 'Carol shouldn't be long. Would you like another drink or will we head in to the Coffee Dock?'

'We might as well go in. I don't usually drink in the middle of the day,' Maggie confessed.

'Don't get the wrong impression; I don't either,' Sandra assured her as she led the way along the carpeted corridor of Jury's Hotel. 'But today being the day that was in it, I thought we might celebrate.'

'Oh, I don't need alcohol today – I've got this.' Maggie waved her cover exuberantly.

'I've got more good news for you.' Sandra sat down at their table and took a menu from the waitress. Maggie did likewise.

'What news?' she said excitedly; this encounter was getting more like Christmas by the minute.

'I've been talking to the wholesalers and I'm getting a really good response. They like the cover, they love the title and they like the sound of the story-line. Maggie, this could be really big. What am I saying? This *will* be really big. Easons and Hughes & Hughes are hoping to do window displays. That's fantastic for an unknown author and we're already discussing signing sessions. We're going to launch in the UK in the spring. Our UK publicist is working on a tour and Carol and I are going to have to get out there and hype *City Woman* for all it's worth. Just hurry on with your rewrites and get your next one started. They're asking about your follow-up already.'

Maggie was stunned. Looking for a second novel, window displays, hype and wholesalers, launches, publicity tours, signing sessions. This was the kind of thing she read about in interviews with Barbara Taylor Bradford and Danielle Steele and Maeve Binchy – and here it was happening to her!

'Maggie, it's only starting, believe me!' Sandra declared happily. 'But you've got to be one hundred per cent committed if you want to make it. You're going to have Marcy breathing down your neck for editorial, and you're going to have Carol and me on your back for sales and marketing. Don't think it's easy. It's not, but it's a great challenge. I love getting my teeth into something like this. I love building up a new author. It gives me such a buzz.'

Maggie envied Sandra her enthusiasm for her career and her freedom to go where she liked and do as she pleased. She was unattached and totally happy with her lifestyle. She had a townhouse in Glasnevin and was always jetting off to London on business. Then there were the trade fairs and conferences she attended all over the world. Sandra Nolan had the ideal life, Maggie decided ruefully, as she watched the other woman making a note in her bulging Filofax.

'Sandra, darling, what are you doing here?' a plummy voice demanded, and the sales and marketing director was being air-kissed on both cheeks by an extremely glamorous, very thin, heavily made-up, bejewelled woman. The scent of Opium was overpowering. With a shock, Maggie realized that it was Angela Allen, the bestselling novelist who headed Enterprise's stable. Based in the Isle of Man, she kept a mews in Dublin.

'Angela! Hi, I might ask the same of you,' Sandra smiled and then introduced Maggie.

'It's a pleasure to meet you. I've enjoyed all your books,' Maggie said politely.

'Ryan . . . Ryan. Oh yes! you're the new find, aren't you? I heard about *City Woman*. Terrific title. Best of luck.' Angela sounded enthusiastic but her eyes were cold and Maggie got the feeling that she didn't really mean it.

'We must do lunch some day, Sandra. You can take me to Dobbins the next time I'm in town. I've just come from RTE. I had to record an interview for an arts programme. It will be transmitted in two weeks' time. I won't join you. Jonathan is waiting for me over there. We're just having coffee.'

Angela smiled sweetly, blew some kisses on the wind and glided along to where her husband was sitting. Every eye in the restaurant was upon her and she knew it and gloried in it.

'That will be you one of these days,' Sandra murmured slyly. Maggie looked at her and laughed. It was quite obvious that Angela wasn't too happy about 'the new find'. For some time now her crown had been slipping and Maggie had found her last two novels definitely disappointing. There were a lot of new writers around, nudging her from her top position in the bestseller lists. Maggie was fresh blood, new talent. No wonder Angela hadn't been too friendly.

'Sorry I'm late, loveys.' Another voice intruded on her thoughts and Maggie looked up to see a rotund, smiling woman plonking herself on the chair opposite her. 'I'm Carol, and you must be Maggie. I've been so looking forward to meeting you.'

'Hello.' Maggie smiled and knew immediately she was going to like this friendly woman. Carol was nothing like what she had imagined a top PR person to be. Glamorous she was not. Her curly brown hair was liberally sprinkled with grey, she wore no make-up apart from the merest touch of lipstick and mascara, but her skin was soft and creamy and unlined, despite the fact that she was in her mid-fifties. She wore a simple flowered cotton dress and carried a huge soft leather bag, out of which she took a file for Sandra. Earth mother was how Maggie would have described her.

'That book's a winner,' the earth mother said matter-of-factly, as she handed Maggie a file similar to Sandra's. 'I'm starving, loveys. Should we eat before we get down to business?'

'Good thinking,' agreed Sandra, who ate like a horse and never put on a pound. 'Angela's here having coffee with Jonathan,' she murmured.

'Oh, what a drag! I suppose I'd better go and pay homage,' Carol groaned. 'It's enough to put anyone off their lunch . . . even me.' She gave a hearty chuckle and headed in the direction of the bestselling author.

'She's nice, isn't she?' said Sandra. 'The two of you are going to get on great. Carol likes no-nonsense people. Angela's a bit highly strung and she can be difficult at times,' she explained diplomatically.

'I understand,' Maggie said.

The three had a jolly lunch and by the time Maggie left she was on cloud nine. Carol said that she urgently needed some biographical notes about Maggie so that she could include them in the publicity pack that she was preparing for the media. Her suggested campaign seemed to please Sandra, and Maggie just couldn't believe that such good luck was happening to her. She looked at her watch. It was gone three-thirty. She decided she'd just pop in to see Terry before heading back to Wicklow. She was dying to share her good news with him. Window displays, signing sessions. Wowie! This was big time; this was *it*! It was really unbelievable. For a moment Maggie felt incredibly happy and she hugged it to herself. It was like waking up on Christmas morning when she was a child, knowing that Santa had come. It was like the day she got engaged and like the first time she held her babies – that rare, precious, happy feeling when nothing matters and you're high as high can be. It doesn't happen very often in a lifetime. Make the most of this, she told herself as she strode out to her car.

'Jesus, Maggie, what are you doing here? The VAT inspector's arrived to do a spot-check and I'm up to my eyes. Is there something wrong with any of the kids?' Terry was not in a good humour.

'No, no, they're fine,' Maggie said hastily, her bubble beginning to subside.

'Well, what's wrong?' Terry asked irritably. 'I thought you'd be long gone by now.'

'Nothing's wrong. Oh Terry, I've just had the most marvellous lunch. I met Angela Allen and then Carol, the publicist, and it's really going to be exciting. They're talking about having window displays and doing signing sessions and publicity tours and look,' she bubbled, taking her cover out of her bag with a proud wave and handing it to her husband.

'Lovely, lovely, it's great.' Terry hardly glanced at it. 'Look, Maggie, I'm really up to my ears. You can tell me all about it at the weekend. I've got to bring this lot out to that little bastard. He can sit in the front office – he's not coming in here.' With that he marched out the door with an armful of files and left her alone and crestfallen in his office.

Had Terry no idea how important this was to her? OK, she knew that VAT inspectors were most unwelcome visitors, but even so, to dismiss the cover of her first novel with barely a glance was hurtful in the extreme. She would never have done that to him. When he had started up his financial consultancy after they had returned home from Saudi she had been behind him every step of the way, making sure that he never had to worry about anything at home, despite the fact that she had just had twins. She had made sure that his domestic life was always serene, his meals always on the table, his clothes washed and ironed for him. He never had to do housework because he was working so hard and Maggie understood how necessary it was to get things going. She hadn't moaned, she had just mucked in and did what she had to do. Why, now, when she needed it, couldn't he be as supportive of her? The trouble with Terry was that everything had to revolve around him. His little dramas with VAT inspectors were far more important than his wife's novel.

Maggie straightened her shoulders, put her cover carefully back in her bag and walked out the door of her husband's office. Terry never even noticed she was going. He was explaining something in a file to the inspector and was all charm and smiles.

Well fuck you, mister! Maggie thought, anger beginning to replace her disappointment. You can just go to hell as far as I'm concerned because I've had it with you. She strode out to the foyer and waited impatiently for the lift. Angrily, she jabbed the buttons on the two elevators. If Terry Ryan thought for one minute that Maggie was going to go on being the good little wife that she had been for the past six years, he could go and scratch himself. Before she had married him she had been vibrant and happy and full of life. And look at her now: fraught, harassed, full of guilt because she feared she was neglecting her children and him. She should be over the moon with excitement because of the great opportunity she had created for herself. Maggie marched into the lift, the doors closed silently behind her and she descended smoothly to the ground floor of the large modern office building. She ran down the steps and five minutes later was driving back towards the city and not in the direction she had intended before her encounter with her husband.

She wasn't going back to Wicklow this evening: she was going to phone her mother and ask her to keep the children overnight. Nelsie would probably moan, but let her! Maggie had always been more than a good daughter; now she was calling in her markers. She was staying in the city tonight, because tonight was the start of the rest of her life. If Terry didn't want to be part of it that was his loss.

As she drove along Baggot Street she felt her resolve strengthening. For too long she had been living in a vacuum. Her spirit had slowly been eroded and she had ended up frustrated and vaguely unhappy. She loved her children; they meant the world to her and she would never neglect them. But by God she owed it to herself to have a life for herself as well. She didn't want to slide into middle age, bitter and regretful that she hadn't taken her chances. From now on she was going to take her writing and the opportunities it provided seriously. This was not a

306

game any more — nor a hobby. This was business and she was going to embrace it all: the writing, the marketing, whatever was called for. Terry didn't understand and he never would, but there was someone who did. Maggie pulled over and stopped the car beside a phone booth. She was on double yellow lines but she didn't care. One quick phone call was all it would take. Rooting in her bag, Maggie found the number she was looking for.

Twenty-Five

She saw Adam before he saw her. She had seen him drive into the car-park, from the umbrella-shaded table she was sitting at in the beer-garden of the Addison Lodge. She knew it was ridiculous and corny and the reaction of a sixteen-year-old but her heart had started to pound, her mouth got dry and her palms started to sweat.

'You idiot, Maggie!' she murmured, but there were only a couple of tourists and a grandmother and two grandchildren in the garden, and they gave no indication of having heard her.

She watched as Adam uncoiled himself from the car, hungry for the first look of him. Had he always been that tall, that broad? Maggie was a tall woman herself but she had always had to tilt her head to look up at Adam Dunne. He loped across the car-park with that lithe rangy stride that she knew so well and then he saw her and stopped and smiled, and for the second time that day she felt ridiculously happy. Her own mouth curved in an answering smile and it was as if there were no-one else in the universe, let alone the world. The noise of the traffic faded away; the other people in the beer-garden might as well have dissolved into thin air. Maggie and Adam's eyes met and they held each other's gaze for what seemed like an eternity.

'Hi,' she said, suddenly shy.

'Hello, Maggie.' Adam leaned down and kissed her gently on the cheek.

'I'm sorry about not ringing when I said I would. I—'

'Maggie, you don't have to apologize for anything,' he said quietly. 'I had no right to ring.'

'I'm glad you did.' Maggie looked him straight in the eye. 'I missed you, Adam.' Maybe she was mad; no maybe about it: she *was* mad. This man was footloose and fancy free, a decade younger than she was, and she knew it would be the easiest thing in the world to fall in love with him. By arranging to meet him, she had taken that first dangerous step. But it felt so very good to see those dark-lashed hazel eyes smiling down at her, to look at him smile and to know that he was as glad to see her as she was to see him.

'How's your little girl?' Adam pulled out a chair and sat down beside her.

'She's fine, Adam, back to normal.' Maggie couldn't take her eyes off him. He looked so lean and muscular and healthy, his tawny hair streaked with blond after weeks spent working in the sun. She fought down the urge to run her finger along his jaw and across his mouth.

'Would you like another drink?' He indicated the shandy she had been drinking.

'OK,' she agreed, wishing she felt more in control of the situation. She was acting so gauche, more like a lovesick teenager than a mature woman in her mid-thirties!

'Relax, Maggie.' Adam leaned over and patted her hand. 'I'm even more nervous than you.'

Maggie laughed and relaxed instantly. He knew her so well, it was uncanny. That was what had drawn her to him all those months ago when they had started going to his writers' group together. She watched him as he went into the bar to order the drinks and knew she should take to her heels, get into her car and scorch down to Wicklow. Make up your mind now, Maggie: go, or stay and face the consequences, she argued silently with herself. The strength of her reaction to seeing Adam for the first time had shaken her. She realized that what she felt for him was no mere fleeting physical attraction. She took her car keys and the book-cover out of her bag. She badly wanted to show it to him and tell him her news. If she used the keys he wouldn't find out about her novel until some time in the future – perhaps not until he saw it in a bookshop – and that wasn't what she wanted. If she left now, she'd have some chance of making her marriage work. Maggie thought of Terry's reaction when she had popped in to see him with the cover. Taking a deep breath she put her keys back in her bag and placed the cover of *City Woman* on the table in front of Adam's chair. She could feel the tension ease out of her body and when Adam came out she was smiling.

'I half-expected you to be gone, you know,' Adam said, half-seriously, half-joking, as he placed the glass of shandy in front of her.

'It was touch-and-go,' she admitted, taking a satisfying draught of the cool tart drink.

'What made you stay?'

'I was thirsty,' she said flippantly and met his steady gaze. 'I stayed because I wanted to, more than anything in the world.' The look in his eyes made her catch her breath.

'I missed you like hell: all I could think of was coming home to see you again.' Adam gave a deep sigh. 'Maggie, I don't know what you've done to me. All I know is that I'm as confused as bedamned.' He sat down, took a gulp of his beer and put his glass down. His eye caught the cover in front of him.

'Hey! Hey! What's this?' A stunned look crossed his face and then he was leaping out of his chair and pulling her to her feet. 'You're being published! You did it! Oh Maggie, Maggie, Maggie, I'm so *proud* of you.' She was enveloped in a bear-hug that squeezed the breath out of her lungs and she hugged him back, wishing the moment would never end.

'I want to hear everything,' he said, his eyes dancing with delight. They sat down again and Maggie, unable to keep the grin off her face, told him all that had happened from the moment she had sent off her precious manuscript to Enterprise Publishing until her lunch meeting that day with Sandra and Carol.

'This is unbelievable,' he kept saying over and over. 'You're going to be published. I always knew you could do it, Maggie, you've got real talent. It's just great.'

'I feel I'm in a bit of a dream myself,' Maggie confessed. 'I shouldn't really be here at all, you know. I've still got rewrites to do and my editor is screaming for them.'

'The famous deadline strikes again. It's a different

ball-game when contracts are signed, isn't it?' Adam reflected. 'You're not doing it for fun any more, Maggie; it's big business now.'

'Yes, it's a bit scary when you think of all the money that's being spent.'

'Ah, scary nothing, Maggie Ryan. You're well able for it. Publishers aren't the St Vincent de Paul, you know: they don't do these things for charity. They know bloody well they've got a bestseller on their hands and of course they're going to spend a lot of money promoting it and you. Otherwise they would never publish so soon after taking it on. And why? Because there's money in it for them — that's what they're in business for.'

'Mmm, maybe you're right, I hadn't thought of it like that,' Maggie said cheerfully. 'I know nothing about publishing.'

'Well, lady, it's time you learned because it's going to be your scene for quite some time to come.' He drained his glass. 'Would you like another drink?'

Maggie shook her head. 'Oh look, Adam,' she said, pointing, 'look at the bride. She must be having her pictures taken in the Botanic Gardens. God, I haven't been there since I was a child.' They watched a bride in a flowing white gown step out of a white Rolls-Royce. Her veil fluttered and the lemon-gowned bridesmaids fussed around, their laughter carried on the summer breeze.

'Come on and we'll go for a stroll before we have something to eat.' Adam stood up and reached out a hand to pull her to her feet. Lightheartedly, Maggie stood up. What a lovely way to spend a summer's afternoon, she thought happily. They crossed the busy road and walked towards the big dark green wrought-iron gates. 'I must bring the children here some day,' Maggie said as she watched a child in front of her skip excitedly towards the little drinking-fountains. They had always been a source of great fun when Maggie and her brothers had been brought to the gardens as part of their annual visit to the city. Immaculate beds of flowers and shrubs dotted the lush emerald lawns and ahead of them the great domed curve of the glasshouses glittered like diamonds in the afternoon sun. The bridal party stood under a magnificent oak tree as the photographer arranged the bride's train to his satisfaction and one of the bridesmaids sneaked a quick puff of a fag.

Adam and Maggie stood with other onlookers admiring the scene for a time and then, taking her hand as if it was the most natural thing in the world, Adam led her along the winding path towards the river. Maggie smiled as she saw a sign outside one of the glasshouses saying that perambulators were not allowed. 'Look, Adam, even the signs are still the same. It's so Victorian, isn't it?'

'You should bring the children here in the autumn; they'd love it! The trees are glorious and the leaves underfoot are so crunchy and crisp. I've often seen red squirrels collecting nuts.'

'It's shameful, really, not making the most of the amenities we have in the city. I'm always a bit wary in the Phoenix Park, which isn't that far from us. This is much nicer: there's no traffic, it's really peaceful and it's free! Definitely, when we come back from Wicklow, I'm going to bring them here for an afternoon.'

They walked on under the leafy trees as Adam told her about his work in the UK and how Telecom were offering yearly contracts for people who wanted them. 'The money's great, but I missed my friends and I missed you.' They had reached the rose-garden and the heady scent of the hundreds of blossoming roses enveloped them. Maggie leaned her head on his shoulder.

'I missed you too, Adam. I tried hard to put you out of my head. I couldn't. I know I shouldn't be here with you but I don't care any more. It's like hitting my head off a stone wall with Terry: he has no idea of the emotional support I should be getting from him. He has never given it and he never will – marrying him was a big mistake in my life. I care for him; anybody who knows Terry couldn't but. But I don't love him any more. When I got the news about being published, you were the first person I wanted to tell. I don't know what it is about you, Adam, but you seem to know what's in my mind; you understand about my writing – you just seem to understand me.' She smiled up at him. 'And, boy, am I confused . . .'

'Don't ask me to explain it, Maggie, because I can't. We just clicked that first time we met. You do that with people sometimes. With you I feel free to be totally myself and that's a rare thing. I feel we've known each other for a lifetime and I wish to God you weren't married.' Adam looked dejected.

'Well I am, and there's nothing can be done about that. I have three children to think of, but, Adam, I'm entitled to some happiness! We all make mistakes but that doesn't mean we have to stop living or that we're never entitled to another moment's happiness. I'm making a fresh start in my life today. I want you to be in it. You know how I'm fixed; you know the constraints I'll be under. What you decide is entirely up to you, Adam.' Maggie looked him straight in the eye.

For answer, Adam bent his head and very gently kissed her on the lips. A light, soft, sensuous kiss that took her breath away and made her long for more.

'Let's go home,' he said huskily.

'Oh yes,' Maggie murmured against his mouth, opening her lips wider as his tongue teased her lips and the soft inside of her mouth before flicking gently against the moist velvet of her own tongue. They parted, dazed. 'You know where the house is; so follow me in your car and drive carefully,' Adam instructed.

'I'll do my best,' she said shakily. His kiss was unlike any other she had ever had and it shook her to the core of her being. Terry was always a very passionate aggressive lover and she had forgotten how erotic a very gentle, exploring kiss could be.

They walked across the weir and back up between the glasshouses towards the exit. When they reached the car-park, Adam opened her door for her and before she got in he drew her to him. 'Be happy,' he breathed softly against her lips, making her want to taste him all over again. But he wouldn't let her. Pressing his index finger softly against her mouth, he said, 'Soon,' and went over to his own car. Maggie was so aroused she had to calm herself by taking several deep breaths. Adam lived in a two-up-two-down redbrick house in Drumcondra, only five minutes away, which was just as well as Maggie drove in a haze of desire, intent on being with him as soon as she could, and with scant care for the rules of the road. She parked behind him and followed him into his hall, aching to have his arms around her.

'Do you want to eat first?' he asked and she gave him a dig in the ribs.

'Oh, Adam, stop teasing me,' she said breathlessly.

He laughed and, taking her hand, led her up the stairs. 'I never do anything on the first date,' he joked as he led her into the bedroom. 'You're an awful bad influence on me. I hope you'll respect me in the morning.'

'I will. I will.' Maggie pulled him to her, hungry for him.

They kissed again, a long slow lingering kiss that made her heart thud against her ribs as she arched herself against him. Very slowly he began to undress her, easing her dress off, brushing aside her bra straps with butterfly-light kisses as his mouth followed the wisps of lace down to the hollow between her breasts.

'Oh Adam!' she moaned in a frenzy of impatience, as she pulled off his shirt and, unbuckling his belt, drew his jeans down over his hips.

'We've all the time in the world,' he murmured as he unclipped her bra and let it fall to the floor. He tenderly caressed her breasts, his tongue flicking her nipples. The warmth of his breath made her burn with desire. He eased her down on the bed and lay down beside her, stroking and caressing her whole body. His lips following his fingers, under her breasts, over her belly, down along her inner thigh. Gently he stroked a finger inside the lacy wisps of her briefs and Maggie gasped with pleasure. He slid them down her legs with one hand, his other fingers tantalising her with feathery touches and caresses that made her groan in mindless pleasure. For a long time he kissed and caressed her so sensually and erotically, until the sensations were almost unbearable. Only then did he enter her, bringing her quickly to the most powerful orgasm she had ever experienced. Then he came too, his face buried in her hair, calling her name over and over.

'I'd forgotten it could be so good,' Maggie murmured, as she lay in the circle of his arms a little while later, totally relaxed and contented. As well as being such a generous lover, Adam was also very responsible when it came to contraception.

Adam raised his head and gazed down at her, his hazel eyes warm as he studied her, glowing and flushed after their love-making, her tousled auburn hair so striking against the white of the pillow, her green eyes heavy-lidded and slumberous and sensual, her full red lips just asking to be kissed. 'Maggie, you are so beautiful. You taste like honey, so sweet and wet and warm. We'll just have to spend tonight reminding you of how good it can be, now won't we?' Bending his head, he parted her lips in a kiss that brought all those wondrous sensations rushing back.

Twenty-Six

'I can't believe I did it; I can't believe I went to bed with Adam but oh girls . . . it was lovely.' Maggie was having lunch with her two friends and Devlin and Caroline were agog as she told them of the events of the previous day. 'Do you think I'm awful?' she asked a little uncertainly.

Devlin shook her head. 'No, Maggie, of course not. Just be careful. You could be letting yourself in for a lot of heartache.'

'Well, Devlin, at least I'm prepared to take that chance,' Maggie said calmly. 'Adam cares for me a lot and I'm not pushing him away the way you're pushing Luke away. Better to have loved and lost and all that. Loving and being loved is the most precious thing in the world.'

'Don't lecture me, Maggie,' Devlin snapped.

'OK.' Maggie turned her attention to her Caesar salad.

'I think it's nice the way he is so supportive about your book.' Caroline reached across and gave Maggie's hand a squeeze. She bit her lip. 'Richard and I are going for an annulment. Charles is dying of cancer and he's going to Boston to be with his brother. Richard is going with him and will stay with him for as long as he's needed; so I'm going to be on my own. Maggie, I think you're dead right to have your affair with Adam. If someone loves you, make the most of it: grab it with both hands. There's nothing worse than being alone, and you can be married to someone and be utterly lonely. I know; I was.'

'Caroline, I'm so sorry. Why didn't you tell us before now?' Maggie was shocked. 'You hadn't made any decisions like that before we went away for our weekend and that was only a couple of weeks ago.'

'I found out only when I came back from Wexford. Charles told Richard that very day. I think he's right to go with him. Charles and he love each other and at a time like that you need all the love you can get. Poor Charles, he's a lovely man. I'm going to miss him,' Caroline said sadly.

'What are you going to do?' Devlin asked in concern.

Caroline shrugged her shoulders and smiled. 'Who knows? Grab life by the throat in my usual adventurous fashion,' she said dryly.

'If you need us, we're here,' Maggie said firmly. 'Aren't we, Devlin?' She looked her friend in the eye.

'Of course we are,' Devlin said warmly. 'And Maggie . . . I'm sorry I snapped.'

'You should try and lighten up a little bit, Devlin, just for your own sake. Don't let your business affairs overwhelm you. There's more to life than work.'

Devlin gave a wry smile. 'Well, looking at you, that's obvious. You arrived here grinning from ear to ear, whatever you were up to last night!'

'Don't knock it till you've tried it,' Maggie said tartly. 'Believe me, Devlin, a couple of long lustful nights with Luke is just what you need.' She laughed as her friend's jaw dropped. 'Look, it's not just about sex,' Maggie explained. 'Don't think that for a minute. Even though that was terrific because Adam was totally concerned with my pleasure – which is a change for me, I can tell you. It's the sharing and the support and the emotional sustenance that mean so much, especially when you haven't had them for so long.' She smiled at Caroline and Devlin. 'It's like being reborn. You probably think I'm as mad as a hatter. Maybe I'm not explaining it very well but for the first time in a long while I feel that I have some control of my life. There is happiness of a sort for me.'

'And you deserve it more than anyone,' Caroline affirmed.

'Maggie, do you know something,' Devlin laughed, 'you're an incorrigible romantic. Isn't she, Caroline?'

'One of us has to be,' Caroline replied with a hint of a smile. 'One of these days I'm going to go looking for a bit of romance myself – anything has to be an improvement on my experiences.'

'Now *that* would make a novel for sure,' Devlin murmured wickedly. 'Could you imagine the reaction of the glitterati. The gossip columnists would have a field-day. The things they write about people. Mind, if they heard some of the things I've heard since opening up here, they'd be gobsmacked. Do you see your one over there in the pink-and-grey leggings? She's married to Hugh McHugh the financier and they're absolutely loaded. She spends her time shop-lifting. She was caught trying to slip a silk camisole into her bag without paying for it down Grafton Street, and she's notorious in town for it. And the one she's talking to, Leslie Delahunty — she's only six weeks married and she was caught by her husband in bed with her father-in-law. Maggie, I'm telling you: you need step no further than City Girl for inspiration for your novels.'

'Whoever said "truth is stranger than fiction" sure knew what he was talking about,' laughed Caroline. 'Did you hear about Rita Dillon?'

'Noooo!' exclaimed the other pair. 'What's she done now?'

The rest of the lunch was devoted to a very satisfying gossip as the three of them caught up on all the news that travelled like bushfire around the luxurious environs of Dublin's most exclusive health and leisure complex. Finally, Maggie had to call a halt as she had told her mother she wouldn't be too late in collecting the children. Nelsie had been very gracious about keeping her grandchildren overnight when Maggie had phoned her the previous evening to say she was unavoidably delayed in the city. Knowing her mother, Maggie had no doubt that she would demand her pound of flesh at some date in the future. Nevertheless, she was grateful to her and didn't want to take advantage.

She hummed to herself as she sped down the Bray dual carriageway. There wasn't much traffic and she was in Rathnew in less than an hour. She stopped at the supermarket and bought a box of Black Magic for Nelsie, who had a weakness for the dark chocolates, and some jelly babies and Smarties for the children. As she drove towards Brittas, she was sorry the journey was almost over. She had enjoyed it, particularly the solitude which she never seemed to have much of these days. It had been nice and relaxing listening to Ronan Collins on the radio playing romantic music, which brought back vivid memories of the passion and pleasure of the night before. A record of Elvis Presley singing 'Can't Help Falling in Love' came on and Maggie sang away, thinking of Adam and how good it had been to spend the night with him. She had promised, that morning as they parted, to phone him daily, and if she could persuade her mother to take the children once more she intended going back up to Dublin to spend even an afternoon with him.

Humming and smiling at the memories that were so fresh in her mind, Maggie drove into the site and drew up outside her mobile. She climbed out of the car and ran lightly up the steps of the veranda. She wanted to take off her posh dress and wear something more appropriate for the farm, as no doubt the kids would want to feed the hens and help with the milking. Vaguely, she noticed a little girl and a petite blonde woman on the end of the veranda surrounding the mobile opposite. Lady Muck must have arrived, she thought fleetingly, as she unlocked the door and rushed inside, undressing almost as she went. Ten minutes later, dressed in a pair of denim shorts and a sleeveless T-shirt and loafers, Maggie was racing down the steps again and into the car. She had been so anxious to get changed and on her way that she hadn't noticed the look of shocked recognition on the face of her new neighbour.

Twenty-Seven

As Marian Montclare looked out the kitchen window
of her luxurious mobile, she could not believe her
eyes. It was Maggie MacNamara. Well, obviously she
was married now, so MacNamara was probably no
longer her surname, just as Gilhooley was no longer
Marian's. What the hell was she doing in the
next mobile? Didn't someone called Cassidy own
it? Imagine having spent the best part of twenty
thousand pounds for a luxury mobile and site, only to
find herself side by side with her erstwhile friend.
Maggie was really the last person she wanted to see. It
had been fifteen years − no, more − since they had
parted on bad terms. Deep down, Marian acknowledged that at least Maggie had made an effort to save
the friendship. Her pride had not allowed her to
accept the offer of reconciliation. As far as she was
concerned, Maggie had ruined their friendship by
accusing her of treating her like a doormat, just
because of a silly mix-up over holiday arrangements.
That had pierced Marian to the core; for Maggie, who
had always looked up to her and been as close as a
sister, to criticize her like that had been unthinkable.

She watched as the other woman got into her car.
Although it was hard for her, Marian had to admit

that Maggie looked a million dollars. Such a change from the tomboy she had known. When she and Maggie were going to school together, all Maggie had ever worn was jeans in the winter and shorts in the summer and her thick auburn hair had a flyaway wildness that her friend had never been able to control. The radiant woman who had run up those veranda steps in her chic tailored dress, with a figure and tan worth dying for and a short sophisticated hairstyle, was light years away from the Maggie she remembered. Nevertheless, Marian had recognized her immediately. Obviously the same couldn't be said for Maggie, but then she had been in such a rush that she had hardly glanced in her direction.

Almost as a reflex action, Marian got up from her lounger and retired to the privacy of her mobile to come to terms with the shock. She hoped she was mistaken, until she saw Maggie running down the veranda steps in a pair of shorts and a T-shirt. Then she knew without a doubt that like a bad penny she had returned to her life. It was not a pleasant thought; in fact it was most unsettling. How she was going to handle their inevitable encounter she had no idea. And they would surely meet unless she stayed skulking in the mobile for the duration of the holiday. She wondered what Maggie's husband was like and what he did for a living. Obviously he wasn't as successful as her own husband, Alex, Marian thought with satisfaction. After all her former friend was only driving a Starlet; she herself drove a Volvo. The dress had looked expensive undeniably; with shorts and a T-shirt you couldn't tell. But then Maggie had never been a great one for clothes.

Marian always liked to start from a position of superiority and she felt fairly certain that Alex and she were one of the most affluent couples on the site, if not indeed *the* most affluent. That thought cheered her up somewhat and she walked into her bedroom and flung open her wardrobe. Time to change. What would she wear that would look glam but casual? What would make a good *statement*, as they said on fashion TV? She scanned the rows of clothes on the racks and drew out an outfit that caught her eye. It consisted of mint-green and blue tie-dyed Lycra leggings and matching fitted gauntlet top, worn under a mint-green silk chiffon overshirt. She'd got it in Pia Bang just before she came down to Wicklow. It was ideal, though perhaps she would not wear the overshirt. It might be just a bit OTT in the middle of the afternoon; she wanted to make a statement — not a newsflash! Marian smiled wryly. She had never thought she'd end up wanting to impress Maggie, the one person she had always been able to be herself with. But now after all that had happened between them . . .

She'd let Maggie see how well she had done for herself, without their friendship. She had made it right to the top of the social ladder: married a successful wealthy broker, had one gorgeous child and lived in a big house in Foxrock. She never admitted that she came from a not very posh suburb of Cork but always said West Cork instead. Oh yes! Marian Gilhooley Montclare had come a long way and she wanted to look her very best when she met Maggie MacNamara, or whatever she was called now.

*   *   *

'Can we go and stay with Gran again soon?' Mimi asked from the back of the car. 'We had bwilliant fun.' Maggie grinned to think she had been so worried about the children. She had phoned her mother's twice from Adam's to make sure everything was OK and that they weren't pining.

'If Gran doesn't mind, of course you can, pet! Did you enjoy yourself, Michael?' She addressed her son, who was guarding a plate of fresh homemade scones as if they were the Crown jewels.

'Oh Mammy, it was brill. I helped Grandad to milk the cows. I wish we lived on a farm all the time.'

'Mammy, I've a thong for you.' Shona was not to be outdone. 'I'm thpecial becauthe I'm thpecial,' she sang in her little baby voice that made Maggie smile.

'You're special because you're special. That's a lovely song, Shona. Where did you learn that?'

'It's really a hymn, Mammy. She just doesn't know all the words,' Mimi explained as they drove through Redcross and past Johnson's and Saint Mary's and on to the main road. It was marvellous to see the kids again, Maggie reflected, as they started to sing the hymn Mimi was going on about. Honestly, you'd think she'd been gone a month rather than a day but when they had run out to greet her and smother her in hugs and kisses it was the greatest thing.

They were all singing the 'special' hymn as Maggie drove up to the mobile. There was much laughing and excitement as the children tumbled out of the car. Michael started doing his handstands on the grass and Shona had to be in on the act. Mimi, because she was wearing a dress, stood demurely at the veranda with her mother pretending to be all grown-up.

326

'Anybody like to go to the beach?' Maggie asked casually.

'I would!'

'I would!'

'Me would!'

Thus shrieked the trio in turn and they galloped up the veranda steps to get into their togs. Maggie laughed as she walked up behind them. A little girl peered shyly around the corner of the mobile opposite and Maggie smiled at her. She appeared to be just a little older than Mimi and was dressed in a gorgeous frilly sundress with matching hat. Maggie smiled at her. 'Hello.'

'Alexandra, where are you?' said someone with a rather posh accent and Maggie smiled to herself as she remembered Cathy's title Lady Muck. Alexandra wasn't your run-of-the-mill common-or-garden name either. A petite blonde woman came around the corner of her veranda.

'Hi,' Maggie gave a friendly smile, looking up from her bag, where she was rooting for her keys. It was something in the way the other woman was looking at her that made Maggie look again. Her brows drew together in a little puzzled frown. That face was terribly familiar from somewhere. She looked again. 'Good Lord!' she ejaculated. 'It's Marian. It's Marian Gilhooley, isn't it?'

'Hello, Maggie,' Marian said coolly and turned her attention to her daughter. 'Darling, you know you're not allowed on that side of the mobile, we have to respect others' privacy. Come up to the veranda and play with Mummy.' She smiled a vague uninterested smile in Maggie's direction and then glided around to

327

the main part of her veranda and out of sight.

Maggie stood with her jaw open.

'Come on, Mammy! Are we going?' Mimi danced up and down impatiently beside her.

'Yes, sure. Come on inside quick and get ready.' Had she imagined it or had she just seen Marian Gilhooley, friend of her schooldays. Get a load of that accent! When she knew Marian, she had had a lovely Cork lilt. Now there wasn't a trace of it. It was pure South Dublin. It was hard to credit. And obviously, after all this time, Marian still did not wish to let go the past. Maggie shrugged. 'Oh well, that's her problem,' she muttered as she organized swimming-togs, rings, buckets and spades and, as well, some biscuits, lemonade and banana sandwiches for a picnic tea. When she came back out to pack everything in the car there was no sign of Marian or her little girl.

Sitting on the beach, as the late-afternoon sun warmed her back and the children splashed happily at the edge of the sea, Maggie reflected on her recent encounter. Imagine meeting Marian Gilhooley again after all this time. It was such a small world. At the time when Marian had ended the friendship, Maggie had been devastated, because Marian had been like the sister she never had. But the old saying that time heals all wounds had proved true and Maggie, while regretting the loss of the friendship, had put the past behind her and got on with her life. She felt that she had made every effort at reconciliation but Marian had rebuffed her each time. Maggie, never one to hold a grudge, had ended up feeling sorry for the other girl and eventually she forgot all about her.

Now, meeting again, it didn't surprise her that

Marian was cold and unfriendly. She was obviously defensive and if she didn't want to be friendly it was no skin off Maggie's nose; she wasn't going to force anything. The situation no longer bothered her. Marian had looked great though, with her sleek bobbed blonde hair and her obviously expensive designer gear. More power to her, Maggie reflected, as she turned her attention to Mimi who was covering her toes with a bucketful of sand. 'Play with me, Mammy.'

'Of course I will,' she said, smiling and catching her daughter in her arms, and beginning to tickle her amid much squealing and laughter.

Several times during the week, she and Marian passed and greeted each other politely. Each time she saw her, Marian had a new outfit on and her make-up was always immaculate, her hair perfectly groomed. Her poor daughter was always dressed to the nines and Maggie felt sorry for the little girl that she wasn't allowed to join in the rough-and-tumble with the rest of the kids.

She was sitting on her veranda the following Friday, doing the last of her revision, anxious to get as much done before Terry arrived for the weekend, when she heard Marian calling her name frantically. 'Maggie, Maggie, quick! It's Alexandra: she's choking. I don't know what to do. Maggie, help me!'

Maggie was out of her seat like a bullet, racing across the dividing lawn and up around to the other woman's veranda. She could hear the great gasping whoops of the little girl as she fought to get air into her lungs. Her face was already turning blue. Maggie, recalling her nursing training, stood behind the child, put her arms around her diaphragm and applied the Heimlich manoeuvre. The obstruction lodged in the little girl's throat shot out to the other side of the mobile and with tears streaming down her cheeks she gulped in great gasps of air.

'Now, now you're fine! There's a good girl,' Maggie soothed her. Doing the Heimlich on a child was dicey enough: there was always the danger of cracking a rib or two as their bones were so soft, but as she ran her hands expertly over the child's ribcage, Maggie knew everything was all right.

Marian put her arms around her daughter and looked up at Maggie, her face as white as a sheet. 'Thanks, Maggie. I don't know what to say,' she whispered and promptly burst into tears.

'Stop that, Marian,' Maggie said firmly, seeing that Alexandra was beginning to howl even louder at the sight of her mother in floods. 'Come on! I'll make you a cup of coffee.' She knelt down to the little girl and said cheerfully, 'Alexandra, would you like to come over to my mobile and see my little girl's Little Mermaid doll?' Alexandra stopped howling.

'Yes, please,' she said excitedly.

'Is that OK with you?' Maggie asked Marian calmly. For a moment their eyes met and then Marian dropped hers and nodded her head silently. 'I'll bring her over and make you a strong cup of coffee; a small drop of milk and no sugar if I remember rightly.'

'You've a good memory,' Marian said dryly.

'Oh, it's just that you were always the same as my mother with tea and coffee,' Maggie said lightly and at the mention of Nelsie the other woman blushed under her make-up.

'How *is* your mother?' she asked awkwardly.

'She's well – ageing a bit, slowing down, but well, thank God. How are your parents?' Maggie tried to be as matter-of-fact as possible. She knew Marian was feeling uncomfortable now that the drama was over and things were back to normal.

'They're . . . they're good,' Marian said tersely, and her tone had more than a hint of frost.

'Look. Sit down, Mar, you've had a shock. I'll bring Alexandra over to my place and I'll be back in a jiffy,' Maggie said briskly, taking the child by the hand and leading her out the door and down the steps of the veranda. It was quite obvious to Maggie that Marian was feeling uncomfortable with the situation. If Alexandra had not choked, Marian would have ignored her for the duration of her stay and they would have parted, probably never to see each other again. But now, Marian obviously felt she had to be civil at least and she wasn't liking it much.

Maggie felt slightly angry. What was the big deal, for God's sake? Couldn't Marian for once in her life be adult about a situation and let bygones be bygones. She hadn't changed a bit from when they were at school. Maybe she didn't want her little girl playing with Maggie's children, but the child had had a shock and the best thing for her was to forget about it as soon as possible by being distracted by something nice and normal. If she had stayed with her mother both of them would have ended up in hysterics. Although, as Maggie had to admit, Marian was usually very level-headed in a crisis, it was a different kettle of fish when your child was involved. As quickly as it had surged, her anger faded. If Marian wanted to be friends, fine; if she didn't, well, it wouldn't cost Maggie any sleepless nights any longer. She had got over that years ago.

'Look, Mimi, Michael, Shona, this is Alexandra, I've brought her over to play for a little while. Mimi, will you show Alexandra your Little Mermaid doll?'

Her three children stared at the newcomer. Alexandra, who was at least a year older than Mimi, put her thumb in her mouth and stood shyly, sucking it.

'Mammy! she's sucking her thumb an' she's bigger than me,' Mimi exclaimed.

'*Mimi!*' Maggie glared at her elder daughter. Trust her. 'Alexandra has no little brothers and sisters to play with so I want you to be nice to her and show her how well-behaved you are and how good you are at sharing. OK?'

'OK, Mammy,' chorused her offspring, as Mimi, in charge of the situation, took the little girl by the hand and led her over to the toy box.

'Would you like to see my Likkle Mermaid doll?'

'Yes please,' Alexandra nodded, her ringlets dancing up and down.

'You can play with Thomas the Tank Engine if you like,' Michael offered generously and Maggie smiled to herself as she made the coffee. Kids were great: they had no side to them. Pity adults couldn't be the same.

Marian was on her mobile phone when Maggie walked in with the coffee but as soon as she saw her she told the person at the other end that she would call them back later.

'There's no need to cut short your phone call,

Marian, I'll just give you your coffee and let you relax,' she said.

'Oh . . . oh, I was just calling Alex, my husband, to tell him what happened. I thought he might be able to come down tonight instead of tomorrow but he can't. Business commitments and all that.' There was a hint of bitterness in the other woman's voice.

'Oh, I know all about it. It's a bit of a drag, isn't it?' Maggie sighed. 'Although, miracle of miracles, Terry, my husband, is actually leaving work early to miss the traffic, I'm expecting him any time now. But to be honest, I'll believe it when I see it.'

'What does your husband do?' Marian sipped her coffee and started to relax.

'He's a financial consultant,' Maggie informed her.

Marian suddenly noticed that Maggie hadn't got a cup of coffee herself. 'Why aren't you having coffee?'

'Ah, I didn't feel like it. I thought you might like to relax by yourself,' Maggie said casually. They looked at each other. Marian swallowed and two bright spots highlighted her cheekbones. 'Please sit down and have a cup of coffee with me, Maggie,' she said but this time her gaze didn't waver and the expression in her eyes reminded Maggie of the Marian she had once known and loved.

Maggie smiled, a broad melon-slice grin. 'Thanks, Mar. I'd like that very much.' In spite of herself, Marian grinned back and then they were hugging each other. All the years of estrangement slipped away and it was as if their silly row had never happened.

Twenty-Eight

'I'm not putting Maggie up against Janet Stevens. She'd sink like a stone,' Sandra Nolan said vehemently. She was sitting in the boardroom of Enterprise Publishing at the emergency meeting she called when she heard the news that was turning their publishing schedule upside down.

'Why the hell is Janet Stevens coming out in October? The Americans *always* bring her out for the summer market — that's why we held on to *City Woman* until October!' Jeremy said irascibly. The news had made him very angry. He had great plans for *City Woman*, but Sandra, who was the best marketing person in the business, was right. There was no way a first-time author could be put head to head with an established and very popular author who sold millions.

'Seemingly, Janet felt she should be getting a higher royalty after all the books she's sold for Arthur Martin Publishing,' said Sandra, 'and even though she was half-way through the book, she refused to sign the contract. They thought it would just be a formality and they never thought she'd get stroppy. She's usually so placid.' Sandra was always up to the minute in publishing gossip.

'Obviously she got the royalties she was looking for then,' Marcy said glumly, feeling very sorry for Maggie, who was going to be so disappointed.

'And how!' grimaced Sandra. 'Not only did she get her royalties; she insisted on two hundred and fifty thousand just to sign the contract.'

Jeremy winced. 'Keep that to yourself, for God's sake! We don't want any of our lot getting ideas. I hate hearing things like that.'

'When do you want to go with it now?' Marcy asked.

'I think,' said Sandra slowly, 'that we should postpone it until November of next year. We'll get the Christmas market, and launch the paperback the following summer and her second hardback in October of the same year. As far as I can see from what's coming out next year, November is our best time. Because we'll have the two hardbacks out within the space of a year, plus the *City Woman* paperback, we can do a media blitz and the momentum will keep going for the second one. In one way Arthur Martin has done us a favour. Believe me, in a couple of years' time it will be Arthur Martin who'll be saying they can't put Janet Stevens up against Maggie Ryan,' finished Sandra firmly.

'Who's going to tell Maggie?' sighed Marcy. 'She really slogged her guts out to get *City Woman* ready for us when I asked her to.'

'I'll tell her,' Sandra said. 'It's my department's decision and I'll explain all the facts to her.'

'Treat her to lunch. Buy her flowers. Make a fuss of her,' Jeremy instructed. 'I'm as disappointed as she's going to be.'

'I will,' Sandra assured him. She was known for her great ability to smooth ruffled feathers.

'Hell! Buy her a bottle of champagne too – a decent bottle,' Jeremy growled, and brightened up a little as Marcy squeezed his hand. Sandra, who was phoning Locks restaurant to make a lunch reservation for the following Friday, did not notice.

'So you see, Maggie, it's not in your best interest to publish *City Woman* when we wanted to because of this new development,' Sandra said gently.

Maggie felt the food in her mouth turn to sawdust, her heart sank like a stone and she tried hard not to cry. The disappointment she felt was almost physical. She knew that Sandra was right, that she wasn't being mucked about, but it still didn't make the news she had just been given any easier to swallow.

'I know you're terribly disappointed, Maggie,' Sandra said sympathetically, 'and, believe me, this is as big an upset for us as it is for you. There's nothing I can say that's going to make it any easier. But your day will come. Don't worry.'

'Can I stick it that long?' Maggie said dispiritedly. 'Do you really think I should bother carrying on with the second one?'

'Yes! Yes,' Sandra urged. 'This is just a setback, Maggie, believe me.'

'You can say that again!' Maggie gave a sigh that came from her toes.

'You're not writing? Why not?' Marcy's crisp tones came down the line. It was a week after the dispiriting lunch with Sandra. Maggie's holiday in Wicklow was over and she was back in Dublin.

'Ah, I'm not in the humour,' Maggie declared.

'Really!' Marcy's tone was disapproving. 'Let me tell you, Maggie, this is what separates the men from the boys, the women from the girls. Anybody can write a first novel. It's getting on with the second one, and then the third and fourth that proves that you are a real writer. I never had you figured for a quitter.'

There was silence as Maggie digested this. 'I'm not a quitter,' she responded angrily. Who the hell did Marcy Elliot think she was?

'Prove it then,' Marcy said coolly. 'Have your next chapter on my desk by Friday week.'

'I'm going into hospital to get my tubes tied on Friday week,' Maggie snapped.

'Fine. Have it done by Thursday week then.'

'Right,' Maggie growled and hung up. What a bitch that Marcy one was. As hard as nails. The cheek of her calling her a quitter. Well, she *wasn't* going to write that chapter before she went into hospital and that was that.

She wished that ordeal was over too. The letter with details of her appointment had been waiting for her when she arrived home from Wicklow and Terry was prepared to take a week off work, so anxious was he for her to have the operation done. She might as well get it over with, she decided. It would be one less worry in her life.

She went into the kitchen and stood glowering at her typewriter. Ten minutes later she was tapping away on it. 'I'll show you if I'm a quitter or not, Ms Marcy Elliot,' she muttered angrily.

On the following Thursday week, she arrived in Marcy's office and plonked forty pages of manuscript on her desk. Marcy grinned. 'I put the iron in your soul, didn't I – calling you a quitter!'

'Bitch,' retorted Maggie, but in spite of herself she laughed. Now that her equilibrium was somewhat restored she was able to see that Marcy had motivated her wonderfully. She was a hell of an editor!

'Relax now when you're in hospital and make the most of the few days' peace and quiet. You'll be raring to go when you get home,' Marcy said teasingly. But knowing her, Maggie felt she was half-serious.

'It's all over now; you're fine,' Maggie heard the nurse in the recovery room tell her. She sank back into slumber with a vague sense of relief. At least she'd never have to worry about getting pregnant again. Maybe she could write about it some time in a novel; it was something that lots of women had to make a choice about. She'd discuss it with Marcy, she decided, as she fell fast asleep.

PART TWO

Caroline's Story — II

Twenty-Nine

'Have you got your passport? Have you got a copy of your visa? Have you got your tickets?' Devlin ran through Caroline's checklist.

Caroline took her KLM ticket folder out of her bag. 'They're all here and I've got my traveller's cheques and my sterling.'

'Right then, come on,' said Devlin.

'Are you ready, Maggie?' Caroline called.

Maggie appeared at the kitchen door, holding her head. 'Oh God, I'll never drink red wine again,' she moaned.

'I think I've heard *that* refrain a few times over the years since I've known you,' said Caroline.

'Will I ever learn? At least you don't suffer from hangovers these days!'

'And I had some humdingers, believe me,' Caroline said sombrely. 'Life is much simpler for me without drink. I just hope I never fall off the wagon!'

'Well, you shouldn't have any problem in Abu Dhabi,' Devlin remarked cheerfully. 'Drink isn't allowed there, sure it isn't?'

'Actually it *is* allowed. Abu Dhabi isn't restricted like Saudi – or so I'm told. Bill said they have great parties there: it's a very social place by all accounts.'

As she spoke, Caroline finished filling out her luggage-tags.

'I had some of the greatest hangovers ever invented in Saudi, despite that fact that it was dry,' said Maggie, remembering some of the home-brews she'd tasted when she had lived on a compound in Riyadh as a newly-wed. 'But you're right, Caroline; you can't compare Abu Dhabi with Saudi. The rulers in the Emirate are very enlightened: they even allow people of other religions to practise. It's a very cosmopolitan city. It may be only thirty years old but it's really well laid out and so green and picturesque. The Corniche is fabulous, Terry and I walked along it at sunset one evening when he had to go there on business and it was breathtaking. Caroline, you're going to have a ball.' She beamed at her friend.

'Do you think I'm mad to go?' Caroline said doubtfully.

'Don't be daft,' retorted Maggie. 'This is the chance of a lifetime. Make the most of it, for heaven's sake. And Caroline . . .' Maggie pointed to the traveller's cheques. 'Treat yourself! Gold is fantastic value and so are the silks and the sportswear, and you can get designer labels for half-nothing . . . Oooh, I wish I was going with you.'

'I wish you were too,' Caroline said. Now that the big moment had come, she was having second thoughts.

'Nobody will be going anywhere if we don't get a move on,' retorted Devlin, nipping Caroline's doleful-ness in the bud.

Caroline took a deep breath. 'You're right, Dev, let's get the show on the road.' They left Devlin's apartment, where they had all spent the night, and as they walked across the gravelled courtyard Caroline cast a glance at the penthouse in the opposite block, where she had lived since her marriage. She had no regrets about leaving it. The for-sale sign was planted firmly in the lawn; the sooner the penthouse was sold the better. For her, the sale would signify the end of her marriage and the start of her new life. Richard had wanted her to continue living there, but it had never been a home to her. It had been a place of great unhappiness, beatings, heavy drinking and her awful suicide attempt after discovering that Richard and Charles were lovers. Even living there after Richard had gone to the States with Charles, she hadn't enjoyed it. She wanted a place of her own and when she had made the life-changing decision to work for six months in the UAE, she and Richard had decided to sell up. The estate agents she had worked for were doing the sale free of charge and were confident of a quick sale. The proceeds would then be divided between her and Richard. With that, and whatever money she saved in Abu Dhabi, Caroline intended to buy herself a small townhouse.

'Get in, Caroline,' Devlin said gently, knowing what was going through her friend's mind. Caroline got into the front seat and as Devlin drove out on to the Clontarf road, she didn't look back.

There was little traffic on the roads at six-fifteen a.m. and Caroline looked across the Liffey at the lights of Dublin port twinkling in the dark. She wouldn't see them again for at least six months but right now the thought didn't bother her. She was heartily sick of Dublin at this minute. Sick of answering the phone to all Richard's phoney jet-set friends who were dying to know where he had gone without telling any of them and even more anxious to know why she had not gone with him. She had overheard gossip at City Girl that Richard had run off with DeeDee O'Neill, the actress he had been with in the Gaiety Theatre, that night so long ago, when Caroline met him for the second time.

She had gone into the Coffee Dock with Devlin one morning and seen Lucinda Marshall, the tabloid gossip columnist, who had a greatly exaggerated view of her own importance, seated with her VBF Andrea Walsh, the well-known neurotic, who had married a much older man for his money and was now spending it with gay abandon, much to his dismay — particularly as she seemed to develop a migraine every time he suggested sex and they were now sleeping in separate rooms.

'Darling,' Lucinda had immediately greeted Caroline in that peculiar drawly accent of hers. 'You look stunning. How is that gorgeous husband of yours and where on earth is he? I need some legal advice.' To her own surprise and Devlin's delighted amusement she had retorted coolly: 'Richard doesn't do libel, Lucinda, but I'll tell him you were enquiring after him when I'm on the phone to him tonight.' Lucinda's jaw dropped as Caroline and Devlin moved on to Devlin's corner table.

'That's one of the few times I've ever seen Poison Pen Marshall speechless, Caroline. Congratulations! I'm really thinking of not renewing her membership. I want my clients to be able to come here in peace and not have to be worrying about her and her snide comments in that thing she calls a social column.'

346

'I bet I'll feature in it after this,' Caroline sighed. 'Look at the face of her; she's furious.' They glanced over to where Lucinda and Andrea were glowering at them.

'Oh don't mind them, Caro; they're pathetic,' Devlin urged, but the following Sunday, the heading in Lucinda's gossip column was '*Careworn Caroline Candidate for Marriage Break-Up?*'

Caroline smiled to herself as Devlin swung left off the Malahide road on to Griffith Avenue. Maybe she ought to start a rival gossip column called Abu Dhabi Diary. That would really knock the wind out of Lucinda's sails. The only people who knew Caroline was going away were Devlin and Maggie, her father and her two brothers, and Richard and Charles. She couldn't face any questions and she wasn't yet ready to announce to all and sundry that her marriage to Richard was over. That was why she had decided in such haste to take this job. She wanted to get away — needed to get away — to try and make some sense of what was happening in her life. In a sense, Charles's illness had forced her and Richard to face up to the realities of their own lives. It had given her the kickstart she needed to get out of the cocoon that had been her life since she had come out of the drying-out clinic. Making the impetuous decision to accept Bill Mangan's offer was so totally out of character for her that at times she still felt as though she were dreaming and that she would wake up to find everything as it was before.

'Are you all right there, Caro?' Maggie's voice came from the back of the car. 'You're very quiet.'

'I'm fine, Maggie,' Caroline responded lightly. 'It's

just a bit early for scintillating conversation.' In fact, her insides were like jelly and her right leg was actually shaking. 'Have you any advice for me?' She tried to ignore the butterflies that were galloping around like a herd of elephants in her stomach.

'Well, you're going out at a nice time of year; the temperatures will be in the high seventies and low eighties, you lucky thing,' Maggie said enviously. 'Imagine, Devlin, this one will be lying on a beach and swimming in the Arabian Gulf in the middle of November when we're shivering over here for the next four months.'

'I'd love to be you.' Devlin smiled across at Caroline.

'Let's see now, what advice have I got for you?' Maggie spoke aloud. 'Well, you're going to a country that's not too rigid: so you can pretty much wear what you like as long as it's fairly respectable. For example, don't wear your skimpy low-cut T-shirt and mini when going shopping in the souk. You'll find it's a totally different culture and as long as you remember that you are a guest in the country and that their ways and their customs are the norm, while yours are strange but tolerated by them, you should be fine. Lots of people go to these countries and try to retain their ways of living or won't accept the rules, and they end up in trouble or very unhappy. I've seen it often. I found it difficult at times myself when I lived in Saudi, but they are totally off the wall there,' Maggie failed to stifle a yawn. 'Sorry, Caroline,' she apologized. 'It's old age.'

'Huh, it's too much red wine,' snorted Devlin.

'Do you think I'll stick it, Maggie?' Caroline asked.

'Of course you will, Caroline,' Maggie said firmly. 'Just look on it as an extended holiday. You'll have a ball. It's such a different way of life. It gets a bit unreal sometimes. When I first flew out to Saudi, I felt as though all my problems were left at home. You know: the worry and hassle I had with my mother that time after her operation when I had to come home from America. My mother and father were very opposed to me going to Saudi with Terry and they gave me a terrible time over it. But the further away from home I got on that plane, the more my problems seemed to recede. So *you* just go to Abu Dhabi and take this six months as a breather away from everyone. Away from the annulment and Richard and selling the penthouse; away from the likes of that ridiculous Marshall woman and that awful set she writes about. Just go and enjoy yourself, and believe me, my girl, when you come home in six months you'll be a different woman.'

'I wish . . .' sighed Caroline.

'I'm telling you,' Maggie said earnestly. 'I saw girls coming out to Saudi, nurses and secretaries and the like, who wouldn't say boo to a goose, and after a couple of months of having to fend for themselves they were different women. Do you know something?' She sat up straight. 'I'm getting great ideas for a new novel here.'

'Maggie Ryan!' expostulated Caroline, laughing. 'Don't you dare put me in a novel.'

'As if I would,' snorted Maggie as Devlin scorched along the dual carriageway. The lights of the airport came into view and a Boeing 737, coming in to land, roared over the top of the car.

They all grew silent as Devlin turned into the airport and before long they were parked in the multi-storey car-park. Devlin took charge of unloading the luggage. As they paused at the crossing in front of the entrance, Caroline took a deep breath. The November air was sharp and clear and frosty, and she inhaled deeply. It would be quite some time before she inhaled cold air again. The stars twinkled against the blue-black sky and a silver sliver of moon was suspended in the darkness. The next time she saw those very same stars and that curved moon, she'd be thousands of miles and several time-zones away, she reflected, as she manoeuvred the luggage trolley into the terminal building.

The Aer Lingus flight to Schiphol Airport, Amsterdam, was checking in at Section 2, Devlin read from the monitor, and before Caroline knew it, the formalities were over and they were having a quick cup of coffee in the snack bar.

'Well, it's too late to back out now.' Caroline tried to keep her spirits up but her smile faltered. 'I'll miss you two so much. I wish I was going to be here for the launch of *City Woman*.'

'I wish you were, too, Caro,' Maggie said gently. 'It won't be the same, but really, this is just what you need.'

'Caroline, this time next week when you're sunbathing and living the high life,' said Devlin, giving Caroline's fingers a reassuring squeeze, 'you'll hardly believe your luck and you'll be feeling so sorry for us. It might get too much for me and I'll have to come out and visit you.'

'Oh really? Would you, Devlin?' Caroline said

eagerly, her face brightening. 'Oh that would be really something to look forward to.'

'Well, we'll see how things go,' Devlin responded lightly. 'I'm up to my tonsils in work with Belfast and everything.'

'Oh, I know you,' Caroline said, deflated. 'Something will come up and you won't be able to go. You'd want to be careful you don't turn into a real workaholic. Isn't that right, Maggie?' she appealed to their friend.

'That's right. I'm always saying it.'

'Oh don't be ridiculous,' said Devlin, running her fingers through her blonde hair. 'Come on, Caro,' she said briskly, 'if you want to buy some papers and have a look around the duty-free you'd want to get a move on.' Caroline had to laugh.

'What am I going to do without you to organize me in Abu Dhabi?'

Devlin had the grace to look abashed. 'Sorry, I didn't mean to sound so bossy; do you want me to get you a paper?'

'Do you know something, Dev, I don't think I'll bother. I'm heartily sick of the recession and unemployment, and men pontificating about women's affairs.'

Maggie agreed. 'I'll tell you one thing. I made my own choice about my body, without any interference from popes, cardinals, bishops, politicians, lawyers or even my own husband. I got my tubes tied and I don't for one minute regret it. So you're right, Caro: don't go buying a paper and depressing yourself with all the bull that's being dished out. Go off and enjoy yourself and forget about everything that's going on here. Life's too short . . .'

So Caroline treated herself to *Vanity Fair* and *U* instead and then it was time to pass through the boarding-gate and Maggie and Devlin were hugging her and promising to write. As she passed her hand luggage through security, she caught her last glimpse of her two best friends with their noses pressed against the glass partition and their thumbs up, urging her on to her great adventure. She waved for as long as she could see them and then she rounded the curve into the duty-free and they were gone. Caroline was on her own.

Two hours later, as the Aer Lingus 737 still sat on the tarmac, she was beginning to get slightly frantic. They had boarded at seven-thirty, and had just been preparing to taxi towards the runway when the Captain's deep and rather attractive voice announced that the computer had gone down at Schiphol Airport, and that the airport could not handle incoming flights until the problem was resolved.

Maybe it's an omen, Caroline thought to herself. Maybe I'm going to miss the connection; maybe I'm mad to be going. I'll just get off the plane and ring Bill Mangan and tell him it was all a mistake.

'Good news, ladies and gentlemen: we've been cleared for take-off,' announced the gorgeous voice, and without further ado the plane headed towards the runway. Minutes later they were airborne and there was nothing to do but sit back and enjoy the ride.

It seemed like no time before they were descending over Holland, and Caroline peered out of the window, anxious for her first glimpse of Amsterdam. Apart from trips to Paris and London with her husband, and that giddy first holiday abroad with Devlin, Caroline had not flown much and this was all new and exciting. Unfortunately there was a lot of cloud and it was raining, so her first impressions of Holland were of huge flat rectangular fields with no hedges and trees as there were at home – just every inch utilized for crops – and long narrow canals. Then there was a very straight wide-laned motorway and the runway was coming up to meet them. Somehow, she felt slightly disappointed.

But Caroline had no time to dwell on her first impressions of Holland because a stewardess was urging her to the front of the plane, and as soon as the door opened she instructed Caroline to follow her as she raced down the passageway towards the huge terminal building. Panting, Caroline followed the young woman who was side-stepping passengers and luggage trolleys with the agility of a gazelle. Caroline had a vague impression of long white corridors and huge windows looking out onto tarmacs crowded with planes, moving walkways, big yellow and green signs. All rushed past her as she hurried along but she kept her eyes on the Aer Lingus hostess until they arrived at a transit desk and the smiling young woman handed her over to the care of the KLM check-in.

The young man took one look at her tickets and said urgently, 'I'm sorry, I can't check you in here. The flight has been called. Please hurry. Gate D.' Once again, Caroline took to her heels, peering frantically ahead for Gate D.

'Madam! Madam!' she heard a male voice calling and turned around to see the desk clerk running after her waving her tickets at her. 'You forgot these, Madam.'

'Thanks, thanks very much,' Caroline said, completely flustered. Oh you're great, just great, she told herself, as she carried on in the search for the elusive Gate D. Five minutes on your own and you go and forget your tickets. This was not the way she had envisaged things at all. She had so wanted to be calm and efficient as she transited at Schiphol, just as Devlin would have been. Mind, ten minutes to transit when the normal time is about fifty does make a difference, she comforted herself, as she arrived at her boarding-gate and was promptly checked in and issued with her boarding-card.

It was Caroline's first time on a wide-bellied jet and when she finally settled herself in her assigned seat she looked around her with interest. It was an Airbus 310 with eight seats across, and compared with the 737 it was enormous. Before long they were airborne and she had time to think again. Maybe all her rushing wasn't a bad thing: she'd not had time to panic and wonder if she had made the right decision. Now it was too late: she was on her way to Abu Dhabi, to live and work there. She resolved to start enjoying herself from that very moment. The girls were right: this was something that would happen only once in a lifetime. She took the hot towel from the stewardess and wiped her face and hands. It was very refreshing. She sat back and enjoyed her meal and afterwards the in-flight movie. Then, surprisingly, she fell asleep, and when she awoke they were preparing for their descent into the Saudi city of Dahran. The lights spread out beneath them in the desert winked and glinted while the crescent moon seemed to dip and dance when the plane banked sharply as it lined up for landing.

As they taxied up to the terminal, Caroline stood up to let the man beside her get out. During the early part of the flight they had chatted and she discovered that he, like her, was arriving in a strange country to work on contract, although he was staying for a year. At least she had the comfort of knowing the man she was going to work for; her companion did not know a soul where he was going.

'Good luck, Caroline.' He shook her hand warmly. 'If I ever get to Abu Dhabi, I'll look you up.'

'Make sure you do,' Caroline said with a smile, wishing he was travelling on with her. He seemed a nice young man and after sitting (and sleeping) beside him for seven hours, she was sorry to see him disembarking.

They remained on the tarmac for about an hour while the Saudi police came on board to check the plane. Caroline was able to peer out of the oval window at the beautiful Arabic architecture of Dahran Airport. The arches and minarets of the terminal building looked so exotic, compared to the businesslike buildings of home.

As they took off for Abu Dhabi, Caroline knew that the start of her new life was less than an hour away. There were only about thirty passengers remaining on the aircraft, most of them businessmen. One middle-aged woman was travelling alone and she smiled across the seats at Caroline. In one of the centre-row seats an Arab man was pulling a pristine thobe over his head. Fascinated, she watched as he arranged his

Arab headdress. In his business suit, he had been a portly nondescript man. In his white robes, he seemed to exude an almost stately presence and for the first time, Caroline realized that she was going to be part of a totally different culture.

Tense with excitement, anticipation and not a little apprehension, as the landing-gear clunked down and the 'Fasten seat belts' sign came on, Caroline looked out the window eagerly. Like jewels in black velvet, the lights of Abu Dhabi shimmered on the long straight airport road that crossed the desert. The city in the distance looked like something out of Disneyland. She knew it was on an island connected by a bridge to the mainland. Very soon she'd be crossing that bridge on the way to her new home for the next half-year. This is it: I'm here, she thought excitedly, as the great jet shot down the runway of Abu Dhabi Airport and then taxied to a smooth halt outside the terminal building. Gathering her bits and pieces together, Caroline took a deep breath and followed the man in front of her down the aisle to the exit.

Her first sight of Abu Dhabi Airport almost took her breath away. The arrivals hall was decorated with the most beautiful mosaics of greens and turquoise. Caroline stood staring at this vision, which was like something out of the *Arabian Nights*. This is beautiful, she thought with delight, admiring the splendour before her eyes, and, although she would have liked to linger, she could see the rest of the passengers disappearing from view and, anxious not to be left behind, hastened to catch up with them.

Bill had instructed her that when she got to

immigration control she was to go to the big glass partition and he would throw her visa over to her. As the control booths came into view, Caroline peered anxiously ahead of them to see if she could see Bill in the knot of people who stood behind the partition waving white visas at the arriving passengers. Her eyes scanned from right to left and back again. What would she do if he wasn't there, she thought in a panic. And then she saw him, a big grin on his ruddy face as he waved the precious paper at her and threw it over the partition. A wave of relief swept over her. Bill was there; everything was fine.

Twenty minutes later as she stood waiting for her baggage to arrive, Caroline acknowledged that while she might have got to Abu Dhabi in one piece, her luggage had not. Forlornly she watched as all the other passengers reclaimed their cases until she was the only one left. Unsure what to do, she bit her lip in anxiety. She had three big cases with clothes and enough cosmetics to last her for the six months and not one of them was to be seen. A customs official pointed her in the direction of lost luggage and a yawning official was taking down the details of her missing bags just as the KLM rep arrived.

'Don't worry about it at all,' the young woman reassured her. 'I'll give you an overnight bag and an allowance and we'll deliver your baggage to your door most likely tomorrow. This often happens; it's nothing.' Feeling somewhat bereft, Caroline passed through customs with her hand luggage and met Bill at the other side of the partition.

'No luggage? Ah well, no doubt it will turn up

tomorrow. Come on! Let's get you home. Nell has the place all ready for you and she'll be here for a few days to show you the ropes. I've to fly to Bahrain for a couple of days on business and then I'll be back myself.' They walked through the airport doors. A blast of hot, humid air hit Caroline and she inhaled the scents of this new country.

'It's warm, isn't it?' she breathed.

Bill looked at her in surprise. 'I thought it was cool enough actually. Don't worry — you'll acclimatize soon enough. If you were here in the middle of summer you'd find it hard, but it's very pleasant now.'

It was a drive of about thirty kilometres from the airport but in the air-conditioned Mercedes it took no time and very soon they were crossing the bridge that took them from the mainland out to the island where the capital city was situated. Soon they were driving through suburbs and then as they moved further along Airport Road, apartment blocks and high-rise buildings started to appear. Then Bill was swinging off the main road into a residential area and Caroline could see the minarets of a huge mosque, its mosaic dome gleaming in the moonlight. He turned right and pulled up outside an apartment block and Caroline realized that this was where she was going to live for the next six months. 'Well, what do you think?' Bill asked cheerfully.

Caroline gazed around her. 'It's certainly different, that's for sure,' she said with a smile, as she stepped out of the car and felt the blanket of hot air envelop her again. Posh it wasn't, compared to where she had lived with Richard: there were no penthouses in this apartment block. But as a dark-haired smiling girl waved at her from the first-floor balcony, Caroline felt she was going to like it. She followed Bill up the stairs, eager to see the inside of her new home.

Thirty

A high-pitched sound woke her. She turned over and buried her head in the pillows but the noise continued. Was it someone singing? One of her brothers, at this hour of the morning? What on earth was he up to? Caroline dragged herself back to consciousness and sat up, yawning. Bleary-eyed she reached for her bedside lamp. It wasn't there. Comprehension dawned and she shook her head at her stupidity. Of course she wasn't at home: she was in Abu Dhabi and that musical wailing that was amplified across the city must be the famous call to prayer.

So that was what it sounded like! Caroline had read about the muezzins calling the faithful to prayer five times a day from the mosques, and now she was hearing it for the very first time. A little tingle of excitement ran up her spine. Who could believe that she, timid and unadventurous Caroline Stacey Yates, was lying in a bed, in an Arab country, thousands of miles from home, listening to the call to prayer. Only that she knew better, she would have told herself she was dreaming.

She lay back against the pillows and immersed herself in the sound. All over the Islamic world, no matter where they were or what they were doing, practising Muslims would face towards Mecca and begin to pray. It was a bit like the Angelus really, Caroline mused, snuggling down into the bed, but the Angelus bell was nothing as exotic as this. She became aware of another sound, a low whirring, and had to think for a moment what it was. Of course, the air-conditioning.

Nell, Bill's secretary, whom she was replacing, and in whose guest-room she was sleeping, had laughed when Caroline had said how hot it was. 'I'd better put the AC on, so,' she smiled. 'I think it's quite cool myself and you'll get used to it too.' Caroline found it strange that Bill and Nell thought the weather cool. To her, it was like a very hot and humid summer's night. If this was what it was like in their winter, she didn't dare imagine the heat of the summer! Just as well she was staying only until the spring. Otherwise, she'd never stick it, she thought, as she flung off the sheet and lay beneath the cooling breeze of the AC. Nell had actually put a duvet on the bed for her, which she removed immediately. How on earth was the other girl going to stand the chill of home in November, with the rest of the winter to follow?

Nell was nice, Caroline thought. She had been smiling as she stood at the door waiting for them while Bill, carrying Caroline's hand luggage, led the way up the stairs to the first-floor apartment. A petite dark-haired girl, Nell had huge brown eyes that sparkled with good humour.

'Welcome. Welcome.' She had flung open the door wide and ushered Caroline in. A slightly puffed Bill followed. Caroline had walked through a tiled hall into a large sitting-room decorated in soothing shades of cream and brown. A slight breeze ruffled the muslin curtains that covered the windows and Caroline could see exotic plants trailing along the balcony.

'Sit. Relax,' urged Nell as she rushed out to the kitchen and brought in a tray with tea and sandwiches. 'I thought you'd feel like a snack so I made some club sandwiches. I brought you this.' She grinned at Bill handing him a can of chilled beer and a glass. 'I thought you might need it after your exertions on the stairs, with you having a lift in your plush pad and all.'

'Boy, I sure do,' Bill puffed, wiping his ruddy face with a handkerchief. 'I'll have to get fit. Definitely!'

'If you came down to the Irish dancing on Tuesday nights, I'm telling you, Bill, you'd be as fit as a fiddle,' laughed Nell, sitting down beside Caroline on the sofa.

'Could you see me?' snorted Bill, gulping down the cool beer. 'Girls, I'll love you and leave you. Caroline, I have to go to Al Ain tomorrow—' he looked at his watch '—today,' he amended, 'So I probably won't see you until Friday. But Nell is going to take you to the office in the afternoon and show you around. She'll be here until next week so you'll be fine.' He put out his hand and shook hers. 'Get a good night's sleep.'

'I will,' Caroline assured him.

'Nell, don't keep her up yakking all night. She'll probably have a touch of jet-lag. Don't forget she's been flying since early this morning.'

'As if I would,' exclaimed Nell indignantly.

'As if you wouldn't,' declared Bill as he walked into

the hall. 'I know you when someone comes over from home.'

Nell winked at Caroline, 'I'll have her in bed in half an hour, O master. Good luck in Al Ain.' She closed the door on Bill and came in and sat down by Caroline. 'I'm dying to hear all the news from home but I'll restrain myself until tomorrow. I know you must be knackered, especially having had to hang around because of your luggage,' she said sympathetically, as Caroline yawned in spite of herself.

'It's been a long day,' Caroline agreed, telling Nell all about the delays at Dublin Airport and how she had made the connection only by the skin of her teeth. She rooted through her large hold-all and handed Nell a box of handmade Lir chocolates. 'I thought you might like these, and I've brought you some magazines: *U, Woman's Way, Image*, just so you can see what's going on at home. I should have brought the papers, but they're so full of bad news I just didn't bother.' Caroline felt like kicking herself for not thinking that Nell might have been interested in reading about the news at home.

'Don't worry about it; sure I'll be home this day next week and I'll hear it all then. But thanks very much for the chocolates and the mags. I'm going to take them to bed with me.' Nell took Caroline's empty cup and plate from her. 'Come on; I can see you're wall fallin'. I'll show you your room, and you can have a shower and get into bed. And you don't have to worry about getting up in the morning. I'll come home from the office around one and we can have lunch together and a good chat. Then I'll bring you down to introduce you gently to the circus that's going to be your life for the next few months. How does that grab ya?'

'That sounds fine,' Caroline smiled back, liking this live wire and wishing that she wasn't going home at all.

Nell had shown her to a small guest-room decorated in blues and white. It was very soothing and Caroline liked it immediately. Nell pointed to a blue-tiled bathroom across the hall. 'I've got an en suite and the room is much bigger. So you can move there when I'm gone. I hope you'll be warm enough,' she added doubtfully. 'There are blankets in the top of the wardrobe if you need them.'

'God, I'm baked,' Caroline assured her, mightily relieved when Nell switched on the AC. She had been so glad to have that shower. Her clothes were stuck to her from the heat and the long hours of travelling, and she stood for a good twenty minutes under the refreshing spray. Wrapped in a towelling robe that Nell had given her, Caroline had stood peering out through her bedroom window at the strange new environment. Across the street, she could make out several small shops on the ground floor of apartment blocks. Up to her right she could see the airport road where they had turned off. No doubt it would be much easier to get her bearings in daylight. It was hard to believe that the same crescent moon shone over Dublin city, thousands of miles away.

The neat blue KLM overnight bag caught her eye and she opened it to find a little treasure trove: nightshirt, slippers, black eyemask, four headache tablets in a little case, needle and thread and small scissors, moisturizer, toothbrush, toothpaste, sachets of washing-powder, razor and aftershave, deodorant, shampoo, plasters, tissues, toothpicks, nail clippers, emery boards, and even a little game of draughts. They had thought of everything. Caroline was delighted with it. It would come in very handy in the future for overnight stays and no doubt she'd have her luggage tomorrow, if what she had seen so far of KLM's customer service was anything to go by. Having dried her hair, she slid into bed and fell instantly asleep, to be woken a few hours later by the muezzin's amplified call.

After a while the keening of the muezzin ceased and Caroline drifted back to sleep, relaxed in the thought that she could have a lie-in in the morning. That would help alleviate any jet-lag she might feel because of the four-hour time difference.

The insistent ringing of a phone woke her and she jumped out of bed half-asleep. She padded out into the hall towards the sitting-room, where the sound was coming from.

'Hi, it's me!' Nell's voice floated cheerfully down the line. 'Sorry to have to wake you but I've been on to KLM and your luggage is in Cairo.'

'I'm in Cairo!' Caroline said groggily.

'No, no, you're in Abu Dhabi! Your luggage is in Cairo,' Nell said soothingly as Caroline began to wake up properly. 'I'm sorry I had to wake you but someone from KLM is on the way over to get your case keys. They'll need it for customs. And they promise they'll have your luggage delivered by lunchtime. I'll see you then. Make yourself at home. Raid the fridge for breakfast and go back to bed.'

The carriage clock on the bookcase told Caroline

that it was just gone nine. That meant it was five a.m. Irish time. Nell had been in the office since seven-thirty. They started work early in these parts and Caroline realized that she too would have to get used to the habit. She was trying to decide whether to go back to bed or get up when a knock at the door announced the arrival of a man from KLM. Giving him the keys, she closed the door, yawned widely, forbade herself to look out the curtained windows of the apartment because she knew if she saw the sun she'd never go back to bed, poured herself a glass of fresh orange juice, drank it in two gulps and went back to her comfortable divan. Five a.m. was just not the time to get up, she decided, but she promised herself that she would no longer compare times with home. From now on it would be Abu Dhabi time only.

When she woke again, she felt completely rested. Alert and excited, she flew to the window to get her first look at the city in daylight. Brilliant sunshine and the bluest of blue skies greeted her and it was hard to credit that it was almost the middle of November.

Across the street, men in white thobes stood chatting outside a small supermarket. Traffic whizzed up and down the airport road further along. Another supermarket, Bashir's grocery, was brisk with customers. Indian and Pakistani women in their colourful saris seemed to glide in and out and the Arab women in their black abayas looked mysterious and exotic.

Nell had told her that Thursday was the start of the weekend in the Arab world and that Friday was the holy day. Most people were off work but Bill's office was open seven days a week and Nell sometimes worked at the weekend if they were particularly busy. She then took her two days on the Saturday and Sunday. Caroline would be doing the same.

Walking down to the sitting-room, Caroline drew the curtains, opened the balcony windows and stood squinting in the bright sunlight. A blast of hot air hit her and she stood on the balcony inhaling the scents of the flowering shrubs and the aromas of coffee and spices that were wafted along on the warm breeze.

Suddenly conscious of the fact that she was hungry, she decided to have breakfast. Nell had set the table for her in the small cream-and-yellow dining-room. Beside her cup were some newspapers and magazines and a little note that said, 'There are croissants and bread in the fridge and cereals and eggs in the press. Enjoy!'

Caroline heated the croissants, made herself a piece of toast and took them and her pot of tea into the dining-room. It was quiet in the apartment. There was a peaceful aura about the place with its comfortable, worn furnishings that were in such contrast to her own sterile high-tech penthouse. Richard had employed an interior designer to decorate it before they were married but Caroline had never liked the harsh, modern furnishings and decor. She was going to enjoy living in this homely apartment with its airy, spacious rooms.

She passed a very pleasant hour munching away on her breakfast as she read a copy of the *Gulf News*, one of the Emirate's English newspapers. It was a lively newspaper that covered world affairs as well as the news from the neighbouring Emirates and the Gulf area.

A section in the information guide showed maps of the Gulf giving the weather forecast in the area, and she was fascinated to see a little diagram giving details of rising sand as well as wave height in feet. She wondered if she would ever see a sandstorm. After all, Abu Dhabi was built out of the desert. The temperatures were in the high eighties and if the high eighties was winter weather, God knows what the temperatures would be in high summer. Then she noticed a little column that gave the times for prayers. She learned that the prayer that she had heard the call for in the early hours was called Fajr and that, very soon, she would hear the call for Dhuhur, the midday prayer. Then there would be Asr, the afternoon prayer, and Maghrib, the evening prayer, and then at about ten-past seven the Isha, the last prayer of the day.

Nell had left her a little news-sheet of an international women's club that gave the most interesting details of various clubs and classes she could join during her stay in the Emirate. With mounting interest she read about badminton and book discussion groups, bowling and bridge, computers, contact and conversation groups, cookery and handicrafts, mah-jong and rug appreciation and tennis. There was news about a day safari to the Sharjah souk and an intriguing piece titled 'Flying Carpet' which told of a planned trip to Syria, as well as shorter trips to areas of interest in the Gulf.

She was definitely going to get involved in *something*, she told herself firmly. She was not going to spend her time like a little dormouse in this exotic city. The time had come to spread her wings. The distinctive, wailing sound started and she smiled, pleased with herself to remember that it was the call to Dhuhur.

Energy surged through her and swiftly she cleared up her dishes, showered and dressed. She awaited Nell's homecoming eagerly because she was dying to ask her a thousand and one questions. More than anything, however, she was really looking forward to her trip to the office and to her first glimpse of this Islamic city with its magnificent mosques and multi-storeyed buildings, its palaces, and souks, and flower-filled parks. The garden of the Emirates, Abu Dhabi was called. Soon she would discover why. With mounting excitement Caroline watched white-robed men converge upon the nearby mosque. Nell had told her it was called 'The Big Mosque'.

'Hurry on, Nell,' she murmured. 'I want to be out there. I want to be part of it all.'

Thirty-One

Nell drove skilfully along the wide-laned highways of Abu Dhabi and Caroline admired the way she refused to be cowed by the horn-honking taxi-drivers and the huge Mercedes and Range Rovers. The traffic was fast and frenzied and Caroline knew she'd be totally intimidated.

The roads themselves were wide and the shrubbery and greenery took her breath away. The roundabouts were spectacular with their displays of flowers and emerald grass. Nell had skirted the city and was taking the scenic route to the office, to give Caroline an idea of the place.

Caroline watched as dozens of workers trimmed hedges, laid camel dung and weeded the flower beds all along the route.

'National Day is coming up and the place is always decorated beautifully then,' explained Nell. 'You're really seeing the city at a nice time of the year. It's pretty, isn't it?'

'It's such a surprise, I can't believe how green it is,' Caroline remarked.

'That's thanks to Sheikh Zayed. He loves greenery and he's had millions of trees planted. I think he's really enlightened. Look at these roads. Aren't they super! If we had a road system like this at home we'd be doing really well. It's hard to believe the city is only about twenty-five or thirty years old.'

'Wow!' exclaimed Caroline, impressed. 'Who is Sheikh Zayed? I've heard the name before.'

'He's the ruler of Abu Dhabi,' Nell explained as she swung left at a roundabout and drove down a tree-lined highway, 'and the head of the UAE – the United Arab Emirates. Abu Dhabi is the capital. This area is where most of the sheikhs' palaces are. You see those high white walls. See if you can see the palace inside.'

Caroline craned her neck eagerly and caught a glimpse of a sumptuous building. Ornately Arabic in design, it looked magnificent. A guard in a hut kept watch over the entrance barrier. 'Were you ever in a palace?' she asked eagerly.

Nell laughed. 'Never, unfortunately. The locals keep very much to themselves. Of course there's enormous wealth here because of the oil. That's why you saw those Pakistanis and Egyptians and Filipinos doing all that manual work. They have to work very hard but the wages are far better here than in their own countries. Most of them can send money home. The same with the Filipino maids. Some are like part of the family; others are treated badly.'

An enormous car pulled up beside them at the traffic lights and Caroline saw a robed man with a neatly trimmed beard staring straight ahead.

'Is he a sheikh?' Caroline asked, intrigued.

'I don't know if he's a sheikh. You know that only a member of the royal family is entitled to be called a sheikh. In Saudi they're called princes; here they're sheikhs.'

371

'Oh.' Caroline was surprised.

'It's mostly the sheikhs, their wives and families who live in the palaces. In that compound we've just passed there are about five big houses. All the sons and their wives live there too: they even have their own family mosque. The women are very traditional, covered from head to toe.'

'How awful,' Caroline said.

Nell drew the car to a stop beside a little roundabout that had a flowering tree in the centre.

'I don't know,' Nell smiled. 'There's an awful lot of misconceptions about Arab women. They're not the downtrodden species the West thinks they are. Arab women have great power in their own homes. When they marry they don't take their husband's name; they don't wear a wedding-ring. Whatever they have in their dowry is theirs alone and cannot be touched. And you'll probably notice that they're dripping in gold. Their gold is their investment and it is a matter of pride with men to buy their wives gold so that others can see what good husbands they are.'

'Even so, I think being wrapped up in a veil and not being able to go where you want is a bit restrictive,' Caroline mused.

'Well, you know,' countered Nell, 'the veil gives you great privacy. No-one can see behind it but the wearer can see all that's going on. Here, where you have to get used to being stared at, a lot of women wear sunglasses not only to protect themselves from the sun but to hide behind as well. The veil of the West I call them. I've often been tempted myself to buy an abaya and mask. Sometimes I think it would make life much simpler here.'

Caroline stared out the window of Nell's red Honda Civic. They had driven out of the city and were on a road that had water on both sides. There was hardly any traffic and it was very peaceful.

'This is called the breakwater,' Nell explained. She pointed to a strange-looking shop. 'That's a dhow restaurant. The food is gorgeous; you should try it out when you're here. Doesn't the city look nice in the distance? You know, of course, that the city is built on an island?'

'Yes, I read that, and you can really see it from here. It's lovely.' Caroline drank in the sight of the high-towered city gleaming in the sun, as the waters of the Arabian Gulf glittered green and turquoise on all sides.

The Arabian Gulf, she said again to herself. It sounded so exotic. She had heard so much about it during the Gulf War, and here she was, standing on its shores. Caroline felt like doing a little dance of excitement. To think that she had flown to Schiphol and changed planes all by herself. And then arrived in Abu Dhabi ready to take up a new job. She was proud of herself. Other people might not think it was such a big deal but it was the most challenging thing she had ever done in her whole life.

'Sometimes I bring my lunch here if I feel like a bit of peace and quiet,' Nell said. 'It's only seven or eight minutes away from our offices on the Corniche. I think the view is superb. Not that you'll have much time to enjoy it,' she added laughing. 'Come on. I'll show you where we are.'

Nell hadn't exaggerated about the view, Caroline decided, as she stood in the tenth-floor office, with its banks of equipment, including a fax machine, constantly sending and receiving. She gazed at the panorama across the six-lane highway with its dividing line of emerald grass, edged by neatly clipped hedges, and laid out with flower beds full of startling yellow zinnias and whiter than white lilies and lush flowering hibiscus. Beyond was a large promenade outlined by luscious parkland and gardens, and dotted with ornamental pools and high-spraying fountains. This was the famous Corniche that Maggie had told her about. Seven kilometres long, it curved in a semi-circle along the waters of the Gulf. Caroline was dying to explore its length.

The next few hours passed in a haze of facts and figures as Nell gave Caroline an outline of what would be expected of her as Bill's office administrator. Nell explained that Bill worked all over the Gulf. He owned a construction company that had developed over the years into one of the busiest firms in the Levant.

'Bill never went in for the usual practice of bribing officials to get contracts or underquoting so that there wasn't enough to finish the job – as is a frequent practice in this neck of the woods,' Nell informed Caroline as she explained the filing system to her. 'You must remember that up until the early sixties when Sheikh Zayed became ruler, there was no city here. All that you see here—' she waved out the window to where the molten sun turned the tinted-glass façade of the towering Arab Monetary Fund Headquarters building to gold '—all the infra-structure, roads, offices, hospitals, have been built since then. Well, naturally, there were more than a few shysters around ready to rip off the locals: architects, builders and the likes, and consequently lots of the houses and palaces that were built in the early days are falling to bits. The thing with Bill is, if he does a job he does it properly. You'll see, Caroline; he's a real perfectionist. At first he didn't get many contracts because he charged more than his competitors but the work he did has lasted and over the years his reputation as a builder with integrity has grown enormously. And, my dear,' Nell continued dryly, 'that's almost a contradiction in terms, because the building fraternity are certainly not known for their integrity. Bill's reputation has grown and grown, not only here, but all through the Emirates as well as Oman and Qatar. And with the phenomenal development of these states, he's involved in construction work all over the place. He's rarely in the office; that's why he needs someone reliable here. You'll manage fine. Maria and Filomena, both Filipinos, are the other two staff and I think you'll get on with them.' Nell smiled as she read a fax that had come through.

'That's from Bill in Al Ain: he wants me to rearrange a flight for him to Bahrain tomorrow and fix the accommodation in the Hilton: we won't see him until Sunday evening.' She shook her head. 'Caroline, you'll spend your time arranging and re-arranging flights and accommodation and itineraries. He'll drive you nuts but he's the best in the world,' Nell said fondly as she began calling to see what flights were available.

Caroline spent the afternoon with Nell, trying to assimilate all she was telling her. No doubt she would get used to it in time, but as she listened to Nell explaining how to go about getting visas for the foreign employees Bill would be sponsoring, she couldn't help the spasms of panic that engulfed her, as she struggled to remember the strange-sounding names of the people she would have to contact. By this time next week Nell would be gone and she would be in charge. Would she be able to handle it?

Nell saw the expression on her face and laughed. 'You'll be grand; stop worrying. The girls will be here and Bill's not an ogre. Now I think we've done enough. I don't know about you, but I'm starving. Let's go and have a bite to eat.'

It was just turning to dusk as they left the building and the sunset was breathtaking. The whole city was tinted red-gold and the sun, an enormous red orb, was sinking rapidly. It was so different from home: there was no twilight and in minutes, it was dark. The refreshing breeze that had been blowing seemed to die away in an instant and as they walked towards one of the main shopping areas of the city Caroline found the humidity intense.

She was wearing a light silk blouse and a flowing cotton skirt but even with those light clothes, rivulets of perspiration ran down between her breasts and her hair stuck damply to her forehead. Caroline was amazed that Nell, who was dressed in a heavy Lacoste T-shirt and pale denim jeans, strode along briskly. It was clear that the heat didn't bother her at all.

'Don't worry: you'll get used to it,' Nell assured her as Caroline blew a little breeze down the vee of her blouse. They walked until they came to a wide street full of shops and offices. Nell led the way into the marble foyer of the Novotel Centre Hotel and Caroline was immensely relieved at the cool of the air-conditioning.

'I brought you here because it's handy for work, the food is good and you can have snacks or a meal depending on what you fancy. This street is called Hamdan Street. There's a lovely shopping mall just beside us called the Hamdan Centre. You might like to have a look around after we've eaten. I'll take you to Salam Studio and Stores; it's just across from BHS. They have a huge range of sunglasses, and they've lovely ones just in. You really do need a decent pair of shades here. The sun is so bright and we're not used to it.'

After they had ordered, Caroline sat back and relaxed. It was like being on holiday really, except that in a week's time she would be on her own. It was a daunting thought, but at least she now knew her way from the office to Hamdan Street.

'Will you have a glass of wine, Caroline?' Nell enquired.

'No. No thanks. Just iced water for me,' Caroline said. 'I don't drink.' She didn't feel like announcing that she was a dried-out alcoholic. Some things were best kept to oneself.

'Oh.' Nell was surprised. 'Pity. I was going to bring you to a ladies' night before I go.'

'What's that?' Caroline was intrigued.

'All the big hotels have them,' Nell explained. 'The one in the Sheraton is in a bar called the Tavern – that's on Sunday. The Zakher Tower one is on Mondays in The Ship. Harvester's is in The Holiday Inn on Tuesday, The Meridian's is on Tuesday as well and the Hilton has one on Wednesday in Hemingway's. The ladies get two drinks free and you meet all sorts of people. It's a night out if you're in the mood. Of course if you don't drink, there are soft drinks.'

'It sounds interesting.' Caroline wasn't sure if it was exactly her scene.

'At the beginning, it's great – it's a novelty. There's so much going on in this city you could be out every night of the week at all sorts of functions.' Nell popped a piece of bread-roll into her mouth. 'When I came here first I was never in and I was permanently wrecked. So after the first six months I copped on and calmed down. To be honest, after a while you begin to realize that you're seeing the same old faces, and you understand that you're not on holidays: you're working as at home and you start getting into a routine. But having said that, it's still a great place to work and I don't think I can ever see myself settling down at home again.'

'Don't you get lonely?'

'Ah yes,' said Nell nodding. 'I miss my family, and now and then I have a day or two when I get a tremendous bout of homesickness. But, Caroline, then I just go to the beach on my next day off, lie on a lounger and order a Pimms. Now imagine doing that at home. Or going on a weekend trip to the Buramini oasis or up to Dubai to do a bit of shopping or taking a dhow trip to an island in the middle of the Gulf. No, this is the life for me. It's a bit unreal but I love it.'

'You'll be freezing when you go home,' Caroline laughed, as she tucked into a huge fluffy omelette which was accompanied by the most colourful salad she had ever seen. 'Winter came very early this year and it was bitterly cold when I was leaving.'

'I know; I dread it,' Nell moaned as she speared an olive. 'Although I must say I'm getting a bit excited now and it will be great to be home for Christmas.'

'You'll be out of hospital by then?' Caroline asked, a bit unsure if she should have mentioned the topic. Nell's reason for going home was to have surgery and Caroline didn't want to appear too nosy.

'Oh, I'll have had the first operation by then and I'll go in for the second one some time in mid-January,' Nell said cheerfully.

'Oh, you poor thing! I didn't realize you had to have two operations.' Caroline was shocked, and very impressed at the other girl's coolness about going under the knife.

'It's a real pain in the ass getting your bunions done,' Nell sighed.

'*Bunions!*' Caroline's jaw dropped. She had been imagining all kinds of operations, but never bunions.

'I know. I'm mortified,' Nell confessed, giggling, 'but they've just been getting worse and worse and they are so painful. The specialist told me I should have them done or I'll be in real trouble by the time I'm forty. I'll be on crutches for weeks: he'll do one foot first and then the other. So I decided to have it done at home. I'm going to buy a house while I'm there. I'll have time to organize that too. And I'd like to spend some time with my parents. They're getting on a bit and I've been gadding around the world since I left school.' Nell looked enquiringly at Caroline.

'And what made you come out here for six months? Or am I being nosy?'

Caroline shook her head. 'Of course not. My husband and I are separated . . . well, we're going to divorce actually. You know, one of those foreign ones, seeing as there is no divorce at home.' She smiled wryly. 'I believe a man only has to say, "I divorce you" thrice in the Arab world and it has legal effect. Anyway, I just felt I needed to get away. And here I am.'

'I'm sorry, Caroline: that's tough,' Nell said sympathetically.

'It's the best thing, really,' Caroline said briskly. 'My marriage was a disaster but at least we've come out of it friends. This is a whole new opportunity for me and I'm going to enjoy it.'

'You will, Caroline! As I said earlier, life here is a bit unreal. It's as if you leave all your problems behind you. You work, you shop, you socialize. You don't have to worry about property, because you're not allowed to own any. You have such a choice of material goods that shopping can become addictive. But it's such fun! You meet your friends for as long as they're here. It's a very transient world and it's exactly what you need at the moment. It will give you time to think, time to make plans and when you do go home you will have a very different perspective.'

'Well, that's what I'm hoping,' Caroline replied, as she swallowed the last mouthful of omelette. Much refreshed by their meal and chat, the girls lingered a while for coffee and then Nell took her to the Salam Studios to buy her sunglasses. Earlier in the day Caroline had changed some traveller's cheques into dirhams, the currency of the Emirate, and of course she had her credit card. Eager to do her first bit of shopping, she was overwhelmed by the choice of sunglasses: Cartier, Christian Dior, RayBans, Fabergé, YSL – all the labels at various prices, but far far cheaper than they would be at home. Nell made her try on a multitude and they had great fun before Caroline finally selected a classy pair of RayBans.

'I'll look like Jackie Onassis,' giggled Caroline as she slid into the car beside Nell. They had decided to call it a day, as Caroline was beginning to wilt a bit.

'They're lovely on you, very sophisticated, very glamorous. Don't worry – you'll get a hell of a lot of wear out of them.' Nell plonked herself in the driver's seat and started the engine. Caroline sat gazing out at the lights and the sights of the city, fascinated by the men in the white thobes and the veiled women. Timid by nature, she knew it was going to be a bit of an effort for her to explore this exotic city on her own, but explore it she would. She'd never have an opportunity like this again.

They were walking up the stairs to their apartment when a tall blonde girl with the most striking green eyes passed them on the stairs. She was wearing a floral print dress with a fitted bodice, and a slim black jacket. She looked like a model.

'Hiya, Féile,' Nell saluted her. 'You're looking like the cat's pyjamas! Where are you off to?'

'Hi, Nell,' the other girl said, and Caroline immediately recognized a familiar accent. 'I'm going to the President's dinner.'

'Ah, yes, that's on tonight. I tried to get tickets for it but I'd left it too late. They were all sold out. I thought Caroline might have enjoyed it. Féile, this is Caroline; Caroline, Féile Morris. She's one of our neighbours.'

'Hi, nice to meet you.' The other girl gave Caroline a firm handshake and smiled broadly. 'You don't know how thrilled we are to be getting rid of this one for a while.'

'Give over,' said Nell with a grin.

'I'm having a *Coronation Street* night tomorrow if you want to come. I got a video from home,' Féile remarked. 'Although you're probably right up to date, Caroline, having just arrived.'

'No I'm not, actually,' Caroline laughed. 'I missed all of last week's because I was doing the rounds saying goodbye to people. I'd love to see it.'

'Great, we always have a good night when the *Coronation Street* video arrives. A few of us get together and have a drink and a bit of a laugh. You'll get to meet some of the girls and I'll be able to tell you all about tonight. It's usually a very good night and with Pat at the helm, no doubt it will be one of our best. Will you come with Nell?'

'I'd enjoy that, thanks.' Caroline accepted the invitation with delight.

'See you tomorrow, then. I'd better rush. I'm late and you know when you really need one it seems like an age before you get a taxi.' Féile glided down the stairs and out into the night.

'Féile's a pet. You'll really like her. She's a terrific neighbour and very kind too. She's going to show you around a bit when I'm gone.'

'Is she?' Caroline was pleasantly surprised.

'Oh yeah,' Nell said matter-of-factly, as she

unlocked the door. 'When I told her you were coming and that I'd only be here for a week, she volunteered. That's Féile all over, softhearted. But she's great fun, Caroline. You'll have such crack with her. She's famous for bargaining. She can keep the straightest face. I'm hopeless. I always get a fit of the giggles.'

'What's the President's dinner she is going to?' Caroline was intensely curious, and envious of the elegant young woman who had so confidently marched out into the night to hail a taxi in this exotic city that had all the brashness of the West and all the mystery of the East.

'It's the Irish club,' Nell explained, drawing the curtains and putting on the kettle for some coffee. 'You'll have to become a member. It's a terrific way to meet people from home and keep in touch, and it's nice to go down on Tuesday nights and have a jar and join in the dancing if you want to. I like it very much although some people don't bother with it at all.'

'It sounds like a good idea to me. I never knew that there was such a thing here.'

'Oh yes indeedy: the St Patrick's Society of Abu Dhabi is one of the best associations here. I couldn't get tickets to the dinner. They were snaffled up because the Irish events are so popular. I'll bring you to next Tuesday's meeting and introduce you to Pat Jawhary, the president. She's hosting the dinner tonight. The ambassador will be there and a special guest from Ireland. Pat is very enthusiastic and very proud of being Irish. She's really done a lot since she's become president. I think she's great; you'll like her.' Nell handed Caroline a mug of coffee.

'I'm sure I will.' Caroline was looking forward to

meeting the woman Nell had spoken so glowingly about.

As she lay in her bed reflecting on the events of the day Caroline felt much more optimistic about being on her own. So far she had met Féile Morris, her new neighbour. Caroline smiled in the dark as she thought of the blonde young woman. It was very strange, but somehow Féile reminded her of Devlin when she had first known her. A carefree happy-go-lucky Devlin before tragedy had taken its toll. Féile had the same confidence, the same sense of style as the young Devlin. A few weeks out here would do Devlin all the good in the world. Determination gripped her: if it was the last thing she did, she was going to get Devlin Delaney out here on a holiday. But she'd wait until she was accustomed to the place so that she could really show Devlin around and give her a good time.

And even though she shrank a little at the thought of meeting a whole load of strangers, she *would* go to the Irish club with Nell on Tuesday night, and the following Tuesday when she was by herself she'd take a deep breath and go on her own. That would be one night of the week filled. No doubt the Irish club would hold other functions too. Well, she would go to them as well. She was determined not to be her usual shrinking violet self here. God knows, she had spent her life with Richard going to functions with the so-called cream of Dublin society. She had gone to galas and openings, launches and lunches, and hated them all, and had drunk to give herself courage. Well, not any more! In Abu Dhabi she was going to go to events on her terms because she actually wanted to go, not because she was Richard's wife and had to go. It would take nerve. She would not be able to have a few vodkas beforehand to give herself Dutch courage.

The thought of Nell and Féile, two young Irish women who had grabbed life by the horns and were shaking it for all they were worth, gave her courage. If they could do it, and hundreds more like them, the least she could do was give it a bash.

Pat Jawhary sounded like an interesting woman. How long had she lived out here? Such a contrast in names, Pat, so Irish, Jawhary, so Arabic; Caroline was looking forward to meeting the president of the St Patrick's Society of Abu Dhabi. Wait until she wrote to them at home and told them about it. They wouldn't believe it. But it was nice to know that there was a place she could go to where Irish people gathered, and feel a little bit more at home in this fast-paced high-rise city. She fell asleep smiling.

Thirty-Two

'How do you do, Caroline?' said a woman with a soft Kerry accent. 'Welcome to the St Patrick's Society and welcome to Abu Dhabi.' Caroline found herself looking into the friendliest, kindest eyes she had ever seen. This was Pat Jawhary, the president of the Irish society. She was petite and very striking, with hair the colour of burnished copper and big blue eyes that sparkled with animation. Her accent was so rich and musical that Caroline could have listened to her speaking all night.

'We'll make sure you have a good time here; don't worry,' Pat said with a laugh. 'Only the driest old stick going would fail to enjoy herself in this city. Isn't that right, Nell?' She winked at the other girl. Turning to Caroline, she fixed her with a blue-eyed gaze. 'You will come next week now, won't you?' Pat said warmly. 'Even though Nell won't be here. Quite a few new people have arrived in the past few weeks and I want to make sure that everybody gets to know at least some people so they won't feel lonely during their first few months. Anyway it's nice to have a network of friends and acquaintances.' Caroline felt instinctively that Pat was a person who cared about people. Nell had told her that she had been a midwife and Caroline, even on this short acquaintance, felt if she was ever to be in labour, she'd very much like a woman like Pat Jawhary to be delivering her baby.

She had been a bit apprehensive about coming to the weekly Tuesday night meeting. A roomful of strangers had always intimidated Caroline. But having met Pat and a few other members, she realized she need not have worried. As she had discovered in the past few days, people were always delighted to meet someone from home, someone with news. Before she knew it, Pat and Nell had partnered her with a cheerful engineer called Mike, for the Walls of Limerick.

'I'm not very good at this,' she confessed as the music started.

'That makes two of us,' said Mike with a grin, as he clumped around the floor like a young elephant. It was hilarious and also intriguing to watch olive-skinned men from a different culture taking part in Irish dances. Round they danced, laughing at missed steps, and breathless from the exercise, and when it was over they all retired, thirsty, to the bar.

Sipping the Coke that Mike brought her, Caroline looked around at the laughing, chattering people and felt she could be in any bar at home. Except that it was much cosier than a pub. Comfortable chairs dotted the large room. Soft wall-lamps cast a comforting glow and a French window led to a tiled patio. It was the social club of the Corniche hospital and the Irish society used it on Tuesday nights. As she viewed the various groups of relaxed people, Caroline decided that she liked the easygoing atmosphere and thought

387

happily that it wasn't going to be an ordeal to come here once a week.

'Are you enjoying yourself, Caroline?' she heard Pat ask as she pulled up a chair. 'It's such a pity you couldn't have come to the President's dinner: we had a marvellous time.'

'Féile told us all about it,' Caroline said smiling. 'I believe there was dancing on the tables and everything.'

'Oh that's the sign of a great party in Abu Dhabi,' Pat laughed, 'but we'll have lots more events that you'll have to come to. We have a mince-pies and mulled-wine evening for Christmas and we'll surely have a dhow trip or an outing to the desert before you go home next spring. You'll enjoy it here, Caroline: Abu Dhabi is a very friendly place and I love seeing girls come out from home and have a ball.'

Caroline wondered if she would ever achieve such an aura of self-confidence. They chatted over another drink. Pat told Caroline how she had been a midwife in the Rotunda, before going out to Saudi to work as a midwife and later as head of a department in a big American hospital. Afterwards she had come to Abu Dhabi with her husband, Akram, and little son, Eamonn. Caroline judged that Pat was only in her early thirties, but hearing all she had done in her life, she felt completely inadequate. All Caroline had ever done was to leave home and share a flat for a happy time with Devlin, before rushing into a marriage that had turned out to be the biggest mistake of her life. And all because she had been so afraid of being left on the shelf! How stupid she had been! Looking at all these independent young women who were making their own choices, living the kind of lives they wanted to live, seeing the world, experiencing other cultures and throwing off the stifling mantle of insular thinking, she wanted to emulate them.

Caroline knew that taking this job was the most important step she had ever taken. So when Pat asked her if she would like to join a silk-painting class, she immediately said yes and later in the evening when Féile suggested she join her badminton club, she found herself agreeing.

'Oh God! I'm going to have a hell of a hangover,' moaned Nell as they took a taxi home several hours later. Because it was her last night, everybody had been buying her drinks.

'Don't worry; at least you don't have to get up for work in the morning,' Caroline remarked as the driver drove past the imposing Sheraton Hotel. The previous night, Bill had taken Nell and herself and the other two girls in the office to the Inn of Happiness, the Chinese restaurant in the Sheraton, as a treat before Nell went home. They had had the most superb meal in the exotic red-and-black restaurant and Caroline promised herself she was going to go there again.

The following morning, she padded around the apartment, making sure not to make any noise so as not to disturb Nell. It was a beautiful morning out and she stood on the balcony marvelling that the sun was so hot and the sky so blue in the middle of November.

She also found it so incongruous to go into the huge co-op that stocked everything from Christmas cards to Kerrygold butter and see all the Christmas decorations, or to listen to Christmas music being played in

Spinneys, the large English shop, and then to come out to the oven-blast heat and the blazing sun.

'Morning!' A cheerful voice interrupted her musings. For someone suffering from a hangover, Nell looked remarkably well. Seeing Caroline's quizzical look, Nell laughed. 'I'm not as bad as I thought I'd be: lots of water and an Alka-Seltzer last night and some orange juice this morning did the trick. So since we have the day off and I'm all packed and organized, what do you say we catch a few rays? I'd better top up the tan for going home. I have to make them all pea-green.'

'I'd love that,' said Caroline eagerly. She hadn't been to the beach yet and she was dying to go swimming in the Arabian sea.

Twenty minutes later they were driving through the suburbs and past the enormous sheikhs' palaces to the Intercontinental Hotel.

'You have to be a member of a beach club, unless you just want to go to the ladies' beach,' Nell explained as she expertly negotiated a huge round-about covered with flowers. 'This one is one of the most exclusive. Bill pays our membership as a perk for working unsocial hours. It's terrific, Caroline: there's tennis and squash, a gym and saunas, and you can do water sports like windsurfing and paragliding off the beach. It's lovely to come down here on your mornings off, particularly if it's midweek when it's not packed. I usually try to come once a week, just to flop and relax and be by myself for a while. It really renews you.'

'I'd say!' exclaimed Caroline, as they turned left off the carriageway and drove down to a marina that was full of luxurious yachts and sleek motor cruisers, the like of which Caroline had only seen in films. Nell parked the car and led the way to the entrance of the beach club. She handed Caroline a card. 'This is your membership card and you are entitled to bring two guests if ever you want to.' The smiling man at reception handed a pair of thick fluffy towels to each girl and then Nell was leading Caroline past the tiled shower- and changing-rooms out to a verdant lawn, beyond which were two rows of loungers with luxurious emerald cushions that just invited a body to sink into them. Shaded by palms, the club was like something out of an exotic travel brochure. A long crescent of white sand curved along the coast, fringing the aquamarine waters of the Gulf. At the edge of the lawn was a large circular shaded bar, where patrons could order drinks or tea and coffee or snacks. Lucinda Marshall, eat your heart out, thought Caroline in amusement. This was the nearest to paradise she had ever been.

'You like it?' Nell spread her towels on a lounger and stepped out of her sundress to reveal a black bikini and tanned smooth skin. 'Ooohhh, I'd better make the most of this,' she sighed, oiling herself with Hawaiian Tropic. 'It will be grey skies and cold weather for the next few months.'

'I think I'll go for a swim first,' Caroline decided, as she was feeling quite warm. Pulling off her shorts and T-shirt, she stepped out of her sandals and walked down to the water's edge in her turquoise bikini. The sand was hot under her feet and with a sigh of pleasure she waded out into the crystal-clear waters of the Gulf and dived in. It was bliss. The water caressed her body

391

as she swam and floated. Later she lay on her lounger and let the sun warm her cooled limbs as she fell into a peaceful slumber under the shade of her palm fronds.

The girls spent the day at the club, chatting, snoozing, swimming, eating and drinking and when it was time to leave, Caroline took a last look around, knowing that she was going to spend many happy hours in this gorgeous place.

They did some last-minute shopping for presents that Nell wanted to bring home and then it was back to the apartment to get ready for Nell's departure.

As she stood with Bill behind the glass partition at Abu Dhabi airport, waving to Nell until they could see her no longer, Caroline tried to ignore the vague knot of apprehension that twisted her intestines. She had met lots of people, she had the Irish society and Féile and Pat and most of all she had that beautiful beach. Thousands would give anything to be in her shoes.

'Will you be all right on your own?' Bill cast a glance in her direction as he pulled up outside the apartment.

'I'll be fine, Bill,' Caroline assured him confidently.

'Well, you have my number: use it if you need to.'

'I will, Bill; don't worry.' Caroline gave him a quick peck on the cheek.

'Good night, good night, Caroline,' her boss blustered, but Caroline could tell he was pleased. Despite his gruff exterior, he was as soft as butter.

'I'll see you in the morning, Bill, bright and early,' she promised, and waved as he drove off.

It was strange going into the apartment without Nell being there, but in another way it was nice being on her own. She made a pot of tea and some toast and pottered around for a little while and then, knowing she had to make an early start, she went to bed and almost before she knew it, she was asleep.

'Don't be a coward!' Caroline spoke severely to her reflection in the mirror. Big brown eyes under a feathery fringe of black hair stared doubtfully back. She was trying to get up the courage to drive to work rather than get a taxi. 'Start as you mean to go on.' All her paperwork was in order and the keys to Nell's Honda Civic were lying on the dressing table. She picked up her map of Abu Dhabi and ran her eyes along it. On paper her route looked relatively easy. It was a straight road to the city. Airport Road would be no problem. There were no roundabouts until she got to the big one opposite the Cultural Foundation where she would have to turn on to Zayed the First Street, and then all she had to do was to turn right at Khalid Bin Al Waleed Street, near the British Embassy. Then she was on the Corniche and the rest was a doddle. Still she dithered. She had seen the erratic driving. Would she keep her nerve with all the beepings and lane-hopping that were part and parcel of driving in Abu Dhabi? She looked at her watch. It was almost seven-fifteen; she'd want to hurry if she wanted to be into work on time, whether driving or taking a taxi. Caroline knew that if she took a taxi today, she'd never drive in the city. So, taking a deep breath, she picked up the car keys and closed the door behind her.

Opening the car door, Caroline sat in, only to remember with a deep sense of shock that the car was left-hand drive! Exiting on the passenger side, she was sorely tempted to lock the doors and hail a taxi but her stubborn streak came to the fore and with a hasty prayer to her mother in heaven, she got in and started up the engine. It was a bumpy start, to say the least, as she clutched at an unfamiliar gear and tried to remember that her handbrake was on her right side rather than her left. Cautiously she edged out, her gears jarring unmercifully as she slowed to a halt to let some traffic pass. Then the car cut out. Cursing vehemently, Caroline started up the engine and then shot out on to the street and turned left on Airport Road. The traffic was fast-flowing but she kept to the slow lane and proceeded at a steady pace. She passed the white walls of the open-air mosque where everyone gathered to celebrate Eid al Fitr, the great three-day celebration after the long fasting of Ramadan. She would be here for the next Ramadan which would start some time around the end of February. During that month, all Muslims had to fast from sunrise to sunset and non-Muslims, such as herself, would have to refrain from eating in public or anywhere they could be seen by Muslims in daylight hours.

Although she knew Pat lived somewhere nearby, she didn't dare look around but kept her eyes firmly on the road ahead. 'Remember the traffic lights are overhanging,' she muttered, as a taxi-driver shot in in front of her. As she got closer to the city centre, the traffic intensified and sweat prickled her brow and upper lip.

'Omigod! Omigod!' she breathed as she was tooted at impatiently from behind. 'Creep, jerk!' she swore, her palms sweaty against the wheel. 'Keep to the right; keep to the right; O Sacred Heart of Jesus, get me to work safely.' Caroline prayed to herself the whole way into town. The roundabout at the Cultural Foundation came into view and she slowed down to negotiate it, only to invite a torrent of hoots and beeps.

'Piss off, the whole shaggin' lot of you,' Caroline growled as she shot around the roundabout and turned left onto Zayed the First Street. It was with immense relief that she finally drove on to the Corniche and saw the haven of her office building.

Standing in the lift as it glided silently up to the tenth floor, Caroline tried to compose herself. Her crisp white cotton blouse and tailored black trousers still looked good in the mirror in the lift. Despite her traumatic journey, she didn't look as flustered as she felt. At least she had a good idea about how the office worked. Nell had been very patient and thorough at explaining; so she wasn't too apprehensive about her first day without her.

'Morning,' Bill greeted her as she walked through the door into the office.

'Morning, Caroline,' Filomena smiled sweetly. Caroline wasn't sure that she particularly liked Filomena, who could be a bit smug and superior and didn't like to be asked to do things.

'Morning, all,' Caroline returned their greetings cheerfully.

'You had no problems getting here?' Bill cocked an enquiring eyebrow.

'None at all,' Caroline sat down at Nell's desk.

'You took a taxi.' Filomena made a statement rather than asked a question.

'Not at all,' Caroline said. 'I drove.'

'Ha!' exclaimed Bill. 'That's thirty dirhams you owe me, Filomena. I knew Caroline would drive in.'

'What's this?' she asked in amusement.

'Filomena was so sure you wouldn't drive that she bet me thirty dirhams. She should know better than to bet with me, eh, Filomena?' Bill was as pleased as if he'd won a grand.

'Know-all!' Filomena snapped, and Caroline felt a secret sense of satisfaction that she had proved her wrong. It would be interesting to see how the typist behaved when Bill was not in the office and Caroline was in charge. An instinct just told her that Filomena was someone she was not going to like. There was something bossy about the younger girl and it was perfectly obvious in the few days that Caroline had been at the office that Filomena resented her presence and, understandably, probably felt that she should have been left in charge of the office during Nell's absence. However, she did not have Caroline's linguistic skills nor her experience of office administration. Caroline hoped there would be no unpleasantness between them and that Filomena would not take advantage when Bill was away.

It was a hectic day. Bill had secured a contract to build a palace for a sheikh in Oman and Caroline spent the day on the phone getting quotations from suppliers. At lunchtime, Filomena decided that Caroline and Maria should have first lunch and she would have second. Caroline knew she was being tested.

'That's very kind of you, Filomena,' she said pleasantly. 'I'm dying for a bite to eat. We'll let you go on first tomorrow.'

'Oh I don't mind looking after the office: I'm used to it.' Filomena was as sweet as sugar.

'Oh, fair is fair!' Caroline said firmly. 'Isn't that right, Maria?'

'Oh yes,' Maria affirmed, much to Filomena's chagrin. Caroline gave a mental sigh of relief, feeling that she had handled the situation quite well. Maria was a gentle soul and it was obvious that Filomena, if she were allowed, would boss her around. Nell had made sure that didn't happen and Caroline, seeing the way the wind was blowing, decided she would continue to keep Filomena in her place.

'Caroline, would you like to come to the Pizza Hut on Khalifa Street?' Maria asked. 'It's not far from here and they do very tasty food.'

'I'd love to, Maria,' Caroline agreed, glad to get out of the office for an hour and delighted that she'd have company for lunch.

'But you brought sandwiches,' Filomena interposed.

'Oh, I feel like a pizza and I can show Caroline around as well,' Maria said as they walked out to the lift.

Filomena was annoyed with herself. She realized that she had made a mistake throwing Maria and Caroline together but she had thought that Maria would have her usual sandwich in the office before going out for a walk along the Corniche. It had never entered her head that Maria would ask Caroline to go to lunch; she was such a mouse normally.

In a thoroughly bad humour, Filomena assaulted her keyboard, prompting Bill to enquire, as he walked through to his own office, if she was still sore about the thirty dirhams.

'Huh!' She kept her head down and ignored her boss, much to his amusement. Bill had a pretty good idea of what was wrong with her and it would be interesting to see how Caroline handled the situation. So far, she was doing fine and he was very pleased that she had driven to work this first day. She would be able to use the car to get around and it would give her a chance to see the Emirates properly.

By the time she got home that evening, Caroline was on a high. She had come by a different route which, although it had four roundabouts, had meant that she did not have to go into the city centre. As long as she stayed in the slow lane, she was fine.

'I did it! I did it! Easy-peasy,' she hummed to herself as she undressed. 'First day over and I did fine. Good girl, Caroline,' she applauded herself, thrilled at the way the day had gone and proud of the fact that she had taken the car.

It was bliss to stand under the cooling jets of water. She washed her hair, slipped into a robe and sat down with a cup of coffee to read the *Gulf News*.

A knock on the door surprised her and when she opened it Féile was standing there.

'Hi, how are you getting on?' asked her neighbour, smiling. 'How did the first day go? I see you took the car.'

'Come in, come in,' bubbled Caroline. 'I'm still on a high after it all. I can't believe I drove into the office, but I'm just so glad I did!'

'I thought you'd be wrecked,' laughed Féile.

'I'm not. I feel I've loads of energy. If you knew me, you'd know what an achievement this is for me. I'm a bit of a mouse at home. I used to avoid like the plague driving in O'Connell Street, and even having the first day in the office without Nell over and knowing that I did a good job is a great relief. I won't be dreading it or the journey to work any more.'

'Caroline, I'm telling you: you'll go home a different person. Being in a city like this and learning to fend for yourself gives you loads of confidence. I'm here three years now and I'm a totally different person from what I was when I came out. So make the most of it and enjoy it! Talking of enjoyment, how would you like to pop over to the souk for a while? Nell told me she hadn't had the chance to bring you. I'm going myself for an hour or two.'

'Oh, that would be a real treat! I'm dying to go there. I've heard so much about it.'

'Have you had your dinner yet?' Féile enquired.

'Ah, I'll get something when I come back,' Caroline replied.

'Come over and have a bite with me,' Féile said easily. 'It's nothing exotic – just pasta and a side salad – but it will save you cooking.'

Caroline accepted the offer gratefully and as she dressed, reflected on how kind her neighbour was. Nell had obviously asked Féile to keep an eye on her, but giving her her dinner was above and beyond the call of duty. Caroline resolved to have the other girl

399

over later on in the week. And to think she had been worried that she would be lonely. Maria had gone to lunch with her, she was having dinner with Féile and then going to the souk: it was still like being on holidays.

This impression was reinforced as she strolled around the exotic streets of the souk with Féile. They had taken a taxi and then walked across the huge white winding pedestrian bridge known as the Twirly. Illuminated with strings of lights, it led to an Aladdin's cave of narrow shop-filled streets. There were glittering gold shops, fabric shops with the purest of silks and chiffons, electric and watch stores, oriental gift stores, rug and tapestry shops and exotic grain and spice shops which scented the air with the most aromatic scents. It was a shopper's paradise and Caroline was in her element. 'I'm going to get some silks, and I want some good runners oh! and look—' she pointed out a Little Mermaid doll that sang, '—that would be perfect for Mimi, Maggie's little girl.' Féile urged caution, reminding her that she was going to be there for some time and that she should shop around and see where the bargains were to be had.

'Look at that!' Caroline was still agog, staring at a jet-black hairpiece hanging outside a little knick-knack shop. 'Is that real hair?'

'Yes, they have them all over the place,' Féile remarked as the owner, a small dark-skinned man, came rushing up to them rubbing his hands.

'You like? You like? You want to buy; very good price I give you.'

'Just looking,' Caroline smiled.

'Real hair; you feel; real hair.' He took Caroline's hand and rubbed it along the hairpiece.

'No I don't want to buy, thank you,' Caroline said politely.

'Very, very good price!'

'Have you got one this colour?' Féile interrupted, pointing to her blonde tresses.

The man glared at her. 'No.'

Féile gave an eloquent shrug and moved off. Caroline followed. 'You brat,' she laughed.

'It's the only way,' grinned Féile. 'I can see I'm going to have to take you in hand or else you'll be buying everything you're offered.'

In the end, after a really enjoyable evening, Caroline went away with fresh-roasted ground coffee which had been flavoured with cardamom and saffron. She also bought some bhar, an Arabic mixed spice, and some sticks of incense and a piece of sandalwood, which she sniffed the whole way home in the taxi.

It had been a day of personal triumph for her and she fell asleep full of plans for further explorations of the souk and looking forward immensely to a trip on a dhow, to which she had been invited by Féile and her flatmate Ger.

'Richard, it's wonderful! I'm having a ball. I love the job, I've made friends. Listen: I went on a dhow trip last week and it was fantastic! We just sailed off to a little island and dropped anchor. We swam and had a big barbecue and a sing-song afterwards. And next weekend I'm going up to Dubai to do some shopping. I've even started to play badminton.' Caroline's voice came floating down the phone and despite the distance of many miles and the static and the pauses caused by the time-gap, it was impossible to miss her enthusiasm.

Richard couldn't believe that the laughing, outgoing, fun-loving person at the other end of the phone was his gentle, self-effacing wife. But had he not made her life a misery because of the way he had treated her? He had made her question her own womanliness, her sense of self. Listening to her at the other end of the phone helped ease the burden of guilt he carried from the marriage.

'How is Charles, Richard?'

'He's here, Caroline. I have you on speaker, so he's been hearing about all your exciting times, too.' Richard smiled at the gaunt man sitting opposite him at the kitchen table.

'Caroline, I'm fine, Richard is taking great care of me and my brother is making sure I have no pain. It's snowing here in Boston at the minute. It's like a scene from *The Snowman*. I'm sitting beside a roaring fire, looking out the window, while Richard is making a fish chowder for lunch. What more could a body ask?'

'Well, I'm just getting ready for bed. It's very balmy, the sky is clear and the stars seem very near tonight.' Caroline had to laugh, amused at the complete contrast of time and weather between Boston and Abu Dhabi.

They talked a while longer and then Richard confirmed that he would phone the following week, as they took turns to make the weekly call. As the chowder simmered gently on the stove, Richard poured a glass of wine for himself and Charles and sat down at the table with him.

'I can't get over Caroline. Can you?' he asked his companion.

Charles took a sip of the Bordeaux, savouring its full fruity flavour.

'I'll admit I was a bit concerned when she told us she was taking off for Abu Dhabi to work. Caroline is so unworldly. I was worried about how she would cope on her own in a strange city and in a different culture.' He looked Richard straight in the eye. 'To be honest, I was afraid she'd go back on the bottle. Caroline always needed a crutch. Isn't it wonderful that the need is gone and she's doing so well on her own?'

'I'm really pleased. I made such a mess of her life that I never thought she'd get over it, but she has, hasn't she, Charles?' Richard needed the affirmation.

'Richard, you've got to stop looking back. Forget the past unless it's happy and look forward. You've got to put the guilt aside. What's done is done but you can make amends to Caroline by always being there when she needs you. Believe me: knowing there is someone you can turn to, whatever the circumstances, is one of life's greatest blessings.'

The older man spoke earnestly, leaning over and taking Richard's hand in his own. 'If you do for Caroline what you've done for me . . .' He leaned back in his chair and sighed contentedly. 'In a strange way, you know, I think everything is really working out for the best. Caroline is living the life she missed as a teenager and young girl; she's doing all the things she never had a chance to do before she married you, when she was looking after the family home. You and I have this lovely time here, with no-one to bother us. Here

403

it doesn't matter that we're gay and we don't have to look over our shoulders or worry about our legal reputations. I'm very happy here, Richard, despite the cancer and everything. I've never known such peace. I love our little house, I love our walks, I love going shopping. I love just sitting here in the kitchen with you looking out at the blizzards. This is a rich, rewarding time for me, I want it to be the same for you. I want you to have this time to look back on and say it was one of the best times of your life. Do you think you'll be able to say that, Richard?'

Richard went over and embraced his lover. 'I'll be able to say that, Charles, without reservations. We're going to have such good times. It's great we've got the pool and we'll be able to do barbecues ourselves again. Caroline's not the only one who's going to live it up,' he said lightly, kissing Charles on top of his head before going over to give his chowder a stir and sprinkle in some seasoning.

'That sounds lovely,' Charles agreed. 'Hurry up with that chowder: it smells divine.' Richard buttered several slices of fresh brown bread and dished out the chowder, making sure to keep the portions small. He knew Charles would only manage a few mouthfuls; his appetite was getting smaller and smaller, despite Richard's best efforts.

'Get that inside you.' He placed the steaming dish in front of Charles, and then threw a couple of logs on the fire. 'When you've had your nap, we can finish that bugger of a jigsaw.'

'Oh, it's a bugger all right,' Charles agreed, catching Richard's eye. They laughed together, as the flames roared up the chimney, illuminating the kitchen with a warm orange-and-yellow glow, as the sky darkened outside and the wind howled and great flurries of snow whitened the window panes.

Warm and contented, Richard and Charles ate their chowder in companionable silence, while across the world, Caroline battled through the first wave of loneliness and homesickness to hit her since her arrival in Abu Dhabi. Richard and Charles had seemed so happy together and the picture Charles had painted of the blizzard outside and them inside with the roaring fire had left her longing to be part of it. She missed them both. It was most unlikely that she would ever see Charles alive again. The previous time she had talked to Richard, Charles had been asleep and her husband confided that the older man was deteriorating slowly.

They seemed so far away; home was so far away. She missed Devlin and Maggie badly. She had had letters from both of them in the previous week, giving her all the news. Caroline tried to resurrect her earlier bubbly humour. She remembered Nell's solution to homesickness and decided that tomorrow, her day off, she would go to the beach. Even in the few weeks she'd been here, she had noticed a dropping in the temperatures. She might as well make the most of the warm weather while it lasted. It was starting to get much cooler at night. She was actually sleeping under the duvet. Or maybe it was just that she had finally become acclimatized. The thought cheered her up slightly and she picked up the book Féile had given her as a present. It was called *Mother without a Mask* and it was all about the women in an Abu Dhabi family and all their traditions and culture. Compared to her own world it was like something out of the *Arabian Nights*. Passing the palaces of the sheikhs and sheikhas now, having read over half the book, Caroline felt that much more familiar with their denizens' private and hidden world. As she read of the Sheikha and the Youngest Son and the Second Son and the Sheikha Grandmother and Um Hamed and her beautiful daughter Shamza, Caroline's homesickness faded and she snuggled down in her bed, knowing she could read as long as she liked. She didn't need to be up at the crack of dawn. Tomorrow would be spent on the beach.

Thirty-Three

There was a howling gale and it was lashing rain. It had been a very cold night and Caroline thought grumpily as she scraped the burnt bit off her toast that if she'd wanted this weather she could have stayed at home. The weather had been bad for the previous week and in the *Gulf News* that morning there was actually an article about the weather, giving advice to the residents of Abu Dhabi about how to cope. A doctor in the emergency department of the central hospital was advising people to take Vitamin C and wear clothes that were suitable for the weather. Caroline had seen people wrapped up as if for the Arctic. Fifty-eight degrees wasn't that cold, she reflected, but she supposed that for the residents of the Emirates, this kind of weather, which wouldn't have aroused comment at home, was extraordinary.

Devlin had phoned a few days before and filled her in on all the news – and weather – from Ireland. She told Caroline that Maggie and Terry were having rough times between them and that she couldn't see the marriage surviving. Then she had mentioned that some journalist had been giving her a hard time. All in all Devlin had sounded terribly cheesed off.

Her call had left Caroline vaguely depressed. Now

she was here a little over two months, and the euphoria of her first couple of weeks had worn off. Although she was enjoying herself very much she supposed she couldn't expect to be in great humour all the time. The uncertainties over the Gulf didn't help. Bill had gone to Oman for the week.

The traffic was brutal, which did not improve her mood, especially as Filomena gave a superior sniff and glanced at her watch when Caroline arrived ten minutes late for work. Relations had not improved between her and the other woman, as Caroline had become more accustomed to the job and had needed to rely less on the younger woman for information. Well, today, Caroline decided, she was in no humour for Miss Filomena and her carry-on. There were two large cheques to be lodged. She'd give them to Filomena right away. That would get her out of her hair for a half-hour or so while she and Maria got through typing several bulky contracts that had been on her in-tray for the last week. She was asking Maria to do them with her because she was a far better typist than her workmate and was extremely careful and accurate. Nothing could be Tipp-ex-ed out on a legal contract and Filomena never seemed to be able to type a document without resorting to the magic white bottle. Caroline filled out all the necessary forms and took the cheques over to Filomena's desk. The sloe-eyed Filipino girl raised her head from what looked like a personal letter.

'Yes?' she said insolently.

'I'd like you to take these to the bank now please, Filomena,' Caroline said politely, handing her the envelopes containing the cheques.

'Oh that's Maria's job,' Filomena drawled, handing them back.

'Maria and I are going to be up to our eyes with those contracts and as you seem to have nothing to do at the moment but write personal letters, I'd like you to go to the bank,' Caroline said firmly.

'I'm the senior typist: I should be doing the contracts,' said Filomena defiantly.

They stared at each other, and Caroline felt her insides quiver. If she backed down on this, she might as well admit failure in the job she was appointed to do and go home to Dublin.

It took every ounce of her willpower to keep her gaze and her voice steady. 'You know as well as I do, Filomena, that both you and Maria have the same position in this office and that there's no such thing as a "senior" typist. You also know that there can be no errors in a legal document and I'm sure you'll admit that every document that I have asked you to type since I came here contained several typing errors. I'm afraid that's just not good enough. That's why I'm asking Maria to help me with the contracts. It means she will not have time to go to the bank today.' She handed Filomena back the cheques.

'I'm going to speak to Bill about this when he gets back,' Filomena muttered.

'Fine,' Caroline said coolly. 'In the meantime, if you could lodge these and then start on the office supply orders, please.'

Furious, the younger woman grabbed the envelopes and her coat and marched out of the office, slamming the door. Maria gave Caroline a sympathetic smile. 'Don't mind her. Would you like some coffee?'

'I'd love some,' Caroline said fervently, drained after the encounter. Normally it took Maria only about half an hour to do the lodgements, but Filomena strolled in two hours later. Caroline said nothing but when lunchtime came she said to Filomena, who was sitting in icy silence at her desk, doing the office supplies, 'I'm sure that since you took an early lunch you won't mind if Maria and I take ours now. We won't be late,' she added pointedly. Filomena's jaw dropped. She was stunned at this behaviour to say the least. She hadn't figured that Caroline would exert her authority the way she had. She knew that if Bill found out about the way she had behaved today there'd be trouble. He had made it very plain that Caroline was in charge when he was out of the office. Well, she wouldn't push her luck, she decided, but she was damned if she would give that Irish girl an easy ride.

Richard was exhausted. Charles had not been at all well that day. When his brother called, he sat with Charles for several hours and before he left he took Richard aside and said that maybe the time was coming when Charles would have to go to hospital.

'He doesn't want to go,' Richard said agitatedly.

'I know,' the oncologist said kindly. 'Cancer patients never do. I've increased his morphine dosage. Make sure that he doesn't get dehydrated.'

Charles had fallen asleep that evening, but Richard could not relax, although he felt terribly tired himself. He was almost afraid to go to sleep in case he wouldn't hear Charles if he called for him in the night. In the weeks after Christmas, Charles's

410

condition had worsened and fear gnawed at the younger man. He knew the time was coming when he was going to have to face the thing he most dreaded.

'Don't think about it until it happens,' he muttered miserably, as he rubbed his neck muscles to try and loosen the knots of tension that had gathered there. He had deliberately blotted out the future, planning barbecues and picnics for the summer. The planning of them had kept him going, postponing the thought of what was inevitable.

'Richard,' he heard Charles call weakly and was at his bedside in two steps. There was something different about his friend's face. He couldn't explain it, but it filled him with fear.

'Will I call Mark?' he asked, taking Charles's hand. It was icy-cold and he rubbed it between his palms, trying to infuse some warmth into it.

Charles shook his head and smiled. 'There's no need. I have no pain. I'd like to go into the sitting-room for a while and sit by the fire and look at the tree.' Even though it was mid-January, the Christmas tree was still up, because Charles liked sitting in the soft glow of the twinkling lights and watching how the flames from the fire cast warm shadows on the walls and ceiling. His eyes couldn't take harsh bright light any more, and if the tree had to stay up until June, Richard didn't care.

He carried Charles gently into the sitting-room and settled him on the sofa in front of the still-flickering fire. He threw on some kindling and together they watched the flames rise brighter and higher.

'Thank you, Richard, for everything,' the older man said, with a weary smile.

'It's I who have to thank you, Charles,' Richard said fiercely. Why had those words of thanks seemed so final? Why did things seem so different tonight? They had sat here like this many times before. Why did Richard have this feeling of dread?

Charles lay back against his cushions and Richard tucked the rug closer around him. 'You're awfully cold, Charles. Will I get a quilt?' he asked anxiously.

Charles took his hand, and Richard grieved at how frail those hands had become.

'A quilt wouldn't make any difference, dearest Richard; it won't be long now.'

'Don't say that!' Richard said angrily. 'You've got to fight it.'

Charles sighed, 'I don't want to fight it any more. I don't mind now.'

'But aren't you afraid?' Richard could not understand the other man's attitude. He was terrified of death.

'No.' Charles shook his head. 'You get a peace that takes all the fear away. I don't fear going to meet my Maker. He made me what I am. I did my best in life, I tried never to hurt anybody. That's all anyone can do. Promise me, Richard, you'll hold your head high and not be ashamed of who and what you are. God made you and me what we are. He'll give you courage as he gave it to me. Have a happy life, Richard. Look everybody in the eye as I did. Stand by Caroline, just as she'll stand by you. Promise me.'

'I promise. I promise.' Tears streamed down Richard's face as he held Charles close.

'It's not so bad,' Charles murmured and, closing his eyes, he drew several short shallow breaths and then gave the smallest sigh. There was silence and Richard knew he was dead.

'Oh Charles, Charles, don't leave me on my own. I'm scared, I'm scared as hell,' Richard cried, great gasping sobs, knowing that he had lost the one person who had truly loved him with a wholehearted, generous, undemanding love. The only person who had never expected him to be anything he wasn't. Richard bowed his head over his best friend and cried.

By the time Caroline got home she had a thumping headache. She was also feeling a bit queasy and she couldn't decide if this was as a result of her run-in with Filomena or the spare ribs she had eaten at lunchtime. She was due to go to her silk-painting class and normally it was one of the highlights of her week: she really loved her new hobby and she enjoyed having a coffee afterwards with Pat Jawhary, who was a classmate. But at the moment she just wasn't in the humour so she dialled Pat's number with the intention of telling her that she wasn't going. The line was engaged so she went into the bathroom and ran a bath. Maybe it would perk her up.

Now that she was on her own, self-doubts began to set in and she brooded about the situation with Filomena. Would she be able to maintain her authority? What would she do if the other girl openly defied her? How was it that she had never behaved like that with Nell? Caroline remembered her schooldays so long ago, when Ruth Saunders, the class show-off, had bullied her mercilessly. Not physical bullying but the tormenting and needling that gave a whole new meaning to the term mental cruelty. Filomena reminded her of Ruth: she had that same sly malicious quality. She had got the better of Ruth, though, at a class reunion. Caroline gave a wry smile as she stepped into the bath. She hoped she could do the same with Miss Filomena.

She had dozed off in front of the television set when the persistent burr of the phone jerked her back to consciousness. 'Hello,' she murmured drowsily.

'Hello, Caroline. It's me,' she heard her husband say and, with a sense of shock that jerked her back to instant wakefulness, she realized he was crying.

'What's wrong? What's wrong?' she said frantically.

'It's Charles.'

'Oh no! Oh God no.' Caroline's stomach gave a sickening lurch. Although she had known it was inevitable, now that it had happened it seemed unbelievable. At the lowest point in her life, Charles had been like a father to her. He had been a strong shoulder to cry on when she had needed one and was always ready with an encouraging word and sound advice. Now she would never see him again, would never experience the familiar tweedy pipe-smoking smell of him when he enveloped her in a bear-hug. Bereft, Caroline cried with her husband.

When he hung up, she felt terribly alone. How she wished she were at home. Then at least she could have gone to stay with Devlin or Maggie. She didn't really know anyone here well enough to share her grief with. How could she explain about the unusual relationship she had had with her husband's lover. If

Féile had been there she would have knocked on her door, but she had gone home to Ireland for a couple of weeks' holiday. Caroline knew Mike wouldn't mind her calling him. They had seen a lot of each other at various functions, since that first meeting at the Irish society, and Mike would have liked their relationship to develop further. But Caroline was happy just to be friendly with him: she had no desire to get involved with a man so soon after her disastrous experience with Richard. If she rang Mike, he might get the wrong idea. He would see it as a deepening of their relationship and right now she didn't feel she could cope with that.

Agitatedly, she paced up and down the lounge as all the old horrible feelings of panic came surging back. It had been so long since she had experienced a panic attack that, when it hit her, it seemed all the more terrifying. Her heart started to pound, she felt dizzy and sick and her breathing quickened.

'Oh God, please don't do this to me, please don't let me lose it after all this time.' She didn't even have a tranquillizer to calm her down. A powerful desire for a drink engulfed her: just a brandy to knock her out, send her to sleep and stop this awful shaking fear. Nell had brandy in her drinks cabinet. Surely one drink couldn't harm her.

Slowly she walked over to the sideboard where Nell kept her drinks. Hands shaking, she took out a tumbler, opened the brandy and poured herself a generous measure. The rich never-to-be-forgotten smell of expensive cognac made her palms sweat and her mouth dried in anticipation of that first sip. The phone rang and she was so sorely tempted to let it ring, but she was afraid it might be Richard again. She lifted the receiver and heard Pat's warm tones at the other end of the line.

'Caroline, you weren't at class. Is everything OK? Are you sick?' came the kind Kerry voice that was so much a part of Pat's personality.

'Oh Pat,' Caroline blurted. 'I'm an alcoholic and I'm standing here with a glass of brandy in my hand and I'm so scared. Help me, please, help me!'

Thirty-Four

'Put the glass down, Caroline,' Pat said very calmly and firmly. 'I want you to pack an overnight case. I'm on my way over to collect you this minute.'

'Oh, I couldn't put you out like that,' Caroline said. 'I'll be fine, I'll be fine,' she added shakily.

'Caroline, I'm not leaving you alone in this state,' Pat declared. 'I know Féile's at home on holidays, so you have no-one in the building. I'll be over in less than ten minutes and you're not putting me out at all. Go and empty that brandy down the sink and put the bottle away. Come back to the phone and tell me when you've done it.'

Caroline's hand shook as she carried the glass out to the kitchen. She was strongly tempted to take a slug of the sweet-scented amber liquid. Even one small sip. For long seconds she held the glass in her hand and then, with the greatest reluctance, she turned the tumbler upside down and watched the brandy drain down the sink. Slowly, she walked back to the phone.

'Did you do it?' She could hear the note of anxiety in the other woman's voice.

'It's gone. I poured it down the sink,' Caroline said heavily.

'Good girl. I'm on my way now,' Pat said, and hung up.

Caroline stood as though in a daze. Why was she not exhilarated that she had thrown out the brandy? All she could think of was that lovely golden cognac draining down the plughole and what a waste it was. She could have drunk that brandy. *One* glass wouldn't have sent her over the edge.

'It would, it would, look at you, you're craving it. And you haven't touched a drop for months. Just look at you: the first time you have to face up to something you go running to the bottle. You're pathetic!' Caroline sank to her knees and bawled like a baby. Surprisingly, after a couple of minutes of uninhibited weeping, she felt a little better. At least the heavy weight on her chest seemed to have dissipated with the release of her emotions. The knowledge that Pat, who lived less than a mile away, was on her way to collect her, galvanized her. Wiping her tear-streaked face with the back of her hand, she rushed into the bedroom to get dressed. She had just slipped into a pair of jeans and a sweatshirt when the doorbell rang. Hastily she ran a comb through her hair and went out to open it.

Pat stood there, concern etched on her face. 'Are you OK? Did you take a drink?' she asked, putting a comforting arm around Caroline. At the sympathy in the other woman's voice, Caroline dissolved into tears again. Pat closed the door and led her in to the sofa. 'You're going to be fine; don't worry about a thing.' Pat Jawhary had the most reassuring voice in the world. No doubt she had said exactly those words to desperate mothers-to-be as they suffered the woeful pains of labour.

'I'm really sorry for dragging you over here. I feel such an idiot,' Caroline confessed, as she struggled to regain her composure.

'Don't be a bit sorry,' Pat said crisply. 'That's what the president of the St Patrick's Society is for.' Her eyes twinkled and in spite of everything, Caroline couldn't but feel at ease with her. With Pat, there was no bullshit; what you saw was what you got. What Caroline saw was a very caring person who was genuinely concerned about her predicament.

'Now, have you packed an overnight bag? You're staying the night with me,' Pat announced, picking the bottle of brandy up and putting it away in the sideboard.

'I couldn't put you out like that,' Caroline protested again. 'I'll be fine, honestly.'

'You're not putting me out in the slightest. Come on.'

Caroline was mortified. 'But . . . but I can't go waltzing in on top of you . . . I'm sure a distraught female is the last thing your husband wants in the house after a hard day in the office.'

'Akram's in Bahrain on business, but if he wasn't, he would have been here with me to collect you,' Pat said firmly, and Caroline could see that there was no point in arguing with the determined Kerrywoman. To tell the truth, she was glad not to have to spend the night on her own. She wasn't sure if she would have the willpower to leave that brandy bottle in the sideboard.

She sat in silence as Pat drove through the darkened

streets, and then they were passing the Open Mosque. After they had passed the Indian school, Pat turned left and drove up to her enclosed villa.

The scent of the huge frangipani tree in the centre of the lawn never failed to delight Caroline, and even tonight, in her stressed state, she was able to appreciate the great tree's unique beauty.

'It's beautiful, isn't it?' Pat smiled as she locked the big gates after them. 'I'll always associate the scent of frangipani with Abu Dhabi.'

'Pat, are you sure I'm not putting you out?'

'Caroline, believe me, you're not. Now, come on in and I'll show you to your room. Then you and I are going to sit down and you can tell me what's upsetting you so much that you feel you need a drink. If you want to, of course, that is,' Pat finished with a smile.

'Thanks, Pat, I'd appreciate that very much,' Caroline answered quietly.

She led the way through the hall and up a wide, plushly carpeted stairs. On the wall facing her Caroline saw a big, framed silk painting. It was a beautiful study of a woman kneeling at a stream, looking very pensive. Slender reeds grew along the river-bank, leading the eye up to the delicately coloured sky. It was one of the most exquisite silk paintings that Caroline had ever seen.

'Pat! Did you do this?' she exclaimed. 'It is absolutely gorgeous. You're really talented. I'll never be that good.'

'Yes, you will, if you keep going to your classes,' the other woman said encouragingly, as they carried on up the stairs. 'This is your bedroom.' Her hostess led her into a luxurious pink-and-white en suite bedroom. A huge bed dominated the room, complete with a white wicker headboard and matching bedside lockers. It was elegant, yet restful, and the stamp of Pat's tasteful style was unmistakable.

'Just settle in. I'm going down to put on the kettle,' Pat said, and closed the door gently behind her. When Caroline was alone, she sat on the huge bed and tried to compose herself. It shocked and unnerved her that she had fallen so disastrously to pieces on hearing about Charles's death.

'But, my dear, it's only natural!' Pat exclaimed after she had heard the long, sorry saga which had burst out of Caroline like water from behind a dam. They were sitting in Pat's kitchen drinking cups of hot, sweet coffee. 'Why should you be surprised at your reaction? My God, Caroline, if I'd been through what you'd been through that brandy would have got short shrift. Don't be so hard on yourself,' Pat said gently. 'Look, I've checked the times, and there's an AA meeting at St Andrew's tomorrow night. Why don't I go with you?'

'Thanks, Pat. I'd appreciate that very much.'

Somehow she got through work the next day. Pat had not wanted her to go, offering to phone in and say that she was sick. But after the carry-on with Filomena the previous day, Caroline did not want the younger woman to think that she was chickening out. Going to work was the best thing to keep her mind off her problems and especially off the thought of going to the AA meeting. It was always the same: she hated going to the meetings, but once she got there she was always very glad she'd gone. Pat was being very supportive and Caroline knew she was lucky to have made a friend like her in Abu Dhabi. It had been such a relief to talk about everything and they'd had some good laughs as Pat told hilarious tales about her time as a midwife in Dublin. She had insisted that Caroline spend another night at her house.

As the time approached for her to leave for the AA meeting, Caroline got more and more tense. 'Come on,' said Pat briskly, seeing her agitation. 'Let's get it over with.'

Half an hour later, in the midst of a group of people, some of whose faces were surprisingly familiar, Caroline stood up and cleared her throat.

'My name is Caroline,' she murmured, and caught Pat's encouraging gaze. 'My name is Caroline,' she repeated clearly for all to hear. 'And I am an alcoholic.'

Thirty-Five

'Are you enjoying the Eid?' Mike raised his voice above the din of the crowd.

'It's fabulous,' Caroline declared. 'I've never seen such food.' They had gone to a party in the Hilton for the celebration that marked the end of Ramadan. It was over two and a half months since her dark night of the soul, and with Pat's, Féile's, Mike's and AA's help, she was back on track again and enjoying life in Abu Dhabi to the utmost. Sometimes she felt a bit guilty about enjoying herself, but as a kind of defence mechanism she had pushed Charles's death to the back of her mind. Richard was back in Dublin and she spoke to him once a week, but, on her counsellor's advice, would not let him burden her with his woes.

'You're too far from home to be able to do anything about it and it's futile for you to be worrying out here. Besides, you must stop that pattern of taking on everyone else's troubles and brushing your own under the carpet. Your troubles are just as important as anyone's, so worry about yourself for a change.' Thus went the firm but sympathetic advice she had been given.

Not that she had too much time to worry, these days. The weather, which had been very rainy, overcast and surprisingly cold until nearly the end of Ramadan, had picked up, and there were loads of activities to take part in. Caroline had gone for a weekend's camping with Mike and some of his friends to the Liwa, the largest oasis in the area, which was about a six-hour drive from Abu Dhabi. The scenery had been breathtaking after they left the Al Ain Road and turned right on to the Ruwais Road to follow the coast to Tarif. The oasis, its villages surrounded by magnificent sand dunes that turned to a deep red-gold in the sunset, was the most exotic place Caroline had ever been. At night the stars seemed so near in the pitch-blackness that she felt she could almost reach up and pluck one out of the sky. The peacefulness of the desert, particularly at sunrise and sunset, was really special among the many wonderful memories of her stay in the Emirates.

She was aware that her time in Abu Dhabi was slipping away quickly and so she crammed in as many experiences as she could: trips to Dubai and Sharjah and, nearer home, to Al Ain, the university city and birthplace of Sheikh Zayed. Caroline was also looking forward immensely to Devlin's impending visit and was going to do her utmost to give her friend the holiday of her life.

After that, she was going to Nepal for ten days with Féile and some other girls. When they had asked her to go, she had said yes immediately. It was so easy to travel from Abu Dhabi to the other countries of the Middle East, to India and to Africa, and Caroline knew she would never have such an excellent chance again.

She realized that she would have to make lots of

decisions when she got home – like where she was going to live, now that the penthouse had been sold and the proceeds divided between her and Richard. She also knew that she would have to get a job. But Caroline pushed all these thoughts to the deepest recesses of her mind. She wanted very much to enjoy her last few weeks in Abu Dhabi and she made a conscious decision that for once in her life she would not worry about the future, that she would try to forget the past and instead enjoy the hour and the minute and the day.

It was a strategy that was proving successful. She relished every day, every new experience she had, knowing that in six months it would all seem like a wonderful, fading dream. It saddened her to think that her time in the Emirate was coming to an end, but in another way she was very much looking forward to going home and starting anew.

'Come on. Stop daydreaming!' Mike interrupted her musings, grinning at her. 'We've got a lot of dancing to do if you're going to exercise away that feed you've just had.'

Caroline grinned back at him. She had grown extremely fond of the bearded engineer to whom she had been introduced on that Tuesday night so long ago – her first Irish night. When she explained to him that she was recovering from a very damaged relationship and was interested only in friendship, Mike took it on the chin and declared that if that was what she wanted, that was what she would have. He had been true to his word and never once overstepped the boundaries she had drawn. Their friendship had developed into a warm bond of affection. Mike dated other women, and Caroline was glad of that because it took away the pressure. Right now she was happy just to be single and free with no-one depending on her. Her self-confidence was growing all the time. She had discovered that being on her own was not a disaster and could actually be quite pleasant. All in all, she was a far more stable woman than the fragile, apprehensive person who had arrived out in the Emirate almost six months before.

Maggie had forecast that she would be a changed woman when she came back, and she was right. She had taken hold of life, just like Nell and Féile and Pat and all the other wonderful Irish women she had met. She no longer felt a failure. She had met the challenge presented to her by fate, and met it well. She would go home to Dublin renewed and invigorated, and ready to face all the necessary decisions. It would be a triumphant homecoming. Like the proverbial phoenix rising from the ashes, her new self would emerge and never again would she be the timid, self-effacing, appeasing creature of before. Caroline had at last discovered a sense of worth, which was immensely liberating.

Richard had suggested that they buy another place together. He was handling being on his own very badly, but although she felt sorry for him and could empathize with what he was going through, Caroline told him gently but firmly that her answer was no. It was almost a year and a half since she had seen her husband. The time and distance had loosened their bonds of habit and dependency. There was no going back; she didn't want that. She was her own woman now and nothing or no-one would change that. She would proceed with the annulment and divorce no matter what. Not that she needed the bits of paper to tell her what she already knew. Caroline Yates was a free woman for the first time in her entire life. No-one would ever take that freedom from her again.

'Are you going to dance?' Mike exclaimed in exasperation.

'Lead on, Fred Astaire. If you want dancing, then dancing you shall have.' Caroline laughed as her partner swung her out on to the dance-floor. She felt young and carefree and happy. She felt like dancing all night.

Maggie's Story – II

Thirty-Six

'Excuse me. Sorry.' Maggie edged her way into the crowded lift in the ILAC Centre, her arms aching from the bulky parcels she was carrying. She was doing her Christmas shopping and she had been in town since the shops had opened at nine. When the lift disgorged some equally burdened shoppers at the first floor, she was grateful for the extra space. Down below, she could see just how crowded the centre was. Maggie sighed, knowing that as soon as she had dumped her parcels in the boot of the car, she was going to have to go down herself and battle her way into Dunnes. She still had to get all the children's new outfits for Christmas Day, plus presents for her own and Terry's nieces and nephews, not to mention his mother and her parents and brothers and sisters.

Maggie had put her foot down when Terry asked her if she would get the presents for the girls in the office as well. He was so cool, her husband, and he had not been a bit pleased when she told him he was lucky she was doing all the rest of the Christmas shopping. Right this minute, she was sorely tempted to go and buy gift vouchers for everybody. Still, she comforted herself, at least she had got all the Santa toys, although she had to remember to get batteries for Shona's Lights Alive, or there'd be tears on Christmas morning.

Maggie left the lift at the next floor. Even at nine that morning there had been a queue to get into the car-park. She didn't like multi-storey car-parks, finding them terribly claustrophobic, but today it was the handiest option. She had already filled the boot once before this morning.

Ten minutes later she was taking the lift down again, but rather than face the throngs in Dunnes straight away, she decided to have a cup of coffee and a croissant at La Croissanterie, go through her list and focus on what exactly she needed. She decided, as she munched the hot snack, that she was going to stick rigidly to her list and not be side-tracked by anything else. No browsing; just get what she needed and out. On a Saturday like today it was the only thing to do.

An hour later, as Maggie emerged through the portals of Dunnes, she felt as though she had gone ten rounds in a prize-fight but she had succeeded in her quest and once again she found herself in the lift making the journey up to her car.

Next on her agenda was Evans, a shop that sold clothes for the larger woman. She was going to buy some nice long-sleeved cotton nightdresses for her Gran and Terry's mum, who were both on the stout side. A box of chocolate-covered Brazils and a cheque for twenty pounds each would complete those two presents.

She rang home to remind Terry to collect his suit from the cleaners; he'd need it that night for the office party.

'How are the kids?' She could hear squeals in the background.

'Cut that out, the pair of you,' Terry roared.

'What's going on?' she asked wearily.

'They're arguing about one Christmas stocking being longer than the other.'

Maggie grinned. Now he knew what it was like being stuck with children who were up to ninety with excitement at the impending visit from Santa. 'What's Shona doing?'

'She's spent the entire morning kneeling in front of the fire staring up the chimney. Here she is now to say hello. She's her daddy's good little girl.'

'Hello, Mammy.' Maggie's heart lifted at the sound of her toddler. 'I saw Santa Plause's fairy.'

'Did you?' Maggie feigned amazement. 'I'll be home soon and I've got something nice for you.'

'For mine own self?' Maggie could imagine Shona's huge blue eyes getting wider. She loved getting any little treat and she'd look adorable in the little pinafore and blouse Maggie'd bought for her.

'For your own self,' Maggie assured her.

'I'd better go and separate these two before murder is committed. Whoever invented Christmas should be shot!' Terry cut in, as the rumpus in the background got louder.

'Don't forget your suit,' she reminded him again before hanging up.

Outside in the crisp, biting air, the cacophony nearly deafened her. The traders, the buskers, the carol singers all added to the unique atmospheric chaos that was Henry Street at Christmas time.

It was a very weary Maggie who greeted Adam in

433

the subdued elegance of Clerys Tea Rooms. They had arranged to meet there and it was such a joy to sit down and take the weight off her aching feet.

'You look bushed!' Adam said sympathetically, reaching across to give her hand a squeeze.

'I am,' she sighed. 'All I want to do is to go home and get into a hot bath and crawl into bed afterwards. But Terry's office do is on tonight so I'll just have to glam myself up and try to get into a party mood.'

'Poor Maggie,' Adam said with a smile. 'If you moved in with me that would be one less problem you'd have to worry about.'

'How could I move in with you, Adam?' Maggie asked irritably. 'I've three children. I can't split up our home. I can't walk out on them. You know that.'

'Bring them with you,' Adam said, so cheerfully that Maggie just had to laugh.

'And where would we all fit in your little house?'

'We'll buy a bigger one. Now that you're going to be a bestselling author, between the two of us we could manage a mansion in Howth or Killiney.'

'I won't be a bestselling author until this time next year — that's if they don't change their minds again,' Maggie said glumly.

'They won't,' he said reassuringly. 'And anyway they did it only in your best interest.'

'I know that, Adam. It would just have been nice to see my book on the shelves this Christmas.'

'At least you're being published, which is more than you can say for me,' he said lightly.

Maggie was immediately contrite. 'Oh Adam, I'm sorry for being such a moaning Minnie. Have you had any luck at all? You were going to phone the publishers. Did you call them?'

Adam nodded. 'Yep, I did.'

'And?'

'They're having something called an acquisitions meeting the week before Christmas. I'll know early in the new year.'

'I'll be keeping my fingers crossed for you,' Maggie declared, 'but at least you've got this far; at least your book hasn't been returned out of hand.'

'Two bestselling authors: we'll be able to afford to move to the southside,' he teased.

Their closeness, and the tea and muffins, revived her and she was much more cheerful as they walked out the North Earl Street entrance together.

'So, are you going to be able to come over to me at all this week?' Adam asked, not very hopefully.

'Well, Terry's looking after the children all day today; knowing him, he'll think that should let him off the hook for the rest of the week. Look, I'll phone you on Monday. I might say I'm having a meeting with Marcy or Sandra some afternoon next week. I'll try to arrange for Josie to look after the children if she'll do the extra afternoon.' Usually Josie was very obliging, but coming up to Christmas was always a busy time.

'Do your best, Maggie,' Adam urged. 'I'll take a half-day's leave.'

'You know I will,' she promised. An afternoon all to herself with Adam, sitting in front of the fire in his bedroom and then making love in the big, old-fashioned double bed with its gleaming brass bedstead was like the promise of paradise in her hectic life.

Adam bent down and kissed her lightly on the lips. And Maggie kissed him back, quite unaware that Marian Montclare, who was on her way into Clerys to buy her mother-in-law a Windsmoor suit, was staring at them from the other side of the street, and in grave danger of getting lockjaw.

Thirty-Seven

'I'm sorry Dev,' Maggie apologized. 'I'm a bit disorganized. We got back from Wicklow only half an hour ago.' She was unloading a pile of dirty clothes from a black plastic sack and stuffing it into the washing-machine.

'Stop fussing, Maggie! I'm perfectly capable of filling a kettle and making us a cup of tea. Don't start treating me like a guest, for God's sake. And don't *mention* Belfast to me!' As Devlin spoke, she stepped over two biscuit-tins that were on the floor and began to fill the kettle.

'Oh, I must put these out of the way,' Maggie murmured distractedly, picking up the two tins. 'Ma filled these up with mince-pies for me.'

'Oh yum,' Devlin said. 'I have a real weakness for mince-pies.'

'You can have them all,' Maggie announced. 'I'm heartily sick of turkey, ham, pudding and all the rest of it. In fact Christmas just gives me the pip!'

'And tidings of comfort and joy to you too,' Devlin murmured.

'Sorry. I've had a sorely trying time, Dev, and I feel like exploding.'

Devlin reflected a moment. 'Let's see: you've just

come home from Wicklow and you're like a demon. Hazarding a guess, I'd say it was not all happy families on Walton's Mountain.'

'You can bloody well say *that* again,' growled Maggie. 'How that girl isn't half-way to the North Pole with the toe of my boot up her arse I don't know.'

'Aha!' said Devlin, 'that could only be Sourpuss Susy. What's your dearly beloved sister-in-law been up to this time?' Devlin loved hearing about the antics of Susy, Maggie's most recently acquired sister-in-law.

'Dearly beloved, my hat! I just can't stand that ignorant little bitch. Christ above, I don't know how I restrained myself. I swear I developed an ulcer in the space of a couple of hours from trying to keep my mouth shut.'

'Look, go in and sit down. I'll bring you a cup of coffee and we'll relax in the sitting-room until Terry brings the kids back from McDonald's. You can tell me all about what's bugging you.'

'But *I* invited you to stay: *I* should be making the tea,' Maggie protested.

'Oh, give over and go and sit down. I'll be with you in a minute. Put the Christmas tree lights on and start the fire. We'll enjoy a bit of peace and quiet. What time is Caroline coming?'

'Some time this evening; she's gone visiting her aunt.' Maggie couldn't help grinning.

Devlin threw her eyes up to heaven. 'God! Poor Caro! Imagine having to put up with *that* for the afternoon. She has her aunt, you have the dreaded Susy and I have Grandpa Delaney. You see, we all have our little Christmas crosses to bear!'

'Ha, ha,' retorted Maggie dryly, but in spite of herself her mood started to lighten.

'Here, get that inside you,' Devlin ordered ten minutes later, handing her an Irish coffee.

Maggie's eyes brightened. 'What a brainwave, Devlin Delaney! Why didn't I think of that?'

'Oh well, you had other things on your mind; obviously Sweet Sue has surpassed herself this time. Tell us all.' Devlin curled up on the sofa and took a sip of her drink. She loved hearing the gossip from Wicklow.

'Sweet Sue is right,' Maggie snorted. 'Although to look at her with those limpid blue eyes, you'd think butter wouldn't melt in her mouth.'

'What colour is the hair these days?' Devlin enquired, dipping her little finger into the cream on her coffee and licking it.

'Oh, it's kind of straw-blonde highlights with a perm. I don't know where she gets her hair done but she looks like a right little old granny.'

Devlin guffawed. 'Sorry, Mags. It's just that when you get going about Susy I have to laugh!'

'I can tell you that you wouldn't be laughing if you had her in your family, the ungracious little cow,' Maggie retorted. 'Honest to God, Devlin, but she had a puss on her all over Christmas. And the rudeness of her! All I can say is, thank God I was brought up, not dragged up. Who does she think she is, going on like Lady La La with her airs and graces? What is she but a jumped-up barmaid? Not that I've anything against barmaids,' she added hastily. 'I was one myself during my school holidays . . .'

'Her parents bought the Wicklow Hills Lounge and Restaurant on the main road, didn't they?' Devlin interjected.

'Oh they did,' Maggie sighed. 'You'd think it was the Horseshoe Bar in the Shelbourne the way she goes on about it. And it's only a dirty old kip, you know. I wouldn't drink in it if I was paid. But sure, what other way would it be? You know her father plays poker? They haven't a penny: whatever they make in the pub he loses at cards.

'Her mother's a nice woman. I feel sorry for her and Susy is no help to her at all. What Patrick saw in her I'll never know, but she got her little claws into him good and deep. By God, if ever there was a henpecked husband, it's my brother Patrick. Terry overheard her about an hour after they arrived for tea at Gran's, telling Patrick she was going straight home whether he liked it or not. And it's a pity she didn't, because she ruined the evening for everyone.'

'Why? What did she do?' Devlin grinned.

Maggie took a slug of her Irish coffee before continuing the saga. 'Of course, they were having a row before they arrived. I copped that immediately when I was on the phone to them earlier in the day. I mean, OK, if you're having a row, fine! Let's face it: Terry and I haven't been getting on great recently. But you don't make other people uncomfortable by inflicting your domestic disagreements on them. You put on the best face and you keep it between the two of you – well, that's if you've any manners. But of course she hasn't,' Maggie declared, much to Devlin's amusement. 'Well, by the time Terry and I arrived with the kids, she was sitting there with a face on her that would curdle milk, looking daggers at everyone.'

'Little madam,' Devlin murmured. She had met Susy on a few occasions and thoroughly agreed with Maggie's assessment of her: rude, spoilt and thoroughly selfish. It wasn't like Maggie to make those kinds of comments, but Devlin had to admit they were perfectly justified.

'Remember the time just after they got engaged when I was staying down at the farm with you for a few days? She came to visit and I asked her if she'd like a cup of tea.' Devlin laughed at the memory. 'You'd think I'd asked her did she want Paraquat. She's a bit peculiar, isn't she?'

'Peculiar isn't the word: she's spiteful, that's what she is! Do you know what the fucking little wagon said to me?' Maggie fumed. ' "When's the famous novel coming out? I thought you were supposed to be published months ago? Mam was dying to read it. She thinks it's great that I'm married to someone who's related to an author. You *are* going to be published, aren't you? Or was it all an April fool?" '

Devlin's eyes widened. 'The catty little so-and-so.'

'She's lucky she's not sporting a new set of false teeth, I can tell you,' Maggie retorted. 'And, you know, the sickening thing is that when I first mentioned about being published, she was all around the town telling people. No doubt when *City Woman* comes out it will be "my sister-in-law the famous author". Oh woe is me!' Then Maggie laughed as she began to relax and enjoy her chat with Devlin. 'That's if she's still talking to me. Although, to be perfectly honest, I couldn't care less if she never spoke to me again. In fact, after her carry-on at Gran's I hope she won't, the little hypocrite!

'It's just, Dev, that poor Gran had gone to such trouble, and she's not really able for it. She's very rheumaticky but she loves to have the family around her, especially for that one day at Christmas. She couldn't even enjoy the couple of hours with the lads and myself because of that Susy and her shenanigans, sitting there like Lady Muck with a face on her that would trip a duck. I don't know why Patrick lets her get away with it, because I'll tell you one thing, Dev, if he treated her family the way she treats mine, she wouldn't stand for it. Honestly I wouldn't dream of treating Terry's mother other than with respect. Terry and I were disgusted, and so were Lillian and Anthony. Susy actually had the bad manners to start a row with Patrick out in the scullery and she could be heard all over the house. Poor Gran was getting upset. So I went out and told them to have some manners and cut it out and stop making a spectacle of themselves.'

Devlin was amazed that anyone could be so rude. 'What did she say to you?'

'She told me to fuck off back up to Dublin and mind my own business. I said, "You're upsetting my grandmother and that *is* my business. You should be ashamed of yourself." '

'And what did she say then?' Devlin laughed.

'What *could* she say? I was right and she knew it. Oh, she knows what I think of her all right. But I did feel sorry for Gran. She's coming up to me with Ma and Da for New Year's Day and I'm going to make such a fuss over them.'

442

'You do that, Maggie,' Devlin said, getting up and giving her friend a hug. 'And don't let that other one get you down. She isn't worth the worry. Imagine going on like that, the spoilt little brat. That's total immaturity.'

'She's thirty-five years of age, for God's sake! She's four years older than Patrick.'

'Exactly!' said Devlin. 'Imagine a woman in her thirties behaving like that! It's pathetic! Just think: some day she'll be a grandmother and a mother-in-law and what goes around comes around. May she get the sons and daughters-in-law she deserves, just as bad as herself. And, no doubt, she'll look like a great-granny then. Now, what do you say to another Irish coffee?'

'You're a great mate, Delaney. Lead on to the kitchen,' laughed Maggie, her bad humour evaporating at the picture of her silly sister-in-law that Devlin had painted.

They were sitting laughing and chatting, on their second Irish coffee, when Terry opened the door and three little bodies hurled themselves on Devlin.

Mimi hugged Devlin tightly. 'Auntie Devlin! Auntie Devlin! Are you staying on your holidays tonight?'

'I certainly am,' laughed Devlin.

'Did you bring us presents?' Michael asked shyly.

'Michael!' exclaimed his mother.

'I certainly did, Michael! Let's go get them.'

'I lobe you, Manty Devlin,' Shona declared.

'I love you too, pet.'

'I love you too, Devlin,' grinned Terry. 'Did I get a present?'

'Wait and see.' Devlin turned to Maggie. 'Hey, Mags, how about if I wash this gang and get them ready for bed, Terry can start the dinner: he's a dream cook—' she fluttered her eyelashes at her friend's husband '—and you go and write a few pages. I'd say you've enough for a chapter at least.'

Maggie snorted. 'You're a bad egg, Devlin Delaney.'

'Maybe I am,' chuckled Devlin, 'but I bet there isn't one person who reads your book who won't say, "Oh, I know someone exactly like Susy MacNamara." '

'Well, you're probably right,' laughed Maggie. 'Why don't I go and put it to the test?'

'Every cloud has a silver lining,' declared Devlin, as she was dragged out to the hall to get the presents.

'Maybe you're right,' murmured Maggie an hour later, as a totally new character appeared in her second novel. It's amazing, she thought, but bitches are so much easier to write about. Look at Ria Kirby. But this one's even better than her. Marcy's going to *love* this!

Maggie's fingers flew over the keyboard. Now she was actually looking forward to meeting Marcy early in the new year with her next instalment. Before Devlin's visit, she had been dreading it. She hadn't written anything since her last meeting with her editor just before Christmas. Now there was no stopping her. She smiled to herself as she wrote, 'Cissie Lyons wore her hair in a style that made her look like a little old granny . . .'

*　　*　　*

'You should have seen the face of her when I said,
"When's the famous novel coming out — or is it all
an April fool?"' Susy MacNamara smirked at her
friend Harriet, from behind the bar at which Harriet
was sitting on a high stool. 'Imelda!' She waved an
imperious hand at the young girl who was standing at
the other end of the bar. 'Serve this gentleman,
please.'

'Why don't you serve him your bloody self instead
of standing there gabbing with Harriet Anderson —
who's only sitting listening to you in the hope of
getting a brandy,' Imelda muttered to Neil, the
barman. Nevertheless she did as she was bid. She
needed this job, even if it was a torment working for
Mrs high-and-mighty Susy MacNamara. Soon, she
promised herself, her day would come and she'd be
able to tell Susy to get lost.

'What did Maggie say?' Harriet leaned forward
with feigned eagerness. She'd been there twenty
minutes already and there wasn't a sign of a drink
being offered. All Susy had done was rabbit on about
her horrible in-laws. She didn't know how lucky she
was to have in-laws, even if they were horrible — and
Harriet knew that the MacNamaras were pretty OK,
no matter what Susy said. The trouble with Susy was
that she had such an inferiority complex that she
was always dwelling on imagined slights. When
she worked in the County Council, no-one had got on
with her there. One minute she'd be talking to you,
all smiles and charm; the next she'd ignore you or
barely say hello. Her moods had been extremely
unsettling and made for a very unpleasant atmosphere
in the office at times. It was a great relief to all her

colleagues when she resigned from her job after her father bought the pub. Mark Bennett had actually sung the 'Hallelujah Chorus' when she signed off for the last time and the next day they'd bought a cake to celebrate. Harriet kept in contact only because it meant that she didn't feel such a spare thumb going to the pub on her own. At least she could talk to Susy when she was behind the bar. *And* get a free drink – if the younger woman was in a magnanimous humour. Harriet cast an envious glance at the solitaire engagement-ring and extra-wide gold wedding-ring on Susy's pudgy third finger. How she had managed to ensnare Patrick MacNamara, who was several years younger than her, and a gentleman to boot, mystified Harriet!

She herself, just turned forty, had more or less given up hope of ever entering the married state, after a hard-fought battle that saw her going out every weekend for the previous twenty-five years in search of a man. Oh, she still got dressed up and went out whenever she could. Still gave her stock response of being a 'career woman' to the inevitable questions about when she was going to 'give people a day out'. Harriet hated the term 'career woman', hated knowing that she was going to be stuck in the County Council until it was time to collect her pension. Deep down, Harriet felt an utter failure because no man had ever asked her to marry him, and it looked now as if no man ever would. That was why it was so irritating to hear Susy MacNamara narking on about her in-laws. How would she like it if she were stuck on the other side of the counter in Harriet's position?

Harriet came to in time to hear Susy declare, 'I just

446

can't stand these ones coming down from their big fancy houses in Dublin, swanning around, doing the lady. I suppose when the great novel is published she'll be arriving in a chauffeur-driven Mercedes. Herself and that Delaney one.'

'Who?' asked Harriet glumly. So far there was no sign of a freebie. She'd give it five more minutes, buy herself a gin and tonic and go home to watch TV.

'You know, her friend who owns City Girl, the ultra-posh women's leisure complex up in Dublin.'

'Oh yeah,' Harriet sighed. Frankly, she couldn't care less if Susy was talking about the first woman Pope.

'She's a friend of Maggie, you know.' Susy popped a handful of peanuts into her mouth and pushed the dish towards Harriet. 'Have some.'

'Thanks very much.' Harriet's tone was Sahara-dry but Susy didn't even notice.

'I've met her a few times. Another consequence who thinks she's *it*! I remember once after we'd got engaged, she was staying at the farm for a few days and she was going around as if she owned the place. Making herself at home, offering me tea! I mean, after all, *I* was the one who was coming into the family. *I* should have been making tea in the MacNamaras' kitchen, not some blow-in from Dublin. I'm telling you, when you get married you're stuck with your husband's family and friends as well. Stay single as long as you can.' Susy loved saying that, from behind the security of her wedding-ring of course. She knew very well that, barring a miracle, Harriet was unlikely to get married now; she was too long in the tooth.

Bugger you, you superior cow! Harriet thought

furiously. She smiled at Susy. 'Well, it *is* nice being footloose and fancy-free, having my evenings to myself to do as I please. I'd hate to have to work at night like you do. I suppose you might as well not be married at all really,' she added sweetly, 'if Pat's working all day and you're working all night.' Ha, she thought as she saw the expression on Susy's face, good enough for you.

She slid off the bar stool. She was damned if she was going to add to Susy's profits tonight. 'I think I'll go and get a Chinese meal and sit in by the fire. There's a great film on tonight. Ta ra, Susy.' Harriet waved and departed briskly.

It's well for you, thought Susy dourly. Wouldn't *she* like to be sitting in front of the fire eating a Chinese takeaway. If only Patrick would take over the running of the pub lounge and restaurant. After all he was a Swiss-trained chef. He'd be in charge just as much as he was in the kitchens of the hotel in Wicklow where he worked.

They had been fighting about it all over Christmas but he was adamant that he wasn't giving up his job. Well, she was still not speaking to him, and wouldn't until he came round to her way of thinking. She'd made that quite clear to him. *And* if he thought she was going to put up a façade for his family, she had certainly dispelled the notion at his gran's tea-party. She had told him exactly what she thought of him, until that Maggie bitch had the gall to interfere. Who the hell did she think she was, anyway? Just because she was having a novel published she thought she was the bee's knees. Well, Susy wasn't impressed by her and she'd let his family see that she wasn't too impressed by Patrick either. In fact she couldn't stand the whole bloody lot of them. Susy was delighted to hear of Maggie's publishing setback. It would give her great pleasure if the book was an unmitigating flop. And what was more, when Maggie invited them to her annual New Year's Day family dinner, she was just not going to go.

Thirty-Eight

'Won't you stay the night now and not go rushing back to Wicklow? It will make the day less tiring for Gran as well.' Maggie was talking to her mother on the telephone, making arrangements for her New Year's Day dinner.

'Oh well, all right,' Nelsie agreed, and Maggie knew she was smiling at the other end of the phone. 'What time do you want us to come?'

'Look, leave early in the morning when there won't be much traffic, and it will give you time to relax when you get here. Then you can stay the night so Dad can have a few drinks with Terry and Anthony, and Terry's brother-in-law.'

'Are Anthony and Lillian bringing the children?' Nelsie asked eagerly. She loved her grandchildren.

'Yes, they are,' Maggie assured her. 'My gang are in a tizzy of excitement at seeing their cousins.'

'Ah, it will be a nice day; I'm looking forward to it,' Nelsie declared. 'I hope Susy will be in better form than she was at your gran's.'

There was silence at the other end of the phone and then Nelsie heard her daughter say calmly, 'I don't care if she's in good form or not, she's not coming to my house with her bad manners, Ma. If she and

450

Patrick can't behave properly in company, that's *their* problem. I'm going to a lot of trouble so that you and Dad and Anthony and Lillian and the rest of you will enjoy yourselves. I do *not* intend for Miss Susy to create an atmosphere in my house now or ever . . . so, Mother, I didn't invite them.'

'Oh Maggie, they're family,' Nelsie demurred.

'Precisely, Ma! And when they behave like family, they'll be treated like family,' Maggie said firmly.

'You know, Maggie, you're right,' Nelsie said quite cheerfully after a minute. 'Patrick has made his bed and he must lie in it. And if he wants to change it, it's up to him. Why should we all have to suffer? Now, do you need mince-pies or will I bake a few scones or sausage rolls?'

'Oh, a few sausage rolls would be lovely, Ma. But don't go to any trouble, now.'

'I won't, dear. See you on New Year's Day.'

'See you, Ma, God bless,' Maggie said fondly, and hung up.

She was very relieved at her mother's attitude. Obviously Nelsie had had enough too. Terry had backed her all the way when she decided not to invite her brother and his wife.

'Thanks be to God,' he laughed. 'I couldn't sit looking at her sour puss for another evening.'

So it wasn't only herself, Maggie reflected, as she hoovered the guest-room. And even if it *was*, she decided, she still wouldn't invite Susy. She was too old to put up with the crap her sister-in-law dished out. Lick your arse one minute, cut the nose off you the next, and treating poor Gran like dirt. It just wasn't on. Let Patrick put up with it if he wanted. In fact it wouldn't bother her if she never saw Susy again. The thought cheered Maggie up and she hoovered with vim and vigour, looking forward to having the two families to dinner. Terry's sister and her husband and children were nice people and Terry, to give him his due, was a very good host. At the moment, Maggie and he were not arguing as much as before. She wondered if the postponement of the publication of her book had made her new career seem less threatening to him.

She was already well into her second novel, but with Christmas and everything she hadn't had any time to write, except for the couple of hours she had spent at the typewriter the night Devlin was there. Actually, that couple of hours had really got her going, and once Christmas was over, she was dying to get stuck in again. Maybe the reason Terry was in better humour was because she hadn't been writing. Maggie sprayed Sparkle on to the Sliderobe mirror and buffed it off. If her husband thought she was going to ease off her writing because she'd had a setback, he was mightily mistaken. He could just get used to the idea that she had a career too and that she intended making a success of it.

Maggie was making one big new year's resolution, she decided. She wasn't going to take any more crap from anyone. Not from Terry, not from her publishers and certainly, most certainly, not from moody Susy. On the phone beside the bed, she dialled Adam's number, after making sure that nobody was within earshot. Terry was going to take the kids to Funderland for the afternoon. She had a few hours free; she hoped her lover would be free as well. He'd be

interested to hear about her new year's resolution.
Adam was always telling her she was too soft. From
now on, for a change, she was going to put her own
feelings first. Having a dinner party without madame
was the first step. Her phone call to Adam was the
next.

'Come on, gang, into the car, or it will be dark before
we get to Funderland,' Terry urged as Mimi, Michael
and Shona scurried around putting on hats, coats and
gloves.

'Sure you don't want to come?' he asked Maggie.
'Remember the first year we were going together, we
went to Funderland and had a ball?'

'Yeah, I remember,' Maggie said, and her eyes were
sad.

'Come on, the house looks fine. Leave it and we'll
go to McDonald's!' Terry suggested enthusiastically.

'No, you go on. I've a few bits and pieces to get in
Superquinn still, and I might call on Marian. I
promised I'd call to see her over Christmas.' Maggie
would never call on Marian without an invitation, but
it seemed like a good excuse.

'Sure, aren't we going to dinner to her house the
Sunday after New Year's Day?' Terry reminded his
wife.

Maggie was a little flustered. 'Oh yes, I forgot.
Look, Terry, you go. I've a million and one things to
do, anyway,' Maggie said, as she buttoned Shona's
coat and put on her gloves and scarf. She stood waving
after her family, a big smile on her face, and Terry
smiled himself at the sight of their three children
waving excitedly from the back seat.

Apart from being annoyed with Susy and Patrick, Maggie was in remarkably good form these days. It was great, because when Enterprise had told her they were going to postpone publishing her book, she'd been like a bear with a sore head. At least she hadn't her head stuck to the typewriter this past couple of weeks. Except for that afternoon when Devlin had insisted she go and write.

He couldn't help it, but it really bugged him when he came in from work and she was out in the kitchen tap-tap-tapping away. That was all she ever did, tap-bloody-tap-tap-tap. She hardly ever came out to dinner with his clients, whereas she used always to accompany him or else entertain them at home. Oh, she still gave the odd dinner party, but nothing like before. Now that she'd got out of the habit of writing, she mightn't bother as much in the new year, and they could get back to normal. The thought cheered Terry up immensely. He was pleased with the way she was rushing around making sure everything was right for the gathering on New Year's Day. He was looking forward to it himself. He liked having the two families together; it was great for the kids to play with their cousins, and now that Maggie had decided not to invite Susy and Patrick, there'd be no strained atmosphere. He wouldn't have to be spitting out every word and polishing it before he spoke to Susy in case she took offence. Everyone could relax and the crack would be great.

Susy was in the horns of a dilemma. She wasn't talking to her husband, she couldn't find out whether Maggie had invited them to dinner for New Year's

454

Day or not, so she could say she wasn't going. Every time the phone rang she rushed to answer it, so she could have the pleasure of refusing Maggie's invitation personally.

By New Year's Eve, she was like a demon. Patrick was at work, the lounge was crawling with customers and Imelda had phoned in sick. She was exhausted when she got home and irritated to find Patrick already in bed and snoring. She slept in the spare room, as she had done for the previous week. Not that she slept much, she was far too annoyed. If the Ryans thought that they could invite her and Patrick to a meal at the last minute they had another think coming. And she'd make sure Maggie knew it when she phoned in the morning to invite them to dinner.

She was thoroughly miffed when Patrick poked his head through the door at nine-thirty to say that he was on his way to work. He had decided to work overtime.

'Oh, so you'd prefer to work overtime than spend New Year's Day with your wife,' she shrieked at him.

'Correct,' snapped Patrick, and marched out the door.

'And what about if your dear sister invites us to dinner?'

'You go. I know how much you love being with my family,' he called back and she heard the door slam.

Almost speechless with rage, Susy lay back against the pillows. She was starving. Usually Patrick brought her up her breakfast in bed. Now she was going to have to get it herself.

She waited all morning for the phone to ring, then after lunch, a thought struck her that made her eyes open wide. She dialled her mother-in-law's number. The phone rang and rang. Lips tightening into a thin line, she dialled Anthony and Lillian's. The same.

Taking a deep breath, Susy dialled Maggie's number.

'Hello.' Terry's deep voice answered. In the background Susy could hear sounds of gaiety, laughter, and children shrieking.

'Hello,' Terry repeated. 'Anthony, could you close the sitting-room door. I can't hear a word. Oh thanks, Nelsie,' Susy heard her brother-in-law say.

'Hello,' Terry said cheerfully again.

Susy hung up. The fuckers! They were having the new year's meal without her and Patrick. The absolute nerve of them. How dare Maggie Ryan snub her like that. How dare she! By golly, she'd get even with her, see if she wouldn't, Susy vowed, as she sat staring at the phone.

'Pull the crackers, pull the crackers!' Mimi shrieked. The happy crowd gathered around Maggie's big dining-table complied with much laughter and fun and squeals of delight from the children. When they all had their multi-coloured party hats on their heads, Terry's brother-in-law, Harry, stood and held up his glass.

'A toast,' he said. 'To Maggie, for serving up this banquet and giving us all a lovely, relaxed jolly day. Here's to great success with her writing. I'll tell you one thing,' he beamed, 'Maggie's a great cook and I always look forward to coming here for my dinner on New Year's Day.' His wife guffawed. It was well known that she couldn't cook to save her life but she didn't mind in the slightest admitting it. 'So, Maggie and Terry, here's to many more new year's feasts in your house. I know I speak for all of us when I say how much we enjoyed it.' Catching her mother's eye, Maggie grinned, as Nelsie gave the tiniest wink.

She stood up and raised her glass, 'Well, thank you, Harry, for your kind words. I do look forward very much to having you all here next year.' Maggie smiled as she looked around the table at her nearest and dearest. 'Here's to family,' she toasted.

'To family,' echoed the rest as they raised their glasses.

'It went very well,' Terry said later that night, as Maggie undressed and slid into bed beside him.

'It did,' she agreed. 'Harry was in great form and Ma and Da were able to relax and Gran thoroughly enjoyed herself. Not inviting the other pair was the best thing I ever did.'

'Susy won't be too pleased,' Terry said with a grin, putting his arm around his wife.

'I'm deeply worried,' Maggie replied dryly.

Terry yawned. 'Ah well, they missed a great party; that's all I can say, Maggie. Harry was right; you're a terrific cook.'

'You're not so bad yourself.' Maggie smiled in the dark. Seconds later, her husband was snoring. Wide-eyed, she lay awake. Today had been a really good day. Terry had done his utmost to make sure that all the guests had enjoyed themselves and he had spent hours playing with all the kids. He had always been very good at that kind of thing; it was one of the traits that had most attracted her to him.

To tell the truth, she was feeling a bit guilty. What

would they have thought if they knew that she was having an affair with a man ten years her junior. She'd felt a bit of a hypocrite toasting the family.

Oh stop! Terry would never have let feelings of guilt affect his affair with Ria, she argued silently with herself.

You're not Terry. The thought popped unbidden into her mind. Stop thinking about it, enjoy it while it lasts, she ordered herself. Maggie was too much of a pragmatist to imagine that there was going to be any future in her affair with Adam, although he had urged her to consider moving in with him, children and all.

Would it work? Could it work? Restlessly she tossed and turned, knowing that a time was coming when she'd have to make some very important decisions.

Thirty-Nine

'Way to go, Mrs Ryan!' Terry's eyes widened in admiration and he gave a long appreciative wolf-whistle as Maggie appeared at the sitting-room door, all ready to go to dinner at the Montclares'.

'Black really suits you, Maggie. You look gorgeous,' Josie declared.

'Thanks, Josie, and thanks a million for babysitting for me tonight,' Maggie said warmly.

'Do you know something, Maggie?' the older woman sighed. 'I'm actually looking forward to a peaceful night by myself. Dan's mother came to us for Christmas. Every year I say I'm not having her, let one of her other sons have her, and every year I give in. I'm fifty-four years of age with my family raised and I can't even watch what I want to watch on my own TV when she's there, the old bat. Isn't that pathetic?' She gave a wry smile.

'Don't talk to me about in-laws,' Maggie said sympathetically. 'They can be a right pain in the butt!'

'All the years I've known her and tried my best to be nice to her but she makes no effort at all,' moaned Josie.

Maggie grimaced, as a mental picture of a scowling

Susy flashed through her mind. 'I know exactly. Although I'm lucky as regards my own mother-in-law. I get on fine with her.'

'Well, mine's at home in a huff because I've gone out, but if I didn't get away from her I'd probably end up strangling her. As well as saving my sanity, you've probably saved her life,' Josie said with a grin. 'So, off with you. Enjoy your night out and let me enjoy mine.'

'Yeah, Maggie, time's pushing on,' Terry put in.

'Oh Lord, I forgot my watch and rings. I won't be a minute. You go on and get the car out of the garage. Sit down,' she said to Josie. 'Relax and have a drink and watch whatever you want on TV.'

Maggie ran upstairs to get her jewellery. She slid her engagement- and wedding-ring on to her finger, and fastened her watch. She pulled her fringe down a little more on her forehead and ran her fingers along her eyebrows. When she looked at her reflection in the mirror she was pleased with what she saw. Knowing Marian, the dinner party would be a very posh affair and, without being vain about it, she knew she looked her best. She'd treated herself to a gorgeous, slinky, black cocktail dress that she'd seen in Arnotts the week before Christmas, and although it had cost an arm and a leg, it clung in all the right places and was very slimming. It had an off-the-shoulder neck-line and an elegant fifties air that had attracted Maggie to it in the first place. She was wearing a pair of the finest denier barely-black stockings and elegant black suede shoes. She'd even had her hair blow-dried. The pearls at her throat and ears finished off the look perfectly and the overall effect was very classy.

Maggie smiled to herself in amusement as Terry drove through the city, still festive with Christmas lights. Was she actually trying to impress Marian? It looked like it. In the old days she wouldn't even have thought about having her hair done for a dinner with Marian, but these were not the old days and her relationship with Marian was totally different from what it had been. In their youth, Maggie had quite happily followed where Marian led, always impressed by what she had perceived as her friend's sophistication and savoir faire. This had suited Marian, who always liked to feel she was impressing people. In that respect she had not changed one bit: if anything she was even more conscious of her image. Maggie, on the other hand, was at the stage of her life when she didn't give a hoot what others thought about her. She was what she was and people either liked it or lumped it as far as she was concerned.

Marian, she could see, had found the new more assertive Maggie a little difficult to get used to. While it was nice to be on speaking terms with her again, Maggie knew that their relationship would never be of the calibre of her friendship with Devlin and Caroline. Marian had grown even more reserved in the years since they had last met, and it was only rarely that she let her guard down at all. To tell the truth, Maggie sometimes found her hard going. Marian was not relaxed. It was as if she felt it of the utmost importance to keep up her façade of brittle sophistication at all times. Since their reacquaintance, Maggie had never seen her in the same outfit twice or without perfectly applied make-up. Marian was all talk of how successful Alex was, and what she had

461

bought and where she had been on holidays. When she heard that Maggie was a close friend of Devlin Delaney she had been extremely impressed.

Tonight was the first time that Maggie would visit Marian's house. Although they had kept in touch by phone and met in town for coffee several times since the summer, and although Maggie had had Marian and Alex over to dinner twice, this was the first occasion the hospitality had been reciprocated.

Maggie was *dying* to see the Foxrock mansion that she'd heard so much about. Alex's elder brother and his American wife, Clarissa, would also be at the dinner party. Maggie had got the impression that Marian wasn't enamoured of her brother-in-law's wife.

'A bit loud,' Marian had confided in one of her few unguarded moments. Maggie took this to mean that she was a woman who enjoyed herself in an uninhibited kind of way. Marian would never be uninhibited, although she'd been a much more relaxed and easy-going person when they'd been friends in their young days.

After taking her degree in UCD she had gone into marketing for a couple of years and then she had become a researcher in RTE, for both radio and television programmes. That was where she had met her husband. She had had to interview him for a series of business programmes on TV, and when the broadcasts were over, he asked her out.

Marian had spoken about her time in RTE with great enthusiasm and Maggie felt it was a shame that she'd given up her job after she got married. It was obvious to Maggie that part of her friend's trouble was that she was bored, despite all the entertaining and all the expensive holidays she had with Alex. Her husband hadn't wanted her to continue working after they'd married, Marian confided in Maggie, and at first, she said, it was a real treat being able to do as she wanted. But although she didn't say it, Maggie knew that the thrill of this had worn off and Marian was at a loose end.

'Couldn't you go back part-time?' Maggie had suggested.

'Maybe.' Marian had been non-committal, and Maggie had left it at that, knowing that Marian did not want to discuss it any further.

Alex's brother, Edward, was a lawyer in Atlanta, and the loud Clarissa worked for one of the state's welfare agencies. From what Maggie had heard of her, she sounded like a lively woman. All in all, it might prove to be a very interesting evening.

Marian checked the dinner table once more, looking for flaws, making sure that the place settings were evenly spaced, and that the bowl of red roses, white gypsophila and green ferns was precisely at the centre of her round mahogany table. Red, white and green, the Christmas colours, were her theme colours, carried right through to all the decorations. The tree was an elegant picture, with red and white bows so striking against the deep green of the foliage. No gaudy balls and tinsel for Marian, just small white lights and her red and white bows. 'Less is more,' was Marian's motto this year and simple wreaths of holly entwined with white ribbons were her only other decorations. She had candelabra with red, white and green candles.

She was extremely pleased with her minimalist approach. Maggie would surely be impressed.

It was very important to Marian that her dinner should be a great success. She wanted Maggie to see how well she had done for herself. To see what taste and style she had. To see what a lovely, elegant house she was mistress of. Nobody could deny that it was a hell of a lot more elegant than Maggie's Castleknock home. Not, Marian thought, that there was anything wrong with Maggie's house. It was very nice, if a tad in need of repainting. But there had been toys everywhere except the sitting-room, which admittedly was very cosy and pretty. In her house, Alexandra had a playroom, and was expected to play with her toys there, and there alone. Toys all over the house would have driven Marian bananas.

She was so pleased with the new conservatory that they'd recently had built. That was why she'd waited so long before inviting Maggie to dinner at her house. She'd wanted everything to be just so, and there was nothing worse than having the signs of workmen around the place.

Everything was fine, she reassured herself. Alex was taking care of the wines. All she had to do was to go upstairs and slip into the new burgundy velvet dress that Alex had bought her for Christmas to go with the ruby earrings and necklace he had given her on their last wedding anniversary.

Walking past the guest-room occupied by Edward and Clarissa, Marian wrinkled her nose in distaste. That one was smoking again, she fumed. God, she was as common as dishwater. Marian loathed smoking and would not permit it under her roof. If anything went wrong tonight, it would be because of big-mouth Clarissa. Once she had drunk a few glasses of wine, she'd say anything. Maybe she should have waited until they'd gone home before inviting the Ryans, but her visitors were here for another two weeks. By then, the season would be over and she wanted Maggie to admire her house complete with its tasteful Christmas decor.

What Edward saw in Clarissa, Marian could not imagine. From the way he was always pawing her, she could make a guess at one thing, she thought primly, as she closed her bedroom door behind her. They'd been married for twenty years or more – you'd think they'd have more sense. If Alex mauled her the way Edward mauled his wife, she'd slap him across the face. Maggie and she would probably get on well, Marian thought crossly, remembering her friend and the good-looking blond man she'd seen her kissing outside Clerys.

Marian had never really enjoyed sex that much. You had to reveal too much of yourself. And Alex, like herself, was a reserved, controlled type of person. They understood each other perfectly. Nevertheless, remembering the glow in Maggie's eyes, and the lustre Clarissa always seemed to have, Marian wondered wistfully what it would be like to be consumed, body and soul, by lust for a man. It was something she had never experienced and, she thought with a vague sense of dissatisfaction, it was something she was certainly never going to experience with Alex.

What on earth had got her into this frame of mind, Marian wondered with irritation, as she slipped the

465

dress over her immaculately coiffed hair. She was perfectly happy the way she was . . . totally in control. She had a wealthy, supportive husband, a beautiful little girl, a fine house, a big car and money to do as she pleased. What more could a woman want? Her mouth tightened as she heard Clarissa give one of her husky chuckles. It wouldn't surprise Marian one bit if they were doing it right this minute.

'Stop pinchin' my ass, you horny devil,' Clarissa reprimanded her husband with a grin, as she drew deeply on a cigarette. She leaned out the bedroom window and exhaled a long thin stream of smoke. 'Gahd! I needed that. I know she's your brother's wife, honey, but Jeez, I dunno how I'm going to put up with her and her airs and graces for another two weeks. Can't we say we're gonna do some sightseeing or something and get the hell outta here and stay in a hotel?'

'Alex would be really hurt, Clariss. I haven't been home in five years. Just stick it out until next week and we'll go and spend a few days in Kerry,' her husband urged. 'OK?'

'Oh Gahd, Teddy, the things I do for love!' Clarissa said with a grin. 'I wonder what this friend of madame's is like. Probably another right royal asshole. When I heard she *had* a friend you could have knocked me down with a feather!'

'Clarissa, stop being a bitch,' Edward ordered, his eyes twinkling.

'I love it when you order me around, you great big hunk you.' Clarissa grabbed her chubby little husband around the waist and planted a big kiss on his lips.

'You'd better get dressed,' he declared.

'Don't you mean undressed?' Clarissa gave a hearty chuckle, removed her bathrobe and twirled it around her head as if she were Salome doing the dance of the seven veils. 'Come on, babe, we're on vacation. Let's jiggle those bedsprings!' She giggled. 'I'm a post-menopausal woman and I'm in my prime.'

'You're telling me!' Her husband enthusiastically put his arms around his voluptuous wife, who, even after twenty years of marriage, could still turn him on like the first time.

'Very impressive,' Terry remarked as they drove up the gravel-lined drive of Manresa, the Montclares' imposing Victorian house in Foxrock. 'This guy isn't short of a bob or two. He has a hell of a good client list.' Terry drew the car to a halt. 'He was telling me all about it the last time you invited them over for dinner. He's not a bad contact to have at all, Mags,' Terry said with satisfaction. He was looking forward to the evening immensely. Good food, good drink no doubt, a man with whom he had a lot in common, businesswise . . . and Maggie at his side, looking sensational, a million dollars. It just went to show what she could do when she made the effort. Tonight when they got home, he'd make sure to show his appreciation, he thought happily.

All in all, it hadn't been a bad Christmas, although Maggie had been furious at the carry-on of Susy and Patrick at her gran's. But Susy had picked the wrong cookie to tangle with when she started her shenanigans. If Susy thought for one minute that Maggie would stand quietly by and let her treat Patrick's

467

family like dirt, she had made a mighty big mistake. She was very loyal, was his Mags, he thought appreciatively. She'd never let on anything about his affair to her own family, which made things much easier for Terry. He genuinely liked his in-laws. They didn't interfere or make great demands of Maggie and himself. It could have been very awkward if they had ever come to know about Ria.

Susy was a different kettle of fish. She never had a good word for Patrick and actually gave out about him in front of all of them. Sometimes he felt like telling her to put a sock in it. If she was his wife, he knew what he'd do with her. Patrick was a hell of a good husband. He cooked meals and did housework on a regular basis. Terry'd never have put up with that. Sure, he'd cook the dinner occasionally and do a bit of cleaning if Maggie was sick, but not every day of the week. The trouble with Susy was that she always had to be the centre of attention, with everyone running right, left and centre to do her bidding and make a fuss of her. He wouldn't stand for it if Maggie carried on like that. Not that she would anyway, he thought fondly: she was a very supportive partner. His sister-in-law didn't know what being a wife meant.

All in all, apart from her obsession with what she called her 'writing career', Maggie wasn't a bad old wife at all. They'd had their bad times but they'd got over them and at least they weren't fighting these days.

He reached out and squeezed her knee. 'Did I ever tell you you've got very sexy knees?' Terry asked, enjoying the silky feel of her stockings.

'Stop it, Terry!' His wife slapped his hand away. 'Someone's opening the door.'

'Come on then, shift your gorgeous derrière,' Terry said cheerfully. He'd play footsie with his wife under the table when they were having dinner, he decided. It would help him stay in the mood for what he had planned for later on.

'It's a beautiful house, Mar. You've great taste,' Maggie said in admiration as she followed her friend downstairs after the guided tour. It was like something out of *Homes and Gardens*, all pale plain carpets and swathes of ruched and frilled curtains. The carpets wouldn't have lasted long in Maggie's house with *her* three, she thought in amusement. And the master bedroom, with so many fitted wardrobes and units surrounding the huge bed, was not to Maggie's taste. It would be a bit like sleeping in a kitchen, she felt.

'What do you think of Clarissa? Isn't she something else?' Marian threw her eyes up to heaven and made a droll face.

'I think she's nice,' Maggie murmured diplomatically. Actually she thought the American woman was great gas and highly intelligent.

'Oh, but she never knows when to shut up. She's got an opinion on *everything*. To tell you the truth, Maggie, I'll be glad when they're gone back home.'

'I know. It can be a bit of a strain having visitors for a long stretch. Can I do anything for you?'

'I've everything under control, I think.' Marian led the way into her state-of-the-art kitchen, from where the most delicious smells were emanating.

'Tell me,' she said, cocking her head to one side in that characteristic way of hers that Maggie had been familiar with since she first knew her. 'Who was that you were kissing outside Clerys just before Christmas?'

Maggie stared at Marian in shock and felt her insides go cold. That was a bloody stupid thing to do, kissing in public like that, but of all the hundreds of thousands of people who were in town that day, trust Marian to have seen them!

Marian was looking at her, waiting for an answer. If it had been like the old days when they knew everything about each other, Maggie would have confided in her. But times had changed, they had changed — and so she merely said, as casually as she could, 'That's Adam. He's the one who introduced me to the writers' group. He's an old friend.'

'And a dear one, by the looks of it,' Marian remarked tartly.

'Oh God!' Maggie thought to herself. Or, as Clarissa would say, oh Gahd!

'Shouldn't we join the others?' she murmured.

'Of course.' Marian smiled knowingly, leading the way into the lounge.

Clarissa beamed at her. 'Maggie, your gorgeous husband here tells me you're having a book published, I guess you must be thrilled. Sit here and tell me all about it.' The other woman patted the sofa beside her and, grateful for the respite, Maggie sat beside her.

'What's it called, honey?'

'I called it *City Woman*. It's coming out next November.'

'Waal, that's surely what I call an achievement. I wish you the very best of luck with it.'

'Thanks very much, Clarissa, I'll send you a copy when it comes out,' Maggie promised the friendly, enthusiastic woman at her side.

Despite her shock in the kitchen, Maggie enjoyed the dinner. Clarissa and Edward were very witty, warm people and Terry, who was always good in company, was thoroughly enjoying himself. Alex, despite his suave exterior, revealed a dry sense of humour, and there was plenty of laughter and interesting conversation. Maggie, who had been a bit tense during the first course, started to relax. Because she was driving home, she wasn't drinking at all, but the rest of the company imbibed freely and by the time they were sipping their Irish coffees after dessert everybody, even Marian, was relaxed and full of bonhomie. She was getting on like a house on fire with Terry, who had turned on the charm for her. 'Your husband is flirting with me,' giggled Marian, and Maggie realized she was slightly tiddly.

'Don't be taken in,' laughed Maggie, 'Terry is an incorrigible flirt. He flirts with everyone.'

'Well, he can flirt with me any time! A woman likes to be appreciated.' Marian beamed at Terry, her cheeks slightly flushed, her eyes bright. 'I'll have an affair with him while you're having an affair with that Adam guy.'

The colour drained from Maggie's face and she stared at her tipsy friend in horror, giving an involuntary gasp.

Marian immediately sobered up and her hand flew to her mouth. Clarissa met her husband's eye

471

in dismay and then, with a discreet flick of her wrist, knocked over her glass of red wine, shrieking dramatically, 'Oh Gahd, what a clutterbuck I am. You can't take me anywhere, Teddy,' as the vivid red stain seeped into the pristine white of the tablecloth.

'Not to worry, Clarissa.' Alex came to her rescue and started mopping with his napkin.

'Why don't we finish our coffee in the lounge,' Marian suggested quickly.

'Oh yes, do let's. And it's my turn to flirt with Terry; you've been monopolizing him all night,' Clarissa said brightly, linking Terry's arm and giving Maggie an imperceptible wink.

Maggie could have hugged the other woman for her intervention. She was an astute lady and a kind one too. With great skill and charm, she kept the atmosphere light for the remainder of the evening and, glancing at her husband occasionally, Maggie comforted herself that he hadn't even noticed what Marian had said. He seemed his usual exuberant self. Nevertheless, she was glad when he suggested they make a move an hour or so later, saying that they didn't want to keep their babysitter up too late.

'Maggie, I'm terribly sorry. It just slipped out,' Marian whispered as they went upstairs to get the coats. 'I didn't do it on purpose. You believe that, don't you?'

'I know you didn't,' Maggie said with a sigh. For all her pretension, Marian hadn't a malicious bone in her body. Maggie knew that it had been a slip of the tongue as a result of too much wine.

Marian ran her fingers through her hair in agitation. 'I don't think Terry noticed anything.

Not with the fuss Clarissa was making about the wine.'

'Stop worrying about it,' Maggie said firmly. 'Clarissa handled the whole thing very well by upsetting that glass deliberately. She's one nice lady.'

'She certainly surprised me tonight,' Marian admitted. 'There's more to her than meets the eye.'

'Well, *I* wouldn't mind having her for a sister-in-law,' Maggie declared, as she slipped into her coat and took Terry's navy overcoat and scarf from the closet where they were hanging.

'It was a pleasure to meet you, honey, and the best of success with your book.' Clarissa enveloped her and Terry in turn in a bear-hug, as they stood at the front door.

'Happy New Year,' the Montclares all called as Maggie and Terry got into the car. Maggie switched on the ignition and drove slowly down the drive. 'That was a nice evening. Clarissa and Edward are a lovely couple,' she remarked as they emerged on to the main road.

Terry turned to look at her and his eyes were cold slits of fury. 'You bitch, Maggie! You're paying me back, aren't you? You're carrying on with that bloke from the writers' group! And don't bother to deny it — it's written all over your face!'

Forty

Maggie drove steadily on. She had often wondered what the moment would be like when Terry found out about her affair. But she could only give half her attention to her own plight because there was a lot of traffic and she needed to keep her wits about her. In a way it was a relief that he knew. Maggie was not by nature at ease with lies and deception, so she had found them the hardest thing to handle. Now Terry knew – it was all out in the open. Where it would lead, she tried not to think.

Of course, she was quite aware of the feelings he was experiencing this minute: the rage, the hurt, the sense of betrayal. Oh, she knew *exactly*. She recalled how she'd felt the day she'd discovered Ria Kirby, in her house, in her shower, with her husband. At least, she thought bitterly, she'd conducted her affair outside their home.

'By Christ, but you're cool, Maggie,' Terry fumed, interrupting her musings. 'You don't even try to deny it.'

'Why should I? It's true,' Maggie said flatly, as she geared down and stopped at a set of traffic lights.

Terry looked at her with hatred. 'How long have you been sleeping with the bastard?'

'What difference does it make, Terry? What difference does the date, the hour, the minute make?' she snapped.

'It makes a hell of a bloody difference,' he shouted at her. 'I want to know. I want to know how long you've been making a fool of me, how long you've been going between his bed and mine?'

'Since last summer, if you *must* know. We haven't been having an affair as long as you and Ria were, I haven't been making a fool of you as long as you were me,' Maggie spat.

'You bitch, you bloody spiteful bitch. You make me sick!' Terry turned away from her and Maggie jerked the car forward as the lights went green.

She was so tempted to yell, 'Now you know what it's like; now you know what I felt like. Sauce for the goose is sauce for the gander,' but she held her tongue. There was no point in engaging in a screaming match in the car. It was hard enough to concentrate on her driving as it was.

In a silence that palpitated with anger, resentment and even hatred, they drove home to Castleknock. Terry barged into the house before her and marched up the stairs.

'Hi, Josie!' Maggie popped her head through the sitting-room door and tried to keep her tone normal. 'Are we very late?' She was hoping against hope that Josie wouldn't be in the humour for a chat.

'You're grand, Maggie. Did you have a good time?' Maggie saw with relief that Josie was packing away her knitting.

'It was lovely. It's nice having a meal served up to you.' She tried to smile, but felt like bawling her eyes out. 'Were the children all right? Terry was bursting to go to the loo, and he's going to look in on them,' she fibbed.

'As good as gold, Maggie. I enjoyed my evening, but I'd better get home and face the music. I wouldn't put it past that ould rip to be up waiting for me.' Josie slipped on her coat and kissed Maggie on the cheek. Maggie went to the door to wave her off. As the little yellow Mini, Josie's pride and joy, disappeared into the night, she closed the front door, switched off the downstairs lights and walked slowly up the stairs. She walked into her bedroom and stood rooted to the floor at the sight that met her eyes.

'What do you think you're doing?' Her eyes widened as she saw Terry filling a suitcase with her clothes.

'I'm helping you to leave this house. Just get out, Maggie. Go to your lover. I never want to see you again. How could you do it to me, Maggie? How could you betray me?' Terry was nearly incoherent.

Fury surged through Maggie. 'Now, *you* listen here to me, buster. The cheek of you to tell me to get out of my own home. Who the hell do you think you are? You bloody hypocrite. What about you betraying me with that lousy wagon, Ria Kirby?'

'Oh, and you had to get your own back, didn't you?' Terry raged. 'You just couldn't wait to jump into the sack with some creep to even the score.'

'How dare you, Terry Ryan!' Maggie walloped her startled husband across the face. 'Adam isn't a creep and I didn't jump into the sack with him. I knew him for a hell of a long time before I had an affair with him. I'll tell you why I'm having an affair with him.

476

And it isn't to even any scores,' she said contemptuously. 'That's not my style, it's yours. The day I started my affair with Adam was the day I went into your office to show you the cover of *City Woman*. You couldn't be bothered even to look at it,' Maggie accused him bitterly.

'How the fuck could I look at it?' he roared. 'Hadn't the bloody VAT man just arrived unannounced doing one of his sneaky spot-checks. What was I supposed to do – just drop everything because you arrived?'

'Keep your voice down! You'll wake the kids,' Maggie said furiously. 'That's just the point I'm trying to make. You would never ever drop everything because of me. I'm way down on your list of priorities, Terry, and always have been. When I'm with Adam, he treats me as if I'm special. He's interested in what I am and what I'm doing with my life in a way that you've never been.'

'Ah, don't give me that crap, Maggie. You're living in cloud-cuckoo-land. I work my butt off to give you and the family a reasonably affluent lifestyle and it isn't easy. We've three children to clothe, feed and educate. You can't expect me to behave as if we're still on our honeymoon.'

'Oh, what's the point?' Maggie said wearily. 'You haven't a clue about what I need emotionally. I'm just wasting my breath.'

Terry paced up and down the bedroom floor. 'Oh, for Christ's sake, Maggie, grow up! We've got three fantastic kids. I have a good business so we don't have any worries about money. We've someone who comes in every Friday so you can have time for yourself.

You're having a book published. You've got it made. Anything else is a bonus. How would you like to be Caroline? What's *she* got, for crying out loud? Look at Patrick and Susy – they're miserable. How would *you* like to live in that purgatory they call a marriage? We're doing well, Maggie, and if you can't see that you're blind.'

'I'm not talking about the kids or the house or what we've got materially. I'm talking about *us*. You and me, Terry. Whatever we had when we married is gone. I need more from you than you give me,' Maggie cried.

'You're looking for the moon, Maggie, and you'll never have it. Go and stay with your lover-boy; he'll give you all the emotional support you feel I'm depriving you of,' Terry snarled.

Slowly, deliberately, Maggie walked over to their en suite and picked up the soft mat that lay at the door. 'Do you see this, Terry?' she asked calmly. 'This is a doormat; you wipe your feet on it. Well, I've got news for you, mister. I'm *not* a doormat and you aren't going to wipe your feet all over me. If you want to leave this house, *you* go, because I'm not going anywhere. I've three children to look after and this is my home.'

'A fine mother you are,' Terry sneered, 'carrying on with another man.'

'Well, I suppose I could say the same about you and another woman,' she said contemptuously, taking her clothes back out of the case and hanging them in the Sliderobes.

Terry glared at her. 'Are you going to finish with that bloke?'

478

Maggie turned around and faced him squarely. 'That, Terry, is a matter that has nothing to do with you,' she said coldly. 'As far as I'm concerned, what I do from now on is none of your business, because, for me, our marriage is over.'

Forty-One

'He just can't handle it! At all,' Maggie said ruefully to Devlin and Caroline almost a month after Terry's discovery of her affair with Adam. 'I mean, I was supposed to accept that he had had an affair with Ria Kirby and then forget all about it or pretend it never happened. Men!'

The three of them were having a long-overdue lunch: Devlin and Caroline had been up to their eyes for the previous month because of the opening of Belfast City Girl, and had spent most of their time in the North. Caroline had travelled down from Belfast that morning to attend to some personal business and was due to go back the next day. The friends had decided that lunch was a priority, to catch up on all the events in their busy lives. Devlin and Caroline already knew of the disastrous dinner party at Marian's. Now, as they sat at a quiet window table in Locks Restaurant, Maggie was bringing them up to date on developments.

'If women had the egos men had, we'd be in serious trouble,' Caroline reflected.

'It's his pride, you see,' Maggie fumed. 'I was *his* woman and another man has had what he considers to be exclusively his. That's what annoys me about it.

He's not devastated because I found the emotional support I needed from another man; he's just upset because I *slept* with another man. They take sex so bloody seriously. Terry thinks I did it to get my own back on him.' She sighed.

'And didn't you — a little bit?' Devlin probed gently.

'No, I didn't,' Maggie said indignantly.

'Just a teeny bit?' Devlin arched a quizzical eye-brow.

'Whose side are you on?' Maggie snapped.

'I'm sorry that two people I care for are so utterly miserable,' Devlin retorted. 'I'm not taking anybody's side, but if you'd stop being so self-righteous you'd see that there are faults on both sides.'

Maggie was shocked at Devlin's straight talking.

'I think you're being a bit hard on Maggie, Dev,' Caroline interjected.

'Well, you must have known how Terry'd react if he found out — and he was bound to find out some time or other,' Devlin pointed out.

'He had an affair first!' Maggie argued vehemently.

'Well, two wrongs don't make a right,' Devlin said calmly, 'and by that statement, you've more or less admitted that because he had an affair first, you felt that it was perfectly all right for you to go ahead and have one to make things even.'

Maggie leaned across the table and glared at her friend. 'What would you do if you found out that Luke was having an affair?'

Devlin was taken aback.

'Well?' demanded Maggie, annoyed at her friend's sanctimonious attitude. She had come to lunch looking for sympathy and succour; she hadn't expected a lecture.

'I'd probably never speak to him again,' Devlin said.

'Well, that's what I felt like when Terry had his affair, but I *did* speak to him and I tried to put it behind me. I even let him back in my bed and he took it all for granted. Took it as his due, even. So yes, maybe you're right, Devlin; maybe there was an element of getting my own back with Adam, but I'd never ever have considered an affair if Terry had been faithful to me!' Maggie burst into tears.

'I'm sorry, Maggie. Don't cry.' Devlin was genuinely contrite. 'What's the old saying about not judging a person until you've stood in their shoes? I've no business pontificating.'

Maggie wiped her eyes. 'I'm always pontificating to you, aren't I?' she said wryly to Devlin. 'You're entitled to do it. If we've something to say to one another, we've always said it out straight. That's one of the reasons the three of us have stayed friends.'

'What do you think is going to happen, Maggie?' Caroline asked. 'Are you going to leave Terry? Are you going to stay with Adam?'

Maggie pushed her plate away; she had no appetite. She had asked herself the same question over and over. Some days she was certain that she was going to leave her husband and bring the children with her to Adam's. There were other days when she was going to tell Terry to sell the house and make up her mind to live in Wicklow, just herself and the children. Most of the time she felt trapped. How could she uproot the children from their home, their playschool, their friends? They loved their father and he loved them. It wouldn't be fair on them. What was fair? What was right?

'Caroline, to tell you the God's honest truth, I don't know what the hell I'm going to do,' she said wearily.

'This is really good. It's even better than *City Woman*.' Marcy pointed to the sheaf of pages in front of her. 'It's as if she's writing from a deeply personal point of view. There's great empathy there. The readers are going to love this one.'

'Great,' Sandra said with satisfaction. 'I'll take a copy of it and read it myself. I love the title . . . *A Time to Decide*. It's very snappy, very intriguing. I can't wait to start selling it in.'

'With the way Maggie's writing we'll have a third book way ahead of schedule. It's really flowing out of her. She's writing like a fury. Have you spoken to her lately?'

Sandra shook her head. 'Not since we took her to lunch before Christmas. I suppose I should telephone and see how she's getting on. It's just that I don't need to get anything organized with her for a few months yet and I wouldn't like her to think I was hassling her. That's *your* job,' the sales and marketing manager said, grinning. 'It has been ages though, so maybe I'll give her a call. She likes to hear the publishing news. That's what I like about Maggie; she's interested in it all.. Not just what pertains to herself and her own books.' She threw a questioning look at Marcy. 'Was there any particular reason you asked me if I'd phoned Maggie?'

'No,' Marcy said slowly. 'I was just wondering if you'd been in touch.'

'Is anything wrong with her?' Sandra asked in concern.

Marcy frowned. 'I don't know. You know Maggie; she's usually a very *up* kind of person. Lately, I feel she's under some kind of pressure. She hasn't said anything but she's not herself.'

'But she's writing?'

'Terrifically well,' Marcy reiterated.

Sandra took the thick wad of pages from the editor's desk. 'I'll have this photocopied for myself. I'm looking forward to reading it now. If *A Time to Decide* is as good as you say, then whatever pressure Maggie's under is obviously good for her writing. So let's hope it lasts,' she remarked cheerfully.

'Can I have popcorn, Mammy?'

'Where are your manners, Michael?' Maggie reminded her son.

'Sorry, can I have popcorn *pleassse?*' He put an extra-special emphasis on the please and Maggie hid a smile.

'Can I have Coke please, Mammy?' Mimi made sure to have her manners.

'We'll all have some.' Maggie cuddled Shona to her and was rewarded by a sloppy kiss. 'Right, let's go,' she ordered. After her lunch with the girls, she had decided to bring the children to the pictures as a treat. The atmosphere at home had been horrible for the previous few weeks and she was sure they could sense it. Children were very intuitive like that. Mimi had even asked why Maggie was sleeping in the guest-room and not in her own bed and Maggie had explained that she was writing a new book and she had moved into the other bedroom so she could type at night and not keep Daddy awake. To her relief, her daughter seemed to accept her explanation, and sometimes before she went to bed at night, Maggie let her type some letters on the screen of her word processor, which now reposed on the bedside locker in the spare room.

She hadn't actually lied when she'd said she was writing, because her writing was the only thing that gave her any comfort at the moment. Immersing herself in her characters' lives released her briefly from the unhappiness of her own. Often she went to bed at nine so as not to have to sit in the sitting-room with Terry in that simmering cauldron of silence that often erupted into harsh words, accusations and recriminations.

She wrote until the early hours of the morning, spurred on by her anger, her resentment and her fear. Because she *was* fearful about her future. She knew things couldn't go on like this for ever and if she did leave Terry or he left her she wanted financial independence. Terry would maintain the children – she had no fears for them – but she didn't want to be beholden to him in any way, and if her writing career took off at least she'd have some money of her own.

Adam was urging her to come and live with him, but in her heart and soul Maggie didn't think it would work out. Adam, her dreamer, had such unrealistic notions. Adam couldn't cope with three lively children running around demanding to be fed and entertained, no matter how much he protested that he could. Adam was a bit of a loner – that was why having an affair suited him. Maggie could recognize that. Of anyone she had ever known, he was the most self-sufficient person in terms of not needing other people's company. Adam was quite happy to write, play with his computer, and see her whenever she could get time to be with him. If he had to put up with the wear and tear of family life, she wasn't sure if their idyll would stand the strain. Their love affair was not based on reality. It was a paradisiacal few hours once a week, in which real life did not rear its ugly head.

If she were totally honest with herself, she mused, as she drove past St Peter's Church en route to the Santry Omniplex, she would have to admit that it was easy for Adam to give her the emotional support she craved, especially with regard to her writing. He had no other pressures or commitments to worry him or absorb his time. If he was in Terry's position, trying to maintain momentum in his business and provide emotional and material security for his three children – all of which, Maggie recognized, Terry did very well – would he be able to keep up the level of support that she had grown so dependent on?

It was a question that had given Maggie much food for thought these past few weeks. She sighed deeply. Devlin hadn't put a tooth in it when she declared at lunch that there were faults on both sides. It wasn't a very nice thing to have to admit. But maybe she was so concerned with her own needs and desires that she had neglected Terry. What was it that Devlin said? Two wrongs don't make a right. Perhaps if she had given a bit more instead of dwelling on her own hurts and resentment, things might have worked out for them. Should she have been as assertive as she was, particularly in the last couple of years? Was it selfish to put herself first now and again; after all, she had as much right as her husband to develop her career and grow as a person. Surely that was not the crime that Terry seemed to think it was. She had given him a hundred per cent support when he'd started out in business. He could have done the same for her. She'd always put herself out for *him*, she muttered resentfully, as she drove past Dublin City University. A group of students crossed the dual carriageway, laughing and joking on their way to The Slipper pub, and Maggie envied them their carefree gaiety.

'What did you say, Mammy?' Michael piped up from the back of the car.

Maggie feigned cheerfulness. 'Nothing. I was just talking to myself.'

'Are we nearly there?' Mimi demanded. 'I can't wait!'

'And I can't wait mine own self,' Shona added her tuppenceworth. Maggie felt a fleeting moment of happiness. She loved her children, with their innocent needs that were so easily fulfilled: feed them, clothe them, keep them warm and dry and lavish love on them. Oh, of course there were days when she could strangle the three of them, but they were good affectionate kids, and watching them develop their individual personalities was a source of great joy to her . . . and to Terry. When she had suggested going to the pictures, you would have thought she had offered them the moon. A trip to Disneyworld wouldn't have caused as much excitement.

'We're nearly there,' she assured them. There were squeals of excitement from the back seat. No matter what happened, she thought firmly, their happiness would be paramount.

'Can I go to the toilet?' Mimi asked, as Maggie paid for the four of them.

'Of course you can. Come on, we'll get the popcorn when you're finished.'

'Can I go? I'm bursting.' Michael suddenly discovered that he too had an urgent need to do wee-wee.

'We'll all go,' Maggie decided, leading them across the airy foyer of the cinema, past the snack kiosk and into the immaculate pink-and-grey ladies toilet.

'I wish Daddy was here,' Michael announced forlornly.

'Why, pet?' Maggie asked gently, as guilt scorched through her.

Her son raised his big brown eyes to her and gave a sigh. "Cos then I could go into the men's toilet instead of being stuck with all these women,' he declared in a most hard-done-by tone. There was no answer to that, Maggie thought!

They all thoroughly enjoyed the Disney cartoon, and sitting in the darkened cinema, the three children wide-eyed with excitement, Maggie put her worries aside for a while and joined in the fun.

Driving home in the deepening dusk, Maggie wondered if Terry would be home from work yet. They'd have to talk. Although she'd said their marriage was over as far as she was concerned, the needs of their children had to be considered and they couldn't continue ignoring each other or fighting, as they'd been doing for the past few weeks.

A thought struck her. It was Nelsie's birthday the day after tomorrow and her mother always liked to get a card through the post. She'd get one in the Winkel on the Rise. Five minutes later Maggie pulled into the well-stocked newsagents. It had been in this very shop a few years before that she had bought the magazine featuring the novel-writing competition that had made her sit down and write *City Woman*. Of course, the children all wanted to come in with her but she didn't mind; they could pick a card for their gran as well and she'd buy the stamps there and post the two in the box outside. She'd noticed that there was an eight o'clock collection so the cards would get to Wicklow in plenty of time. She'd bring her mother down her present at the weekend.

She selected a pretty card with a thoughtful verse for her mother, and watched in amusement as her three youngsters argued over the selection of cards for a grandmother before finally making their choice. Maggie paid the smiling woman behind the counter, wrote her greetings on the card and let the twins stick the stamps on the envelopes. On a spur-of-the-moment impulse, she bought three lottery tickets and let the children scratch them. When they discovered that Michael's card had won him ten pounds, there was great excitement, and they drove home singing, 'We're in the Money.' Now that Maggie had made up her mind to talk to her husband, she felt marginally more positive about things. What the outcome would be, she had no idea. If Terry was still sulking she could forget it, but maybe he too would have come to the realization that talking was the only way to settle things.

'Can I buy Daddy something with some of the money?' Michael asked from a position immediately behind her left ear.

'I've kept him some popcorn,' Mimi announced proudly.

'Yes, you can buy your daddy something. We'll stop at the shop in the village. And you're a kind girl, Mimi, to keep some popcorn for your daddy.' Maggie eyed her children in her rearview mirror, noting their proud smiles at her praise. God bless their innocence, she thought with a pang, as she turned left off the Navan Road towards home.

Forty-Two

'Why don't you move in with me?' Ria Kirby suggested, leaning across the table to rub his hand seductively.

Terry sighed and shook his head. 'What about the kids? It's not that simple, Ria.'

'Of course it is!' the curvaceous black-eyed woman retorted. 'She's having an affair; she doesn't love you; you don't love her. There's no point in being miserable. You can always arrange to spend time with the children.'

Terry stood up from the table and helped his companion on with her coat. 'I'll see, Ria; I'll be in touch. I'd better get back to the office.'

'Spend the night with me?' she invited. 'It makes no difference now whether you go home or not. Come on, it's Friday. You won't have to get up for work in the morning and I'll pamper you and bring you breakfast in bed.' Ria smiled suggestively.

Terry's eyes brightened. 'Sounds like just what I need. You always *did* know how to look after a man, Ria,' he said, smiling at her.

'Remember how I always liked to drink champagne in the bath?' she murmured huskily. 'I have a bottle at home.'

'You haven't changed a bit,' Terry declared admiringly. 'I'd really better go, Ria. I'll phone you.' He held the door of the restaurant open for her and walked her to her car.

'Do that!' She smiled sexily, showing a tantalizing few inches of plump thigh as she got into her Nissan Micra and zoomed out of the car-park.

Terry grinned. She was one fast woman in every sense, Miss Ria Kirby, and he had always been very attracted to her. She worked hard and she played hard and he was glad he'd phoned her and invited her to lunch. It was nice to be appreciated and it was very rewarding to be still fancied by his ex-mistress.

Maggie wasn't the only one who could play around, he thought grimly, as he sat into his Saab and headed back to the office.

He still found it hard to believe that his wife had actually slept with another man. He would never have considered her capable of infidelity. Terry had always thought that he could count on Maggie's total loyalty and commitment. A man having an affair was different – and he'd only got involved with Ria when Maggie was pregnant and not very interested in sex. As far as he was concerned, it had just been a bit of a fling. But Maggie had not seen it like that at all. She had made a song and dance about commitment and trust and fidelity. And then, after all her giving out? She upped and went and did the same thing herself.

It made his blood boil when she went on about the emotional support she got from this other bloke. Was she mad? As a man, he knew that the creep she was sleeping with was only enjoying a bit on the side. 'Emotional support, my hat,' he muttered, driving around St Stephen's Green. Who did she think she was fooling? She had done it to get back at him. He should have known, of course. She'd lost weight and had her hair styled differently and sometimes seemed to have a glow about her when she came back from a so-called meeting with her editor. Terry had put it down to the excitement about that novel of hers. She'd made a right fool of him. And then the cheek of her when he asked her if she was going to give the bloke up and she told him it was none of his business. Her own husband, whom she was deceiving – and it was none of his business! By God, but those feminists had a lot to answer for, for putting notions into women's heads. There was many a woman who would be glad to have what Maggie had, he thought resentfully, pulling into the car-park behind the office. A lovely house, a generous husband, and three lovely kids. Terry's frown vanished as he thought of the children. This carry-on was not good for them. Only the other day, when he'd snapped the nose off Maggie, his little son had put his arms around Terry's neck and said anxiously, 'Don't be cross with Mammy, Daddy. It makes me feel funny in my tummy.' Both of them had been horrified. Their one remaining bond was the love they had for their children. Terry would do anything rather than cause them grief.

He might bring them to the zoo this weekend and make a fuss of them, he decided, as he sat behind his desk and eyed the file he had been working on with something less than enthusiasm. Maybe Maggie would come too, and they could put aside their bad feelings and give the kids a good time. That was, if she didn't have a date with lover-boy, he thought bitterly. If she'd said she was going to end the affair he might have forgiven her eventually, but knowing that she was still seeing the bastard just stuck in his craw. He'd never have dreamed that they would end up like this, he thought miserably, as he turned his attention to a letter from the tax inspector saying that his client owed eighty thousand pounds in unpaid taxes. His client was in a fine bloody mess, and his marriage had broken up too. Life was a bitch, Terry thought, as he bent his head and tried to make sense of the figures in front of him.

'You're in great humour, Ria,' Joan, one of the girls in the office, declared, listening to her supervisor humming the Roy Orbison hit, 'Anything You Want You Got It'.

'I'm always in great humour,' Ria retorted. 'I'm gasping for a cup of coffee. I'm going up to the canteen. If a phone call comes for me, make sure to put it through.'

'There's obviously a new man on the scene,' said Anne, the typist, with a grin. 'I know the signs.'

'Did you hear her: "I'm always in great humour." She's hilarious! No wonder she's still on the shelf at forty – no man would put up with her moods,' Joan snorted. 'She's not the only one who's "gasping for a cup of coffee". And she's only come back from her lunch!'

'That's one of the perks of being a supervisor: the more you earn the less you work,' agreed Anne. 'Maybe this new guy will whisk her up the aisle and she'll take her gratuity and leave us in peace.'

'You may as well dream here as in bed,' Joan said

dryly. She'd seen Ria's men come and go. Why should this one be any different?

Ria sipped her black coffee and smiled happily to herself. To think that Terry had called her and invited her to lunch! It had been a bolt from the blue, a very welcome bolt. Of all the men she had ever dated, Terry Ryan was the one she had really fallen for. She had met him when she was out in Saudi in the eighties, and their subsequent affair had been the best time of her life. When Terry had ended it, after they had come back to Dublin and his wife had caught them making love in the shower in their bedroom, Ria had been devastated. She had always secretly hoped that one day he would leave Maggie for her. Now, after hearing the sorry saga of his wife's affair, Ria couldn't suppress the hope and excitement that bubbled inside her. She had been thrilled to hear that Maggie was having an affair, although to tell the truth she'd never have thought that Miss Goody Twoshoes had it in her. It was obvious that Terry was disgusted about it. Well, the more angry and disgusted the better. That would suit her purposes admirably. This time he wouldn't be too eager to go back to his wife, and she'd make sure that he wouldn't want to. Oh yes! Ria thought happily, she could just visualize that gold ring on the third finger of her left hand.

Although she often claimed she would never wash a man's socks and that being an independent woman was the only life for her, Ria knew well that if any man who was half-fanciable proposed to her, she'd accept like a flash. Who'd want to work in the Civil

Service for the rest of their life, for God's sake? She thought Joan and Anne in the office were mad to be working when they had husbands who could keep them. Imagine being able to stay at home all day and sleep in as long as you liked and then watch TV to your heart's content. That's what she'd do if she was married. And then in the afternoon she'd dress, put on her make-up and make her husband take her out to dinner. Cooking was not Ria's forte.

Please let him ring me, Ria sent up a fervent prayer to the heavens as she took out an emery board and began to shape her nails.

Maggie's car wasn't there, Terry noted glumly, as he drove into the drive. He was hungry – he hoped Josie had something nice for the dinner. Today was her day to clean the house and take care of the kids while Maggie was off 'having time to herself'. There were no lights on in the front of the house. They must be all out in the kitchen at the back. He let himself into the house, expecting to be leaped upon by his offspring, but all that greeted him was silence. No children, no Josie, no dinner. Nothing. The doorbell rang and Terry opened up to find the girl from next door standing in his porch, holding a beautiful arrangement of peach roses.

'These are for Mrs Ryan. The delivery man left them in our house because there was no answer here this afternoon,' she informed him cheerfully, thrusting the flowers at him. 'Bye, Mr Ryan,' she smiled, and skipped off down the drive. There was no card with the flowers and suddenly a red rage engulfed Terry. That fucking fancy-man of hers was sending flowers to his wife at their house! He flung the flowers across the hall, thundered up the stairs and into his bedroom. Throwing open drawers and wardrobes, he shoved clothes into a case. Maggie had the nerve to say she wasn't a doormat. Well, by God, neither was he! To hell with Maggie; he was going to go to a woman who had always appreciated him. Ria Kirby would never treat a man like dirt. He ran back down the stairs, still fuming, and slammed the front door behind him.

Terry's car wasn't there, Maggie observed, as she brought the car to a halt outside the front door. She didn't know whether she was glad or sorry. She was a bit tired and was looking forward to getting the children to bed and sitting in front of the fire to watch the *Late Late Show*. The hall light was on, though, so Terry must have come home and gone off again. Maybe he'd gone to get himself a Chinese takeaway, although she'd left him a hotpot ready to be popped in the microwave.

Opening the front door, she followed her children inside and stopped short when she saw the peach roses strewn across the hall. What the hell was going on, she thought in confusion.

'Look at the lovely flowers, Mammy. Why are they on the floor?' Mimi asked.

'I don't know, pet.' Maggie bent down to pick them up, wondering who they were from and how they had got scattered all over the hall.

A minute later the doorbell rang, and she found her next-door neighbour on the step with a small white envelope in her hand. 'Maggie, I sent Charlotte over with flowers that were delivered for you when I saw Terry's car in the drive. She dropped the card in the porch, so here you are. Have to fly! Jonathan is taking me out for a meal and I'm trying to get the gang to bed before the babysitter comes.'

'That's exactly where mine are going this minute,' said Maggie, taking the card. 'Thanks, Stella.' She grinned. Stella was always in a rush, no matter what she was doing. Closing the front door, she slid the little white card out of the envelope and smiled as she saw the note from Devlin. 'Sorry for pontificating,' it said. But why had Terry flung them around the hall? A thought struck her and her lips tightened. The idiot! He must have thought they were from Adam. Her heart sank like lead. So much for her plans for talking things over. If that was the kind of humour he was in, she could forget it.

She gave the children scrambled eggs for tea and after an hour's play got them ready for bed. When she noticed the light on in the master bedroom, Maggie went in to switch it off, and saw the open drawers and wardrobe doors. A queer, sick, heavy feeling came over her. Terry must have taken some of his clothes. But where was he going? He must be leaving her and the children. Why couldn't he even have left a note? Sinking on to the bed, she put her head in her hands and wept. What a way for their marriage to end!

She half-expected him to phone to say he wouldn't be home, but by the time the *Late Late Show* was over, she angrily accepted that he wasn't going to call. He could have at least had the guts to tell her to her face that he was leaving.

Maggie spent a restless night tossing and turning,

before falling into a fitful sleep. She was giving the children their breakfast the following morning when the phone rang. Her heart began to thud and she strove to keep her voice normal as she answered it.

The voice at the other end was not Terry's but her eyes widened at what the man who spoke to her was saying.

'Thank you,' she replied. 'Yes, I'd be very interested, I'll be in that neck of the woods this afternoon, so I'll call — if that's all right,' she said, and smiled as he agreed to the arrangement.

If Terry was making a fresh start, well, so was she, she decided, as she walked into the kitchen to finish her breakfast.

Forty-Three

'You bought a mobile in Wicklow! Congratulations, Maggie.' Adam gave her a hug. His eyes brightened. 'Hey, you know what this means?' He took her hands in his. 'I can take my holidays and spend them with you in the summer. We can be together for three weeks.' Adam was all excited by the idea.

Maggie got up from the sofa and walked over to the window. There was an early-blooming cherry-blossom outside Adam's sitting-room window and the buds were just opening. It was young and fresh and pure, heralding the change of season and the arrival of spring. Usually this would have cheered Maggie enormously, but today she felt desperately sad as she turned to face her lover.

'You can't come down to the mobile, Adam,' she said quietly. 'The children will be there. I can't see you in front of them.'

'But Maggie!' Adam protested. 'Terry's living with someone else. Why can't you do the same?'

'He doesn't live with someone else in front of the children. They don't know of her existence and they don't know of yours. I don't want them to be confused and hurt.' Maggie sighed. 'It's bad enough for them at the moment. Michael cries himself to sleep at night and Mimi's become very aggressive at playschool. Her teacher told me.'

'But what about me? And what about you?' Adam's hazel eyes flashed with hurt and resentment.

Maggie took a deep breath and looked him squarely in the eye. 'I don't think we should see each other any more.'

'*What!*'

'Believe me, Adam, it isn't easy for me to make this decision,' Maggie said wearily. 'I've thought of nothing else, night after night. And *you* can't be satisfied with this type of relationship, either. It's going nowhere.'

'I'm not!' he barked. '*You* know that. You know I want us to be together. I'm fed up with an afternoon here, an evening there. Tea in Clerys, for God's sake! It's pathetic. Now that you and Terry have split, I can't see any reason why we can't be together, at least for three lousy weeks in the summer. Why can't I take my summer holidays and be with you and the kids in your mobile? I mean, it's nothing at all to do with Terry.' Adam was highly indignant.

'Adam,' Maggie explained gently, feeling miserable but knowing that what she was going to say had to be said whether he or she liked it or not. 'My children have got to be my priority at the moment. I have such a huge responsibility to them and I can't forget that. When we go down to the mobile home at the end of May, we'll be there until the end of August. That's three months. I can't see you for those three months. I'm not going to get my mother to babysit in order to come up to Dublin for an afternoon under the pretence of meeting my editor. I can't take the deceit any more.' Her lower lip suddenly wobbled and tears smarted her eyes.

Adam grimaced as he put his arms around her. 'Well, I'll wait the three months, then.'

'Look, Adam,' Maggie said unsteadily. 'This is no kind of a life for you to be leading, hanging around waiting for the few hours I can spend with you. You should have a girlfriend of your own age with no commitments. This is not right for you; you can do much better for yourself.'

'But I love you, Maggie!' Adam said desperately. 'No-one else understands me like you. If it hadn't been for you, I would have gone off my rocker when I got my manuscript back a few weeks ago. I love you,' he repeated. 'I want to be with you. Why can't you and the children come and live with me?'

'Because I won't do that to them. Terry calls every evening to put them to bed. He couldn't do that if I was with you. I won't deprive the children of their father.'

'Even if it means sacrificing us?' Adam asked bitterly.

'I don't want this to happen!' Maggie cried. 'You know how much you mean to me. You must know how happy you've made me. But I can't be totally selfish. I brought those kids into the world and I'm going to do my best for them. And if that means putting my personal life on hold until they're reared . . . well then, that's tough on me but that's the way it's going to be.'

Adam was horrified. 'For Christ's sake, Maggie, this is the twentieth century, almost the twenty-first. Women and men are changing partners all the time!

You can't be serious about putting your personal life aside. You're talking like someone out of your mother's generation.'

'And what's wrong with that?' Maggie flared. 'At least my mother's generation raised relatively stable families grounded in the basic decencies. It's just too easy now to walk away from a marriage because of a few setbacks. My mother's generation had to grin and bear it and for the most part, things worked themselves out. Our generation ups and runs at the first setback.'

'You're never going to go back to Terry!' Adam exclaimed, aghast.

Maggie shook her head wearily. 'I don't know what's going to happen between us. What I do know is that we both want the best for our children – it's the one thing that unites us – and if that means Terry coming home every evening for an hour or two, or coming down to the mobile for the odd weekend, I can cope with that.'

'Well, you're a bloody idiot, Maggie!' Adam said in disgust.

'Maybe,' she said soberly. 'But at least I'm facing my responsibilities as best I can, in order to be able to live with myself.'

'And so I'm getting the bum's rush?' he asked harshly, turning his back on her.

'Don't be like that, Adam,' she pleaded.

'Well, what should I be like?' He turned angrily back to face her. 'Where do my feelings come into this? What about your commitment to me?'

Maggie exploded. 'Adam, when we first fell in love, I warned you I was a married woman with children.

You knew that from the start, and you have no right to expect anything more from me. So stop trying to make me feel guilty. You knew how I was fixed. You knew I'd always put my children's interests first.'

'Do you know something, Maggie?' Adam's lip curled in disgust. 'I feel used, really used. You had your sex and you had all the support from me that I could give you and now you're dropping me like a hot potato because of your kids. Wow! This is a turn-up for the books! I never knew women did this to men, I always thought it was the other way around. Goodbye, Maggie; you know your way out,' he finished coldly.

Maggie was pale with shock. Not in a million years had she expected Adam to react like this. Did he not realize that she was making one of the hardest decisions of her life, a decision that had caused her many sleepless nights. In silence, she picked up her bag and walked out his front door. As she sat into her car, she realized with dismay that she was shaking. She had expected him to understand. Not to like her decision, but at least to understand. Kind, sensitive, intuitive Adam, always encouraging, always supportive. But he had failed her when she most needed his understanding. A shocking thought struck her: Adam had behaved just like Terry, full of *me, me, me*, and wounded ego and pride. That, to her, was the ultimate betrayal of their relationship. She drove through Drumcondra and turned on to Botanic Avenue. Pulling into the hard shoulder by the park, Maggie buried her head in her hands and cried her eyes out.

*　　*　　*

'Well, to hell with you, Maggie Ryan! *And* your bloody kids!' Adam stared angrily out the window and watched Maggie drive off down the road. He had given up a lot for that woman – and for what? To be dropped because she felt her kids were her priority? He couldn't believe she was such a fool. Everybody knew kids grew up and left home and forgot all about the sacrifices their parents made for them. Oh yes, not too far in the future, her children would fly the nest and she would end up one very lonely lady indeed.

He sat down and gazed into space. He just couldn't believe that Maggie had walked out on him. How could she do it just like that, with no thought at all for his feelings? All this time, he thought he was someone really special in Maggie's life and that she needed him – needed his love and encouragement and support, which he lavished unstintingly on her. How often had they sat for hours discussing every aspect of their writing? When she hadn't felt like writing another comma, it had been he, not the kids and certainly not Terry, who had urged her on to get back on track. That had obviously counted for nothing, Adam thought bitterly.

A lump lodged in his throat. He had been so sure that Maggie loved him. He felt a tear slide down his cheek and angrily he brushed it away. What a wimp he was, to be crying about a woman who had used, abused and dumped him. 'Ah, Maggie, why did you do it? Why? I loved you. Don't you know that? I loved you very much.' The lump was nearly choking him and in utter misery, he sat down and cried.

*   *   *

'Daddy, will you come down and see us?' Michael held tightly to his father's arm, as two other pairs of eyes turned anxiously in his direction. Terry shot Maggie a glance and she nodded imperceptibly.

'Of course I will,' he promised. 'We'll have great fun in your mammy's new mobile, and we'll go to Brittas Bay and into Arklow . . . and we might go to Rosslare . . . and even on a ship to Fishguard for the day.' There were screeches of delight at this news. 'Go to sleep now,' Terry ordered, 'because you've to get up early in the morning. I'm going to help Mammy pack the car.'

'Dood night, Daddy,' Shona held out her arms to him and Terry hugged her tightly.

'Won't you come down soon?' Michael held up his face for a kiss.

'I will,' promised Terry.

'I wish you still lived here,' Mimi said angrily, and marched from the room. Terry met his wife's troubled gaze. Maggie looked very tired and down in herself, he thought guiltily. Maybe he should offer to take the children out more at weekends and give her a break. But Ria would go mad. She was already complaining about the way he came home every evening to put the kids to bed.

'I'll go up to her,' he murmured. Mimi was sitting on her bed, hugging her teddy tightly to her. She glowered at her father as he entered the room.

Terry sat down on the bed and lifted his elder daughter into his arms. 'Why are you cross with me?'

'Why do you go away to sleep somewhere else at night? Why don't you sleep here any more? You don't love us any more!'

'Of course I love you, you silly billy. Don't I come home every night to play with you and put you to bed?' he answered lightly. 'And don't I come to sleep some weekends?'

'But why don't you come *every* night?' Mimi insisted.

Terry prayed for guidance. He smiled at the cross little face in front of his own. 'You know your friend Catherine and how her daddy's a detective?'

Mimi nodded.

'And you know that sometimes he has to work at night. It's called doing night duty.'

Mimi looked at her father earnestly.

'Well, I'm doing a lot of night duty,' Terry fibbed lamely.

'But *you're* not a detective,' Mimi protested.

'Oh, but lots of people do night duty. Nurses. Doctors. Telephonists. Lots and lots of people.'

'Well, I wish you didn't have to do it,' Mimi said. But Terry could see that his explanation had given her something to think about.

'Sure, we all have to do things we don't like.' Terry kissed his little girl and tucked her up in bed. 'Now, go to sleep as quickly as you can and then, before you know it, it will be morning and you'll be off on your holidays.'

'Do you wish you were coming?'

'I sure do,' Terry declared, and, to his surprise, he did.

An hour later, the quilts and pillows that Maggie had bought for the mobile home were neatly stashed in the back of the car, and the cases containing all their clothes were arranged neatly in the boot, along with an array of buckets and spades and swimming rings.

'Well, you were always able to pack a car, Terry,' Maggie admitted.

'One of my many attributes,' he said modestly, and his wife laughed.

He closed the boot and locked it. 'Is there anything else you want me to do?'

'If there's any post for me, will you send it on?'

'Sure. Of course.' He paused a little awkwardly. 'Hey, listen. If you like, I could go down on Friday nights and you could come up to Dublin. It would give you a bit of time to yourself to do your bits and pieces and . . . ah . . . I suppose it would give you a chance to meet your chap.' He was a bit surprised at himself for saying that, but fair was fair. Maggie had the kids seven days a week and he knew there was no way she'd ever meet the bloke in front of them. They had agreed that their respective lovers were not to be paraded in front of the children.

Maggie's face flamed in the dark. 'Thanks for the offer, Terry . . . but, actually, I'm not seeing Adam any more. I finished it,' he heard her say quietly.

'Oh! Oh, I see. Well, the offer still holds if you feel like a break.'

Maggie smiled at him. 'That would be nice, I could meet the girls and have a gossip, and I know the kids would love to have you all to themselves.' She caught his eye. 'Won't Ria mind?'

'Kids come first,' Terry said firmly. 'By the way, Maggie, Mimi thinks I'm on night duty like Catherine's da. It mollified her a bit. They're too young to be explaining things to them, aren't they?'

'Yeah,' Maggie sighed, 'but we'll have to tell them some time. Although we can explain things to them until we're blue in the face. They won't want explanations; they'll just want us to be together.'

'Let's say nothing for the time being. Let's give them a good holiday and see how it goes. Have you said anything to your ma and da?' he asked.

Maggie shook her head. 'No, I told only Devlin and Caroline.'

Terry had to laugh. 'Well, that goes without saying!' He'd never seen such close friends as the three of them were. He'd felt a right prat when Maggie showed him the card from Devlin that had accompanied the roses he had thought had come from her boyfriend.

'Have you told your mother?' Maggie asked.

'No,' he admitted. 'I just can't bring myself to.'

Maggie sighed. 'I know. I just don't want to upset them. And it makes it seem all the more final when you actually say it to people.'

'Will we leave it until after the holidays? I'll stay here every few nights. Alone,' he added quickly when he saw her face. 'Just to keep an eye on the place. I don't like it being empty. And when I'm down in Wicklow with you, we can visit your parents' and pretend for the time being that everything is normal.'

'OK,' Maggie agreed, much to his surprise and relief.

'Right! I'd better be off, then,' he said with false cheerfulness. 'Enjoy your time in Wicklow. You look whacked. Try and take it a bit easy. I know that's all right for me to say – I don't have the kids day and night. But I *will* come down and give you a break –

that's if it's OK with you. I have a sleeping bag and I can bunk down on one of the settees.'

'That would be much appreciated,' Maggie answered. 'And the kids will enjoy that; it will be good for them. I think it's best that we try and be as normal as possible under the circumstances.'

'Me too,' Terry said, as he got into his car and waved at her. She waved back and watched him leave before going back into the house.

It was true what she'd said: telling people making it seem more final. Maybe he and Maggie weren't behaving realistically, but at least they were talking and in agreement about not hurting the kids. That was something, and he knew he had Maggie to thank for it. She had made him see reason when he'd been ranting and raving at her after he moved out. Maggie was a very loyal woman, too. She'd never badmouth him in front of the kids, nor he her. And he knew she was terribly hurt that he had started up with Ria again. She had just as much excuse as he had for being bitter. Now that their anger had faded, they weren't getting on too badly, considering everything. He couldn't but be pleased that her affair was over. He was only human, he told himself, as he drove towards Mulligans of Poolbeg Street, where he had arranged to meet Ria and some of her friends for a drink.

To be honest, he was not in the humour for the pub. He'd come to realize that the yuppie lifestyle was not his scene any more. Parties and dinners in restaurants were all very nice occasionally, but not every night of the week. It was Friday night and the place would be packed. Who ever would have thought that the idea of staying at home to watch the *Late Late Show* in front of the fire would actually seem like paradise.

With a deep sigh, Terry began the hunt for a parking spot.

Forty-Four

A blackbird on a fir tree just feet away from her sang his heart out, and Maggie paused in her writing to sit back and savour the beauty all around her. Nestled in a deep hollow among the Wicklow hills, Johnson's Caravan and Camping Park was a Shangri-La that was slowly spreading balm on her bruised and battered spirit. It was July, and the weather, which had been overcast and dull, had suddenly turned glorious. The skies were azure, the trees verdant. In the field behind her mobile home, cows placidly chewed the cud, and rabbits, scampering and scurrying along, were a source of constant delight to the children. They had settled down to the easygoing, almost unreal, way of holiday life, with the amazing facility children have for adapting to new places and new situations.

Maggie turned her head and watched her three offspring playing with some other children from neighbouring mobiles. When she first arrived at the end of May, the site had been very quiet as most of the other owners had schoolgoing children. At week-ends the place would fill up and take on a holiday air, with the sound of children playing, and people cutting the grass on their own patches. The pool and playground would echo to the cries of carefree children and Terry, true to his word, and to the great joy of the children, had come down from Dublin as often as he could.

On Sunday evenings, cars would be packed and families would depart, and Maggie down in her little nook in the inner field would have the place to herself again. After the hurly-burly of the weekend the quiet of Monday mornings was bliss. Maggie found herself becoming much more relaxed as the days turned into weeks.

The first weekend that Terry had come down had been a bit awkward. It hadn't been too bad when the children were still up. Excited at seeing their father, they had fought for the privilege of showing him around. He had been taken on a guided tour of the site and shown the playground and the pool and the shop and the games-room. And, most important of all, the den they had built out of grass and bushes over by the tennis-court.

After they went to bed, exhausted but happy that all was right in their little world, Terry and Maggie were alone together. Both felt awkward and uncomfortable and eventually Maggie said she was exhausted, retired to the double bedroom and closed the door firmly behind her. It was strange knowing that Terry was outside, and she lay alone in the dark and cried unhappily. Adam was constantly in her thoughts. She had written to him, a long loving letter, explaining that she realized she had hurt him and that she understood his anger. She told him she loved him dearly and always would, but that it had been the best thing for everyone for them to end their relationship. She had heard nothing from him —

another heartache to add to the others she was carrying. Knowing Terry was back with Ria had really angered and distressed her, but she'd been angry with herself for her resentment, calling herself a dog in the manger. She had told Terry their marriage was over, she had refused to end her affair with Adam when Terry had asked her, so it was totally unreasonable of her to be annoyed. Nevertheless, she really hated that woman.

Eventually, she heard Terry switch out the lights and get into his bed on the sofa. Only then did she sleep.

When he arrived, Terry asked her if she wanted to go up to Dublin, but Maggie decided against it. Dublin was the last place she wanted to be, and besides, it made the children very happy that they had both their parents' company. So for the rest of the weekend, they had put on the best face they could, and concentrated on giving their children a good time. All the same, Maggie was relieved when Sunday evening came.

'Will I come next weekend?' Terry asked, as the children played outside on the grass. Maggie shrugged and told him it was up to himself.

'I know it's not very comfortable for us, but I'm just trying to do the right thing,' he said a trifle forlornly, and she felt a pang of remorse. After all, the children were ecstatic when they saw their daddy. She couldn't be thinking of herself all the time – and she did have her whole precious week to herself.

'Well, we survived this weekend. I don't see why we shouldn't do OK next time,' she said evenly.

'Look, if you'd rather I didn't come down, just say so, Maggie.'

For one moment she was tempted to say yes, she'd rather he stayed away from her and the kids and just left her in peace in her private paradise. But she thought of the children's excitement when Terry's Saab appeared over the crest of the hill, and she swallowed her resentment and said, as pleasantly as she could, 'Come down by all means, Terry. The lads had a ball, and that's the main thing.'

The following weekend was somewhat less tense. Maggie had to admit that Terry was trying to make things less awkward between them, and they actually sat out on the veranda after the kids went to bed on Friday night, chatting about inconsequential things over a bottle of red wine. They went to visit her parents on the Saturday. Her father and mother were looking forward to seeing their son-in-law. Maggie took the children up to the farm twice a week as it was only a ten-minute drive from the site, but it was Terry who had suggested that he pay a visit, in case they began to wonder why he hadn't been to see them. They had acted out happy families perfectly, and Maggie had half-begun to think that all that had happened in the past few months was a bit of a dream. Reality hit her once again back in the mobile as she closed the door to her bedroom and heard her husband preparing his made-up bed on the sofa.

As June wore on more people began to come to the site to stay, and by mid-July most of the mobiles were occupied. Her immediate neighbours, Yvonne and Donald, had two lovely little girls, Fiona and Caitriona, who had become great pals with Mimi and Shona. There were three cousins of theirs two mobiles up, called Katherine, John and Jennifer. Michael and John had become bosom buddies and the eight children played happily together, much to the satisfaction of their respective mothers.

Maggie got on well with Yvonne and her sister Helen, and they settled into a pattern of taking all the children together to the pool, Brittas Bay or into Arklow or up to the playground in Redcross.

Because Shona and Caitriona were so close in age, Maggie and Yvonne often took them for a walk in their buggies while the older kids played on the site. Maggie enjoyed her walks. At first she and Yvonne had been puffing and panting as they pushed the buggies up and down the hilly, leafy roads. But gradually, their fitness returned, and they walked briskly along to the church of Saint Mary's, which was set on a green patchwork hill about a mile from the caravan park. They would sit in the cool serenity of the pretty village church and enjoy the solitude for a few minutes before attempting the steep hill up to the post-office.

Maggie loved that old-fashioned post-office-cum-shop that sold everything – from school uniforms to Mr Kipling's apple pies. Every nook and cranny was packed with goods, and the little shop was as well stocked as any department store. Needless to say, their offspring would demand a treat, and while the two little girls relished their chocolate Buttons Yvonne and Maggie would each eat a juicy peach and tell each other that they weren't going to eat junk and that they were definitely losing weight. They would walk home by the back road, enjoying the scents and sounds and sights of the beautiful country-side.

At night, Helen would keep an eye on all the children while Maggie and Yvonne did a very fast walk to the church and back. Maggie got on well with Yvonne, a redhead like herself. She enjoyed the company and was delighted with the exercise and the chance to be free of the children for the half-hour or so it took them to do the walk.

The days took on their own routine. Maggie would get the children dressed and fed, do her housework very rapidly and then while the children played, she would sit on her veranda and write for a couple of hours. Then she would take them swimming in the pool. After lunch, if the day was fine, they would all pack into cars and head for the beach for the afternoon. After dinner and playtime, Maggie and her neighbour had their walk. Then she would bath the trio and by eight o'clock, there wouldn't be a sound out of the Ryan mobile. Sometimes Yvonne and Helen would come over to her veranda, or she would sit with them, eating Pringles and peanuts and having a drink. Maggie was usually in bed by eleven. Occasionally she dropped in to Marian at her site on the coast, or Marian dropped over to her. Marian was still torturing herself over her inadvertent remarks at the dinner party, even though Maggie tried to convince her that Terry would have found out about Adam from someone else if not from her. In the end, she asked Marian not to refer to the matter any more. There was no use in crying over spilt milk.

At the weekends all the husbands would appear. Each family would do its own thing until the

Monday, when it was usually just wives and children who stayed behind for the week.

It was a peaceful, easygoing existence, far different to the frenetic pace of her city life, and gradually Maggie found herself regaining some sense of equilibrium. Sitting on that lovely July morning, listening to the blackbird's song, Maggie felt peace envelop her. Whatever happened to her, at least this mobile was hers, and she promised herself that, no matter what, she would bring her children to this glorious place every summer for as long as they wanted. Across the fields, she could make out the winding ribbon of road that led to Redcross. Tomorrow she would visit her parents, she decided.

Helen and Yvonne had offered to take the children to the beach for the afternoon so she could concentrate on finishing the final chapter of *A Time to Decide*. Maggie was very happy with her second novel. All that she had learned from Marcy during the editing of *City Woman* had stood her in good stead, and she felt it was a blooming great achievement that she had all but completed a second novel despite all the traumas of her personal life. *City Woman* was on schedule for a November launch and would be in the shops before Christmas. When she got home at the end of August she would be meeting with her publicist and sales and marketing director to plan the publicity itinerary. In spite of herself, she was becoming excited about it all again, and the great thing was that she'd have her second novel to follow very quickly on the heels of the first.

After waving the gang off, Maggie spent a couple of very fruitful hours, editing what she had written.

She was deeply engrossed in her manuscript when she heard the sound of a car coming down the hill. It couldn't be the lads back already, she thought in surprise, squinting against the sun. Then her heart leapt into her throat as she recognized Adam's car.

Slowly she stood up, as his car drew to a halt. She watched him walk towards her with that panther-like lope that was such a part of him.

'Hi,' she said, unsure of what his reaction would be.

He threw his head back and looked up at her. 'Hello, Maggie. Is it OK to come up and talk?'

'Sure, come on.'

He took the steps on the veranda two at a time. 'Where are your kids? I don't want to make things awkward for you.' He smiled that old familiar smile that made her suddenly ridiculously happy. She'd never thought she'd see him again; she'd thought their bitter parting would be her last memory of him. At least he had come to talk.

'They're at the beach for the afternoon. Come in,' she invited.

'I'm sorry, Maggie, I behaved like a shit.' Adam met her gaze squarely. 'That letter you sent me, I'll always treasure it,' he said gently.

'Oh Adam!' Tears filled her eyes and she buried her face against his chest.

'Don't cry, Maggie. I can't stand it when you cry,' he murmured, holding her tightly.

'I do love you, Adam,' she sobbed. 'I didn't mean to hurt you, but I was thinking of my children.'

'I know you were, I know,' he soothed. 'And you were right. I was angry and I was hurt but that didn't last for long. I could never be angry with you for long,

Maggie. You know that.' He smiled down at her and brushed the tears gently from her cheeks with the back of his hand.

'I'm going away, Maggie, I've signed another contract for the UK. I just wanted to come and apologize for the way I treated you. I want us to be friends.'

'Oh yes, Adam, we'll always be friends. Always,' she said fiercely, hugging him to her tightly. 'I'm so happy you came, I've reproached myself over and over for what I did to you. It killed me to think that we'd parted on such bad terms.' She drew a long shuddering breath.

'You have nothing to reproach yourself with, Maggie, my beautiful, generous, warmhearted Maggie.' He lifted her face to his and kissed her very gently. 'I'll always think of my time with you as a wonderful, happy time with no cause for regret. I hope you'll think the same . . . Promise me you will.'

'I promise,' she said softly, kissing him tenderly.

Shaken, he drew away. 'I'm going to go now, Maggie. I think it's best. I love you, I'll always love you, I hope things go well for you, my love. I'll pray that they do.' He smiled at her, and she knew that as long as she lived she'd always carry the memory of Adam Dunne deep in her heart.

She watched him go and wept, a mixture of grief at his leaving and happiness that he had come back to her. Outside, the blackbird sang his song of joy. You have your children, she told herself over and over. You have your children and you have your career. Now get your ass in gear and finish that chapter and don't let Adam down. The next time he sees your face

520

it will be on the cover of a book. Just get out there and show him that you can do it.

Washing her face in the pure, sparkling spring water that flowed from the tap, Maggie felt as though a burden had been lifted from her shoulders. That she and Adam were friends was all that mattered. The past was behind her now; it was time to pick up the pieces and get on with it.

Devlin and Caroline were coming down for a few days soon. That would help. Her publishers were delighted with her second novel; her children were having the best summer of their lives. She was a lucky woman, she told herself firmly, gathering up her manuscript.

A breeze had risen, enough to blow the hair off her face. The intense heat of the day had given way to the balmy perfection of late afternoon. The scent from the hedgerows perfumed the breeze and the drowsy humming of bumble bees lulled her senses as she eased herself into her lounger and lay back against the cushioned pillows. Later, the fragrant perfume of night-scented stock would envelop the mobile, a fragrance that always reminded her of childhood and the flower beds outside the back door of her parents' house. She had filled the pots on her veranda with the blue-and-purple flower. A lark joined the blackbird. In a minute, Maggie promised herself, she would carry on correcting her final chapter. In a minute . . . Her eyelids drooped, her body relaxed, as images of Adam filled her mind. Slowly the pages of her manuscript slid out of her grasp, as she dropped into a dreamless sleep, in the place where she had found a measure of peace and contentment.

*   *   *

'You're *what?*' Ria couldn't believe her ears.

'I won't be able to come with you to Melanie Kelly's engagement party on Saturday night, I'll be down in Wicklow,' Terry explained patiently to his angry lover, as he knotted his tie.

'Well, come home early then,' she snapped.

'I'm sorry, hon, I can't. We're going to Fishguard for a day-trip. God knows what time we'll arrive back in Wicklow.'

'I've had enough of this crap, Terry,' Ria fumed, flouncing out of bed. 'You're gone every bloody weekend. This is not a goddamned lodging-house, you know!'

'Look, you know I need to have time with my kids,' Terry said sharply. 'I told you that when we first started living together.'

'Well, I've had enough of that too,' Ria shouted. 'It's either them or me. And you either come to Melanie's party or you don't come back here. Make up your mind, Terry.' She glared at him, marched into the bathroom and slammed the door behind her.

'Right, I will. No bloody problem.' Terry was galvanized into action. Dragging his case from the top of the wardrobe, he packed his shirts and socks and underwear and neatly fitted his two suits on top. He'd had enough of living like a twenty-one-year-old. Parties, more parties and yet more parties, until he was heartily sick of them. There was a hell of a lot more to life than sex and parties, he thought grimly. Living with Ria was not the idyll he'd expected. To know me, come live with me indeed.

522

Ria expected him to dance attendance on her morning, noon and night. To bring her here, to bring her there. She couldn't cook to save her life and he was spending a fortune eating out. She couldn't stand it if he decided to watch a bit of sport on TV, and would start parading around half-naked expecting him to start seducing her. He was too old for that, he thought wryly. A man in his early forties was not the goer a man in his mid-twenties, early thirties was, and Ria lived the life of someone in her teens. Terry never thought he'd admit to getting on, but one night last week he and Ria'd been making love and he'd found himself planning to cut the lawns at home, so that they would look tidy if Maggie decided to come up from Wicklow. He'd completely lost his erection and Ria had taken it as a personal insult.

One thing he knew: he'd far prefer to spend Saturday night with Maggie and the kids than at the engagement party of that silly woman Melanie what's-her-name. Even worse would be listening to Ria going on and on about him divorcing Maggie and making things permanent between them. Crikey, he couldn't think of a worse fate. Being married to Ria would be a nightmare. Never being fed or allowed to look at sport, expected to perform – and perform superbly – all the time! It was enough to bring a man out in a cold sweat. He wanted to go home. He missed his kids, he missed his wife, he'd been a bloody fool and it was probably too late now. Maggie seemed quite contented without him. It was a chilling thought. Nevertheless, he was damned if he was staying another minute with Ria.

Terry strode into the bathroom, where Ria had just

finished showering. 'Excuse me! Do you mind?' she exclaimed.

'Just want to get my razor and toothbrush, Ria. Oh and pass me that shaving cream and aftershave out of the cabinet, please.'

Ria was puzzled. 'Why? What do you want them for?'

'Hon, you told me to make up my mind one way or another and I just did,' Terry retorted, exiting the bathroom with his toiletries.

'Are you leaving?' She was horrified.

'What perception, my dear,' Terry murmured, feeling like Rhett Butler.

'You idiot, you gutless, spineless wimp! Run back to your wife who acts like your mother! Run back to your kids! Run back to your stodgy middle-aged rut as quickly as you can.' Ria almost spat the words at him.

Terry picked up his case. 'I'm running,' he said coldly, and left her staring open-mouthed after him.

Ria couldn't believe it! She had made an awful blunder backing him into a corner, issuing an ultimatum to make him choose between his family and her. It was too soon for that and now she had ruined it. Her one big chance and she had blown it. No-one would ever marry her now!

Forty-Five

'Congratulations! It's a great read.'

'Oh! Thank you, thanks very much.' Maggie beamed, her head in a whirl. The woman who had just spoken to her was the typesetter at Enterprise Publishing.

Sandra, the sales and marketing director, took her by the arm. 'You've got to meet Anthony Caffrey. He's *very* important in the book trade.'

'Wait a minute, loveys!' Carol swooped. 'Maggie, you've got to come with me to do a quick interview for *Late Date*. Val Joyce is going to pop in later. He promised he would and I know you're a fan of his. Then Sandra can have you back.'

'Maggie, I want you to meet a few people here,' Jeremy, her publisher, interrupted suavely.

'In a minute, Jeremy, she's mine,' the PR woman said crisply, and guided Maggie to a quiet corner of the restaurant where her book-launch was being held.

The smiling reporter held up the microphone for Maggie to speak into. 'This must be the most exciting night of your life.'

'It certainly is,' said Maggie with a laugh. 'I don't know whether I'm coming or going.'

'Have you a busy agenda for the next few weeks?'

'That's putting it mildly!'

'Give our listeners an idea of the type of thing you'll be doing, Maggie.'

'Well, tomorrow morning, I'm doing an interview on the *Pat Kenny Show* and I'll be in the Shelbourne doing newspaper interviews for the rest of the day.

'On Saturday I'm doing a signing session in Wordsworth bookshop in the Merrion Centre and in Quinnsworth in my local shopping centre. Sunday is free, and then on Monday and Tuesday I travel to Cork, Limerick and Galway for more of the same. On Thursday, it's back up to Dublin to record an interview for *Booklines* out in RTE and on Friday I'm off up to Belfast.'

'You're going to be a busy lady, Maggie,' the attractive blonde woman said, 'but *City Woman* is a rattling good read and I'm looking forward to your next book.'

'Thank you.' Maggie couldn't keep the smile off her face. 'My next is called *A Time to Decide*, and it will be out next year.'

'Congratulations!' The reporter gave Maggie the thumbs-up sign and did a quick rewind to check that the interview had been recorded. Then she was gone and Maggie was back in the fray.

'Excellent,' Carol said with satisfaction. 'I see I can bring you anywhere. Now, look, here's Rik Masters. He's a pain in the ass but he's a great photographer and that's all we care about. Column inches and photographs, lovey, that's our priority for the next two weeks.'

'Carol, darling, good show!' Rik gushed, holding a beringed hand out to Maggie and giving her a limp handshake. 'And you must be the lady of the moment. Seduce the camera for me, darling,' he breathed, and Maggie burst out laughing.

'Lovely, lovely. Wow! Turn to the left. Now, chin down a little, eyes looking at me. Did you ever consider modelling? What divine skin. Serious now. Close your mouth, eyes tilted à la Bacall. Sensational!' Rik kept up the patter as he danced around, focusing his lens on her. Maggie could see Devlin grinning at her in the background and strove to keep her face straight as instructed. She felt such a wally – but she'd better get used to this kind of thing. It was part and parcel of selling the book.

'Fine, fine. Thanks, Carol. Take care, I've got to dash. I'm at a Presidential do next.' Rik sighed dramatically and strode through the throng.

'Excuse me. Would you sign a copy of your book for me, please?' a young woman asked diffidently.

'Certainly.' Maggie was thrilled. 'What's your name?'

'Rachel Taylor,' she replied shyly and Maggie signed the flyleaf for her.

'I hope you enjoy it,' she said.

'Oh I will,' the young woman said enthusiastically. 'I love books like this.' She clutched the thick hardback to her chest and smiled again as someone else came up and asked Maggie to sign another copy of *City Woman*.

'You're playing a blinder.' Devlin glided up beside her and gave her an encouraging pat on the back.

'It's going well, isn't it?' Maggie bubbled.

'It's going fantastic; the atmosphere is terrific.

Point them all out to me now. Which one is Marcy and who's Sandra? That must be Jeremy.' Devlin nodded towards the tall, thin man with the half-moon glasses who was in earnest conversation with the owner of the restaurant.

'That's Marcy.' Maggie discreetly indicated her slim, elegantly dressed editor who was just then speaking to someone on her mobile phone. 'And that's Sandra over there. Isn't she glamorous?' The sales and marketing director was dressed to impress in a beautifully tailored red suit, her shining black bob perfectly cut, her make-up flawless as usual.

'You look pretty good yourself,' Devlin retorted. Maggie was wearing a deep purple three-quarter-length silk jacket over an elegant black cocktail dress. The colour was stunning on her, and Terry's eyes nearly popped out of his head when he saw her.

Terry was over in a corner chatting to her parents and his mother and despite all that had happened between them, Maggie was glad he was there. He had changed quite a lot from the brash devil-may-care Terry. He seemed to appreciate much more the effort she put into the rearing of the children and the running of the home. After leaving Ria, he had moved into a small mews belonging to a friend who was on a six-month course in Germany.

Only yesterday he had amazed her yet again. She had been like a madwoman trying to get organized for the launch and tidying the house for their respective parents' overnight stay. She was in the kitchen making a tart when she heard Terry going into the utility room and saw him reappearing with the hoover. 'Mimi spilt some popcorn she was eating; I'll just clear it up,' he announced matter-of-factly, and went off and cleaned up the sitting-room.

Maggie had stood with her mouth open. Terry, hoovering! Off his own bat! *And* he was cutting the lawns without being asked. *And* he often took up the tea-towel and started drying the dishes as she was washing, something he'd never done before. It wasn't that he was being ingratiating or trying to get in her good books, she'd decided; it just seemed to be because he was now so used to doing things like that for himself in his own place.

He had asked her if she wanted him to come to the launch or not. They still hadn't said anything about their separation to their respective families and Maggie thought it would look a bit odd if he wasn't there. Besides, in a funny kind of way, she wanted him there. When all was said and done, he was still her husband and the father of her children, and she couldn't deny the fact that when he had told her he had ended his relationship with Ria she had been really glad. She had always hated that woman's guts. Now Maggie felt that she was finally out of their lives for good. Maybe Terry felt the same thing about Adam, whom he had never met. At least the rows had stopped and they were getting on reasonably well and he seemed to appreciate the children much more. When he had offered to spend the week at home so she could be off about her publicity, Maggie had been very grateful.

'Are you sure you don't mind?' she asked him anxiously. Not wishing to impose, now that he was no longer living at home, she felt guilty to have him taking time off because of her.

'To tell you the truth, Maggie, it would be a pleasure – and I never thought I'd say that.' He gave a wry smile. 'Living on your own is a bit of a bummer. I miss the kids. I didn't appreciate them when I was living at home and I didn't appreciate you, either. I'm sorry,' he said honestly.

Maggie didn't know what to say. So she just murmured, 'Thanks for taking care of them; I appreciate it,' and left him standing in the sitting-room while she went out to the kitchen to make the tea.

To think that Terry Ryan had actually grown up at last! For her own part, she was happy enough with the way things were. Because she'd got used to depending on herself and getting on with it, she could cope with their separation. Much better than him, obviously. Although living alone was lonely – he was right in that – at least she had the children for company. Would it be simpler all round, she wondered, if she just asked him to move back in? He was spending a lot of time at home lately anyway and next week he'd be there for the full week.

Maggie glanced across the room to where her husband was laughing at something Nelsie had said. He'd be staying at home tonight. Fortunately they wouldn't have to share a bed, because her mother and father were having the master bedroom, and Terry's mother, who had travelled over from the west for the launch, was occupying the guest-room. Maggie was sleeping with Mimi, and Terry was sleeping with Michael. Maybe tonight would be a good night to ask him to come home.

It was the start to her new career. Why not let it be the start of a new life for them? Maggie was much too much of a realist to pretend that starting over would be an easy task, after all that had happened between them, but if not for their own sake, they should try and make a go of it for their children. That was their one great bond. Terry had once accused her of looking for the moon, and maybe he had been more realistic than her in his expectations of their marriage.

She looked at Devlin, her dearest friend. Devlin, who had told her straight that there were faults on both sides. She had been right. Maggie now knew that it was not fair to expect perfection of anyone, and that looking for someone else to make her happy was a recipe for disaster. She had to find happiness within herself and right now she felt pretty good. Anything else would be a bonus.

'Devlin, excuse me, will you? I want to ask Terry something.' She smiled at her friend and then, taking a deep breath, she walked over to her husband, tapped him on the arm and said firmly, 'Terry, could I talk to you a minute?'

Devlin's Story – II

Forty-Six

'Lydia! You look divine!' Lucinda Marshall air-kissed Lydia Delaney, who was arranging a display of satin and lace lingerie in her boutique, Special Occasions, in the City Girl shopping mall. Lydia had got in some new Janet Reger and La Perla stock and soon, she realized, she would have to get in her Valentine's Day stock of teddy bears and hearts and 'I love you' fluffy toys. Right now she was up to her eyes and could have done without Lucinda Marshall's visit. Not that she let on, of course. Lucinda was a good customer, and even after that unpleasantness when Devlin had refused to renew her membership of City Girl, she still bought her underwear at Special Occasions – although she no longer got the special City Girl discount of ten per cent.

'You look very well yourself, Lucinda,' Lydia smiled graciously.

'I just love what you've done here, Lydia; it's a fabulous shop,' Lucinda said enthusiastically, as she fingered a royal blue satin camisole-and-french-knickers set that had a matching lace-edged négligée. 'This is to die for,' she sighed dramatically, using one of her favourite phrases. She always felt very West Coast USA when she said it.

'Oh I simply must have this.' She pounced on an expensive gift-box stationery set and inhaled the fragrant lavender scent. 'Lavender, isn't it superb? It's Andrea's birthday next week. This will be perfect for her: she needs cheering up with that family she married into.'

Privately, Lydia felt it was the family who needed cheering up, having acquired the manipulative Andrea as an in-law, but she refrained from comment and gift-wrapped the expensive stationery.

Perfect, thought Lucinda as she took the exclusive Special Occasions bag from the other woman and handed across her Visa card. She'd present the gift to Andrea in the striking pink-white-and-green striped bag with Special Occasions blazoned across it, and knowing her VBF, she'd be in like a shot to the boutique to find out how much it had cost. Seventy-five pounds was more than a respectable sum to pay for a birthday gift and Andrea would be very impressed. It was a beautiful stationery set, with separate drawers for Thank-You and Thinking-of-You notes, and fragrant quality notepaper with matching lavender envelopes and even a small bottle of lavender perfume. It was genteel, Edwardian-lady almost, and totally wasted on the social-climbing Andrea, who hadn't a genteel bone in her body. Lucinda realized this as she signed for her purchase with a dramatic flourish. When Lucinda's own birthday came around, Andrea, who never liked to be outdone, would have to buy an equally expensive present.

Yes, a good day's work, Lucinda decided with satisfaction, as she put her expenses credit card back in her bag. No doubt accounts would query the sum but when Lucinda explained that it was the carrot that got the horse, they wouldn't be able to say a word. One expensive present bought one lunch in a posh eatery with Devlin Delaney's mother and with luck a few revelations about the proprietor of City Girl that would find their way to the article being prepared – an article that would show the successful young businesswoman in a totally different light. I'll fix you, Ms Delaney! Lucinda thought grimly. The humiliation of being barred from membership of the centre still rankled. Now if only Lydia would agree to be interviewed . . . Kevin Shannon was interviewing Devlin right this minute up in her office, so at least she was out of the way. It would be too awful for words if she came down and caught her with Lydia: she might smell a rat.

Lucinda popped a handmade chocolate into her mouth. 'I'll have a box of these as well, Lydia. Aren't they just delicious?'

'They're Butler's Irish chocolates,' said Lydia, 'and they really are one of my best sellers. Everybody loves them: people buy them for themselves as well as for presents. I often bring a few home myself. Gerry goes mad for them. He has a terrible sweet tooth.' Getting Butler's to supply her had been one of her brainwaves. And what better way to celebrate a special occasion than with rich chocolate with fresh cream fillings. Devlin was always nipping in and filching a few.

'I'll take your biggest box,' Lucinda said. 'I'm having a dinner party and they'll go down a treat.' She took out her expenses credit card again. Might as well be hung for a sheep as a lamb, she decided.

Lydia smiled. She was doing great business with Lucinda this morning, she thought in amusement. Obviously she was a woman who didn't hold grudges: because when Devlin had told her she had revoked the gossip columnist's membership, Lydia hadn't expected to see her again. Not that she was actually in the centre at the minute; the shopping mall was accessible to the public. Further down the ceramic-tiled mall were the glass doors to reception. Only those with a membership card or members' guests could enter there.

'You know, Lydia—' Lucinda turned to Devlin's mother with wide innocent eyes '—why didn't I think of it before? What an idiot I am!' She gave a husky self-deprecating chuckle. 'I'm doing an article about women like us in their late forties-early fifties, who've made successful careers in their later years. You'd be perfect! You're an inspiration to us all.'

'Oh I don't know,' Lydia demurred.

'But Lydia, look what you've done: you've made a great success of Special Occasions and it's *so* tastefully designed and decorated. I remember Devlin saying in some interview or other that you had a great eye for decor. It's super; I might even be able to photograph you here. It would be great publicity for the business,' Lucinda added slyly.

Lydia was hesitant. She wasn't too crazy about being interviewed by Lucinda: she knew she should be extremely wary of her. Like everyone else, she read Lucinda's column, 'The Grapevine', and enjoyed it while still feeling sorry for the unfortunate victims of Lucinda's poison grapes. No! Lydia decided, free publicity or not she did not want to feature in 'The

Grapevine'; she could end up being strangled by its vicious tentacles.

Lucinda saw the doubt in the other woman's eyes. Damn, I've lost her, she cursed silently. She knew if she was to carry this off, she'd want to think of something quickly. As well as everything else, time was running short. She thought fast. It was her forte.

'Of course Lydia, you're no doubt thinking of "The Grapevine",' Lucinda gave another husky chuckle. 'This will not be a trivial or gossipy interview, my dear. This is a new series we're thinking of doing called "Women in Their Prime",' she lied frantically, although now that she thought of it, it wasn't a half-bad idea. 'It will be a full spread in the "Interviews, Reviews, and What's New?" supplement and actually, thinking about it, I'd like to lead off with a serious in-depth interview with you that will concentrate on the business side of things. You're the epitome of the woman we are looking for. Oh, come on, Lydia,' she urged. 'Be a sport and let's show these successful yuppies that they're not the only ones that can do it. Let's show the world that you're not over the hill just because you're over forty.'

It's a long time since you saw forty, Lydia thought dryly, observing the other woman with her perfectly made-up face. She could not conceal the crow's-feet around her eyes despite the face-lifts, or the telltale sag around the chin and that dead giveaway, the wrinkly neck. Lucinda Marshall was a hell of a lot closer to sixty than she was to forty. Perhaps it was the blonde hair that really made her mutton dressed as lamb. It was much too harsh; a nice ash blonde would have been more subtle. Lydia had to admit, however, that Lucinda's figure was excellent and in her Genny mini-skirted red-check suit, her legs were still passable. If you've got it, flaunt it, was Lucinda's motto, and more power to her, thought Lydia in amusement. She herself was dressed in a classically elegant Michael Mortell avocado two-piece which she had had for several years.

'Lydia, come on,' Lucinda wheedled. 'We'll have a jolly lunch. An hour or two will do the whole thing; it will be painless, I promise.'

'Now?' Lydia exclaimed.

'Why not?' Lucinda kept her tone light although she was beginning to panic that Kevin's interview with Devlin would soon be over and she might make an appearance and spoil everything. She felt like strangling Lydia.

'Look, it's just twelve-fifteen. How about we pop over to The Commons? It's only five minutes away. City Girl is so central to all the good restaurants.' Lucinda felt her smile was stuck to her face. She could see that Lydia was wavering. People were so easily swayed when you preceded the word 'interview' with 'serious and in-depth'. On second thoughts, she decided hastily, The Commons was a bit too open for the interview she had in mind. There were too many distractions. The Ladies Who Lunch would be stopping by at her table to greet her like the smarmy sycophants they were, in the hopes of getting a mention in the 'Who's Lunching with Whom' section.

Not that everybody was eager to be written about in that column. Only last week she had mentioned seeing a well-known film director with a young actress from the cast of his current film. Mrs Film Director had not been the slightest bit amused, by all accounts, to read in her Sunday newspaper that her husband was wining and dining a pretty thing who was young enough to be his granddaughter, especially since he had told her he was seeing his accountant. The film director had accosted Lucinda and verbally abused her in the Horseshoe Bar in the Shelbourne, where he liked to sit and pontificate to anyone who would listen to him.

'I'll put you in my next film, see if I don't! You'll be the laughing-stock of Dublin, you talentless hackette. You scribe of scurrility. You dispenser of trivia and trash,' he slurred, his ruddy face even ruddier than normal, his little pig-eyes glowering over the top of the half-moon glasses he affected.

'Darling, if you put me in the film I can guarantee you an Oscar – and God knows you need one,' Lucinda drawled, and a ripple of laughter had run through the bar from a greatly diverted audience of movers and shakers. This was the kind of thing they thrived on. There hadn't been a good to-do there since the episode of the drunken journalists.

'You . . . you medusa of the back page,' the outraged film director had howled.

'Oh, go home and make a film about Mimsy and Pimsy – it's all you're good for,' Lucinda said dismissively, referring to his penchant for boasting about his two obnoxious Pekinese dogs, that were the greatest ankle-nippers this side of the Panama Canal.

The film director gave a strangled gasp and for one heart-stoppingly delicious moment the audience thought he was going to make a lunge for Lucinda and grab her by the throat. Unfortunately, his bosom buddy and sailing companion, an ex-politician who had been in many scrapes, grabbed him by the arm and urged restraint. Both men lurched out the door, as drunk as skunks, the film director clutching at his toupee, which was slightly askew. They left Lucinda the queen of all she surveyed.

No, decided Lucinda, a very small, intimate restaurant was what she needed for today's lunch. She wanted no cock-ups, no interruptions, just Lydia Delaney on her own. 'I know—' she placed a hand on Lydia's arm, '—let's go to The Seven Hills. It's just opened. It's very quiet and intimate and the food . . .' Lucinda kissed the top of her fingers. 'Magnifico. You do like Italian, don't you?'

'Well . . .' Lydia reluctantly agreed, almost overwhelmed by Lucinda's breathless enthusiasm. Now that she knew she wasn't going to feature in 'The Grapevine' she was beginning to warm to the idea. It was flattering to think that Lucinda wanted her to be the first in the series of 'Women in Their Prime'. And just think what a surprise it would be for Gerry and Devlin. She wouldn't tell them about it and then they'd be amazed when they opened their *Sunday Echo*. It would make Gerry proud of her. He was really pleased and supportive about this new venture and to tell the truth, since she had given up drinking and Devlin and she were much closer after all their traumas, Lydia had been at peace and felt so fulfilled. In a way it was like starting afresh, as much for Gerry as for herself. Gerry was a good husband and she had never been much of a wife – and as for being a mother to Devlin . . . Lydia felt a stab of shame. She had treated her daughter so badly, and look how Devlin had forgiven her and encouraged her every step of the way with her boutique. She was a very special young woman. She'd make sure to mention that fact, and acknowledge Gerry's love and support for her as well, in the chat. The past was the past and Lydia was very glad to let it go. She *would* do this interview.

'I'll just get my bag and coat, Lucinda. You really are persuasive. No wonder you're so good at what you do. Rhona, I'm just going to lunch.' Lydia walked over to where her young assistant was arranging a display of red, yellow and white roses. Roses were the only flowers that Special Occasions stocked. Lydia had discovered that many men liked to buy roses to go with the lovely lingerie they bought for wives, girlfriends and mistresses. 'I won't be long, dear,' she murmured. 'If I'm delayed, close up and have something in the Coffee Dock.'

'OK, Mrs Delaney. I'll see you later.'

'Splendid,' declared Lucinda, wishing to God that Lydia would hurry up and get the hell out of the boutique. It was only when they were walking down a frosty, sunlit Grafton Street that the gossip columnist gave a mental sigh of relief and started to relax. Phase One successfully carried out. But Phase Two would be much trickier. She had spent a fortune in Special Occasions. Having lunch in The Seven Hills was not for the financially fainthearted. If she didn't pull this off, she was going to have to deal with a very irate accountant and an unimpressed editor. And people think I have the life of Riley, Lucinda reflected as she led the way into the softly lit, soothing reception area of the plush restaurant just off Wicklow Street. If they made any fuss because she hadn't booked or if she didn't get a table, there'd be hell to pay. Fortunately there were very few restaurants in Dublin where Lucinda Marshall was refused a table. It was more than anyone's job was worth to get on the wrong side of her.

'Miss Marshall! A delight. Table for two?' The smiling young man at reception greeted them. 'Please have a drink at the bar while the maître d' sees to your table.' He ushered them into a small secluded bar where a log fire burned brightly and told the barman, 'Whatever the ladies want, it's on the house.' He left them with Lucinda trying to persuade Lydia to have a Kir, and Lydia refusing very firmly, saying a Ballygowan would do her fine.

Sticking his head into the kitchen the receptionist announced glumly, 'That Marshall bitch from the *Sunday Echo* is out front. Let's take no chances!'

'Mama fuckin' mia,' moaned the chef-proprietor. He was suffering from a severe hangover and he knew it was going to be a hell of a long day. Lucinda Marshall was the last thing he needed right now.

Hell, thought Lucinda, as she observed Lydia sipping her sparkling water. How was she ever going to loosen Devlin's mother's tongue if she sat sipping mineral water! Phase Two was turning out to be a lot trickier than she had anticipated. Excusing herself to go to the powder room, Lucinda slipped into the restaurant and had a word in the maître d's ear.

Forty-Seven

'How sweet!' trilled Lucinda, as she saw the champagne on ice that awaited them at their table.

'Our pleasure, Miss Marshall,' the maître d' said suavely as he seated the ladies.

'Have some, Lydia; do,' urged Lucinda.

'Maybe later,' Lydia said non-committally.

'It's Dom Perignon, darling,' Lucinda said a little tartly.

'So I see,' smiled Lydia. 'Enjoy it, Lucinda.'

Lucinda sipped the champagne sorrowfully. Imagine not getting excited over Dom Perignon; now *that* was sophistication. Lucinda Marshall had never forgotten that she was born on the wrong side of the tracks, in what nowadays would be called a socially deprived family. Deserted by her father, with an alcoholic mother, she had hauled her way up to social prominence by relentless climbing, erasing her background completely and inventing a totally new past for herself.

No-one knew of her past except her first husband, and he was dead. Her second husband, an inoffensive retired architect a decade older than she, had believed every word of the story she had told him: of how her doctor father and artist mother had been killed in a car crash when she was very young. Lucinda often thanked God that she had no siblings to reveal that her mother had died in an asylum. Privately, Lucinda acknowledged to herself that Lydia had natural elegance and sophistication that she could never aspire to no matter how hard she tried. Lydia had been born to it; Lucinda had acquired hers. Lydia Delaney was a very cultured lady, and listening to her as she spoke enthusiastically about her business, answering the questions that Lucinda put to her for her so-called 'Women in Their Prime' interview, the columnist half-wished that she was doing the interview for real.

Doing her Grapevine column gave her a very high profile but she knew that to many she was just a figure of fun and not taken seriously as a journalist. There were times when she chafed at this, times when she longed to show her peers that she could do as good a probing serious interview as the rest of them without resorting to gossip and innuendo. But it was too late now: she was what she was.

'And the amazing thing is, Lucinda, women are buying sexy lingerie for themselves. Lots of my customers are women from City Girl who want to treat themselves to something nice, not because it's what a husband or boyfriend wants to see them in but because they want to have something nice and expensive and sensual to wear. I think that's great, don't you? It's a far cry from when I was a young woman,' Lydia laughed.

'Mmm, me too; my mother would have called me a slut.' The words were out of Lucinda's mouth almost before she realized it. For God's sake, get with it, Lucinda admonished herself. She was not here to empathize with Lydia Delaney: she was here to get the goods on her daughter Devlin. They were waiting for dessert and she noted with satisfaction that Lydia was quite relaxed. Unobtrusively she leaned over and filled Lydia's champagne glass, topping up her own at the same time, while asking a question about whether the current recession was having an effect on business.

Lydia wrinkled her brow and almost absent-mindedly took a sip from the glass of champagne. 'A certain class of people will always have money, Lucinda,' she answered. 'I'm sure you find that yourself. I can't say there's been a noticeable fall-off in business.' She suddenly realized that she had taken a sip of champagne. What on earth was she doing? She hadn't touched alcohol in months. Not since Devlin's accident when she had gone on that horrific binge. After that she had gone into St Gabriel's for a rest, as she called it herself, but in reality to dry out. Lydia had never acknowledged to herself that she was an alcoholic. Sometimes there had been gaps between her binges lasting for months, and she had never allowed herself to get drunk in public. Nevertheless, after her time in St Gabriel's, she had consciously abstained from drink and all in all, she had to admit, her life was much the better for it.

The champagne was lovely, though! The one little glass wouldn't harm her, she reasoned. Really, she was having such a pleasant time. Lucinda was a most charming hostess and she was so interested in Lydia's success. She had always thought of her as a trashy journalist, but there was a serious side to the other woman and from the intelligent questions she was asking about Special Occasions, Lydia could see that there was a sharp brain ticking away behind all the glitz and glamour. She really was quite pleased with the way the interview was progressing.

'What does your husband think about your success?' Lucinda smiled, gazing wide-eyed at Lydia as she refilled the glasses. It was a trick she had perfected over the years. Make eye-contact. Ask the question, and the victims never even notice that their glass is being filled to the brim, while your own is half-empty.

'Gerry's delighted for me,' said Lydia, beaming and taking another sip of Dom Perignon.

'Really! Isn't it wonderful to have a supportive husband!' Lucinda cried, watching in satisfaction as Lydia sipped more of the sparkling golden liquid.

An hour later Lydia Delaney was plastered. Lucinda was amazed at how quickly she had gone from the giggly stage to the faint slurring of the words and the unsteady focus of the eyes. Mind, it had taken another bottle of champagne, most of which Lydia, unbeknown to herself, had drunk.

Very discreetly, Lucinda placed her clutch-bag on the table and pretended to search for a tissue. Casually, she drew her miniature tape recorder out towards the flap, and clicked it on, all the while engaging Lydia in conversation.

'You must be so proud of Devlin,' she murmured. 'All she's achieved after all she's been through. You know, the baby and everything . . .' Lucinda held her breath as Lydia focused on her with some difficulty. Tears came to the other woman's eyes and her lip trembled.

'I am very proud of my darling.'

'I know you are,' Lucinda said sympathetically. 'I have no children of my own, but I can imagine the heartbreak they can cause. It must be so hard being a mother.'

'I wasn't much of a mother, Lucinda, I told her she couldn't come back home with the baby and made her go off to London for an abortion. Oh no, I wasn't much of a mother at all.' Lydia shook her head and two large tears trickled down her cheeks.

Jesus! thought Lucinda, half-shocked, half-excited. This was it! She looked around to see that no-one else was looking and thanked God for their secluded little alcove. Leaning over she reached across and patted Lydia's hand. 'But she didn't have the abortion, sure she didn't?' she asked soothingly. Lydia slowly shook her head and drank another glass of champagne in several quick gulps.

'I told her I never wanted to see her or the baby again. I cast my daughter out of my life and she ended up living in Ballymun. Imagine! How could I do it? I'll never forgive myself. If it wasn't for me, that baby would probably still be alive.' Lydia was quietly sobbing.

'Shush, shush, don't distress yourself.' Lucinda waved away the maître d', who was discreetly hovering.

'What happened to the baby, darling?' Lucinda continued to pat Lydia's hand in a very comforting fashion.

'She was killed in an accident: a juggernaut smashed into the car in Wexford . . . Oh, I can't bear to talk about it. I'll never ever forgive myself for what I did to Devlin. That awful night I told her she was adopted and I accused her of sleeping with a Portuguese gigolo!' She gave a little hiccup. '—And you know Lucinda. It was that bastard, Colin Cantrell-King. He was the father and he wanted to pay for the abortion. I'd love to knife him for what he did to my little girl. He seduced her and used her and turned his back on her when she needed him. Just like I did.' It all came tumbling out like water from behind a dam. Lydia was sobbing harshly and Lucinda was sitting open-mouthed with shock. Devlin adopted! Colin Cantrell-King the father of her dead child! Talk about hitting the jackpot!

Lucinda switched off her tape recorder. She had all she needed to know and a hell of a lot more. Time to get Lydia home before she drew attention to them. 'Let's go to the ladies', pet,' she urged, helping Lydia to her feet. Handing the maître d' her Visa card, she hissed, 'Order a taxi.'

Fortunately, there were only two other couples in the restaurant and no-one in the ladies' room. Lucinda sighed with relief, sat Lydia down in one of the chairs and handed her tissues as the distraught woman sobbed her heart out. She found to her horror that a lump was rising in her own throat at the other woman's obvious distress.

'Stop crying, Lydia,' she pleaded. 'I didn't mean to upset you. Devlin's got over her past. Look at her, she's so well-adjusted and successful, she's put it all behind her.'

Lydia looked at her with red-rimmed eyes. 'Devlin will never get over what's happened to her. She just puts up a very good façade. I know: I'm her mother and no-one can tell *me* anything about putting up a façade.' Lucinda was sorely tempted to ask who Devlin's real mother was. But even she, hard-nosed gossip columnist, felt she could not intrude on this woman's grief and pry into her deepest secrets a moment longer, scoop or no scoop. Now that she had what she was looking for, it didn't feel so great. How would *she* feel if someone got her drunk and winkled her deepest secrets out of her? It was a question Lucinda did not care to answer.

Feeling some responsibility for the state her guest was in, Lucinda got into the taxi with Lydia and asked for her address. Morosely, Lydia gave the required information, her tongue tripping over her words. 'Lucinda, you won't mention any of this in my interview, sure you won't? I shouldn't have said anything, I shouldn't have had the champagne. Promise me.'

'It won't appear in your interview. Not a word.' Lucinda was not telling a lie, she thought uncomfortably. It wasn't Lydia's interview the shocking revelations would appear in . . .

She helped her out of the taxi and into her luxurious house, admiring the exquisite decor and thinking how nice it would photograph for the *Echo*'s 'At Home With—' series. Lucinda could never have dreamt that she was so bad at holding her drink, though. It had been like taking candy from a baby. Phase Two had been more successful than her wildest dreams. She helped Lydia slip out of her suit, removed her shoes and eased her down under the quilt on her queen-sized bed. 'You'll be fine after a little nap,' she assured her.

'Don't report anything I said in the interview.

Promise,' she slurred, and then her voice trailed away and she passed out.

Quietly, Lucinda slipped out of the bedroom and downstairs to the waiting taxi.

'The *Sunday Echo* offices in Leeson Street,' she instructed the driver. The tape recorder in her bag felt like an unexploded bomb and Lucinda wanted to get the information transcribed quickly. She would do it immediately and then . . . later, when she had time to think about it, she would decide what to do with it.

Strangely heavy-hearted and worn out, Lucinda sat back in the taxi and lit a cigarette. To hell with the no-smoking sign; she needed a drag badly.

Forty-Eight

'Hi, Dad,' Devlin said cheerfully. It was always a treat when her father phoned.

'Devlin, could you come home? Lydia's a bit under the weather.' Gerry's voice sounded anxious.

'What's wrong?' Devlin asked in concern.

'She's been drinking again,' Gerry said heavily. 'I came home from work just a few minutes ago and found her in bed, drunk out of her skull.'

'Oh Dad!' Devlin felt sick. 'Why? Why now when things are going so well? The shop is booming, we're getting on fine. What got into her?'

'Will you come over? I just haven't the heart to handle it on my own any more.' Even down the line Gerry sounded tired and old.

'Yes, I'll be over. I'll leave now,' said Devlin. 'See you as quick as I can.'

'Thanks, Devlin. I really appreciate it.' Devlin felt pretty browned-off herself. All those familiar feelings associated with the bad old days of Lydia's drinking surged back with a vengeance. Disappointment, anger, fear, hatred. Why did she have to ruin everything? Just when it seemed that all was well between them and she had everything going for her. What had sent her off on a binge? Devlin rang down to the boutique. Rhona, Lydia's assistant, was still there.

'Rhona, hi! It's Devlin. I was just wondering what time Mum left the shop?'

'Hello, Devlin,' Rhona said cheerfully. 'Mrs Delaney went to lunch around midday. She was supposed to come back but she must have got tied up doing her interview.'

'Her interview?' Devlin said, puzzled.

'Yes,' Rhona said matter-of-factly. 'Some journalist wanted to do an interview with Mrs Delaney about being a successful businesswoman or something.'

'Oh yes,' Devlin lied, pretending she knew all about it. 'Thanks, Rhona, see you.' She hung up, totally mystified. Lydia had never mentioned anything about an interview. What on earth was going on? Well, the only thing to do was to get out to Foxrock and find out for herself. Heavy-hearted, Devlin said goodbye to Liz and left the office.

The traffic was brutal. It was raining and dark and she was stuck in Donnybrook for at least twenty minutes. Once she got on to the dual carriageway the flow would improve, she hoped. She saw some laughing, briefcase-carrying women heading into Kiely's for a drink after work. How could they – and she and Maggie – take a drink and enjoy it, while Lydia and Caroline once they started would end up paralytic drunk, causing hassle and grief all around. Sitting unhappily in the car, she felt like going into the pub herself and for once throwing responsibility to the wind, getting totally langers herself. How would Lydia feel then? Getting blind drunk was just an easy way out of facing responsibilities, Devlin thought resentfully, because drunks knew that there was always someone who would pick up the pieces.

If it wasn't for Gerry she wouldn't set foot in the house. Lydia could have gone and faced the music herself. And if her business in the mall started going to pot because of her drinking, she'd be out on her ear before she knew it. The nearer she got to home, the angrier Devlin became.

It was with immense reluctance that she put her key in the lock of the front door. Gerry, hearing it, came out to the hall.

'I shouldn't have called you; it's not your problem.' He gave her a hug and, as she stood there in his arms, Devlin could have strangled her mother for what she was doing to her long-suffering husband.

'Of course it's my problem! We're a family, aren't we?' Devlin said, hugging him back. 'Where is she?'

'Conked out in bed,' Gerry sighed.

'Oh, well, let her sleep it off,' Devlin said firmly. 'Have you had your dinner?'

'I wasn't really in the humour,' Gerry confessed.

'Come on, I'll cook you an omelette or something light.' Devlin linked her arm in his and they went into the kitchen.

They had just finished their meal and were having coffee when Devlin heard a movement upstairs. It was Lydia going into the bathroom and shortly after they heard her being violently ill.

'I'll go up to her.' Devlin patted Gerry's arm as he sat tense and worried beside her. She ran up the stairs and paused outside the bathroom where her mother was retching miserably. I hate this, thought Devlin, beginning to feel slightly queasy herself, but she took a deep breath and went in and held her mother's head. When it was over and Lydia was sitting flushed and red-eyed on the side of the bath, sipping a drink of water, Devlin said brusquely, 'What happened?'

Lydia shook her head and winced. 'I just took one glass of champagne. I never dreamt I'd get like this . . .'

'Champagne!' Devlin exclaimed. 'Who were you drinking champagne with?'

Lydia sighed, rubbing her temple, her eyes bloodshot and tired-looking. 'Oh, it was with that Lucinda Marshall.'

'*Mum!* Lucinda Marshall! What are you doing getting involved with her? It only means trouble.'

Lydia stood up unsteadily and made her way back to her bedroom, followed by Devlin.

'What were you having lunch with her for?' Devlin sat down on the side of the bed beside her mother and took her hand. Gazing at her, ravaged and ill-looking, Devlin felt her anger evaporate. There was something vulnerable about Lydia right at this minute and Devlin couldn't find it in herself to be angry any more. Lydia raised shamed eyes to Devlin.

'I can't believe I actually got drunk. I refused to have a drink with her beforehand. I wouldn't have wine and because she kept annoying me that it was Dom Perignon I took a glass. Devlin, I swear I never meant to get drunk. I didn't think one glass would have any effect. I must have just kept sipping while she kept refilling it. It must have gone through my system so quickly because I haven't been drinking in so long. Devlin, it's frightening. I'll never make that mistake again.'

And Devlin believed what her mother had just told her. It was such a relief to know that Lydia had not deliberately set out to go on a batter. She knew Lucinda Marshall of old. A couple of drinks to loosen Lydia's tongue was just the way she would operate.

'Why were you having lunch with her?' Devlin asked again, this time in a much more gentle tone.

'She wants me to be the first in a series of interviews she's doing called "Women in Their Prime". It's very flattering really: it's not for her "Grapevine" column at all. It's a serious feature. I hope to God she doesn't mention that I got drunk. I'd be so mortified. Poor Gerry! Does he hate me?' Lydia started to cry.

Devlin put her arms around her. 'No, Mum, of course he doesn't. He just got a fright, that's all. The two of us did. We thought there might be something wrong and that the pressure of the business was getting to you. Because you're not going to start drinking again, sure you're not?'

'Devlin, honestly, I had no intention of doing such a thing and I have no intention of doing it in the future. I don't need it in my life and I'm never touching champagne again. Certainly not in the company of a journalist.' Lydia gave a wry smile. A thought struck her. 'Oh Jesus!' she exclaimed.

'What?' Devlin asked in alarm.

'Oh my God, Devlin. You'll never speak to me again; how could I have been so stupid?' Lydia put her head in her hands.

'What is it? What's wrong?'

'I think she asked me questions about you towards the end. I think I told her about you being adopted and about the baby and the accident.'

Devlin felt her insides go cold. Something was going on with Lucinda Marshall, she just knew it. Revenge was a dish best served cold, the old saying went, and Lucinda was someone who would find a dish of revenge very tasty indeed. She had been furious when Devlin had told her she was not accepting a renewal of her subscription to City Girl. There had been threats of legal action. Solicitors' letters had passed between them but Lucinda hadn't a leg to stand on, especially when cuttings of her articles written about City Girl and its clients had been photocopied and sent back to her legal advisers. Devlin should have known better than to think that that would be the end of the matter.

'Don't distress yourself, Mum; she's a sly bitch. Just have nothing to do with her in the future,' Devlin said comfortingly, trying to put a brave face on it.

'Should I ring her and just say I don't want the interview published?' Lydia raised a tear-stained face.

'It's probably too late for that now, Mum. I think the best thing to do is just let it go. From now on, avoid the woman like the plague.'

'I'm awfully sorry, dear,' Lydia said miserably. 'You'd be better off without me. As a mother I don't seem to be much help to you at all.'

'Don't say that,' Devlin remonstrated. 'Our closeness is very important to me and it's made me so happy this last six months or so. I love you, Mum. I always will.'

'I surely don't deserve you, Devlin.' Lydia kissed her cheek. 'Will you ask Gerry to come up so that I can apologize to him, and then I'll just have to take two Panadol and lie in the dark. I can tell you, Devlin, I've got the mother of all headaches.'

'Poor Mum. I'll send Dad up with a glass of water. You lie down. I might as well stay the night so I'll see you at breakfast. OK?'

'OK.' Lydia smiled. Devlin helped her mother change into her nightdress. Then she went down, gave her father a brief report of the events and sent him up to his wife with a glass of water and two Panadol.

'I don't think Mum's going back on the booze. I do believe her,' Devlin said later that evening as they sat in front of the fire sipping hot chocolate before going to bed. 'But I would love to know what that bitch, Lucinda Marshall, is up to.'

'Maybe she *is* going to do that series of interviews. She'd hardly have treated Lydia to that very expensive lunch otherwise.'

'Hardly,' agreed Devlin, so as not to worry her father. But despite herself she had a feeling of unease that would not go away and that night she found herself tossing and turning restlessly as the problem preyed on her mind.

'Me ma's been trying to ring ya and she wants to know would ya ever give her a buzz.'

'Hiya, Roger! Sure I will. She's all right, isn't she?' Devlin spoke to the good-looking young man who had stuck his head around her office door first thing the next morning.

'Ya know Ma – never a bother on her,' Roger said with a grin. Devlin grinned back. Roger and his twin, Rayo, always had that effect on her. They were unfailingly cheerful and two very popular employees of City Girl.

'I'll ring her this minute,' Devlin promised.

'And tell her I fancy a pork-chop with apple sauce for me dinner tonight,' Roger added.

'Right,' Devlin laughed as he closed the door behind him.

What was up with Mollie, she wondered, as she dialled her friend's number. Mollie O'Brien was like a second mother to Devlin. In fact when Devlin and her baby had lived in Ballymun, she could have been her mother, so kind and concerned was her next-door neighbour. Since Devlin left Ballymun she had stayed in touch with Mollie and her husband Eddie, and when City Girl had taken off, she had asked Eddie, who was a carpenter, to come and work for her and paid for the twins to do life-saving classes. Then Devlin had employed them to run the centre's swimming pool. They did the work with great good humour and efficiency.

'Hello!' Mollie's broad Dublin accent came down the line.

'Hi, Mollie! It's me. What's up?' Devlin responded smiling.

'Howya, luv? I've been trying to get ya all last night. Whose bed were ya keeping warm? Is Luke over?'

Devlin laughed. 'Unfortunately not, Mollie, I stayed with Mum and Dad. What were you looking for me for? Can you not come to the Omni on Thursday night?' Devlin and Mollie met once a fortnight on Thursday nights for late-night shopping. There was coffee in Bewleys and then more coffee as they sat chatting and catching up with the news. It was something Devlin enjoyed very much. Mollie was the salt of the earth and Devlin cherished their friendship. Mollie had grieved almost as much as she had at Lynn's death because Mollie had loved her like her own grandchildren.

'I wouldn't miss our night, Devlin, luv. But what I want ta tell ya is I think ya should know that some little scut has been around here asking questions about ya. I gave him his answer, the little shite, and so did Bernie but I think Bridie upstairs – remember that mad bitch – I think she mighta talked ta him.'

'What kind of questions, Mollie?' Devlin asked in confusion.

'About where ya lived and how long ya lived here and about the baby an' all,' Mollie said grimly.

'But why would anybody go out to Ballymun? Why didn't he ask me here? What does he want to know for?'

'Devlin, luv, I think he was some sort of a reporter: he was a real slimy little geezer with a tape recorder. One of those small ones they use. Bernie told him she'd stuff it up his arse if he didn't stop annoying her; he was terrified of her.' Devlin laughed in spite of herself, remembering what a kind-hearted holy terror her other neighbour, Bernie, had been.

'Something's going on but I don't know what,' Devlin said ruefully. 'Someone's got to Mum as well. You didn't get this guy's name, did you, by any chance?'

'Sorry, pet. He took to his heels when Bernie let fly,' Mollie said regretfully.

'I bet he did,' Devlin said grinning. 'Look, Mollie,

thanks for ringing. I'll try and get to the bottom of this. And I'll see you Thursday as usual.'

'OK, luv, I just thought you should know what's going on,' Mollie said.

'Oh, before I forget, Roger wants a pork-chop and apple sauce for his dinner.'

'Does he now!' snorted his mother. 'Ya shudda seen the state that fella left his room in. Ya can tell him he'll be lucky ta get any dinner at all let alone pork-chops and apple sauce. Bye, luv,' Mollie laughed and hung up, leaving Devlin wondering what exactly was going on.

Picking up her phone she buzzed out and asked Liz to get her Lucinda Marshall on the line.

Five minutes later Liz rang back to say Lucinda was out of the office and not expected in until noon of the following day.

'Don't we have her home number on file from when she was a member?' Devlin asked grimly.

'I'll check,' Liz responded. It was on file and a few minutes later Devlin was ringing it. It was with utter frustration and annoyance that she heard the answering machine.

She spoke coldly after the tone: 'This is Devlin Delaney. Kindly call me as soon as possible. We have a few matters to discuss.' She hung up in bad humour. She had meetings with her accountant and suppliers for the Galway City Girl which occupied her for the rest of the day and by four-thirty she was quite tired. She thought she'd give Maggie a ring and invite herself over to her friend's house for dinner. She was just about to dial when her phone rang. It was Liz.

'There's a Mr Colin Cantrell-King on the line. Will you take it?' Devlin felt her stomach clench into knots: even hearing his name made her feel sick.

'Will you take the call, Devlin?' Liz repeated as Devlin tried to speak but couldn't.

Forty-Nine

'Hello?' How Devlin managed to keep her voice normal she would never know.

Colin's furious tones assaulted her ears. 'What the hell is going on here, Devlin?'

'I beg your pardon?' Devlin said icily. Now that she was getting over the shock of hearing that her former employer, lover, and father of her child was on the phone, she was damned if she was going to let him guess how much he upset her.

'I've had some bitch of a journalist waylay me and start asking questions about you and me and the child you had. I'm warning you, Devlin, I'll sue you if my name appears in any papers or if there's any hint of a paternity claim or an allegation of an affair. How dare you speak to journalists about me! Are you listening to me? Do you hear what I'm saying?' Colin was beside himself with anger.

'*You* listen to me, Colin Cantrell-King!' Devlin, in turn, felt a cold fury engulf her. 'I've never spoken to *anyone*, let alone a journalist, about you. I wouldn't lower myself. You are scum, Colin, the lowest of the low. You were the biggest mistake of my life and I never want to be reminded of it, even by hearing your name mentioned. I don't give a hoot in hell about your threats. Just you stay away from me and don't dare ever to phone me again.'

Devlin slammed down the phone, feeling physically sick. This was Lucinda Marshall's doing. The two-faced bitch! Well, she wasn't going to get away with it. Taking several deep breaths, she flicked through her Rolodex and found the number of the *Sunday Echo*. Briskly she dialled, and asked to be put through to the editor.

'May I say who's calling please. And in connection with what?' came a bored voice down the line.

'This is Devlin Delaney and it's in connection with an article that is being written about me.'

'That would be Features; you've got the wrong number.'

'Could you give me the right number and the editor's name, please,' Devlin said as patiently as she could. If one of her employees had shown such apathy on the phone, Devlin would have sacked him or her on the spot.

She dialled the number for Features and insisted on being put through to Mick Coyle, the editor. Mick was a big, florid, loudmouth who fancied himself as a ladies' man. Devlin didn't like him, despite the fact that he had always been charming when they met at social functions. He was too smarmy for her, hugging women and mauling them. The first time he tried it on with Devlin, she had very coolly removed his arm from her waist and said politely, 'If you don't mind . . .' He got the message and he'd never tried it on again.

'Devlin!' Mick's raspy voice came down the line,

sounding as though she had really made his day by calling.

She came straight to the point. 'Mick, I want to know what's going on.'

'Going on?' he blustered.

'Yes, Mick,' Devlin snapped. 'This article that's being written about me. Why is some little creep going out to Ballymun looking for information? Why is Lucinda Marshall asking my mother and my former boss questions about me? I want this article stopped.'

Mick thought fast and lied through his teeth. 'Don't worry, don't worry. It's only a bit of background information for Kevin Shannon's business piece.'

'Why didn't Kevin ask *me*?' Devlin retorted coldly. 'I could have told him all he needed to know. Mick, I don't want my private life peddled on the pages of your paper, so either stop the article or deal with my solicitors. It's your choice.'

'OK, Devlin, if that's what you want. No article,' Mick declared solemnly.

'Oh!' Devlin was a bit taken aback at his capitulation. Maybe she'd misjudged the man; maybe he had some integrity after all. 'Thank you, Mick, I appreciate that.'

'Anything for you, Devlin,' he said in his most sycophantic tones, then hung up.

Well, that was that, Devlin decided with satisfaction. What a day! Hearing from Colin had really unsettled her. No wonder he was rattling. If any hint of a scandal appeared in the papers it would be an out-and-out disaster for him. Medical consultants, like Caesar's wife, were supposed to be above suspicion.

She buzzed down to Special Occasions, and when Rhona answered she asked to speak to her mother.

Lydia came on the line. 'Yes, Devlin?'

'Do you want to come up and have a coffee with me in the Coffee Dock before I go home? I phoned the features editor of the *Echo* and he told me there'd be no article about me.'

'I'm very glad of that, dear,' Lydia said. 'I'd never have forgiven myself if anything I'd said caused you embarrassment.'

'Well, it won't, so come on. I'll see you upstairs in five minutes.' Devlin decided not to mention the fact that Lucinda Marshall had also been annoying Colin. As she tidied up her desk, she smiled. She'd like to have been a fly on the wall at the meeting between the gynaecologist and the journalist. It would be nearly worth having an article written about her just for the supreme discomfort it would cause him! As far as she and Colin Cantrell-King were concerned, there was no such thing as forgive and forget.

Mick Coyle buzzed his secretary. 'Gillian, get me Lucinda, Kevin and Larry on the double. I want them in here for a meeting. Pronto!'

'Yes, Mr Coyle,' Gillian said politely, from the box her boss had the nerve to call an office.

'Tell them to drop whatever they're doing and get their butts in here. And don't listen to any excuses.'

'Yes, Mr Coyle,' Gillian repeated, giving him a vicious two fingers. 'Yes sir, no sir, three bags full, sir. How high will I jump, sir?' she muttered sarcastically as she began dialling the numbers of the three big names on the *Sunday Echo*.

'Devlin, we're going to have to cut back on costs. We've gone over budget and I don't like that.' Luke fastened his seat belt in preparation for take-off. Devlin yawned. It was the crack of dawn and they were taking the six-thirty flight home from Galway, where they had spent the previous day inspecting the new City Girl complex that was nearing completion.

'I know that, Luke, but at least the building is purpose-built. We don't have to lease it, it's ours. Surely that counts for something!'

'In the long term, yes, but we've got to be very careful that we don't overstretch ourselves. That can cause terrible financial hassle. We've got to make sure we don't develop cash flow problems.'

'I know,' Devlin sighed. 'I'll have another look at the fixtures and fittings and see if we can't do better somewhere else.'

'Have a look at the costings for the pool too. I mean, is it absolutely necessary to have a mosaic mural of Clew Bay?'

Devlin grinned sheepishly. 'I just wanted the best for the place and you'll have to admit that the designs we saw for it were just stunning.'

'There's a recession on, Devlin. Mosaic murals are all very nice but in this economic climate your common or garden bathroom-type tiles will do very well.'

'OK,' Devlin agreed reluctantly. The Galway building had been her brainchild. It was the first time that she had been able to design a purpose-built complex from scratch; with Dublin and Belfast they had been constrained by the architecture of existing buildings.

Devlin and her architect had thoroughly enjoyed the task and maybe they had gone a bit overboard. Devlin knew that Luke was right and this was one of the rare occasions that he had put his foot down. Usually, once he approved the plans, he let her get on with it. Obviously he and Kieran, her accountant, had been chatting. She reached out and squeezed his hand to show there were no hard feelings.

'It's a pity you have to go back this morning. I wish you could have stayed for the weekend,' she said wistfully.

'Me too, but those Dutch businessmen that I'm dealing with are going to be in London today and it's a good opportunity to touch base.' He brightened. 'Maybe you could fly back with me?'

'Don't tempt me,' Devlin laughed.

'Come on, come on. You haven't been over since Christmas!'

'True,' declared Devlin. 'But Friday is always terribly busy in City Girl.'

'You know you're going to need an administrator soon, Devlin,' Luke said seriously. 'You can't run the Dublin City Girl, oversee Belfast and Galway and make more plans for expansion. It's something we'll have to give some consideration to – and sooner rather than later.'

'Definitely,' agreed Devlin, 'but it won't be the same not running the place on a day-to-day basis. I suppose I'll always feel the Dublin City Girl is special, and I'll have to acquire someone special to run it.'

'How about Liz?'

'Oh no!' Devlin exclaimed.

Luke was surprised at her vehemence. 'I think she's a very capable woman.'

'She is,' Devlin assured him. 'And she'd do a great job. But I couldn't lose a superb PA like Liz. She's my right arm.'

'Yeah, I know. I wouldn't like to lose Dianne. She's an excellent PA.'

'How *is* Dianne these days?' Devlin grinned, remembering how cool the other woman always was when Devlin had reason to speak to her.

Luke rubbed his jaw and frowned. 'Well, now that you mention it, she doesn't seem to be herself. She was off sick a while back for the first time since she started to work for me. She seems a bit edgy lately. Maybe she's a bit run down.'

'You're probably working her too hard,' Devlin said wickedly.

'Do you think so?' Luke asked in concern.

'Oh, don't be daft, I was only joking.'

'I'll get her something nice in the duty-free. It might cheer her up.'

It was a short though bumpy flight, and as they started their descent, Devlin peered out the window at the lights of Dublin below them. In the distance she could see the twinkling lights of the airport and the steady flashing of the beacon on the control tower. She could just make out the dark outline of the Ballymun towers rising into the sky and she thought of Mollie and Eddie and the twins and reflected how lucky she was to have friends like them. At least she didn't have to worry about that interview. It seemed like a bad dream – her mother getting drunk, the call from Colin – and even though it had happened at the beginning of the week, she felt as though it had been a lifetime ago. All she wanted to do was to forget about it. Luke had been angry when she told him, and had wanted to meet Lucinda in person to tell her to lay off. But Devlin put her foot down.

The plane was rolling from side to side in the wind as the runway unfolded like a dark ribbon beneath it. Devlin decided on the spur of the moment that she *would* fly to London with Luke. After the week she'd put in, she deserved a little break, and they hadn't seen much of each other since Christmas. And, she further reasoned, Luke flew across the Irish Sea to see her far more than she did to see him. Fair was fair, and she had as much responsibility for nurturing their relationship as he had.

'I hope I can get a seat on the same flight as you,' she remarked, as the plane landed and raced down the runway.

'Great!' exclaimed Luke with pleasure. 'You can always sit on my knee. I'll suffer the discomfort!'

'I bet you would,' Devlin laughed.

By the time Devlin and Luke left the airport and were speeding along the motorway, the rain had stopped and the sun had made a watery appearance. They were on their way to collect some clothes from Devlin's penthouse for her weekend in London. They had had breakfast at the airport and Devlin estimated that it would take her fifteen minutes to get home, ten minutes to pack, and that a taxi would have them back at the airport with time to spare for their nine-thirty flight. Now that she had made up her mind to go, she was really looking forward to the weekend.

She switched on the car radio to listen to the news and especially the weather forecast, which predicted howling gales and rain. Perfect weather for a weekend in bed, Luke teased, as the advertisements came on. Devlin laughed. 'You've a one-track mind, mister.' She leaned over to switch off the radio and almost crashed the car, transfixed by the words that came across the airwaves.

Bright, beautiful and ambitious, the epitome of a modern city girl, Devlin Delaney, well-known Dublin business-woman and celebrity, has made it to the top. But at what cost? In the Sunday Echo *this week, read how she went from being a carefree young socialite pursuing an affair with an eminent medical consultant, to become an unmarried mother living in high-rise Ballymun. Read how tragedy and the horrific death of her baby daughter brought her to the brink of despair and how she clawed her way back to become the success she now is. Read it in the paper that has all the inside stories. The* Sunday Echo. *Your paper.*

'The bastard, oh the fucking bastard!' Devlin whispered in shock, her face the colour of blotting-paper.

Luke's voice pierced the icy fog in her brain. 'Pull the car over! Pull over on to the hard shoulder, Devlin.' Like an automaton she obeyed.

'Luke, why? Why do these things happen to me? Why can't I have some peace in my life? Why am I being punished like this? That bastard told me he wouldn't run any interview. Did you hear that ad? They're out to crucify me.' She put her head in her hands and burst into tears.

Luke put his arms around her. 'It's all right, Devlin. Take it easy.'

'I can't handle this, Luke,' Devlin sobbed. 'I just can't!'

Luke's face was like granite. 'You don't have to,' he said. 'I will . . .'

Fifty

'No, I won't be home today. I won't be home for a few days, Dianne. Devlin needs me here.' Devlin heard Luke talking to his PA. 'Just tell Van der Voek that I'm sorry, I'm unavoidably delayed in Dublin and I'll call him when I get back. I'll keep in touch, Dianne. Bye.' He hung up and smiled at Devlin. 'That's that settled. Now, let's get your solicitor on the line and then we'll have a cup of coffee and plan our strategy. I'm sure we'll have no problem getting a court injunction.'

'Can you believe it!' Devlin shook her head, still in a state of shock. 'How can they do that to me? How can they put my private life up there for everybody to read about? Have I no rights? Oh God, I feel sick.' Devlin began pacing up and down her sitting-room floor.

'Give me your solicitor's number,' Luke said firmly, 'and let's get her over here so that we can see what she makes of it.'

'Luke, you should go home,' Devlin said agitatedly. 'What about your meeting? I don't expect you to cancel all your engagements because of a mess I'm in.'

'I'd expect you to cancel your engagements and

come to my aid if I was in a fix,' Luke remarked calmly.

'Oh!' Devlin was taken aback.

He shot her a questioning look. 'Wouldn't you?'

'Of course I would, Luke. Thank you for that.' Devlin walked over to him and hugged him. 'You mean an awful lot to me, I couldn't imagine life without you. I love you, Luke.' She held him tight, knowing that having him by her side would keep her going no matter what she had to face.

'I never thought I'd hear you say that, Devlin,' he confessed, smiling down at her upturned face. 'All those months that I was crazy about you and you kept pushing me back, I thought: Reilly, you don't stand a chance. When you tell me you love me, Devlin, it just blows me away. I'll never be able to hear it often enough.' He bent his head and kissed her very lovingly and tenderly, and in the circle of his arms Devlin suddenly felt serene and safe. Having had to fend for herself for so long, it was such a comfort to have someone special to share the burden. To hell with the *Sunday Echo* and its readers.

The phone rang and Devlin almost jumped. 'I'll get it,' said Luke. 'It's your mother.' He held out the phone to her.

'Devlin, did you hear the radio?' Lydia sounded not far from hysterics.

'It's all right, Mum. Calm down! I'm calling my solicitor. Luke is here with me and we're going to get an injunction to stop the paper from publishing the article.'

'They don't need to publish any article,' Lydia

fumed. 'That advertisement was enough. Devlin, I really feel this is all my fault . . .'

'Mum, that's enough of that! It's nobody's fault. That paper is a rag and don't you dare let it get to you. Go to work today as normal and forget about it.'

'Will you be in today or are you going to take the day off?' Lydia asked miserably.

Devlin was silent for a minute. To tell the truth, City Girl was the last place she wanted to be after what she had heard on the radio. It would be hard to face everybody, knowing there would be talk.

'Maybe you shouldn't, dear. Maybe you should go away for the weekend: get out of Dublin for a few days until this has all blown over.'

For one moment Devlin was tempted to do just what Lydia suggested, tempted to turn to Luke and say, to hell with it all – let's go to London. But that would have been running away and Devlin had never run away from anything in her life. A sudden sense of resolve stiffened her spine. They weren't going to have the satisfaction of seeing her fleeing or hiding, as if she had something to be ashamed of. It was they who should be ashamed – not her.

'Of course I'm going into the office, Mum. I'll be a bit late because I have to talk to my solicitor but I'll see you later and we'll have coffee in the Coffee Dock. Maybe you and Dad would like to have dinner with Luke and me tomorrow night. I'll see if I can book somewhere nice.' She could sense her mother's surprise and see Luke's face breaking into a grin as he gave her the thumbs-up sign.

'I . . . do you think . . . are you up to it, Devlin?'

'Of course I am. I never felt more like going out for

a meal in my life.' Now that Devlin had decided on a course of action, she was feeling much more positive.

'I'll phone your father and see what he has to say and I'll see you later then,' Lydia promised.

'I like the way you're handling things,' Luke declared. 'Why don't we up the ante and have drinks in the Horseshoe Bar before we go to dinner? Now *that* would really give the glitterati something to talk about!'

'Oh, I don't know, Luke.'

'Come on,' he urged. 'You've the right idea about going into work and going out to dinner. Take it a step further by going for drinks in *the* place to be. Let people see you don't give a damn about the *Sunday Echo* and its grotty little story.'

'Do you know what you remind me of? Do you remember when Rhett Butler dragged Scarlett out of the bed and made her go to Melanie's party for Ashley after India Wilkes had caught Scarlett kissing him?'

'It worked, didn't it,' Luke retorted. 'If you want to come down to the foyer, I'll sweep you up into my arms and run up the stairs with you and ravish you as well.' His eyes twinkled.

'After that ad, I suppose I *am* a bit of a Scarlet Woman!'

'Ouch,' Luke grimaced. 'Another pun like that and I'll need resuscitation. Here.' He handed her the phone. 'Call your solicitor.'

Devlin *needed* him! Did you ever hear anything so pathetic? Dianne paced the office with a face like thunder. What kind of businessman cancelled important engagements because a wishy-washy, pea-brained, clinging bimbo needed him?

Why was Luke so besotted with that Delaney creature when right at his side, day in, day out, he had a woman with brains, class, and beauty, who was his intellectual equal, understood all the stresses and strains of his busy lifestyle and, most importantly, worshipped the ground he walked on. Dianne would *never* insist that Luke cancel business appointments because she 'needed' him, she thought furiously. She didn't blame Luke. Oh Lord, no. His trouble was that he was far too kind, far too softhearted. Didn't she have experience of that? Dianne's cheeks burned in mortification at the memory. It could have been her greatest moment of happiness; instead, it had been the moment of her greatest humiliation.

It had happened the day she left the office early, after she had finally made up her mind to let him know how she felt. She successfully selected some gorgeous sexy underwear, went home and decided to spend the afternoon beautifying herself. She had treated herself to some bath-oils and essences from the Body Shop and she ran herself a scorching hot bath. It was a bitterly cold day and she had been frozen to the bone. Her cleaning woman, Mrs Foster, was hoovering and it pleased Dianne to lie back in the hot scented water and listen to the muted sounds of the Electrolux. Mrs Foster was her greatest luxury. Dianne had always hated hoovering and polishing and doing the ironing and when she had got the job as Luke's PA and started earning a generous salary, moving to a posh apartment block and employing Mrs Foster had been her priorities.

'I'm off, Miss Westwood.' Dianne came back to reality, hearing the cleaner make her goodbyes. She had been having one of her fantasies, the one in which she was a famous pop-singer and Luke was her bodyguard fighting his attraction to her, and she had just come to the bit where he could contain his feelings no longer and was making throbbing, passionate love to her in her jacuzzi. The water had gone cold and, shivering, she jumped out of the bath and wrapped herself in a warm towel. Remembering that she had forgotten to buy coffee and knowing that she would never survive more than two hours without a cup, she stuck her head out the door and asked the obliging Mrs Foster to pop into the supermarket down the road and get her a jar.

Despite the central heating, Dianne felt slightly chilly. She was a very cold creature and hated winter with a vengeance. She slipped into a pair of passion-killer flannelette pyjamas that were worn only on the coldest nights, and wrapped herself in an old but exceedingly warm woolly dressing-gown that her mother had given her when she had first come to London. While she was waiting for Mrs Foster to return she decided to remove the blonde hairs that grew along her upper lip and just at the base of her chin. They were very very faint, but she was conscious of them and wanted everything to be smooth and silky for Luke's kiss. She had bought a new depilatory cream that promised very long-lasting results.

The phone rang and it was Rodney, a merchant banker whom she was using as a stop-gap until Luke came to his senses. He tried to persuade her to let him come and stay the night but she wasn't in the humour and spent ten minutes putting him off. When she had removed the cream, she had discovered to her horror that she had a bright red rash all around her upper lip and chin. She had left the cream on for far too long and the world and his mother would know that she had been using a depilatory on her lip and chin. Dianne was furious. The marks wouldn't fade for at least two or three days so she'd have to stay out of work. Even make-up wouldn't cover it.

A knock on the door had made her curse loudly. Why hadn't Mrs Foster taken her damned keys? In a thoroughly bad humour, she flung open the door to find Luke standing there.

Even now, days later, Dianne felt a rush of heat to her face and her stomach lurch at the memory.

'Lord, Dianne, you don't look at all well. Maybe you've got an allergy of some sort,' he said in concern, staring at her flushed and red-blotched face, as he handed her a bouquet of roses and a huge box of chocolates.

'I think it was shellfish,' she had the presence of mind to mutter, hiding her face in the flowers and making a pretence of smelling them, as great knife-stabs of humiliation penetrated her heart.

'Can I do anything? Do you need a doctor?' Luke asked anxiously. Dianne could have wept. This should have been the fantasy of fantasies coming true. She should have met him at the door in her silk négligée wearing the lovely new underwear underneath. She should have done her dying swan act and pretended to be faint and he'd have had to carry her inside in those strong muscled arms that made her drool. Instead he'd found her in a woolly dressing-gown that had little balls of fluff all over it, and a big blob of spaghetti sauce on the front. The bottoms of her flannelette pyjamas were sticking out, and she had a moustache and beard of raw red skin that were too mortifying even to contemplate.

Luke handed Dianne a jar of coffee and explained that he'd met her cleaner outside and offered to bring up her message. That's how he'd got into the building without disturbing her.

'Go to bed, Dianne, and don't come back for a week,' he said kindly. 'And if you need anything, shout.' She watched him run lithely down the stairs and felt like throwing his flowers and chocolates and the coffee down after him. Then she went back into her apartment, slammed the door behind her, flung everything on the sofa, stubbed her toe on the leg of the coffee table and bawled her eyes out.

Standing in Luke's office, compiling a list of calls to make to people he would not be seeing because Devlin Delaney 'needed' him, Dianne felt like crying all over again. He really was so kind. To think that he had come out all the way from the office to visit her and make sure that she was all right; and to think he had bought beautiful roses and the biggest box of handmade chocolates she had ever seen! It must mean that he cared for her. And to think he had seen her looking like a complete ragbag! It was too much to bear. Sitting in Luke's big leather chair, Dianne wept. Through eyes blurred with tears she caught sight of the framed photo of Devlin that Luke kept on his desk. She could feel anger and jealousy brewing up into a hot, bubbling rage. Picking up the photograph, she smashed it across the desk.

'Bitch! Bitch! Bitch!' she swore, as the glass smashed into a thousand tiny pieces all around her.

'Certainly I can try to obtain an injunction against the paper, to prevent them from publishing the interview,' Monica Finlay, Devlin's solicitor, said in her crisp no-nonsense manner. 'And I'm fairly sure I'll be successful. But I've been thinking, Devlin . . . you've heard the radio advertisement. That will have whetted plenty of appetites. If we get the injunction we're going to have to go to court. The press are going to be camping on your doorstep. Every other gutter publication is going to take up the story. I'm just wondering if you'd be better off to let them publish their damn interview and get it over with . . .' She gave a wry smile. 'You're really in a no-win situation, Devlin. I know they'll be getting away with it, but I'm trying to think what's best for you in the long term.'

'It's so infuriating,' Devlin replied. 'I understand what you're saying, Monica, but I just don't want those bastards to get away with it. What do you think, Luke?' She turned to where he was sitting over by the window.

Luke looked her straight in the eye. 'I feel the same as you, Devlin, but I can see Monica's point. Do you want to be stuck with legal wrangling for months on end? Do you want to have every newspaper in the country annoying you? That ad was very clever but its shock value and that of the interview will last just for the weekend. Next week, it will be someone else, and everybody will have forgotten about you. You'll probably get a few odd looks from the clients in City

Girl, but that will wear off. But if you take legal action, be prepared for a long hard slog.'

'I don't want them to get away with it,' Devlin repeated.

'Right then. If you feel *that* strongly, we'll go for the injunction,' Monica declared.

Devlin was really torn. She didn't want months of legal hassle. She was already getting so many calls that she'd had to take the phone off the hook. The thoughts of being harassed by reporters and photographers was making her ill but, damn them, she wasn't going to let them walk all over her. A thought struck her; a slow smile touched her lips.

'Forget the injunction, Monica. I've just had an idea.' Flicking through her Rolodex, she found the number she was looking for. Eyes sparkling, Devlin lifted the phone and began to dial.

Fifty-One

'It was a very difficult choice to make,' Devlin told the journalist sitting in front of her desk. 'The baby's father was insisting that I have an abortion. I flew to London and actually went to the clinic. Literally hours before the termination was due to take place, I decided I couldn't go through with it.'

In the background, a photographer was lighting up the area around the window overlooking St Stephen's Green, where she was going to have her photograph taken.

She was giving an interview to Sally Briers, a journalist she had known from the very early days of City Girl. She worked for the *Daily Chronicle*, one of the country's most respected and successful newspapers. The *Chronicle* had jumped at the offer of an interview with Devlin, to be published in the next day's weekend supplement, scooping the *Sunday Echo*'s much-advertised exposé.

In a frank interview, Devlin told her story. Not once did she mention Colin. Not that she had to! Anyone who read between the lines of the *Sunday Echo*'s innuendo would realize that he was the father of her baby. There was nothing that Devlin could do about that. That was a matter for Colin and the other paper, so let him handle it as best he could.

'It must have been very difficult for you living in Ballymun,' Sally was saying sympathetically.

'Well, it was my own choice. My parents had no idea that I was living in a flat there. They thought I was living in Drumcondra. My father was always willing to give me financial support,' Devlin explained, wanting to make sure that the interview showed Lydia as well as Gerry in a very positive light. 'And certainly, while living there was far removed from what I was used to, I found great support and kindness among my neighbours there — and I made friends I will always cherish. Ballymun is a much-maligned place.'

When it came to talking about Lynn's and Kate's death, Devlin cried, and Sally asked her if she wanted to stop the interview, but she recovered her composure and went on to recount how, with Luke's help, she had come to terms with her bereavement and gone on to become a very successful business-woman.

'Devlin, I'm going to fly! I'm sure you'll understand that I've got to get this in as quickly as possible. They're holding the front page of the supplement for it. Thank God for modern technology.' Sally was gleeful, knowing that in a matter of hours the interview that she would transcribe from her tape recorder would be safely stored in the computers of the newspaper and ready to be printed. Already, the marketing department had booked last-minute radio slots to advertise the scoop, and Sally had no doubt that Saturday's edition of the *Daily Chronicle* would be sold out. It gave her a great sense of satisfaction to pull a fast one on the *Sunday Echo*, which was despised by the journalists on the respectable newspapers.

Devlin saw Sally and the photographer to the door and glanced at her watch. It was just gone eleven. Everything seemed to have happened so quickly – from the meeting with Monica to her brainwave about calling Sally. After they left, she deliberately walked into every section of the complex, making sure to speak to her staff and clients, letting them see that it was business as usual. Liz was filtering all her calls and the only ones she had taken concerned very urgent business matters. And, of course, one from Maggie, who told her to keep her chin up and ignore the whole shagging lot of them. Her father, too, had been very concerned for her, but Devlin had assured him everything was under control and that she would see him for dinner the following evening. She had managed to book a table in Patrick Guilbauds. Her adrenalin was flowing and she felt very much in control.

She popped her head through the door of Special Occasions. 'Hi, Mum!'

'Devlin! Are you all right, dear?' Lydia looked a bit strained.

Devlin hugged her. 'Never better, Mum. I've just come down to tell you that Luke's taking us to lunch. He's booked a table in The Commons for one-thirty.'

'What!' Lydia exclaimed. 'The Commons? But it's very . . . do you not think it's a bit public . . . considering the circumstances. Why don't we go for Locks? It's very discreet and the food is out of this world.'

Devlin smiled at her mother. 'Oh, I know. It's one of my all-time favourites. Caroline and Maggie and I go there sometimes for lunch and we've often sat until after four. But today is not the day to be discreet, I'm afraid. It's chest out, chin up and best foot forward. Come on, Mum,' she urged. 'We might as well have lunch and get a bit of a laugh out of it, and I might as well make the most of this make-up job Aoibhinn did for me for the photograph earlier on. Luke will be with us; he's a real brick.'

'He's a very nice, supportive man, dear. I'm glad you found someone like him. Do you think they could fit me in for a professional make-up upstairs? There's nothing like a make-up to pep you up and Aoibhinn did a lovely job on you.'

'I'll make sure they'll fit you in. It's handy being the boss sometimes,' Devlin said with a grin. 'See you about one-fifteen.'

'Wow!' Luke exclaimed appreciatively as he marched into Devlin's office to collect his lunch companions. 'No-one would ever believe you were mother and daughter. Sisters, maybe, but *not* mother and daughter!'

'Fibber!' Lydia retorted, but Devlin could see that her mother was pleased.

'Let's hit the town, ladies.' Luke offered an arm to each, and, laughing, they linked him.

'We'll go straight to our table, please.' Luke smiled at Devlin as a waiter took the women's coats. Lifting her chin, she winked at her mother and they walked into the crowded restaurant.

It was, as usual, humming with chat and laughter and the clink of silverware against china. As Devlin, Luke and Lydia were led down the long narrow room to their table, a slight hush descended on the assembled lunchers. Out of the corner of her eye, Devlin recognized two of City Girl's glamorous clients. They were staring at her open-mouthed. Devlin caught Luke's glance. She could see that he too was aware that they were the focus of every eye in the room. They smiled at each other in genuine amusement. He was right; this was much better than skulking at home, as if she had something to be ashamed of.

To her surprise, she enjoyed every mouthful of her lunch, as, she was pleased to note, did her mother. They laughed and chatted among themselves, ignoring the covert glances in their direction.

'The jungle drums will be working overtime,' observed Lydia with a smile.

'Wait until they read the *Chronicle* tomorrow,' Devlin said wickedly, as Luke paid the bill.

Luke leaned across the table and gave her hand a squeeze. 'Lucinda and Co, eat your hearts out!'

'Speak of the devil!' Lydia murmured, and Devlin turned to see Lucinda Marshall swanning through the restaurant in the direction of a well-known TV presenter, who was seated down near the big window at the end of the room. Lucinda was quite aware she was the focus of attention and, graciously accepting it as her due, nodded regally at people. When she saw Devlin, Lydia and Luke her step faltered, and her eyes widened in disbelief. A burgundy flush suffused her heavily made-up face as she encountered the stares of three pairs of contemptuous eyes. Thoroughly flustered, Lucinda stood for a moment as though rooted to the spot, before scuttling past their table.

Devlin smiled at Lydia. 'Thoroughly rattled,

wouldn't you say? I think lunch has been a great success.'

'I think so too. I hope we've put her off hers,' Lydia replied tartly. 'Perhaps I should sent a bottle of champagne over to her table!'

'Lydia, she couldn't look you in the eye. I'm pretty sure she can't look herself in the eye. Forget her; she's trash,' Luke said crisply, but his eyes were kind as he met Lydia's distressed gaze and Devlin could have kissed him there and then for the understanding he had shown towards her mother.

He stood up and pulled out their chairs. 'Come on, girls. I can't have you slacking here for the afternoon. It's back to the grindstone for you pair, I'm afraid.'

'I don't feel like going back to work.' Devlin made a face. 'I'm not used to eating huge lunches in the middle of the day.' Normally when she was out to lunch in the middle of the day she would skip the starter and dessert. Today she'd eaten everything. To tell the truth, after all the goings-on Devlin was beginning to feel a bit wilted.

'I don't really feel like going back to work either,' Lydia said, a trifle glumly.

'This is great!' said Luke in mock-dismay. 'What do you ladies want to do, then?'

'I think I'd like to go to the pictures,' Devlin mused. 'There's something terribly decadent about going to the pictures in the afternoon, especially on a Friday afternoon.'

Lydia laughed. 'Good Lord, it's years since I've been to the pictures. Why don't you go with Luke,' she suggested to Devlin, 'and you'll have a nice afternoon to yourselves?'

'If one plays hookey, we all play hookey,' Luke said firmly. 'What film would you workaholic lady executives like to go to?'

Devlin giggled. She was beginning to perk up again. 'Come on, let's go out to the Omniplex in Santry and then we can have a stroll around the Omni Centre. You've never been out there, Mum. It's very nice. There are good boutiques and I saw some lovely porcelain soap dishes and pot-pourri holders out there in one of the kiosks in the main mall. I thought they might be nice for Special Occasions.'

'*And* if you behave yourself at the pictures, you can have popcorn and an ice-cream!' added Luke.

'You pair are a bad influence on me.' Lydia laughed, suddenly feeling quite lighthearted. 'But I'd love to go to the pictures with you.'

'Let's buy a paper and find out what's on.' Devlin linked her mother's arm and without a backward glance at Lucinda they left the restaurant.

Mick Coyle's pudgy little fingers tightened their grip on the phone as he digested the information being imparted to him.

'She did *what*?' he bellowed, his red nose going atomic.

'Oh, happy day,' sang his secretary to herself. She had heard the *Chronicle*'s advertisement for Devlin's own story on her Walkman at lunchtime and had been awaiting Mick's reaction to the inevitable phone call once the news got around.

'The little bitch!' he swore. 'The two-faced little bitch!'

'Good on you, Devlin,' the secretary murmured as

she bent her head diligently over her typewriter. Moments like this made the rest of her days of drudgery bearable.

'Thank you, Luke, for giving Mum and me such a lovely afternoon.' Devlin snuggled in close as they sat in front of the fire watching the *Late Late Show*. They had thoroughly enjoyed the movie, having the cinema practically to themselves. Then they had strolled around the shopping centre before heading into Bewleys for mugs of milky coffee and cream slices.

'Your mother really enjoyed the film, didn't she? I wasn't sure if it would be her scene.'

'Mum's a different person,' Devlin said thoughtfully. 'She's learning how to enjoy herself again; she's not half as uptight as she used to be. It's really good to see.'

Luke smiled down at her. '*I'll* tell you what's good to see. Watching the two of you together is nice. I saw Lydia looking at you a few times when you didn't notice it. She loves you very much, Devlin.'

'I know, and I love her,' Devlin said with a smile. 'This whole thing is much harder on her than it is on me. I wish she didn't have to go through it.'

'It will soon be all over. You both got through today with flying colours. I bet that Marshall woman is still shellshocked at seeing you in the restaurant.'

'To think that I had the nerve to show my face in public – and in The Commons of all places. Boy, she nearly choked, didn't she? I wonder how she's feeling about my interview with the *Chronicle*,' Devlin said with satisfaction.

'Sick as a parrot, I'd say,' Luke laughed, and then he bent his head and kissed her.

The Delaney women had class, Lucinda had to admit. When she saw them in The Commons, she nearly died. Who would have thought they would have had the nerve to appear in so public a place with advertisements being broadcast on the hour on the radio telling everybody who cared to listen all about Devlin's colourful past.

Devlin had sure as hell outfoxed them, though. Doing the interview with the *Chronicle* was an ace move. Lucinda had been sure she would have handled it through her solicitors and had relished the idea of a legal battle and all its attendant publicity. But Devlin had gone for the jugular, scuppered the *Echo*'s scoop, and was obviously prepared to brazen it out. It was a wonder Mick Coyle wasn't in a coronary care unit. He was sizzling with temper. Kevin Shannon had resigned when he had found out that his in-depth business report on City Girl and its glamorous MD was only a cover for an exposé. Idiot! He'd soon learn that sticking to your principles could be a costly business.

That Luke Reilly guy Devlin was involved with was a fine thing, Lucinda mused, as she typed up an article on 'Sexy Men and Where to Find Them'. She had watched them laughing and chatting in the restaurant and it was clear that he was crazy about Devlin, and *so* protective. The filthy look he had given her had turned her blood cold, even though she had been the recipient of many a filthy look in her career. Lucky old Devlin, she thought glumly. She had it all to live for. What did Lucinda have? A quiet gentle man who had no spark left. And if she wanted to live the life of comfort that she had grown accustomed to, it meant more and more sensational exposés and juicy gossip stories. The competition out there was cut-throat and orders had come down from on high that the gloves were off in the circulation battle.

If she was to keep her position as queen of the gossip columnists, she was going to have to fight for it. Right now, with the memory of the disdainful stares she had been subjected to by Lydia, Devlin and Luke, it was a wearisome and depressing thought. She was getting too old for all that, Lucinda thought dispiritedly. Today she had completely lost her poise, something that had never happened to her before. It had been a thoroughly unsettling experience.

'You should have seen that Marshall woman's face,' Lydia said to her husband as they sipped their hot chocolate before retiring. 'She nearly died. She'll rue the day she was so disgustingly cheap and underhand.'

Gerry gave his wife a warm hug. 'I'm glad you went to lunch with Luke and Devlin. I think Devlin's handling the whole affair superbly.'

'I'll tell you one thing, Gerry,' Lydia said seriously. 'It lifts my heart to see Devlin so happy with Luke. He's the best thing that ever happened to her and if anyone deserves a good man, she does. And I know the blessing it is to have a wonderful husband, even if I did realize it far too late in my life.' Lydia leaned across the kitchen table and kissed her husband on the cheek.

'If they're as happy and contented in thirty years'

time as we are now, Lydia, they'll be doing very well for themselves,' said Gerry, smiling lovingly at his wife.

'Congratulations, Devlin. More power to you.' Trish Duncan, the well-known media consultant, held out her hand to Devlin, as she stood with Luke and her parents the following evening, sipping a drink in the Horseshoe Bar prior to dining in Guilbauds.

'Thanks, Trish,' Devlin replied warmly, returning the firm handshake. Her interview had appeared in the *Chronicle* and Sally had kept to the letter of their conversation. All day she had been receiving phone calls of congratulations and bouquets of flowers from people who wished her well. The warmth of the good wishes expressed by friends and acquaintances had taken her very much by surprise.

As usual, the Horseshoe was packed with movers and shakers and Devlin and the others were quite glad to leave to make the short journey to the plush restaurant. It was nice to sit and linger over their meal, relaxed in one another's company. Devlin was very happy that her parents liked and admired Luke. Later, she and Luke drove Lydia and Gerry home and stayed to have coffee with them. It was well after midnight when they left to go to Devlin's apartment, and as they drove back over towards the northside, Devlin asked Luke if he would drive up O'Connell Street so she could get the Sunday papers from the vendor on O'Connell Bridge.

'Are you sure you want to do this, Devlin?' Luke was not keen on the idea. 'I really don't think you should even consider reading that trash.'

'I have to read it, Luke,' Devlin said grimly. 'I'd prefer to know what's in it.'

'What's the point in tormenting yourself?' he argued.

'Luke, I want to read it and that's all there is about it,' Devlin snapped.

'Fine,' he said curtly, and headed for O'Connell Street. They sat in strained silence. Reaching O'Connell Bridge, Luke slowed the car to a halt and bought a selection of papers, including the *Sunday Echo*. 'There!' He thrust them at her and started the ignition.

A lump rose in Devlin's throat. Her emotions were very near the surface after the strain of the previous forty-eight hours, and she felt terribly tired.

'Don't be mad at me, Luke,' she pleaded.

'I'm not mad at you, Devlin,' he sighed. 'I'm just trying to prevent you from getting hurt.'

'I have to read it,' she said. He said nothing, but a little later pulled the car in on the quay just below Butt Bridge and switched on the interior light. A silver crescent moon dappled the waters of the Liffey, which shimmered like silk as they lapped the quay walls. There was a high tide and the cream-and-black Guinness boats, long a feature of the river, undulated gracefully on the inky waters.

'I love the Guinness Boats,' Devlin commented. Now that the car was stationary, she was strangely reluctant to read the dreaded article.

'I knew a lad who worked on them,' said Luke, who was once a sailor himself and felt solidarity with all things nautical. 'We kept in touch. He went deep sea and he's going to miss his daughter's Holy

Communion this May. I couldn't cope with that. That's one of the reasons I swallowed the anchor.'

'You what?'

'Swallowed the anchor. It's a sailor's saying for when you get a job ashore,' Luke explained with a smile. 'It's very hard to have a relationship or be married when you're at sea.'

'I'm glad you're not at sea,' Devlin said quietly. Then she picked up the *Sunday Echo*, saw the picture of herself emblazoned across the top and turned to the page of the interview. Silently, she read the scurrilous columns. One sentence jumped out at her. 'Although the death of her baby daughter was very tragic, some good came of it, for it was with the massive insurance settlement that she received that Devlin was able to set up the hugely successful City Girl Health and Leisure Complex.' Her face whitened and she gave a little gasp. Wordlessly she handed the article to Luke. He read it, his face growing hard and grim. Leaning across her, he opened her door.

'Get out of the car, Devlin,' he said gently. Mystified, she stared at him. 'Come on, get out. I want you to do something.'

Slowly she did as he asked her, shivering as the chill north wind penetrated her coat and dress. Luke got out and she joined him by the quay wall. He handed her back the paper. 'Now,' he said. 'Throw this garbage in the river and say: "From this moment in my life I will never look back. I will live my life to the full in my present and I will look forward to my future with hope and anticipation." '

'Oh Luke!' She was so touched she could barely speak.

He took her hand. 'Throw it and say the words with me.'

Holding his hand tightly, she flung the paper into the Liffey and spoke the words with his encouragement. Hand in hand they stood in the moonlight and watched her past floating, slowly at first and then faster and faster as it swirled in the current until it disappeared out of sight down the winding river towards the great open sea.

'I really enjoyed that walk.' Devlin shook the sand off her runners before opening the door to the foyer of the apartment. She and Luke had had a lazy day. They had stayed in bed until midday and then he had cooked her a tasty brunch, after which they had sat curled up in front of the fire reading the papers. Around four, Luke had suggested a walk on Bull Island. It was a wild day and they had had to put their heads down and battle against the elements. The wind whipped the waves up to a fury and the spray lashed them as they trudged along the seashore. Devlin's ears, nose and cheeks were numb with cold but she didn't care. She loved the wind blowing through her hair and the invigorating rush of blood to her cheeks as the salty, tangy wind cleared the cobwebs from her mind.

She had her memories of Lynn. She had her career, she had her health, two loving parents, Caroline and Maggie and the joy of her life, Luke. She was lucky and she knew it.

She tucked her arm into Luke's. 'Come on, let's open a bottle of champagne and have a bath to warm us up and a night all to ourselves.'

'You wicked wanton woman,' he laughed.

'Is that a yes?' she twinkled.

'That's a very definite yes.' Luke's eyes were warm and loving as he held the door of the lift open for her. He kissed her soundly as the elevator glided up to the penthouse.

'I'd better check my messages,' she murmured, as she noticed the red light on her answering machine flashing insistently.

'I'll run the bath and pour the champagne.' Luke brushed his lips along the nape of her neck, sending delicious tingles of desire up and down her spine.

'Hmmmm,' she murmured appreciatively, pressing the button on the machine.

'Devlin,' came her dad's voice, sounding strangely tense and harassed. 'I'm ringing from St Vincent's Hospital. It's your mother; she's taken an overdose. Will you come as quickly as you can?'

Fifty-Two

'Why did she do it?' Devlin was distraught. Gerry's eyes flooded with tears and she flung her arms around him. 'It's all right, Dad, she's going to be all right. Thank God you found her in time.'

'Poor, poor Lydia.' Gerry wiped his eyes. 'If I could get my hands on those bitches . . .'

Devlin was instantly alert. 'What bitches?'

'Oh, you know, Angeline Callahan and Jane Kelleher; they're on the committee to raise funds for that new unit in that maternity hospital where Colin Cantrell-King works. They had the nerve to call over this afternoon and demand Lydia's resignation from the committee. The cheek of them. Lydia has raised more money for that unit than the whole bloody lot of them put together.' Gerry, usually an even-tempered man, was beside himself with anger and hurt for his wife.

'This is all my fault.' Devlin was close to tears. Lydia had taken an overdose because of her and her past. She was swamped by a mixture of guilt, fear and terrible anger at the self-righteous society ladies who had humiliated her mother.

'It's not your fault, Devlin. It's those bastards who set you up.' Gerry held his weeping daughter in his arms as Luke stood in front of them, shielding them from view in the busy hospital corridor.

'Why don't we go and have coffee?' he suggested. 'Didn't you say, Gerry, that they were keeping Lydia under observation and that you wouldn't be allowed to see her for a while?'

'That's right, Luke. They've pumped her stomach but they want to keep an eye on her blood-pressure. It's gone sky-high. She won't be brought up to the ward just yet.'

'I'll go and get us some coffee, then. Why don't you go and sit down and try and relax?' Luke said kindly, as concerned for Gerry as he was for Devlin.

'Yes, we'll do that,' Gerry agreed, relieved to let Luke take charge. 'He's one sound man,' Gerry said to Devlin as they walked down the corridor to the TV room.

'He's kept me sane this weekend, that's for sure,' Devlin said shakily. 'Poor Mum! I've ruined everything for her,' she sighed.

'Devlin, if that's the kind of unchristian, uncharitable women they are, Lydia's better off without them and their bloody committee. I think she really didn't want to kill herself. I was in the lounge watching the sports highlights when I heard an awful thump and I found her collapsed half-way down the stairs with the tablet container in her hand. She was coming down to tell me she had taken the tablets: I know she was.' Gerry was insistent. 'You know your mother: she goes off at half-cock sometimes.'

'I know.' Devlin smiled at her father's description of her sometimes melodramatic mother.

'You know,' Gerry mused, 'I think I might take her

600

away on a holiday after all this. We could do with a break. I'll ask her what she thinks.'

'That's a good idea, Dad. I could do with a holiday myself,' Devlin said wryly.

'Why don't you go out to Caroline? You were talking about it at one stage,' Gerry suggested.

'That's a very good idea.' Luke had arrived in time to overhear the last remark. 'A holiday away from everything is just what you need, Devlin.'

'I'll see,' Devlin said offhandedly and Luke raised his eyes to heaven.

It was another hour before Lydia was brought up to the ward. When she arrived she was still drowsy, but looking better.

'I'm sorry,' she murmured, as Gerry and Devlin leaned over to kiss her.

'Just rest yourself, Lydia. Devlin and I are here.' Gerry took her hand in his. They stayed with her for a while until the nurse told them it was time to leave. Devlin went ahead, to give Gerry a bit of privacy with his wife for a few moments. Luke was waiting outside.

'We have to go now,' she told him.

'I was just thinking: should we ask your dad to stay the night with us? I don't think we should let him go home on his own tonight. He could stay with us or we could stay with him. If he comes over to the penthouse he can have the guest-room and I'll sleep on one of the sofas so as not to make him feel uncomfortable.' Devlin was struck once again by Luke's sensitivity and kindness. When his own father had been alive, Luke had always been very good to him, a trait that she had always admired.

'I'll miss you.' She slipped an arm around him and leaned her head on his shoulder.

'We can send erotic vibes to each other,' he said with his usual grin.

'It's a very cold night,' she sighed.

'I'll make you a hot water bottle.'

'You're very good, Luke.' She stretched up to kiss him.

'Actually I'm in line for canonization! Didn't you know that? I'm a saint in the making,' he teased as Gerry joined them.

Her father jumped at the offer of staying with them and Devlin was glad it was Luke who had suggested it.

The following morning, after Gerry had phoned the hospital and been told that Lydia had slept normally through the night and was much better, he and Devlin decided to go to work for a couple of hours. They arranged to meet at the hospital later in the morning. Gerry went off to the bank feeling much relieved and Luke and Devlin had a cup of coffee together before she left for City Girl. She wanted Luke to fly back to London later in the day. He had been extremely good to her, very generous with his time, but Devlin knew he was a busy man and she felt guilty about keeping him from his business.

'Why don't I wait until tomorrow?' he suggested as he tidied up with her after their breakfast.

'Luke, I've got to get on with it, and it's not fair keeping you from work. I'll be fine.'

'I like being here with you, Devlin. One more day isn't going to cause chaos. Dianne could run that company without me; she's a terrific asset. I rarely take holidays so this is my time off. Don't send me back to work. I'm overworked! Think of my health.'

'You're a brat, Luke Reilly!' Devlin burst out laughing. He was impossible to resist. So, happily, she accepted his decision to stay another day.

She arrived into her office to find a magnificent basket of red, yellow and white carnations on her desk, with a card signed by all the members of her staff offering her their support and good wishes. Devlin was very touched by their gesture, her morale boosted by their concern. This whole sorry episode had brought home to her just how many friends and supporters she had and, deciding to keep hold of that thought, she called Liz and got stuck into her agenda immediately.

Two hours later she had achieved a very satisfactory output of work so she didn't mind telling Liz that she was taking the rest of the day off. As she headed for St Vincent's, she decided that she would spend a couple of hours there and then go home to Luke.

Lydia had been moved to the private wing and Devlin walked down the quiet corridor towards her mother's room, deep in thought. She almost bumped into a tall man emerging from one of the private wards and was just about to apologize when she recognized Colin. He had gynaecological patients in most of the private hospitals. He must have been doing his calls, she thought in dismay. They stood for a moment staring at each other, and then he let fly.

'I hope you're satisfied now you've got your revenge,' he snarled. 'I'm the laughing-stock of the profession, my wife's told me to get out, my children despise me and Nurse McGrath's resigned and told me she couldn't in all conscience work with a philanderer. I hope you're bloody happy, Devlin.'

She looked at him. His good looks were fading, but he hadn't really changed much in the intervening years. A little heavier at the waist maybe, but he still had a great physique and although he had much more grey in his hair than when she had been with him, it gave him a distinguished air that many women would still consider very attractive. His life had been destroyed by that article. Although nothing actually libellous had been printed, the innuendo was enough. Like her, Colin was in an impossible situation: if he took the *Sunday Echo* to court, the publicity attached would be a disaster. Even if he did win a case against the paper it would be a Pyrrhic victory.

'I had nothing to do with the *Sunday Echo*'s article, Colin,' she said quietly, aware that two nurses that had passed by were staring at them with ill-concealed curiosity.

'Oh, come on, Devlin,' he said in disgust, 'you don't expect me to believe that you weren't in cahoots with that lot. You must have got a fortune for that article, not to talk about all the free publicity and making muck of me.'

'Don't be ridiculous, Colin,' Devlin retorted. 'Why do you think I gave the interview to the *Chronicle* on Saturday — and I didn't get paid for that either. I wanted the truth to be printed. I didn't want people to think that what that rag of a Sunday newspaper printed was *my* story. I never mentioned your name in the interview that I gave. I never spoke to any journalist about you ever. I have too much respect for myself.'

'Well, why didn't you get an injunction to stop the *Echo*?' he demanded.

'Use your head, Colin. If I had, both of us would have had reporters on our doorsteps morning noon and night. At least it's not going to drag on now after the fuss has died down. It will be a nine days' wonder.'

'For you, maybe,' he snarled. 'I'll have to live with the fall-out for the rest of my life.'

'I've been living with it ever since I got pregnant by you,' Devlin said evenly. 'The reason I'm here today is to visit my mother, who took an overdose as a consequence of that article. Some of the ladies on the fund-raising committee for your maternity unit demanded that she resign from the committee and that just pushed her over the edge. I've lost more than you ever will. I lost my baby and I nearly lost my mother. Don't try to blame me for your troubles. You brought them all on yourself by your actions, just as I did mine.' With immense dignity, Devlin stepped out of his way and with her head held high she continued down the corridor, leaving Colin staring after her.

Colin ran his hands through his hair. He was shocked at the news about Lydia and had to believe Devlin when she said she had nothing to do with that damned article. Despite all the antagonism between them, when he thought of those crystal-clear aquamarine eyes that he remembered so well staring at him with such contempt, he felt a niggle of shame. He had treated her badly, especially in denying their child.

Devlin had too much integrity to kiss and tell and

he secretly admired the guts she had shown in picking up the pieces of her life and making such a success of it. As far as he was concerned, all the status that he had sweated blood for had gone down the drain. It would take him years to get over this. His wife would never forgive him and his current mistress would probably take advantage of the situation to start urging him to get a divorce and marry her. He was getting a bit fed up with her anyway. She was always whingeing about having to be discreet. It was a pity she wasn't a bit more like Devlin, he thought, as he strode out of the hospital, trying to ignore the knowing looks that were coming his way. Devlin had never whined. She had accepted the situation, although she had totally believed him when he told her that his marriage was over and his wife and he were staying together for the sake of the kids.

Devlin had been a corker – she still was, he had to admit as he marched over to his Mercedes in the consultants' car-park. Despite their history, he wouldn't mind a hot night with her in the sack. What a body! And what a shame that he'd had her only the once. It wasn't as if they'd even had a proper affair, he thought, feeling very aggrieved. He put on a charming smile as he passed Stella Richmond, a kidney specialist he often referred his patients to. She cut him dead.

'And fuck you too!' he swore as he got into his car and gunned the engine. 'Self-righteous old cow,' he muttered. He should have known she'd turn on him. Wasn't she one of that Opus Dei crowd, with her bloody holier-than-thou attitude? Well, he'd never refer a patient to her again – that was for sure.

That is, if he had any patients left for referral, he reflected, as he shot past the Merrion Centre on his way to his rooms.

Lydia was sitting against her pillows saying the Rosary, when Devlin, looking more composed than she felt, peered around the door of the room. In a perverse way, she was glad of her encounter with Colin. It had afforded her the opportunity of setting the record straight concerning the interview.

'Devlin.' Lydia laid down her Rosary beads when she saw her daughter and held out her hand.

'Hello, Mum,' Devlin said as she leaned over and kissed her mother's pale cheek.

Lydia gave a sheepish grimace. 'I'm so ashamed, dear.'

'Why did you do it, Mum?' Devlin sat on the edge of the bed, holding her mother's hand tightly.

Lydia sighed and gripped Devlin's hand. 'I don't know really. When Angeline and Jane came and they were so smug, I was furious. I was very angry for the rest of the evening and then I thought I'd really like a drink. And of course we all know what happened the last time I had a drink,' she added bitterly. 'Anyway I went to bed, and I thought about those two madams and then I began to think: what if Gerry's bosses felt the same about him? And then I thought that some of your clients might leave you. I'm afraid I got myself into a right state and the urge to take a drink got stronger and it all got on top of me and I took the pills. After a while when I began to get really woozy, I decided I'd been a bit of an idiot and I got up to go down and tell Gerry what I'd done. I remember getting to the stairs and I'm afraid after that I don't remember too much. I remember getting my stomach pumped; that was ghastly.

'There's something that I remember very well, though, and you'll probably say I was hallucinating or imagining things. But Devlin, as sure as you're sitting here before me, I swear I saw Kate and the baby. They were smiling at me and they looked so happy. They were telling me to go back and I never felt such a sense of peace and serenity as I did then. It lasted for a minute or two and then I remember coming to and having my stomach pumped. You probably think I'm mad, Devlin,' Lydia said a little defensively.

'Actually, I don't, Mum.' Devlin squeezed her mother's hand. 'It's very hard to explain and I wasn't going to say anything to anyone but now that you've brought it up, I've had such a strong sense of them all this weekend. I feel as if they're here taking care of us. I think it was Kate who put it into my head about doing the interview with Sally Briers. Anyway, that's what I want to think.'

'You just keep thinking like that, pet, and so will I, and we'll get through this. I promise I won't pull any more funny stunts.' Lydia met Devlin's eyes.

'We love you very much, Dad and I, you must know that,' Devlin exclaimed. 'If you're down about anything or feel like taking a drink or whatever, you must share it with us. Then we'll know what you're feeling and be there to help. Don't bottle it all up.'

Lydia gave a wry chuckle. 'Do you hear the kettle calling the pot black?'

'I know,' Devlin smiled. 'But I am getting much better. Ask Luke. I'm always moaning to him.'

'It is good to know there are loved ones you can share your ups and downs with. I know you're learning that with Luke and I'm glad. You know something, Devlin, this weekend and especially the visitation of Saint Angeline and Saint Jane has really brought home to me that if people behave like that they're not worth having as friends. Do you know what Mrs Darcy next door did?'

Devlin shook her head. She knew Mrs Darcy, her mother's next-door neighbour, only to say hello to. Mrs Darcy kept to herself in her big detached house and didn't go around poking her nose in other people's business.

'She knocked on the door on Sunday morning with a packet of firelighters which she told me to use to burn any copies of the *Echo* that might come my way. She said you were a lovely girl and a credit to me and I wasn't to take a blind bit of notice of what anyone said. Now, can you believe that?'

Devlin was delighted. 'Isn't she a little old dote?'

'She certainly is,' Lydia replied. 'It's people like that, who stand by you when the chips are down, that are the important ones. Those and family. And I've got the best family in the world!'

'Dad will be in soon,' Devlin informed her mother cheerfully, feeling relieved beyond measure at Lydia's explanation of the overdose attempt. The most reassuring thing was that Lydia had realized that she had made a dreadful mistake and knew that she wanted to live. She could have shaken her mother for giving them such a fright, but Lydia had been through a lot in the last few years and Devlin knew that beneath the sophisticated veneer, her mother was a very sensitive woman who was only learning now how to reveal her emotions.

'I'm glad we had this time to ourselves, dear, and I do apologize for being so stupid. You've enough on your plate without worrying about a neurotic mother.' Lydia hugged her daughter and Devlin hugged her back tightly, rejoicing in their new closeness.

'I'll call tonight, love.' Luke put his arm around Devlin as they stood by the boarding-gate the following morning. She had insisted on bringing him to the airport, wanting to be with him until the last minute.

'I love you.' She held him close and wished that he didn't have to go. Having him with her for the past few days had been such a treat and it had been such a relief to share all her trials with him. It had been the weirdest weekend of her life, but one thing had come out of it: Devlin had realized that Luke played a very important part in her life, and she just couldn't imagine what that life would be like without him.

Well, at least Lydia was out of hospital and seemingly none the worse for her experience, Luke reflected, as he sat on the plane awaiting take-off. He had really felt for Devlin this past weekend, with all she had had to endure. It had made him feel so powerless not being able to prevent all that dreadful ordeal. He hated going back leaving her to shoulder everything but he knew Devlin: she'd cope, although Devlin had had to cope with more than her fair share. Luke just wished he could stay to help her. The past few days had brought them much closer together, closer than he had ever thought possible. At least he had that consolation, he thought, as the jet thundered down the runway and lifted its huge bulk into the grey misting clouds.

Dianne let herself into the office and enjoyed the feeling of being there all by herself so early in the morning. It was just gone seven-thirty, but she wanted to get to work early to make sure everything was just right. Luke was coming home today and she was longing to see him. Whatever crisis Ms Delaney had been going through must be over, or else he had come to his senses and decided that Miss Wishy-Washy was not for him. As happy as a lark, she laid out all the reports she had prepared for Luke in his absence and placed on his desk a neat sheaf of letters that required his signature. Her mouth tightened as she glanced at Devlin's newly repaired picture. She had replaced the broken glass after her outburst the other day. It had been a very satisfying little tantrum, but on reflection she had decided that it would be better to have Luke find everything just as he had left it. One of these days it would be *her* photo that adorned Luke's desk. 'See if it isn't,' she said viciously to Devlin's smiling image.

Luke had said on the phone the day before that he would take a taxi directly from the airport to the office. He'd probably be hungry, Dianne thought, as she ground the coffee beans. In another hour or so she'd order fresh croissants from the deli.

'Dianne, you're the best in the world!' Luke smiled at her an hour and a half later, as he walked into his office to the enticing smell of freshly percolated coffee and croissants, freshly baked. Dianne glowed. How she wanted to run into his arms and hug him tightly to her. With superhuman restraint, she kept her composure and played it cool, pouring his coffee and handing him a crisp linen napkin as he sat behind his desk.

'Oh, Dianne, would you do something for me?' Luke smiled – that attractive crinkly smile that made her melt.

'Of course,' she responded warmly. 'Anything!' And she meant *anything*, she thought longingly.

'Would you have three dozen pink roses sent to Devlin at her office, to be delivered as soon as possible?' he said, before taking a bite out of one of the croissants.

Dianne couldn't believe her ears. I hope it bloody chokes you, she thought savagely, as she saw Luke's even white teeth taking another bite out of the croissant. Pink roses indeed!

'He's been very supportive, Maggie. I'd never have got through this without him. You should have seen the beautiful bouquet of roses he sent me today. They just took my breath away.'

Maggie poured out the tea for them. 'He's a lovely bloke. Don't let him go.'

Devlin smiled at her friend. Despite her own marital problems, Maggie had, as always, provided a strong shoulder for Devlin to lean on. She had insisted on Devlin coming over to be pampered for the evening and now that the children were in bed, they were settling down to a good natter. It was such a relief for Devlin to kick off her shoes and lounge in front of a roaring fire. It had been a particularly hectic day; she had to give a talk to aspiring female entrepreneurs about setting up their own businesses, as well as carry on the normal management of City Girl.

After the publicity of the weekend, facing a large group of women was the last thing she wanted to do. It had taken every ounce of grit and determination she possessed to get up in front of the curious group and speak enthusiastically about setting out on the rocky road to a successful business. She was very frank about the pitfalls she had personally encountered, even mentioning how becoming a so-called celebrity had made her a target for the likes of the *Sunday Echo*. When she finished speaking, Devlin was touched and gratified to receive a standing ovation, and many of the women approached her over coffee and biscuits, to sympathize with her about the article and to tell her they thought she was great. The goodwill of the women she met gave her a great lift. But, as she explained to Maggie, she was weary, really drained, and the idea of going out to Abu Dhabi to Caroline was becoming more and more inviting. The thought of leaving all her worries behind her for a couple of weeks was bliss, and Caroline's letters and phone calls had been very enthusiastic in their descriptions of the exotic Emirate.

'I think you'd be mad not to make the most of the opportunity to visit while she's still there,' Maggie declared. 'She'll be home soon enough now. Go and forget everything and spend a fortune on yourself – and get a tan to make us all pea-green with envy! Caroline will be thrilled skinny if you do. I know she's enjoying herself out there, but it can get lonely, and especially with the way things are for her now . . . God, I'd be gone like a flash if I could. Go, Devlin, go!' she urged, laughing.

'You know something, Maggie?' Devlin stretched her limbs and smiled. 'I think I just might!'

Fifty-Three

Caroline was waiting for her as she promised she would, on the other side of the big glass partition. She was waving Devlin's visa at her, a huge smile wreathing her face.

'See you in a minute!' Devlin exclaimed, as she reached up and Caroline dropped the visa over the partition and then said a few words to an olive-skinned man beside her. Blowing her a kiss, Devlin went back to the passport control queue. She couldn't believe how stunning Caroline looked. Her eyes were so clear and healthy and she had a golden tan that really made her glow. Her hair was gorgeous worn like that, longer than Devlin remembered, soft and silky to her shoulders. She looked so . . . Devlin tried to think of a word that would suit Caroline's new image. Zestful, that was it. She looked full of beans, her eyes dancing with excitement as she caught sight of Devlin. It was hard to believe that this confident woman was the same person as the timid and apprehensive girl Maggie and she had taken to the airport the previous November.

About twenty minutes later, when Devlin had collected her luggage and cleared customs, the friends were finally face to face, hugging each other and laughing and hugging each other again.

'My God, Devlin, you look shattered!' Caroline exclaimed, as she stood back to look at her best friend. 'What on earth have you been doing to yourself? Look at the circles under your eyes! Now listen to me—' she linked Devlin's arm and led her towards the arrivals exit '—you are going to flop for this holiday. You're going to do nothing for the four days you are in the Sheraton except eat, sleep and sunbathe, and then, when you come to stay in my place, I'll bring you sightseeing and shopping. OK? That man I was talking to at arrivals was from the hotel. He came with your visa and your room is all ready for you. So it's R&R big time for you. OK?' she repeated.

'OK,' echoed Devlin with a grin. She was beginning to feel better already.

The thought of this holiday had really kept her going. Caroline had advised her to wait until the beginning of April so that Ramadan would be over, and it seemed to Devlin that February and March had been the longest months of her life.

They walked out of the airport and Devlin felt as if a blanket of heat had suddenly been wrapped around her. 'Whew, it's warm!' she exclaimed.

Caroline looked at her in surprise. 'I thought it was a bit chilly tonight compared to last week,' she declared, leading the way to a red Honda Civic.

Devlin laughed. 'You talk like a native.'

'You'll get used to the heat very quickly. I did,' Caroline assured her. 'But it's nothing to what they experience in the summer – or so I've been told.' She opened the hatchback and hauled the suitcase into it.

'Get in, I'll switch on the AC for you,' she said, beaming at Devlin.

Devlin couldn't get over the way her friend drove them out of the airport complex and on to the straight six-lane highway that cut through the desert to Abu Dhabi. Watching her negotiate the traffic, smoothly changing gears and operating the left-hand drive as if she were born to it, Devlin was mightily impressed.

'I'm dying to hear all the news! Did you bring the papers? Did you bring the *Coronation Street* video? Did you bring the Tayto crisps?' Caroline shot the questions at her as she drove at speed towards the city.

'Yes, I've brought everything you asked me to bring. I've brought all last Sunday's papers.'

'Sometimes you think all that's happening in Europe and the States is happening on another planet. It's a bit unreal here, like coming to a different world,' Caroline confessed, as they drove along the highway that stretched before them like an inky-black ribbon. 'It was just what I needed though,' she said, smiling at Devlin. 'Everything was on top of me. I couldn't think what to do with myself. Out here I've had a real chance to think. I had to stand on my own two feet, and I did it, and now I'm looking forward to going home and doing something with my life.'

'I'm really glad for you, Caroline. I never thought you'd stick it. But, by golly, you have — and look at you!' Devlin declared admiringly as they arrived at the outer suburbs of the city. 'A city woman ready to take on the world. Maggie need look no further for a heroine for her novels.'

'Idiot,' laughed Caroline. 'But I can tell you one thing, miss! *You're* not taking on the world. *You're* going to forget about everything except getting a suntan. I'm not allowing you to go home until those circles have disappeared and you've a bit of colour in your face and a few pounds on your hips. You look like a skeleton.'

'Don't exaggerate,' Devlin remonstrated.

'It's not much of an exaggeration, either,' Caroline said firmly. 'Maggie was right about you being a wreck.'

Devlin grinned. 'All right, I give in! No more lectures, I'll lie by the pool and stuff myself for the duration.'

'There's a lovely pool at the Sheraton. Wait until you see it. It's like paradise there. And I can't *wait* to bring you to the Intercontinental Beach Club. Devlin, you'll think you've died and gone to heaven. I'll really miss it all when I go home, but I've made some great friends out here and I'll be able to come back on holidays. That will be something to look forward to.'

'Ooohhh, I'm getting excited.' Devlin giggled lightheartedly. 'It was freezing cold and there was a howling gale when I left home this morning. Imagine, I'll be sunbathing tomorrow!' Devlin gazed out the window at the skyscrapers and mosques of Abu Dhabi, wondering if she were dreaming.

'Well, here we are,' Caroline announced a few minutes later, driving up to a huge, elegant hotel. It was built of sand-coloured brick and very cleverly designed to give an aura of the exotic, an aura Devlin was beginning to associate with all the beautiful Arabic architecture she had so far seen.

The softly lit marble foyer was luxurious. Devlin, who loved staying in hotels, was really pleased that she had agreed to Caroline's suggestion of getting her visa sponsored by the Sheraton and staying there for four days before going on to Caroline's flat. The four days would give her the perfect opportunity to wind down, and then Caroline would have a few days off work and they would really have a ball.

She checked in with a minimum of fuss, impressed by the friendly courtesy of the staff even at that late hour. It was with great anticipation that she followed the porter to her room.

'Oh Caroline, it's lovely,' she said enthusiastically, staring around in delight. Caroline tipped the young Indian some dirhams and gave a smug smile.

'I thought you'd like it. Now, aren't you glad I made you take a tourist visa? It will do you the world of good to stay here for a few days before coming over to rough it with me.'

Devlin flew over to the French windows and flung them open. 'Oh look! Oh wow!' she exclaimed at the view. Below was an enormous pool, illuminated by sparkling fairy lights. Surrounding it were gardens full of luscious shrubs. In the distance, lights from the city cast a dusky pink glow into the jet-black sky, and just beyond the fringe of beach, three dhows sailed serenely in the Arabian Gulf, which was illuminated by a silver crescent moon. It was like a scene out of the *Arabian Nights*.

She turned and hugged Caroline tightly. 'Caroline, it's gorgeous. I'm very happy to be here.'

'I was so excited driving out to the airport. I've often heard some of my friends here saying "I'm having a guest," and watched them waiting impatiently for the visitor's arrival, but I never really understood the great anticipation. Now, having someone from home myself, I can really see what all the fuss is about. It's great. It's like Christmas coming. I hope you really enjoy every minute of your holiday, Devlin. I won't stay too long because you must be exhausted after the flight.'

Devlin did a twirl. 'I'm not a bit exhausted! I *was* when I got off the plane, but I'm on a high now and I'm starving. Stay and have some supper. What time is it here?'

Caroline glanced at her watch. 'It's just gone one in the morning, but I'm sure they do a twenty-four-hour room service.' She handed Devlin a folder containing all the information relating to the hotel.

They decided on a club sandwich, and twenty minutes later were facing a mouthwatering mountain of tasty salad and cold meats and cheeses. 'It's scrumptious,' Devlin murmured, with her mouth full.

'Some things never change,' giggled Caroline, tucking in. 'When we're together, we're always eating.'

'Pity Maggie isn't here,' Devlin said, taking a drink of tea, which, to her surprise, was also delicious.

'How's *City Woman* going?' Caroline asked excitedly. 'I'd have loved to be at her launch. Wasn't it brilliant it went to number one so quickly? I was thrilled when she sent me out a signed copy.'

'It's selling like hot cakes, and the new one, *A Time to Decide*, is coming out this autumn. I think she's magnificent the way she's held it all together. Combining motherhood and her writing career is a tough one, but she's determined. You know Maggie when she gets the bit between her teeth! Now tell me all about what's happening to you.' Devlin smiled affectionately at her friend.

They stayed nattering for about two hours until Caroline insisted on Devlin going to bed. She wanted to go into work early in the morning so that she could finish early to be with Devlin.

By that time, tiredness had hit Devlin like a ton of bricks and she closed the door after Caroline with a delicious sense of anticipation. Sticky after her long plane journey, she ran the bath in the exquisite pink-and-grey mosaic-tiled bathroom, undressed and removed her make-up. Staring at herself in the enormous mirror that dominated one wall, Devlin had to admit that she looked tired and scrawny. It was past time for her to take a holiday and she was going to make the most of every minute of it.

It was one of the most comfortable beds she had ever slept in, Devlin decided, as she sat on her balcony, in the warm, scented breeze, having a room-service breakfast. She eyed the loaded tray in front of her with amusement. She'd certainly put on plenty of weight if this was anything to go by! Devlin had opted for the Continental breakfast, but the basket of oven-fresh rolls, croissants, Danish pastries, muffins and toast that had arrived would have fed a family of four.

The Oriental breakfast on the menu looked extremely interesting too, she mused, fascinated by the unusual names: Foul, Mudammas, Black Olives, Labneh, Arabic bread and Feta cheese. Tomorrow, she might be adventurous and try it, she thought, biting into a yummy Danish pastry with a melt-in-the-mouth custard centre. Beef bacon and beef sausages were offered on the à la carte menu. This was a Muslim country and pork would never be served here.

She read the *Gulf News*, the daily paper that had been pushed under her door, and enjoyed her breakfast. Then, with a happy heart, she tucked the copy of *Emirates Woman*, a glossy magazine that lay on the desk, into her holdall, which also contained her suntan lotion and sunglasses. She was dying to explore the exotic grounds of the beach-front hotel.

Breathtaking was really the word to describe what she was seeing, Devlin reflected twenty minutes later, as she strolled around the glorious grounds. Emerald lawns, dotted with luxury loungers under palm shades, were planted with huge flowering shrubs, the likes of which she had never seen: heavily scented frangipanis, their creamy white blooms dipping to earth, delicate purple hibiscus, bougainvillaea, huge tropical palm trees swaying in the warm, fragrant breeze. The combination overpowered the senses. She gazed around in delight at the crescent of white sandy beach fringing the grounds. The clear, blue-green waters of the Arabian Gulf lapped the shore, and Devlin stared across the turquoise sea reminding herself that Iran, the Emirate's neighbour, was not that far away. It was hard to believe. And hard to believe too that this time two days before, she had been wrapped up in her winter woollies. Now, here she was, under startling blue skies with a white-hot sun beaming down, all ready to turn her skin golden. Laying one of the soft, thick, pink-and-white striped towels that the pool attendant had given her on one of the plush loungers, Devlin slipped out of her beach-robe, oiled herself, and lay back. She had selected a lounger away from the pool area, down on one of the lawns beside the sea, and she lay watching a dhow sail lazily by, enjoying the breeze caressing her body. Caroline was right; this was heaven on earth.

For the four days she was in the Sheraton, Devlin did absolutely nothing but eat, drink, sleep, sunbathe and swim. Worn out by months of hard work and hassle, she really hadn't realized how completely exhausted she was. Caroline, recognizing this, had postponed all shopping and sightseeing trips. Time enough for that when she moved over to the apartment. In a way, Devlin was quite relieved not to have to rush around. Lying on her lounger, swimming in the magnificent pool when she wanted to cool down, she was quite happy to let her mind wander. It was peaceful and reviving. The joy of not having a phone to answer, or people knocking on her door wanting her to make decisions, or even worrying about what to cook for her dinner was indescribable. The most taxing problems she had here were what to eat and in which restaurant in the luxurious hotel: Chinese, Arabic, Indian. Every afternoon after work, Caroline joined her and they lazed by the pool, yakking nineteen to the dozen, before changing for dinner. Caroline took her to the souk and Devlin loved every minute of it, but at her friend's insistence she was always in bed before midnight. She was sleeping like a log and feeling all the better for it. If only Luke were with her, Devlin thought, it would be perfect.

She missed him desperately, longing to share her little piece of heaven with him. They telephoned each other every day, and though Devlin knew her phone bill was going to be enormous, she didn't care. It was worth it to talk to him and tell him what a wonderful, restful time she was having. He was delighted for her and kept urging her to stay even longer than the ten days she had planned. At night, after her day's activities, she used to sit down at her desk with the balcony doors open, and write pages and pages of letters to Luke, telling him how much she was enjoying herself and how much she missed him.

On the last morning of her stay at the hotel, she dived into the Gulf waters and swam out to the diving platform just below the line of bobbing pink buoys that held the shark-net in place. Taking her camera out of its waterproof case, she snapped away, photos to remind her of every bit of her idyllic stay in the beautiful hotel. Later on, it was with regret that she packed her case. Her eye lingered on the desk by the balcony, where she had found a beautiful basket of fruit when she arrived and where there was also a basket of orchids that Luke had ordered for her.

She would miss the friendly smile of Yusef, who came to pull down her bedcovers at night and lay a selection of gold-wrapped handmade chocolates on her pillow before spreading the pristine white prayer-sheet on the floor beside her bed.

This room had been a haven to her and she had made the most of every minute here. Some day she would return with Luke, she promised herself, as she closed the door behind her and walked down the carpeted corridor with Caroline, on her way to her new abode.

'It's not the Sheraton but it's home,' Caroline declared a while later, leading Devlin into the apartment where she had lived since she came to the Emirate.

'It's lovely,' Devlin exclaimed, going from room to room, delighted at last to see for herself what she had tried to imagine from the descriptions in her friend's letters.

'I've really enjoyed living here. I'm going to miss it like anything when I leave,' Caroline said wistfully.

'Just think of the fun you'll have, buying a new place and decorating it,' Devlin said comfortingly.

'I know. I'm looking forward to that. It's just this was my retreat from the world: here's where I made a new life for myself. It will always be special for me.'

'Of course it will,' Devlin agreed. 'And for me as well. The few days I've spent here have been superb. I'm taking so many photos so that I'll always have mementos of it. There's something healing about this place, isn't there?'

Caroline nodded. 'I found that. And you look so much better, Devlin, even after only four days.'

'I feel so much better,' Devlin declared exuberantly as she stood on the balcony and took deep breaths of the aromatic scents of spices and coffees that wafted by on the breeze. 'I know that I've a whole lot of hassle waiting for me when I get home. I know Galway's City Girl has got to be looked at in the context of the recession. But I'll cope with it. Right now, I feel I could cope with anything.'

'I read in an Irish paper that several big employers in Galway laid people off over the last few months,' Caroline remarked as she put the kettle on for a pot of coffee. 'Is that going to make a big difference to you?'

'Well, I'm afraid it will,' Devlin sighed. 'They've laid off hundreds of people and we would have targeted a good number of their female workforce as customers. Luke warned me about overspending there and I didn't take too much notice. Still we'll sort something out – and at least Belfast is doing great so I won't get depressed about things. Certainly not here in Abu Dhabi. What's on the agenda for today?'

'Well, I thought we'd go to my beach club for a change and then I've planned a *Coronation Street* show for this evening so that you can meet some of my friends. More important, we can eat the Taytos you brought over. Tayto crisps are to die for, as the dreaded Lucinda Marshall would say.'

'Don't mention that she-devil's name,' Devlin groaned.

'Sorry,' Caroline said. 'I forgot.'

'Actually, so have I,' Devlin remarked. 'It's all like a bad dream now and a lot of good came out of it. Mum and I are great pals and very close. And I finally realized how much Luke loves me and I know now that I love him very much.'

'I'm so glad for you, Devlin! You deserve someone like Luke. He's a good man and you'll always be happy with him.'

'I know that! I wish he was here to share my holiday – even though I'm having a ball, I'm looking forward to stopping off in London to spend a few days with him.'

'Crikey, she's only here four days,' Caroline teased, 'and she's looking forward to going home already, I must be failing dismally as a hostess.'

'Well, I've never been to a *Coronation Street* party

626

before,' Devlin giggled. 'Maybe it will change my mind.'

In fact the party was great fun. Devlin met Féile, Caroline's friend and neighbour from across the hall, and before the evening was out, Féile had promised to take her to the Eastern Jewellers to buy some gold and – or so Caroline slagged her – to watch an expert in haggling. The Tayto crisps went down a treat, as did the huge curry Caroline had prepared. There was wine, beer and spirits, and Caroline quite happily spent the night sipping pineapple juice. Lively discussions arose about the developments in *Coronation Street*, as they were all up to date with the serial, thanks to their families who regularly sent videos of the programme out to them. Watching Caroline so at ease with all her Abu Dhabi friends, confident, and with a poise she had never had before, Devlin was very happy. Coming to Abu Dhabi was the most positive step her friend had ever taken and it was a decision that had paid dividends.

Caroline had introduced her to Mike, the man she had written about in her letters, and it was clear that they were good pals. He was a friendly, unassuming chap who teased Caroline unmercifully about her cooking. Devlin reflected how nice it was to see her friend enjoying male company, while also being aware that she was her own woman now. Having a man in her life was not the be-all and end-all. Caroline had confided in Devlin that for the time being she was only interested in men as friends. She was certainly in no rush to get into an intimate relationship after her disastrous marriage to Richard.

Laughing and chatting with Caroline's friends

while Arabic music played in the background and couples danced in the sitting-room, Devlin felt light-hearted and carefree. It was ages since she had been at a party, and the crack was mighty.

The rest of her holiday passed in a whirl of sight-seeing, shopping and other parties, until the day before she was due to go home. This Caroline had decreed a 'blitz-on-suntan' day. Lying on a comfort-able lounger, Devlin sipped her Pimms and felt the sun warm on her body. She gazed out over the Arabian Gulf, relaxing after having spent the previous hour windsurfing. She felt that lovely torpor that comes with complete ease and it was hard to believe that she had been there for two weeks. She had needed very little persuasion from Caroline to extend her holiday to a fortnight. Caroline had been so good to her, going out of her way to make sure she enjoyed herself. They had gone to Dubai and spent a fortune; they had had a weekend in the desert – an experience Devlin would never forget. Watching the setting sun turn the golden dunes to dusky pink and feeling the immense stillness all around, Devlin had felt a lovely serenity envelop her.

She had an abundance of new clothes – mostly silks that she'd had made up as jackets by the superb tailors that were so plentiful in the city. And Féile, true to her word, had taken her shopping to the Eastern Jewellers, where she had bought herself a gold filigree chain and matching earrings and bracelet. She had bought Luke a gold signet ring and had his initials carved on it. She had jewellery and silks for her mother and shirts and cigars for her father. Her gift for Maggie was an exquisite little gold dhow on a chain.

But she'd really gone mad buying things for the children and Caroline had warned her that she'd have excess luggage. 'Who cares?' Devlin had laughed, enjoying the spending spree of her life.

'Have another Pimms?' Caroline invited.

'Oh, all right.' Devlin gave in without a struggle. She had really acquired a taste for the refreshing drink and was going to treat herself to a bottle in the duty-free.

'Imagine, the two of us will be home this time next month,' Caroline mused.

'Imagine, you'll be in Tibet this day week!' Devlin laughed. 'You've changed so much, Caroline: going to the Himalayas on your holidays!'

'I know. I feel so much happier and much freer than I've ever been before. Instead of life being a big ordeal it's become a great adventure. You know, Devlin . . .' Caroline leaned up on her elbow and stared across at her from the adjoining lounger. 'I know City Girl is very important to you, and rightly so, but don't let it become the whole of your life. Don't miss out on what Luke can give you and what you can give to him. Of the relationships the three of us have had, I can see yours being the most successful. Neither Richard nor Terry ever gave me or Maggie the support that you get from Luke. Don't take it for granted.'

Devlin stared at the dark-haired girl with the big brown eyes, now staring earnestly at her. Whenever Caroline had given her advice in the past, it had always been the best. Caroline had the knack of getting to the core of the matter. Devlin knew, as she lay there under an Eastern sun, watching the waters of the Gulf shimmer in the sunlight, that she was getting the best advice she had ever been offered. She had had a lot of time to reflect during this holiday, and she knew that what Caroline was saying was absolutely true.

'You know something, Caroline?' Devlin smiled happily. 'You're right!'

The image that was reflected in the big wall mirror in a ladies' room in Heathrow was far different from what Devlin had seen in the mirror in the Abu Dhabi Sheraton a fortnight before. She smiled, trying to picture Luke's expression when he saw her: tanned and glowing with health, in such contrast to the pale, scrawny woman who had left Dublin for the holiday of a lifetime.

She felt refreshed and invigorated and back to her old vivacious self, and she vowed that she would never again let herself go so long without a proper holiday. She had spoken to Liz on the phone just five minutes before, and Liz had assured her that the building was still standing and, although she knew it would come as a dreadful shock to Devlin, City Girl had operated extremely smoothly in her absence and would continue to do so for the few days she was spending in London.

Devlin was not too disturbed to find that she was not indispensable. If what she had in mind went according to plan, City Girl would have to get used to her not being always at the helm.

She traced the outline of her lips with an ice-pink lipstick that really accentuated her tan. So did the mint-green Lacoste T-shirt she was wearing with a pair of white Bermudas. It was amazing how the tan made such a difference to her appearance, giving her a wholesome, healthy air. Eyes sparkling with anticipation, she brushed her lashes with a wand of mascara and sprayed some White Linen on her wrists and at the base of her throat. In a few minutes she'd see Luke, and she was dying to feel his arms around her and his lips on hers.

She opened her bag, took out the little box and saw the gold of the ring glinting in the sunlight. A smile touched her lips as she reflected on the deed she was about to perform. The more she thought about it, the more right it seemed. Nevertheless her heart skipped a beat in anticipation.

Twenty minutes later she had collected her bulging cases and passed through customs. Then she saw Luke, smiling broadly at her, his arms held out in welcome.

Devlin flung herself at him, kissing and hugging him, telling him how much she had missed him.

'What a reception!' He smiled down at her, holding her tightly to him. 'I must make you go on holidays more often.'

Devlin kissed him again and then opened her bag and took out the little box containing his ring. 'I bought this for you, Luke, with all my love.' She opened the box and handed it to him. Raising her clear blue-green eyes to his, she took a deep breath and said calmly, 'Luke, will you marry me?'

Epilogue

'Devlin, love, here's a cup of tea.' She opened her eyes to find her father smiling down at her.

'And it's a beautiful day.' Lydia popped her head around the bedroom door. 'I told you the Child of Prague statue in the garden always works. Don't stay too long in bed; the girls will be here soon. I have my appointment with the hairdressers at nine, so I'd better go and organize myself. I've a million and one things to do.'

'All right, Mother, I'll be up in a minute.' Devlin sat up in bed and ran her fingers through her tousled hair.

'Your mother's in her element. No general could be more in command in his field of battle,' Gerry whispered conspiratorially.

Devlin laughed. 'I'll tell you one thing, Dad. If Luke and I ever have a daughter, she can elope with my blessing.'

'Ah, it won't be that bad once everything is in place,' Gerry assured her. 'The main thing for you is to enjoy yourself, because when all is said and done, your wedding day is the most special day in your life. Forget all the incidentals, all the things your mother is enjoying getting into a flap about. Just think that nearly everyone who loves you is going to be with you and at the end of the day, the one who loves you most is going to be the last person you see before you fall asleep and the first you see when you wake up.'

'*Gerrryee!*' Lydia's voice resounded up the stairs.

'Your mother would do well in Moore Street if it wasn't for her accent,' Gerry chuckled. 'I'm coming,' he called. 'Devlin, before I go, while we have these few moments to ourselves before pandemonium is unleashed, I just want to tell you that no daughter could make a man prouder than you've made me. I thank God every day for giving me a daughter as special as you.' Gerry leaned down and kissed Devlin on the cheek.

'Oh, Dad,' she murmured, overwhelmed at his words. 'Look, you've made me blubber.' Putting the cup on her bedside locker, Devlin wrapped her arms around her father's neck. 'I love you, Daddy. Thanks for everything, and especially for all the support you gave me in the bad times. I know I'm marrying Luke and I do love him, but I'll always be your daughter. I'll always need your love and you'll always have mine.' Devlin spoke from the heart. Her father's arms tightened around her and his eyes grew suspiciously moist. But he said nothing, just hugged her tightly, and then he was gone. Devlin was alone, sitting in bed in the room of her childhood.

'Now, my girl,' she said crossly, wiping away the tears. 'That's the end of your blubbering for the day. You are *not* a weeping willow, you are a very happy bride-to-be, and besides, your mascara will run when you have your make-up on.' She caught sight of herself in the mirror. 'Idiot,' she grinned.

She lay back against the pillows, determined to enjoy these last few minutes of peace. Caroline and Maggie would be here soon. They'd been through it all so they'd know what to expect. She smiled, remembering the weddings of her two dearest friends.

They had a great day the week before, just the three of them. Luke was always teasing her that he was getting three for the price of one and it was just as well he wasn't the jealous type because Maggie and Caroline were bonded to her with Superglue and she to them. The three girls had seen one another through thick and thin and that was why she had wanted their little hen-party to be so special. And it was! Devlin smiled at the memory.

'A chauffeur-driven limo, you exhibitionist you!' Maggie laughed as the three of them left City Girl. They had spent the morning having the works done, compliments of the proprietor. They'd been cleansed, massaged, manicured, pedicured, aromatized, steamed, sauna'd, *everything*, before having their hair done and faces made up. It was a morning such as every woman dreams of and the three had enjoyed every nano-second of it.

They stepped into the long, gleaming limo and were driven the couple of hundred yards to The Commons. 'Today we're going to be Ladies Who Lunch,' Devlin grinned. 'Lucinda Marshall, eat your heart out.' As usual the restaurant was thronged and as the glamorous trio were led to their table there was a lot of elbow-nudging and little murmured asides.

'That's Devlin Delaney. She owns City Girl.'

'She's marrying a gorgeous hunk. I saw him once. I wonder how long it will last?'

'She really thinks she's it, doesn't she? Little tart. You'd think she wouldn't want to be seen dead in public after that article the *Echo* did about her.'

'I believe the mother's a plonkie. Probably driven to it.'

'Who's that with her?'

'Oh that's Caroline Yates. She's married to Richard Yates, that very successful solicitor, but I think they're separated.'

'There's something very fishy going on there. He disappeared for over a year and then she went off somewhere and came back with a tan, looking like a million dollars, dripping with gold. I think she must have been having an affair with someone and it's done her the world of good.'

'You still see them together occasionally and they look happy enough. I wonder why he went away? Do you think there might be some sort of scandal – you know like the ones we've been having lately? Richard Yates – now that would be a shocker!'

'The redhead's the one who wrote *City Woman*. It was brilliant. Now, I don't usually read, I don't have time, but I just couldn't put it down.'

'She must be a millionairess by now. She was on the bestseller list for months. I believe she has another book coming out soon. It's such easy money, isn't it? Just sitting scribbling whatever comes in to your head. I might try writing one myself.'

'I wonder if she came here to do research. I bet The Commons will be in the next book.'

'All eyes are upon us,' grinned Devlin. 'I'd love to be a fly on the wall near some of the tables.'

'Did you see Rachel Kennedy?' Caroline was shocked. 'She's aged twenty years.'

'Her husband ran off with a younger woman and I believe he's trying to sell the house from under her,' Devlin informed her. 'So she's turned to the bottle.'

'I know all about it,' Caroline grimaced.

'Oh, look,' murmured Maggie, 'it's Shaun Archer, the TV personality. Isn't he supposed to be having a rip-roaring affair with Veronica O'Kelly, the woman who owns all those night clubs?'

' "Supposed" is the operative word,' Caroline whispered. 'Apart from the fact that Shaun is such a narcissist that the only one he could ever have an affair with is himself, the relationship with Veronica is just a front. I have it on the best of authority . . .'

'What do you mean?' Maggie was puzzled. 'Who's he having an affair with?'

'Maggie!' Caroline exclaimed. 'You're hopeless.'

Devlin's eyes widened. 'You're not serious. Shaun Archer? What a waste!'

'You mean he's gay?' Maggie was gobsmacked.

'Pat the girl on the back,' giggled Devlin.

They had a giggly gossipy lunch such as only really close old friends can have and then they hit Grafton Street looking for Devlin's going-away outfit. No stone was left unturned, no garment untried, until finally the decision was made and a beautiful, superbly cut Paul Costello trouser-suit was wrapped and bagged.

'God, I hate that grunge look,' Devlin declared as

they sank back into the comfort of the limo and drove out to Clontarf.

It was a beautiful midsummer evening and the breeze was balmy as they sat on the balcony, Devlin and Maggie sipping champagne, Caroline with sparkling mineral water.

'To the new Mrs Reilly.' Caroline held up her glass.

'To the new Caroline.' Devlin toasted her back.

'To us,' toasted Maggie and they clinked glasses and laughed.

Well, she'd really better get up, Devlin decided happily. She couldn't believe that it was her wedding day. When she asked Luke to marry her, he lifted her in his arms and swung her around until she was dizzy, much to the amusement of the other passengers in Terminal Four.

'Yes! Yes! Yes!' he declared, and she knew that everything was going to be fine between them. She had made the right decision. They had spent hours discussing where they would live and how they would cope with their respective businesses. Devlin, who had been thinking about it the whole long flight back from Abu Dhabi, turned to him and said, 'I'm going to ask Caroline to be the administrator of Dublin City Girl. I think she'd be perfect for the job. I trust her implicitly. I'll be able to concentrate on the overall business plan and spend most of my time with my new husband.'

'I'm marrying a genius,' Luke exclaimed, as happy as she had ever seen him. They decided on the earliest possible wedding-date, much to Lydia's dismay. Although Devlin would have preferred a small intimate wedding, she knew that Lydia would have been disappointed and so she let her have her way with the reception, the catering and the guest-list. Devlin didn't care; all she knew was that she and Luke were getting married and she was the happiest girl in the world.

There was hardly a soul around as Luke left Devlin's apartment and strode down the drive and out on to the main road in the direction of Howth. All that could be heard was birdsong and an occasional dog barking and the clink of bottles as the milkman made his early-morning deliveries. The air was fresh, the breeze salty, and Luke walked quickly, anxious to get closer to the sea. He loved to watch the sun sparkling on the water in the hours after sunrise. It brought back memories of his sea-going days. They had been carefree times with one responsibility only: to do his job well. It had been his own choice to come ashore and he had done well for himself, but occasionally there were times when he would give anything to feel the deck of a ship rolling under his feet, to watch the bow diving into the waves and up again and to taste the salt of the sea-spray on his lips.

Maybe some day he and Devlin would just take off and sail around the world. He smiled to himself. It was hard to believe that in a few hours' time he would be a married man. It was even harder to believe that Devlin had asked him to marry her. He had to pinch himself sometimes to make sure it wasn't one big dream.

It made it all the more special that *she* had asked

him. It was the greatest proof that she really did need him. He knew Devlin loved him, but he had always thought that the relationship they were having suited her fine, leaving her plenty of time to develop her business, which was of paramount importance to her. He had longed to ask her to marry him but had never felt that she was ready to commit herself to that permanent relationship.

When she disembarked from that plane, tanned and glowing, eyes sparkling and happy, and asked him to marry her, you could have knocked him down with a feather. He would always remember the shock, the disbelief and then that great wave of joy that had engulfed him. He had never experienced such a sense of happiness before. Luke smiled at the memory as he turned on to the Bull Wall. Across the bay, he could see a cargo ship moving slowly down the Liffey. What a sight, he thought with pleasure, walking briskly along, enjoying the smell and sound of the sea as it slapped up against the rocks. He reached the statue of Our Lady just as the ship was passing the Poolbeg lighthouse and he paused to watch her as she steamed along at the beginning of her voyage. He was beginning a new voyage himself today, he thought happily, as he stood staring out to sea in the quiet solitude of an early Dublin morning.

'Your boss is very kind to pay for our flights and hotel accommodation. Imagine him asking you to his wedding. He must think a lot of you.' Dianne Westwood's younger sister bubbled happily on as she sipped champagne in the first-class section of the Boeing 737 that was winging its way across the

Irish Sea and bringing them to Dublin for Luke's wedding.

Frankly, Dianne felt she was having a nightmare. When Luke came into work the morning after Devlin Delaney had arrived back in London from her holiday in Abu Dhabi, and told her that he was getting married, she had been stunned. How she had managed to utter the words of congratulations she would never know. But she had, and then she escaped to the sanctuary of her own office, and sat numbed and shocked. Twenty minutes later, she typed her letter of resignation. She couldn't stay on, knowing that Luke was marrying Devlin.

She just couldn't bring herself to give the letter to Luke that day, so she had slipped it into her drawer and gone home and bawled her eyes out. If she handed in her resignation she would never see him again. Could she bear that? After a long night of tossing and turning she had decided not to leave. The marriage would never last. She knew it wouldn't. DD wasn't the woman for Luke, and never would be. No, it would end in tears and when it did, he would turn to her, the one who had been at his side through thick and thin. Then Dianne would come into her own and he'd see her for what she was, his loyal, loving soulmate.

When he asked her to the wedding she said yes. It would have been churlish to refuse and he wouldn't have understood her reasons. It would be the worst day of her life but she would carry it off. Dianne had no doubts about that. No-one could carry it off like she could. No-one had her style, her class and her complete professionalism. Luke had once called her the perfect PA. Some day he would call her his perfect woman, she vowed, as the plane circled and began its final approach to Dublin Airport.

Caroline stood humming under the shower, soaping herself all over. She still had her Abu Dhabi tan, she thought with satisfaction, and she was working diligently on keeping it up. It was hard to believe she was home almost three months now. Sometimes she thought her time in Abu Dhabi had been a magical dream. But it was incredible the way things had turned out. When Devlin told her she was going to marry Luke and offered her the position of administrator in City Girl, Caroline had been speechless. To walk into a job like that after spending six exciting months in a foreign country was too good to be true. Her luck was definitely turning, she firmly believed.

Richard had again asked her to consider their buying a place together, and once again she had refused. Her husband was a sad and lonely man and she pitied him, but she had to do what was right for her and she wanted to be free. She had written to the Marriage Tribunal only the week before, to ask them to set a date for her and Richard's psychological assessment. She was determined to make a new start and if Richard couldn't cope with it, that was not her problem.

She dried herself and smoothed Johnson's Baby Lotion on her silky skin. After the wedding was over she would really focus her mind on buying a place for herself. She was renting an apartment on the old Ballymun Road and while it suited her for the time being, especially while she was busy getting to grips with her new job in City Girl, she wanted a place of her own.

She was really enjoying the job. Having done the stint in Belfast and with her six months' experience in Abu Dhabi, she was confident that she could do the job of administrator. It certainly made up for her sadness at leaving Abu Dhabi and all the friends she had made there. After the holiday of a lifetime with Féile and the gang, she had come back to Abu Dhabi and faced the marathon task of packing all she had bought there, as well as what she had originally brought with her. With her silk paintings, her Chinese screens and Oriental rugs, Caroline was dying to have a place of her own to decorate.

Bill had thrown a hooley for her the night before she left and Nell, who had by then arrived back, minus her bunions, said, with satisfaction, 'Well, it's obvious you settled in and made plenty of friends. I knew you'd have a ball.' In true Abu Dhabi style, it had ended with dancing on the tables and then she had been presented with the most exquisite gold charm bracelet that had taken her breath away, and a card signed by everyone she knew. Caroline was so touched that she cried, and she cried again at the airport when she said goodbye to Bill and Nell and Féile and Pat and Mike, who had all come to see her off. They were friends she would have for ever and there was an open invitation for her to come on holiday whenever she wished. Caroline knew it was an offer she would be availing of.

Devlin and Maggie had met her at the airport, and Devlin was bubbling with excitement as she told Caroline of her wedding plans. When she asked her to work at City Girl, Caroline couldn't believe it.

'Well, believe it – it's true,' Caroline hummed gaily as she let herself out of her apartment. She'd better get a move on, she reflected, as she got into her brand-new Honda Civic and headed in the direction of Foxrock.

He really didn't want to go to the wedding. Devlin had never been one of his favourite people and she had asked him to go only because of Caroline, Richard thought glumly, as he drank his early-morning coffee and stared out over Bullock Harbour. He had bought a penthouse there, as he liked the view very much. It was lonely being on his own. He had hoped that when Caroline came back from Abu Dhabi she might consider moving back in with him. Just because they were getting an annulment and divorce didn't mean they couldn't live together like flatmates. He was surprised when she had refused his offer. In fact, he had been totally surprised by the Caroline who had met him several days after her arrival home from the Levant.

She was glowing and healthy, full of self-confidence and much more outgoing. It was hard for Richard to accept that this together woman was the same timid, shy, insecure girl he had married. He was glad for her. He envied her. And if he was absolutely truthful, he resented the fact that she no longer seemed to need him at all. That was hard to bear. Still, he would have to get over it.

Charles would not be pleased if he saw him moping around. But he missed his companion so much. They had grown closer than Richard had ever believed possible. There were no emotional barriers of any sort between them by the time Charles died and those empty months after his death had been the most traumatic period of his life.

His mother had urged him to come and live with her. 'Now we can get back to normal,' she said. 'That Caroline is in foreign places and won't be back to trouble us. Some day you'll find the wife you deserve.'

'Mother,' he said quietly, 'I've told you. I'm homosexual. I'm not interested in finding another wife.' Charles had urged him to be proud of what he was. Well, he wasn't going to go shouting it from the rooftops; he'd never be able to do that. But he was never going to deny himself again, he swore.

Sarah had been furious and disgusted and told him that until he stopped talking in that dreadful manner, she wanted nothing more to do with him.

'That's entirely up to you, Mother,' Richard replied calmly and walked out of the large red-brick Victorian house that had always been a prison to him. Sarah hadn't spoken to him since then; his secretary acted as go-between on business matters. Richard didn't care any longer. He'd been loved unconditionally by the one person who mattered, and if people couldn't take him as he was, that was their problem. He was lonely, though. He had been out of the social scene in Dublin for so long it was hard to get back in to it. Maybe he would go to the wedding after all. He didn't need to spend much time with Devlin; he would just kiss the bride and wish her luck. But he liked Terry, Maggie's husband, and he'd enjoy being with Caroline for the day.

Yes, he'd go to the wedding and enjoy himself. Charles would want that.

'I want to make a new will,' Sarah Yates instructed the solicitor seated at the desk in front of her. 'I want to leave every single penny I possess to the Church.'

'Come on, Mimi. Eat up your breakfast or we'll be late,' Maggie urged her elder daughter as she fed Shona her cornflakes.

'I can feed mine own self,' Shona protested. 'I'm a big girl.'

'I know . . . I know,' soothed her mother, catching a dribble of milk expertly with the spoon. 'But we've got to hurry up to get to the hairdresser because you're going to get lovely flowers in your hair for the wedding.'

'I'd say I'll look like a pwincess,' Mimi said dreamily, as she tried to follow a puzzle on the back of the cornflakes packet.

'I'd say so too. Now, hurry upstairs and get your pyjamas off so I can give you a quick bath.'

'I've had mine, Mammy.' Michael appeared at the kitchen door, wrapped in a towel. 'Daddy gave it to me.'

Thank you, Terry, Maggie thought approvingly. 'Good boy, just get into your clean T-shirt and shorts and then we'll all be changing our clothes over at Auntie Devlin's.'

'Being a pageboy is very important, isn't it?' he asked solemnly.

'Oh very,' she assured him. 'That's why Auntie Devlin picked you — because she knew she could

646

depend on you. Now, run up and get dressed so that we won't be late.'

'OK, Mammy.'

With a glad heart, Maggie watched her little son trip jauntily out of the room. She had been so worried about his behaviour the previous year. Of course it had happened because of her and Terry's separation; Michael idolized his father.

Absentmindedly, Maggie ate what was left of Shona's cornflakes. Devlin was getting married today and she had such expectations. Maggie had once been a bride like that, and then it had all gone wrong. Now she expected nothing, so anything she got was a bonus.

To be fair, Terry was a much better husband and partner since his return. When she asked him to come home on the night of the launch, he had agreed with alacrity, and, she suspected, with relief. She had been so busy on the publicity trail that she hadn't had a minute to talk to him for the next couple of weeks, but he had taken time off work and looked after the children – she had to give him his due.

They had sat down one night and thrashed everything out, absolutely everything. That had been a very healing experience. She told him of her resentment and her unhappiness at his attitude to her career and his treatment of her, and he, in turn, told her how he felt. It had not been pleasant but each had come from the encounter with a new respect for the other's feelings, and they were united in the conviction that getting back together was the best thing for their children. The change in the youngsters had been miraculous. Mimi had reverted to her old, cheery, impudent self and Michael had eventually stopped bedwetting and was losing his tendency to cling to his father every second. Shona, who was a bit young to understand, seemed to have suffered least.

All in all, Maggie decided, the best thing to do was to be positive. Her novel was selling very well and she had got terrific media coverage. She was frequently asked to address writers' groups or to attend launches and promotions. All this was new and exciting for her. The back-up from her publishers had been wonderful and they were now cosseting her through the rewrites of her second novel. *A Time to Decide* was due out in the autumn.

Maggie now employed Josie on a daily basis. The income from her writing gave her freedom, so that she was able to write every day in peace and without feeling guilty, knowing that the children and the house were not being neglected and that there would be an evening meal on the table for Terry. The pressure to meet her deadline was enough, without feeling guilty as well.

Terry and she still slept in separate rooms. She supposed the time would come when they would sleep together again. Maggie wasn't crazy about leading a celibate life, and she knew that Terry definitely wasn't, either, and there were times she longed for a nice kiss and a cuddle. She missed the intimacy of her marriage. Maybe it would return in time. It was best to let things take their course, she decided, as Mimi appeared at the kitchen door covered from head to toe in talc. She was accompanied by Shona, wide-eyed as she tried to explain to her mother that what had happened to her elder sister was an accident.

'I was trying to make myself smell nice for the wedding and it all came out 'cos the top came off,' the little girl sobbed.

'Don't cry, Mimi, I lub you.' Shona embraced her sister and was herself enveloped in a cloud of talc.

Maggie hugged her elder daughter tightly. 'It's all right, love. I'll give you a bath now and fix you up. Sure it was an accident. Not to worry.'

'Not to worry,' said Little Sir Echo comfortingly at her side and Maggie smiled down into Shona's big blue eyes.

'Come on,' she said, 'we'll all have a bath and get ourselves ready for Auntie Devlin's wedding.' Squeals of pleasure greeted this pronouncement as Maggie led the way upstairs.

What on *earth* had Mimi been doing? Terry stared in horror at the floor of her bedroom. He had heard her running, crying, downstairs to Maggie, and come out to see what the problem was. All he had to do was follow the trail of little white footprints. There was talcum powder all over the place. Maggie would freak. He got down on his hands and knees and scooped back as much as he could into the round container.

Michael appeared at his side. 'Women!' he said conspiratorially, rolling his eyes dramatically. 'The mess they make.'

Terry had to laugh. 'You can say that again, son,' he replied, as he went downstairs to get the hoover.

He wondered what the wedding would be like today. He was glad for Devlin. He liked and admired his wife's best friend and another thing that he appreciated about her was the way she had not stopped talking to him when their marriage was in trouble. She hadn't taken sides, although naturally she had been very supportive of Maggie. He hoped her own marriage would be a happy one, because, when all was said and done, there was nothing to beat a happy marriage.

His had been happy until he'd had an affair with Ria, and for that he took full responsibility. Then the tit-for-tat started, Maggie with Adam, him going back to Ria. It had made neither of them happy. Living alone in that mews had been the very worst time of his life. He missed his kids so badly. He hated looking after himself and wondering what to have for his dinner and, more than anything, he hated being in that house on his own, especially late at night. The loneliness of it had nearly killed him, and when he thought of all he had given up – his home, his children and his good wife – he cursed aloud. Because Maggie *had* been a good wife, even when she was writing that book of hers. The children always came first. The house was clean, if sometimes untidy because of the children – he could never fault her for that. This new arrangement of hers with Josie was working well. It was great that her royalties allowed her to pay Josie, and more power to her. He hadn't realized what a big thing this writing career was going to be and it gave him a great thrill when people asked him if he was married to the novelist Maggie Ryan.

He'd been glad, so glad when she'd asked him to come home, and although their relationship was different from before, it wasn't unpleasant. In fact, they had great fun at times, especially with the kids. He was dying to see how they performed at the wedding today. They were lovely children and he felt that he and Maggie were making a good job of rearing them, and that was the important thing.

Maybe the ceremony would bring back memories of their own wedding and the fun they had. Maybe they'd get back together as man and wife in the biblical sense tonight, he thought, ever the optimist. Whistling cheerfully, Terry hoovered up the mess his adored daughter had created. He could hear shrieks emanating from the bathroom where the three females of the house were bathing.

'Women! The racket they make!' Michael raised his eyes to heaven again, as he arrived to give his father a hand.

Terry smiled at the apple of his eye. 'We men just have to stick together, don't we, son?'

'You can say that again,' Michael replied fervently, giving his dad a dig in the ribs. 'Come on, Dad, put your dukes up. Let's make as much noise as them,' he yelled. He roared laughing as Terry picked him up in his arms and started to tickle him.

'Here she comes,' Caroline exclaimed, as the gleaming white Rolls-Royce drove majestically up to the church.

'Oh Mammy! Oh look!' Mimi was beside herself with excitement as she danced up and down.

'Mammy, just tell me again. I walk *behind* Mimi and Shona?'

'That's right, Michael. And Auntie Caroline and I walk behind you.' The three children looked so beautiful, Michael in his suit and the girls in their matching apple-green-and-white-patterned dresses, white shoes and socks and carrying baskets of roses. Caroline and she wore raw silk, apple-green, off-the-shoulder gowns, with yards of skirt billowing in the breeze.

A ripple of anticipation ran through the church, and, up at the altar, Luke loosened the knot of his tie ever so slightly.

Caroline helped Devlin out of the car, arranging the beautiful white brocade of the dress so that it fell correctly over the hoop and stiff petticoats.

Devlin grinned. 'If I don't break my neck in this yoke, I'll be doing well. Is Luke here?'

'Of course he's here.' Maggie grinned back. 'And the poor fella is *so* nervous. Get up that aisle quickly and put him out of his misery.'

'Are we right, then?' Devlin took a deep breath and smiled at her father. 'Don't gallop,' she warned him. 'Hurry on,' she said to the photographer. 'My husband-to-be is nervous.'

Fortunately the photographer knew his stuff. A few minutes later the organ began to play and a hush descended on the congregation as Devlin, looking radiant in her fairytale gown, glided up the aisle on her father's arm. Luke turned to greet her, and when their eyes met, it was as if no-one else existed for them. The glance lasted for just a few seconds but for Devlin that was the moment of their marriage.

Gerry kissed her and shook hands with Luke, and Devlin turned to smile at Lydia in the front seat. Her mother was dabbing at her eyes with a fine lace handkerchief, but when she saw her daughter smiling

652

at her she beamed back and Devlin gave her a little wink. Behind her, she could hear whispers as Maggie told her children what to do next. Devlin handed her bouquet to Caroline, and Maggie joined them up at the altar.

The three friends were together yet again at a special moment in the life of one of them. Devlin smiled at the other two, and they at her, and then she turned to Luke. He took her hand in his, and the priest welcomed them all in the sight of God, to give love and support as Luke and Devlin vowed eternal fidelity as man and wife.

It was a beautiful, moving, spiritual service and when Luke placed the wedding band on her finger, Devlin felt she would burst with happiness. As she walked down the aisle, out into the bright sunlight, holding Luke's hand tightly, Devlin sent up a special little prayer to her daughter.

'Are you all right, Mrs Reilly?' Luke murmured.

'Oh yes, Luke, I'm just fine.' She flung her arms around him outside the church and hugged him tightly. 'I love you,' she whispered.

'I love you too.' His amber eyes smiled down into hers and then they were being showered with confetti before being embraced and congratulated by all. Maggie and Caroline looked on, smiling broadly, as their best friend almost disappeared in a welter of hugs and kisses.

To be continued . . .

CITY GIRL
by Patricia Scanlan

'Will pull at your heartstrings'
Options

DEVLIN: Blonde, beautiful, rich and spoilt. The world is hers for the taking until she encounters the suave, seductive and very married Colin Cantrell-King — who lies, cheats and uses women until he tires of them. Her life is turned upside down . . . and then the unthinkable happens.

CAROLINE: Frumpy, needy and terminally shy, she's terrified of being left on the shelf. Then she meets Richard . . . cold, reserved and with a secret to hide. She makes a decision that has disastrous consequences for both of them.

MAGGIE: Flame-haired, sexy and vibrant. She lives life to the full . . . and then she marries. Her wings are well and truly clipped by the demands of marriage and motherhood. Has she made the biggest mistake of her life?

This is the story of three young women who deal with everything life throws at them, and how, as their enduring friendship sustains them through thick and thin, they start to live life on their own terms.

A Bantam Paperback
0 553 40943 3

A SELECTED LIST OF FINE NOVELS
AVAILABLE FROM BANTAM BOOKS

50329 4	DANGER ZONES	*Sally Beauman*	£5.99
40727 9	LOVERS AND LIARS	*Sally Beauman*	£5.99
50326 X	SEXTET	*Sally Beauman*	£5.99
40803 8	SACRED AND PROFANE	*Marcelle Bernstein*	£5.99
50469 X	SAINTS AND SINNERS	*Marcelle Bernstein*	£5.99
40497 0	CHANGE OF HEART	*Charlotte Bingham*	£5.99
40890 9	DEBUTANTES	*Charlotte Bingham*	£5.99
50500 9	GRAND AFFAIR	*Charlotte Bingham*	£5.99
50501 7	LOVE SONG	*Charlotte Bingham*	£5.99
40496 2	NANNY	*Charlotte Bingham*	£5.99
40895 X	THE NIGHTINGALE SINGS	*Charlotte Bingham*	£5.99
17635 8	TO HEAR A NIGHTINGALE	*Charlotte Bingham*	£5.99
40171 8	STARDUST	*Charlotte Bingham*	£5.99
40296 X	IN SUNSHINE OR IN SHADOW	*Charlotte Bingham*	£5.99
40615 9	PASSIONATE TIMES	*Emma Blair*	£5.99
40614 0	THE DAFFODIL SEA	*Emma Blair*	£5.99
40373 7	THE SWEETEST THING	*Emma Blair*	£5.99
40973 5	A CRACK IN FOREVER	*Jeannie Brewer*	£5.99
50580 7	SOMEBODY'S GIRL	*June Francis*	£5.99
50691 9	FOR THE SAKE OF THE CHILDREN	*June Francis*	£5.99
40819 4	A BITTER LEGACY	*Margaret Graham*	£5.99
40408 3	GONE TOMORROW	*Jane Gurney*	£5.99
40730 9	LOVERS	*Judith Krantz*	£5.99
40731 7	SPRING COLLECTION	*Judith Krantz*	£5.99
40944 1	APARTMENT 3B	*Patricia Scanlan*	£5.99
40947 6	FOREIGN AFFAIRS	*Patricia Scanlan*	£5.99
40945 X	FINISHING TOUCHES	*Patricia Scanlan*	£5.99
40941 7	MIRROR, MIRROR	*Patricia Scanlan*	£5.99
40942 5	PROMISES, PROMISES	*Patricia Scanlan*	£5.99
40943 3	CITY GIRL	*Patricia Scanlan*	£5.99